P9-AGK-264

Clare Boylan is the author of six previous novels and three volumes of short stories. Her novels include *Home Rule* and its acclaimed sequel *Holy Pictures*, *Room for a Single Lady*, *Black Baby* and *Beloved Stranger*, all of which are available in Abacus paperback, as are the widely praised short-story collections, *That Bad Woman* and *The Collected Short Stories*. Non-fiction works include essays on the art and strategy of fiction writing, and *The Literary Companion to Cats*.

EMMA BROWN

Clare Boylan

and

Charlotte Brontë

LITTLE, BROWN

A *Little, Brown* Book

First published in Great Britain by Little, Brown in 2003

Copyright © by Clare Boylan 2003

The moral right of the author has been asserted.

*All characters in this publication other than those clearly in the public domain are
fictitious and any resemblance to real persons, living or dead, is purely coincidental.*

All rights reserved. No part of this publication may be reproduced, stored
in a retrieval system, or transmitted, in any form or by any means, without
the prior permission in writing of the publisher, nor be otherwise
circulated in any form of binding or cover other than that in which it is
published and without a similar condition including this condition being
imposed on the subsequent purchaser.

A CIP catalogue record for this book
is available from the British Library.

ISBN 0 316 72611 7

Typeset in Garamond 3 by M Rules
Printed and bound in Great Britain by
Clays Ltd, St Ives plc

Little, Brown
An imprint of
Time Warner Books UK
Brettenham House
Lancaster Place
London WC2E 7EN

www.TimeWarnerBooks.co.uk

For Carol Shields

ACKNOWLEDGEMENTS

My first and most profound thanks to the legacy of Charlotte Brontë without whom this book would not have been possible. Gratitude is also due to Ian Stringer, who was my guide in Yorkshire and shared his wealth of knowledge of the region and its history; to Jean Haynes, who walked me through Victorian London; to Richard Beswick for encouragement and assistance with original manuscripts. Thanks also to Donna Coonan, Juliet Barker, Lucasta Miller, Jean Bourne, Alan Wilkes, Noeleen Dowling, Patricia Ryan, Hazel Orme, Viv Redman, Andrew Davies, Lucy Luck and, as always, to my agent Gill Coleridge. I am indebted to the Guildhall Library, the Museum of London, the London Library and the Brontë Parsonage Museum; and, for valuable additional information, to many publications, especially: *The London Encyclopedia* edited by Ben Weinreb and Christopher Hibbert; *London: the Biography* by Peter Ackroyd; *The Brontës: A Life in Letters* by Juliet Barker; *London Labour and the London Poor* by Henry Mayhew; *London: A Pilgrimage* by Gustave Doré and Blanchard Jerrold; *The World for a Shilling* by Michael Leapman.

CHAPTER ONE

We all seek an ideal in life. A pleasant fancy began to visit me in a certain year, that perhaps the number of human beings is few who do not find their quest at some era of life for some space more or less brief. I had certainly not found mine in youth, though the strong belief I held of its existence sufficed through all my brightest and freshest time to keep me hopeful. I had not found it in maturity. I was become resigned never to find it. I had lived certain dim years entirely tranquil and unexpectant. And now I was not sure but something was hovering around my hearth which pleased me wonderfully.

Look at it, reader. Come into my parlour and judge for yourself whether I do right to care for this thing. First you may scan me, if you please. We shall go on better together after a satisfactory introduction and due apprehension of identity. My name is Mrs Chalfont. I am a widow. My house is good, and my income such as need not check the impulse either of charity or a moderate hospitality. I am not young, not yet old. There is no silver yet in my hair, but its yellow lustre is gone.

In my face, wrinkles are yet to come, but I have almost forgotten the days when it wore any bloom. I lived for fifteen years a life, which, whatever its trials, could not be called stagnant. Then for five years I was alone, and, having no children, desolate. Lately, Fortune, by a somewhat curious turn of her wheel, placed in my way an interest and a companion.

The neighbourhood where I live is pleasant enough, its scenery agreeable, and its society civilized, though not numerous. About a mile from my house there is a ladies' school, established but lately – not more than three years since. The conductresses of this school were of my acquaintances; and though I cannot say that they occupied the very highest place in my opinion – for they had brought back from some months' residence abroad, for finishing purposes, a good deal that was fantastic, affected and pretentious – yet I awarded them some portion of that respect which seems the fair due of all women who face life bravely, and try to make their own way by their own efforts.

About a year after the Misses Wilcox opened their school, when the number of their pupils was as yet exceedingly limited, and when, no doubt, they were looking out anxiously enough for augmentation, the entrance-gate to their little drive was one day thrown back to admit a carriage – 'a very handsome, fashionable carriage,' Miss Mabel Wilcox said, in narrating the circumstance afterwards – and drawn by a pair of really splendid horses. The sweep up the drive, the loud ring at the door-bell, the bustling entrance into the house, the ceremonious admission to the bright drawing-room, roused excitement enough in Fuchsia Lodge. Miss Wilcox repaired to the reception-room in a pair of new gloves, and carrying in her hand a handkerchief of French cambric.

She found a gentleman seated on the sofa, who, as he rose up, appeared a tall, fine-looking personage; at least she thought him so, as he stood with his back to the light. He introduced himself as Mr Fitzgibbon, inquired if Miss Wilcox had a vacancy, and intimated that he wished to intrust to her care a new pupil in the shape of his daughter. This was welcome news, for there was many a vacancy in Miss Wilcox's schoolroom; indeed, her establishment was as yet limited to the select number of three, and she and her sisters were looking forward with anything but confidence to the balancing of accounts at the close of their first half-year. Few objects could have been more agreeable to her than that to which, by the wave of a hand, Mr Fitzgibbon now directed her attention – the figure of a child standing near the drawing-room window.

Had Miss Wilcox's establishment boasted fuller ranks – had she indeed entered well on that course of prosperity which in after years an undeviating attention to externals enabled her so triumphantly to realize – an early thought with her would have been to judge whether the acquisition now offered was likely to answer well as a show-pupil. She would have instantly marked her look, dress, &c., and inferred her value from these *indicia*. In these anxious commencing times, however, Miss Wilcox could scarce afford herself the luxury of such appreciation: a new pupil represented £40 a year, independently of masters' terms – and £40 a year was a sum Miss Wilcox needed and was glad to secure; besides, the fine carriage, the fine gentleman, and the fine name gave gratifying assurance, enough and to spare, of eligibility in the proffered connection.

It was admitted, then, that there were vacancies in Fuchsia Lodge; that Miss Fitzgibbon could be received at once; that she was to learn all that the school prospectus professed to teach; to be liable to every extra; in short to be as expensive, and consequently as profitable a pupil, as any directress's heart could wish. All this was arranged as upon velvet, smoothly and liberally. Mr Fitzgibbon showed in the transaction none of the hardness of the bargain-making man of business, and as little of the penurious anxiety of the straitened professional man. Miss Wilcox felt him to be 'quite the gentleman'. Everything disposed her to be partially inclined towards the little girl whom he, on taking leave, formally committed to her guardianship; and as if no circumstance should be wanting to complete her happy impression, the address left written on a card served to fill up the measure of Miss Wilcox's satisfaction – Conway Fitzgibbon, Esq., May Park, Midland County. That very day three decrees were passed in the newcomer's favour:

1st. That she was to be Miss Wilcox's bed-fellow.
2nd. To sit next to her at table.
3rd. To walk out with her.

In a few days it became evident that a fourth secret clause had been added to these, *viz.* that Miss Fitzgibbon was to be favoured, petted, and screened on all possible occasions.

An ill-conditioned pupil, who before coming to Fuchsia Lodge had passed a year under the care of certain old-fashioned Misses Sterling of Hartwood, and from them had picked up unpractical notions of justice, took it upon her to utter an opinion on this system of favouritism.

'The Misses Sterling,' she injudiciously said, 'never distinguished any girl because she was richer or better dressed than the rest. They would have scorned to do so. *They* always rewarded girls according as they behaved well to their schoolfellows and minded their lessons, not according to the number of their silk dresses and fine laces and feathers.'

For it must not be forgotten that Miss Fitzgibbon's trunks, when opened, disclosed a splendid wardrobe; so fine were the various articles of apparel, indeed, that instead of assigning for their accommodation the painted deal drawers of the school bedroom, Miss Wilcox had them arranged in a mahogany bureau in her own room. With her own hands, too, she would on Sundays array the little favourite in her quilted silk pelisse, her hat and feathers, her ermine boa, and little French boots and gloves. And very self-complacent she felt when she led the young heiress (a letter from Mr Fitzgibbon, received since his first visit, had communicated the additional particulars that his daughter was his only child, and would be the inheritress of his estates, including May Park, Midland County) – when she led her, I say, into the church, and seated her stately by her side at the top of the gallery pew. Unbiased observers might, indeed, have wondered what there was to be proud of, and puzzled their heads to detect the special merits of this little woman in silk – for, to speak truth, Miss Fitzgibbon was far from being the beauty of the school: there were two or three blooming little faces amongst her companions lovelier than hers. Had she been a poor child, Miss Wilcox herself would not have liked her physiognomy at all: rather, indeed, would it have repelled than attracted her; and, moreover – though Miss Wilcox hardly confessed the circumstance to herself, but, on the contrary strove hard not to be conscious of it – there were moments when she became sensible of a certain strange weariness in continuing her system of partiality. It hardly came natural to her to show this special distinction in this particular instance. An undefined wonder would smite her sometimes that she did not take more satisfaction in flattering and caressing this embryo heiress – that she did not like better to have her always at her side, under her special charge. On *principle*, for she argued with herself: This is the most aristocratic and richest of my pupils; she brings me the most credit and the most profit: therefore, I ought, in justice, to show her a special indulgence; which she did – but with a gradually increasing peculiarity of feeling.

5

Certainly, the undue favours showered on little Miss Fitzgibbon brought their object no real benefit. Unfitted for the character of playfellow by her position of favourite, her fellow-pupils rejected her company as decidedly as they dared. Active rejection was not long necessary; it was soon seen that passive avoidance would suffice; the pet was not social. No: even Miss Wilcox never thought her social. When she sent for her to show her fine clothes in the drawing-room when there was company, and especially when she had her into her parlour of an evening to be her own companion, Miss Wilcox used to feel curiously perplexed. She would try to talk affably to the young heiress, to draw her out, to amuse her. To herself the governess could render no reason why her efforts soon flagged; but this was invariably the case. However, Miss Wilcox was a woman of courage; and be the *protégée* what she might, the patroness did not fail to continue on *principle* her system of preference.

A favourite has no friends; and the observation of a gentleman, who about this time called at the Lodge and chanced to see Miss Fitzgibbon, was, 'That child looks consummately unhappy': he was watching Miss Fitzgibbon, as she walked, by herself, fine and solitary, while her schoolfellows were merrily playing.

'Who is the miserable little wight?' he asked.

He was told her name and dignity.

'Wretched little soul!' he repeated; and he watched her pace down the walk and back again; marching upright, her hands in her ermine muff, her fine pelisse showing a gay sheen to the winter's sun, her large Leghorn hat shading such a face as fortunately had not its parallel on the premises.

'Wretched little soul!' reiterated the gentleman. He opened the drawing-room window, watched the bearer of the muff till he caught her eye and then summoned her with his finger.

She came; he stooped his head down to her; she lifted her face up to him.

'Don't you play, little girl?'

'No, sir.'

'No! why not? Do you think yourself better than other children?'

No answer.

'Is it because people tell you you are rich, you won't play?'

The young lady was gone. He stretched out his hand to arrest her, but she wheeled beyond his reach and ran quickly out of sight.

'An only child,' pleaded Miss Wilcox; 'possibly spoiled by her papa, you know; we must excuse a little pettishness.'

'Humph! I am afraid there is not a little to excuse.'

CHAPTER TWO

Mr Ellin – the gentleman mentioned in the last chapter – was a man who went where he liked, and being a gossiping, leisurely person, he liked to go almost everywhere. He could not be rich, he lived so quietly; and yet he must have had some money, for, without apparent profession, he continued to keep a house and a servant. He always spoke of himself as having once been a worker; but if so, that could not have been very long since, for he still looked far from old. Sometimes of an evening, under a little social conversational excitement, he would look quite young; but he was changeable in mood, and complexion, and expression, and had chameleon eyes, sometimes blue and merry, sometimes grey and dark, and anon green and gleaming. On the whole he might be called a fair man, of average height, rather thin and rather wiry. He had not resided more than two years in the present neighbourhood; his antecedents were unknown there; but as the rector, a man of good family and standing and of undoubted scrupulousness in the choice of acquaintance, had introduced him, he found everywhere a prompt reception, of which nothing in his conduct had yet seemed to prove him unworthy. Some people, indeed, dubbed him 'a character', and fancied him 'eccentric'; but others could not see the appropriateness of the epithets. He always seemed to them very harmless and quiet, not always perhaps so perfectly unreserved and comprehensible as might be wished. He had a discomposing expression in his eye; and sometimes in conversation an ambiguous diction; but still they believed he meant no harm.

Mr Ellin often called on the Misses Wilcox; he sometimes took tea with them; he appeared to like tea and muffins, and not to dislike the kind of conversation which usually accompanies that refreshment; he was said to be a good shot, a good angler. He proved himself an excellent gossip – he liked gossip well. On the whole he liked women's society, and did not seem to be particular in requiring difficult accomplishments or rare endowments in his female acquaintances. The Misses Wilcox, for instance, were not much less shallow than the china saucer which held their teacups; yet Mr Ellin got on perfectly well with them, and had apparently great pleasure in hearing them discuss all the details of their school. He knew the names of all their young ladies too, and would shake hands with them if he met them walking out; he knew their examination days and gala days, and more than once accompanied Mr Cecil, the curate, when he went to examine in ecclesiastical history.

This ceremony took place weekly, on Wednesday afternoons, after which Mr Cecil sometimes stayed to tea, and usually found two or three lady parishioners invited to meet him. Mr Ellin was always pretty sure to be there. Rumour gave one of the Misses Wilcox in anticipated wedlock to the curate, and furnished his friend with a second in the same tender relation so that it is to be conjectured that they made a social pleasant party under such interesting circumstances. Their evenings rarely passed without Miss Fitzgibbon being introduced – all worked muslin and streaming sash and elaborated ringlets; others of the pupils

9

would also be called in, perhaps to sing, to show off a little at the piano, or sometimes to repeat poetry. Miss Wilcox conscientiously cultivated display in her young ladies, thinking she thus fulfilled a duty to herself and to them, at once spreading her own fame and giving the children self-possessed manners.

It was curious to note how, on these occasions, good, genuine natural qualities still vindicated their superiority to counterfeit artificial advantages. While 'dear Miss Fitzgibbon', dressed up and flattered as she was, could only sidle round the circle with the crestfallen air which seemed natural to her, just giving her hand to the guests, then almost snatching it away, and sneaking in unmannerly haste to the place allotted to her at Miss Wilcox's side, which place she filled like a piece of furniture, neither smiling nor speaking the evening through — while such was *her* deportment, certain of her companions, as Mary Franks, Jessy Newton, &c., handsome, open-countenanced little damsels — fearless because harmless — would enter with a smile of salutation and a blush of pleasure, make their pretty reverence at the drawing-room door, stretch a friendly little hand to such visitors as they knew, and sit down to the piano to play their well-practised duet with an innocent, obliging readiness which won all hearts.

There was a girl called Diana — the girl alluded to before as having once been Miss Sterling's pupil — a daring, brave girl, much loved and a little feared by her comrades. She had good faculties, both physical and mental — was clever, honest, and dauntless. In the schoolroom she set her young brow like a rock against Miss Fitzgibbon's pretensions; she found also heart and spirit to withstand them in the drawing-room. One evening, when the curate had been summoned away by some piece of duty directly after tea, and there was no stranger present but Mr Ellin, Diana had been called in to play a long, difficult piece of music which she could execute like a master. She was still in the midst of her performance, when – Mr Ellin having for the first time, perhaps, recognized the existence of the heiress by asking if she was cold – Miss Wilcox took the opportunity of launching into a strain of commendation on Miss Fitzgibbon's inanimate behaviour, terming it ladylike, modest and exemplary. Whether Miss Wilcox's constrained tone betrayed how far she was from really feeling the approbation she expressed, how entirely she spoke from a sense of duty, and not because she felt it possible to be in any degree charmed by the personage she praised – or whether Diana, who was by nature hasty, had a sudden fit of irritability – is not quite certain, but she turned on her music-stool.

'Ma'am,' said she to Miss Wilcox, 'that girl does not deserve so much praise. Her behaviour is not at all exemplary. In the schoolroom she is insolently distant. For my part I denounce her airs; there is not one of us but is as good or better than she, though we may not be as rich.'

And Diana shut up the piano, took her music-book under her arm, curtsied and vanished.

Strange to relate, Miss Wilcox said not a word at the time; nor was Diana subsequently reprimanded for this outbreak. Miss Fitzgibbon had now been three months in this school, and probably the governess had had leisure to wear out her early raptures of partiality.

Indeed, as time advanced, this evil often seemed likely to right itself; again and again it seemed that Miss Fitzgibbon was about to fall to her proper level, but then, somewhat provokingly to the lovers of reason and justice, some little incident would occur to invest her insignificance with artificial interest. Once it was the arrival of a great basket of hothouse fruit – melons, grapes and pines – as a present to Miss Wilcox in Miss Fitzgibbon's name. Whether it was that a share of these luscious productions was imparted too freely to the nominal donor, or whether she had had a surfeit of cake on Miss Mabel Wilcox's birthday, it so befell, that in some disturbed state of the digestive organs, Miss Fitzgibbon took to sleep-walking. She one night terrified the school into a panic by passing through the bedrooms, all white in her night-dress, moaning and holding out her hands as she went.

Dr Percy was sent for; his medicines, probably, did not suit the case, for within a fortnight after the somnambulistic feat, Miss Wilcox, going upstairs in the dark, trod on something which she thought was the cat, and on calling for a light, found her darling Matilda Fitzgibbon curled round on the landing, blue, cold, and stiff, without any light in her half-open eyes, or any colour in her lips, or movement in her limbs. She was not soon roused from this fit; her senses seemed half scattered; and Miss Wilcox had now an undeniable excuse for keeping her all day on the drawing-room sofa, and making more of her than ever.

There comes a day of reckoning both for petted heiresses and partial governesses.

One clear winter morning, as Mr Ellin was seated at breakfast, enjoying his bachelor's easy chair and damp, fresh London newspaper, a note was brought to him marked 'private', and 'in haste'. The last injunction was in vain, for William Ellin did nothing in haste – he had no haste in him; he wondered why anybody should be so foolish as to hurry; life was short enough without it. He looked at the little note – three-cornered, scented, and feminine. He knew the handwriting; it came from the very lady Rumour had so often assigned him as his own. The bachelor took out a morocco case, selected from a variety of little instruments a pair of tiny scissors, cut round the seal, and read – 'Miss Wilcox's compliments to Mr Ellin, and she should be truly glad to see him for a few minutes, if at leisure. Miss W. requires a little advice. She will reserve explanations till she sees Mr E.'

Mr Ellin very quietly finished his breakfast; then, as it was a very fine December day – hoar and crisp, but serene and not bitter – he carefully prepared himself for the cold, took his cane, and set out. He liked the walk; the air was still; the sun not wholly ineffectual; the path firm, and but lightly powdered with snow. He made his journey as long as he could by going round through many fields, and through winding, unfrequented lanes. When there was a tree in the way conveniently placed for support, he would sometimes stop, lean his back against the trunk, fold his arms and muse. If Rumour could have seen him, she would have affirmed that he was thinking about Miss Wilcox; perhaps when he arrives at the Lodge his demeanour will inform us whether such an idea be warranted.

At last he stands at the door and rings the bell; he is admitted and shown into the parlour – a smaller and more private room than the drawing-room. Miss Wilcox occupies it; she is seated at her writing-table; she rises – not without air and grace – to receive her visitor. This air and grace she learnt in France; for she was in a Parisian school for six months, and learnt there a little French, and a stock of gestures and courtesies. No: it is certainly not impossible that Mr Ellin may admire Miss Wilcox. She is not without prettiness, any more than are her sisters; and she and they are one and all smart and showy. Bright stone-blue is a colour they like in dress; a crimson bow seldom fails to be pinned on somewhere to give contrast; positive colours generally – grass-greens, red violets, deep yellows – are in favour with them; all harmonies are at a discount. Many people would think Miss Wilcox, standing there in her blue merino dress and pomegranate ribbon, a very agreeable woman. She has regular features; the nose is a little sharp, the lips a little thin, good complexion, light red hair. She is very business-like, very practical; she never in her life knew a refinement of feeling or of thought; she is entirely limited, respectable, and self-satisfied. She has a cool, prominent eye; sharp and shallow pupil, unshrinking and inexpansive; pale irid; light eyelashes, light brow. Miss Wilcox is a very proper and decorous person; but she could not be delicate or modest, because she is naturally destitute of sensitiveness. Her voice, when she speaks, has no vibration; her face no expression; her manner no emotion. Blush or tremor, she never knew.

'What can I do for you, Miss Wilcox?' says Mr Ellin, approaching the writing-table and taking a chair beside it.

'Perhaps you can advise me,' was the answer; 'Or perhaps you can give me some information. I feel so thoroughly puzzled, and really fear all is not right.'

'Where? and how?'

'I will have redress if it be possible,' pursued the lady; 'but how to set about obtaining it! Draw to the fire, Mr Ellin; it is a cold day.'

They both drew to the fire. She continued:

'You know the Christmas holidays are near?'

He nodded.

'Well, about a fortnight since, I wrote, as is customary, to the friends of my pupils, notifying the day when we break up, and requesting that, if it was desired that any girl should stay the vacation, intimation should be sent accordingly. Satisfactory and prompt answers came to all the notes except one – that addressed to Conway Fitzgibbon, Esquire, May Park, Midland County – Matilda Fitzgibbon's father, you know.'

'What? Won't he let her go home?'

'Let her go home, my dear sir! You shall hear. Two weeks elapsed, during which I daily expected an answer; none came. I felt annoyed at the delay, as I had particularly requested a speedy reply. This very morning I had made up my mind to write again, when – what do you think the post brought me?'

'I should like to know.'

14

'My own letter – actually my own – returned from the post-office, with an intimation – such an intimation! – but read for yourself.'

She handed to Mr Ellin an envelope; he took from it the returned note and a paper – the paper bore a hastily scrawled line or two. It said, in brief terms, that there was no such place in Midland County as May Park, and that no such person had ever been heard of there as Conway Fitzgibbon, Esquire.

On reading this, Mr Ellin slightly opened his eyes. 'I hardly thought it was as bad as this,' said he.

'What! You did think it was bad then? You suspected that something was wrong?'

'Really! I scarcely knew what I thought or suspected. How very odd, no such place as May Park! The grand mansion, the oaks, the deer, vanished clean away. And then Fitzgibbon himself! But you saw Fitzgibbon – he came in his carriage?'

'In his carriage!' echoed Miss Wilcox; 'a most stylish equipage, and himself a most distinguished person. Do you think, after all, there is some mistake?'

'Certainly a mistake; but when it is rectified I don't think Fitzgibbon or May Park will be forthcoming. Shall I run down to Midland County and look after these two precious objects?'

'Oh! would you be so good, Mr Ellin? I knew you would be so kind; personal inquiry, you know – there's nothing like it.'

'Nothing at all. Meantime, what shall you do with the child – the pseudo-heiress, if pseudo she be? Shall you correct her – let her know her place?'

'I think,' responded Miss Wilcox reflectively, 'I think not exactly as yet; my plan is to do nothing in a hurry; we will inquire first. If after all she should turn out to be connected as was at first supposed, one had better not do anything which one might afterwards regret. No; I shall make no difference with her till I hear from you again.'

'Very good. As you please,' said Mr Ellin, with that coolness which made him so convenient a counsellor in Miss Wilcox's opinion. In his dry laconism she found the response suited to her outer worldliness. She thought he said enough if he did not oppose her. The comment he stinted so avariciously she did not want.

Mr Ellin 'ran down', as he said, to Midland County. It was an errand that seemed to suit him; for he had curious predilections as well as peculiar methods of his own. Any secret quest was to his taste; perhaps there was something of an amateur detective in him. He could conduct an inquiry and draw no attention. His quiet face never looked inquisitive, nor did his sleepless eye betray vigilance.

He was away about a week. The day after his return, he appeared in Miss Wilcox's presence as cool as if he had seen her but yesterday. Confronting her with that fathomless face he liked to show her, he first told her he had done nothing.

Let Mr Ellin be as enigmatical as he would, he never puzzled Miss Wilcox. She never saw enigma in the man. Some people feared, because they did not understand him; to her it had not yet occurred to begin to spell his nature or analyse his character. If she had an impression about him, it was that he was an idle but obliging man, not aggressive, of few words, but often convenient. Whether he were clever and deep, or deficient and shallow, close or open, odd or ordinary, she saw no practical end to be answered by inquiry, and therefore did not inquire.

Why had he done nothing? she now asked.

'Chiefly because there was nothing to do.'

Then he could give her no information?

'Not much: only this, indeed – Conway Fitzgibbon was a man of straw; May Park a house of cards. There was no vestige of such man or mansion in Midland County, or in any other shire in England. Tradition herself had nothing to say about either the name or the place. The Oracle of old deeds and registers, when consulted, had not responded.'

'Who can he be, then, that came here, and who is this child?'

'That's just what I can't tell you: an incapacity which makes me say I have done nothing.'

'And how am I to get paid?'

'Can't tell you that either.'

'A quarter's board and education owing, and masters' terms besides,' pursued Miss Wilcox. 'How infamous! I can't afford the loss.'

'And if we were only in the good old times,' said Mr Ellin, 'where we ought to be, you might just send Miss Matilda out to the plantations in Virginia, sell her for what she is worth, and pay yourself.'

'Matilda, indeed, and Fitzgibbon! A little imposter! I wonder what her real name is?'

'Betty Hodge? Poll Smith? Hannah Jones?' suggested Mr Ellin.

'Now,' cried Miss Wilcox, 'give me credit for sagacity! It's very odd, but try as I would – and I made every effort – I never could really like that child. She has had every indulgence in this house; and I am sure I made great sacrifice of feeling to principle in showing her such attention; for I could not make anyone believe the degree of antipathy I have all along felt towards her.'

'Yes. I can believe it. I saw it.'

'Did you? Well – it proves that my discernment is rarely at fault. Her game is up now, however; and time it was. I have said nothing to her yet; but now—'

'Have her in while I am here,' said Mr Ellin. 'Has she known of this business? Is she in the secret? Is she herself an accomplice, or a mere tool? Have her in.'

Miss Wilcox rang the bell, demanded Matilda Fitzgibbon, and the false heiress soon appeared. She came in her ringlets, her sash and her furbelowed dress adornments — alas! no longer acceptable.

'Stand there!' said Miss Wilcox, sternly, checking her as she approached the hearth. 'Stand there on the farther side of the table. I have a few questions to put to you, and your business will be to answer them. And mind — let us hear the truth. *We will not endure lies.*'

Ever since Miss Fitzgibbon had been found in the fit, her face had retained a peculiar paleness and her eyes a dark orbit. When thus addressed, she began to shake and blanch like conscious guilt personified.

'Who are you?' demanded Miss Wilcox. 'What do you know about yourself?'

A sort of half-interjection escaped the girl's lips; it was a sound expressing partly fear, and partly the shock the nerves feel when an evil, very long expected, at last and suddenly arrives.

'Keep yourself still, and reply, if you please,' said Miss Wilcox, whom nobody could blame for lacking pity, because nature had not made her compassionate. 'What is your name? We know you have no right to that of Matilda Fitzgibbon.'

She gave no answer.

'I do insist upon a reply. Speak you shall, sooner or later. So you had better do it at once.'

This inquisition had evidently a very strong effect upon the subject of it. She stood as if palsied, trying to speak, but apparently, not competent to articulate.

Miss Wilcox did not fly into a passion, but she grew very stern and urgent; spoke a little loud; and there was a dry clamour in her raised voice which seemed to beat upon the eye and bewilder the brain. Her interest had been injured — her pocket wounded — she was vindicating her rights — and she had no eye to see, and no nerves to feel, but for the point in hand. Mr Ellin appeared to consider himself strictly a looker-on; he stood on the hearth very quiet.

At last the culprit spoke. A low voice escaped her lips. 'Oh, my head!' she cried, lifting her hands to her forehead. She staggered, but caught the door and did not fall. Some accusers might have been startled by such a cry – even silenced; not so Miss Wilcox. She was neither cruel nor violent; but she was coarse, because insensible. Having just drawn breath, she went on, harsh as ever.

Mr Ellin, leaving the hearth, deliberately paced up the room as if he were tired of standing still, and would walk a little for a change. In returning and passing near the door and criminal, a faint breath seemed to seek his ear, whispering his name –

'Oh, Mr Ellin!'

The child dropped as she spoke. A curious voice – not like Mr Ellin's, though it came from his lips – asked Miss Wilcox to cease speaking, and to say no more. He gathered from the floor what had fallen on it. She seemed overcome, but not unconscious. Resting beside Mr Ellin, in a few minutes she again drew breath. She raised her eyes to him.

'Come, my little one, have no fear,' said he.

Reposing her head against him, she gradually became reassured. It did not cost him another word to bring her round, even the strong trembling was calmed by the mere effects of his protection. He told Miss Wilcox, with remarkable tranquillity, but still with a certain decision, that the little girl must be put to bed. He carried her upstairs, and saw her laid there himself. Returning to Miss Wilcox, he said: 'Say no more to her. Beware, or you will do more mischief than you think or wish. That kind of nature is very different from yours. It is not possible that you should like it; but let it alone. We will talk more on the subject tomorrow. Let me question her.'

CHAPTER THREE

Lest you now imagine all mansions to be mirages, allow me to reassure you, for I, Isabel Chalfont, widow of this parish, have passed a portion of my life in one. I was low born but borne high, and in my aerial view found reason to question all perceived opinions of altitude and attitude.

Some might say I have come down in the world, for my present abode is merely in the 'good house' category. My residence, as I have already stated, is comfortable – a bit too brown from too much wood panelling. I would sacrifice the shade to some brighter paint but my husband always impressed on me the fineness of those panels and that impression has outlived himself. As you will see, I have softened the effect with lamps and mirrors and adorned the surfaces with a good many useless objects which I made myself. The outside of my house is so covered in flowers and creeper as to resemble a little nest. This nest is known as Fox Clough.

Accompany me, if you will, to one of my mirrors. Let us peer into that silver pool and inspect the silent creature who matches gesture for gesture and tread for tread. What cargo do they carry, concealed within the folds of suit or gown, to freight the step and make a secret of the soul?

I see something of a comrade in you. You like a book. Silent revelation on a page pleases you better than a self-bolstering display of verbal spillage. What do you see in me? A well-kept woman insulated by a cloak of tranquillity? A woman who mingles resignation with asperity for a homely bouquet? Do you not take this vision at its face value? Not quite? Very well. We know each other better now. That person I presented is real enough. She is Mrs Chalfont. She has a current version of events. There is another self who bore another name and lies pressed between the pages of time. Her narrative treads a different path. She might once have claimed to have found her ideal in life and to have lost it. Yet who shall weep for a stormy voyage when the ship comes safely into port? The maiden is no more. A woman grew in her place. It is she who greets you now, the naked heart modestly cloaked, the expectations dimmed for economy's sake. Perhaps you have made the same outward adjustments to your inner self. Many would claim that raw passion in a person past their youthful prime sits like tropical flowers in an English garden. My own opinion? You shall have it by and by.

Come into my garden now. Yes, I am a gardener too. Mine is an English garden. Its fair-skinned blooms bask in rain and raise gentle light on a grey English day. No fashionable fuchsias, no carnations homesick for their Himalayan hills! My borders are the borders of an embroidered piece; for spring, bluebells and primroses, for summer, roses and lavender. Here I have made a bower of wisteria. Serenity holds government in this spot. Indignation sleeps and regret is overgrown by honeysuckle and moss and by this tiny, star-eyed flower of blue. What is it called? Forget-me-not. Very well. We shall not forget.

I was born Isabel Cooke in the town of H—, the daughter of a tailor and the eldest of four daughters. My earliest memory is of a tumble of bells that summoned me from sleep. They belonged to a great church right by where we lived, but until I was five or six I thought that church belonged to us and rang its bells for us alone and assembled each Sabbath its congregation to pay us homage. Our own home was two rooms in a run-down dwelling, yet our vistas were of surprising grandeur. The prospect from our lane was of the door and spires of God's abode and when, washed and dressed on Sunday, we paid our visit to its host, He offered from His door a long, refreshing vista of moor and hill and countryside, clear to Castle Hill. A dank alley was our playground (and there were few diversions in that hard-working town, save chapel choirs and bull-baiting), yet we broadened our horizons down by the navigation where huge barges carried people and goods to far-off places and we picked wild flowers and blackberries along its banks. I slept in a bed with my sisters and would have pitied any without so much sibling flesh for comfort. Close by, our parents slumbered and we were never frightened, not even of the ghostly forms upon which my father cut his patterns, and which overlooked our sleep. The second chamber served for workroom, dining-room, kitchen and every other function of family life. You might conceive of this as a chaotic existence, yet it was orderly enough. Our garments hung upon a nail. One in the wash and one to wear was the rule. As there was no surplus there was no disorder. In the mornings, having eaten breakfast, we formed a queue to rinse our cup and dish. Meals being cleared my father cut his cloth upon the table and Mother sewed it. My mother always worked alongside my father, stitching as he cut. We children helped as we could but my parents worked late into the night while we slept.

Our town was famous for its worsted cloth and gentlemen came from as far afield as Manchester and even London to boast the labels of its most prominent tailors. Alas, too many cutters vied for trade and my father, far from prospering, had to struggle for a living. We were poor but I imagined us rich and still think we were. Nourished by love, we could thrive on small rations. I later realized (and rue it even now) that life was not so sweet and simple for my parents and especially my mother. I often remember her red-eyed – not from weeping (for she was a stranger to self-pity) but from close and prolonged labour by meagre light. She had a hard life and willingly forfeited her own aims for her family. I recall an occasion when we visited some better-off household. A plate of meat was set before my mother and my little sister spoke out: 'Mama never eats anything but bread and butter.' Due to the sacrifices of my parents we were able to go to school and my greatest pleasure was to read to them as they worked, as neither had learnt to read or write very well.

My father used to tell us that whenever we felt ill-used we should think of someone worse off than ourselves and count our blessings. His own great blessing, he said, was his trade, for God was also a tailor and our lives were the suits He cut for each one. 'Remember, the life that seems dismal on earth may be one of great splendour in heaven.' (I remember his arm in threadbare sleeve, guiding the shears which bit through fabric with a silky sound like a cat's sneeze.) 'When something happens that causes you to suffer, think of it as a pearl stitched on to your hem.' Often with grievance or with grazed knee, I would sit and contemplate my plain little hem and add another pearl to it and think myself the most glamorous princess on this earth. Coming from such a family I believed the world to be composed of good and I grew up with no fear of life.

If choice were a factor in family hierarchy then I would recommend the place I occupied. An eldest daughter has the twin pleasures of acting as second mother to the little ones and as second sister to her mother. The only drawback to the situation is a belief that one is indispensable and a consequent reluctance to leave home. Yet it was understood that I would work to earn my living and although I loved my home I looked forward to the time when I would explore some fresh corner of the world.

I quitted school at fourteen and passed two happy years in helping my mother with the children and with sewing. In that time we derived harmless amusement from planning my future with as much imaginative speculation as if my prospects were unlimited. In reality, my options were limited to three. I could work at home with my father, enter an industrial works, or go into domestic service. It seemed a stroke of extraordinary good fortune when I came by a situation as nurse governess. Such positions are normally reserved for cultivated girls of the middle classes, but a teacher at my school who liked me had made particular efforts to advance my prospects. These resulted in my achieving a position with the Cornhill family. My charges were to be two children aged six and seven. The house was more than fifty miles distant but I liked its name, which was Happen Heath. From the start I thought of it as Happy Heath. It spoke of open spaces, of air and innocence. If I had to leave home, there could be no sweeter-sounding destination. All the same, the day of parting was very sore. The whole family accompanied me to the staging post. None could speak for sadness although the little children wept. Father had cut me two grey dresses, which made me feel very grown-up and helped me to contain both my excitement at commencing my adult life and my misery at parting with my family.

Picture, if you will, a young lady who has never been outside her own town, nor ever spent a day away from those who gave her life, sandwiched between strangers atop an open carriage in the gathering dusk. All the landscape that was known to me was tossed away behind the wheels. Wind and rain pulled at my hair and let down my new ringlets. Strange towns came and went, dispensing and absorbing unknown travellers. Womanhood seemed very far in the future as I tried to avoid the glances of strangers and wondered what to do if no one came to meet me. I own that I allowed the merciful shadows to mask a few tears.

To my great relief there was a gentleman with my name on a board and two small children dancing at his side. I greeted Mr Cornhill with all due deference until he informed me that he was, in fact, Tom, the driver. In the carriage the children whispered their names – Dorothy and Freddie – and asked me all manner of questions, and I cannot tell you what comfort I derived from the babbling of these two darlings.

The carriage entered a daunting set of gates. A fresh-faced country moon unmasked the scene. Trees stippled this beam as the horse made an arduous ascent. I went very silent and clutched the children's hands for I had never known an approach could be so long. The ground levelled and we drove over a bridge. I heard a rushing sound and peered out of the window. Below us, exquisite in the moonlight, was a racing river. Now the house appeared before us. Nine long windows reflected the view. To me it seemed a palace and as I made an awkward descent from the carriage I was conscious only of my wet hair, my insignificant apparel, my makeshift luggage. We entered by a porch with fan-like green plants in urns and a chequerboard floor, composed of squares of black and white marble; from thence into a hall that itself seemed the size of a mansion. A bright fire was burning. Imagine! A fire in the hall. From pale grey walls sprang moulded garlands of fruit and flowers in the most realistic colours. There was a staircase wide enough for me and all my siblings to walk it hand in hand. So transfixed was I by my surroundings that I failed to notice the arrival of their proprietors.

'Dear Isa, you are welcome.' The voice was soft as summer rain.

Ere I had adjusted to my fairytale habitat I was bewitched by a fresh vision. Although stout, Alicia Cornhill had a porcelain delicacy that characterized all her features, from the pale rose of her cheeks to her blanched fingers. She was dressed for dinner in a gown of rose silk and looked a lovely overblown version of that flower.

'Poor child, you are soaked through.' Her cheek touched the air close to mine. 'Come into the fire and then you may go and change.'

'I have brought no dinner gown,' I apologized.

She gave me a look which I could not quite translate but which quickly became a smile. 'Such matters need not concern you. We shall make every effort to set you at your ease. How do you think you shall like your new home?'

'Very well,' I answered decidedly, and added that I had never dreamed to find myself in so fine a situation. I confessed that such grandeur made me apprehensive but said I would try to take every advantage of my privilege.

A little clap sounded as the young man beside her brought his hands together in applause. 'Well spoken, Miss Cooke. It is clear you know your place in society. You are bound to do well.'

'I hope so,' I said, although his tone discomposed me for it seemed to contain an edge of irony.

'Take no notice of Finch,' Mrs Cornhill said. 'He is a scholar and considers himself superior to us all.'

I now gave my attention to the scholar. He was a tall youth, a year or two my senior, with a pale and somewhat disapproving countenance, this effect emphasized by fierce black eyebrows and wayward hair in matching ebony. I thought his demonstration juvenile and would have liked to let him know that to me he seemed by far the most inferior member of his tribe. Even the whiskery and blustery pater took the trouble to make me welcome. They were as healthy and well-off an assembly as I had ever encountered and I was much taken with all but one.

That same one chose, unbidden, to take my arm and lead me to a reception-room. 'Do you suppose yourself to be suited to this position?' he inquired.

'I shall endeavour to be useful,' said I.

'Beware now, Miss Cooke! Usefulness may not be adequate to the task. The children of the rich are not like other children. They must be held above the crowd by any means; if necessary, by trampling on the heads of others.'

'Children, rich and poor, are held above the crowd, not by trampling on the heads of others, but by a sense of moral purpose such as was given to me by my own parents.' I tried to keep the quake of anger from my voice as I retrieved my arm and made my own way into a chamber where blue silk panels matched an azure ceiling on which a whole paradise of birds had been etched in plaster.

Happily, Finch was not to be a constant presence. He had lodgings at his university and would return home only on occasional weekends. I was rescued from any further hectoring by Mrs Cornhill. This life-sized doll sank on to a primrose damask chaise and, with a gesture so feminine as to be almost flirtatious, indicated another seat. Being wet and dishevelled I was loath to make myself at home. Mrs Cornhill considerately found me a more serviceable perch after which she dismissed the rest of the family with the touching insistence that we ladies were bound to be more comfortable on our own.

For a time she said nothing but merely gazed upon me with pleasure. I felt my terror begin to thaw. What was I thinking in this easeful moment? Was I pondering the inequity of life that some should have so much and others – such as my hard-working parents – so little? No, I had fallen in love with my employer and her milieu. My speculations were restricted to the hope that Mrs Cornhill might soon esteem me sufficiently to let me have one of her cast-off gowns so that I might better fit my new surroundings.

'How do you like children, Miss Cooke?' the lady now asked. I told her I liked them and was well used to them. Upon hearing this she gave a sigh of contentment and I almost echoed it. She asked if I could endure a quiet life. I envisaged sitting in the tranquil garden or walking by the river. I pictured myself (in different attire) in this pleasant room with a piece of embroidery in hand. I conjured up pleasant meals in cultivated company. I answered that I would bear it very cheerfully.

'That is good,' Mrs Cornhill approved. 'That is very good. I can see we shall be the best of friends.' She leant close to confide. 'I, alas, have a limited tolerance of little ones. I have delicate nerves. Therefore,' she added, 'you must be with them at all times. You will take your meals with them and you will appear downstairs only when required to present and supervise the children. In short,' she beamed joyfully, 'you are to be an invisible angel.'

'Yes, ma'am.' I was somewhat subdued by this revelation, and wondered when supper would be as I was very hungry after the long journey.

'And now, Miss Cooke, you may go. You will give the children their meal, conduct their prayers and put them to bed. After that I shall have something sent to you on a tray. I expect you are too tired and excited to be very hungry.'

'Yes, ma'am,' I said.

'You will be lonely on your first evening,' she relented. 'As the daughter of a tailor, I trust you sew tolerably well. I shall send up a little mending to keep your fingers occupied and your mind away from home.'

All the time she spoke she smiled brightly as though imparting the very best of tidings. My little pupils dragged me up several storeys to the nursery, which brought the discovery that the children of the poor may be better off than those of the rich. In contrast to the sumptuous surroundings in which I had found myself downstairs, I now arrived at a small, comfortless chamber with meagre fire and oddments of furniture. I felt sorry for those bright young persons cast out from parental comfort and company but nevertheless had to exercise strong control to avoid pilfering some morsels from their unappetizing supper. My own sustenance, small and cold, appeared in due course but I was too tired and confused to address myself to it and fell into my chill bed promising God a brighter outlook in the morning and an imminent address to Mrs Cornhill's mending.

Happen Heath – that tranquil token to prosperity, which rose proud of the surrounding hills to make its address directly to the sun – contained, unknown to its many visitors, a mouse within the rafters, a human mouse, but sixteen years of age, who had set out upon the great adventure of her life and found that the prescription was for no life at all.

From my lofty eyrie I could hear the bright bustle of the house. Carriages came and went. There were sounds of music and the delicious savour of meals not tasted by myself, for I shared a nursery diet with the children. Parties lit the house with numberless candles and adorned it with people who seemed wonderful to look at, though I never saw them close to. My portion was a glimpse from the banister on the top stair.

From there I tried to feed myself on scraps of eavesdropped conversation. I had no adult company. The household lived in separate layers. The serving staff thought me above them, the family considered me beneath them, and I was compressed in this sandwich of social order, as stifled as a wilting leaf of lettuce. No adult ever spoke to me except when I tried to spend some time in the garden alone and then, very soon, Mrs Cornhill, panting a little, would catch up to say she could not have it on her conscience that I was bored and had a little mending/planting/weeding for me.

Although I executed all that was asked of me, it seemed to irk my employer that I had got off so lightly. If ever she came upon me reading or setting out for a walk she would find some fresh task. She thrust upon me great heaps of sheets and dresses for mending. At night I often felt so tired and homesick that I was obliged to have a good cry.

I said I had no company. That is not quite true. My solitude was occasionally suspended by the appearance of Finch Cornhill. Although he did not seem to like me, the eldest son of the house would not ignore me. When we chanced to share the same space I felt his eyes upon me, seeking, I felt sure, some weakness to deride. Once, he detained me to inquire how I fared. 'Very well,' I lied, for he did not seem one in whom to confide. 'You surprise me,' he replied. 'Perhaps I overestimated you.'

'I think,' said I, with winter in my tone, 'you meant to say you underestimated me.'

One corner of his mouth inclined in wry humour. 'I know what I meant to say.'

His case was not aided by the fact that his mother was never done singing his praises. But I liked the children, whose fresh natures had not yet been afflicted by the snobbery of their parents and I was glad of the opportunity to pass on to these dear little creatures the values I had learnt from my parents.

On a day some six months after my arrival, I was in the nursery with my charges. The dim little chamber stood aloof from summer, yet the narrow window served a modest portion of the season and aroused in me a mood half miserable and half ecstatic. I read aloud part of a favourite poem, *Rokeby*, by Sir Walter Scott, and asked the children if they knew its meaning. A dead silence followed. Freddie yawned and Dorothy gave me a look of reproach (for she considered the exploitation of the brain in such a pretty head an unfair abuse). The thought came over me that I was to spend the best part of my life in this bondage, forced to suppress my intelligence, my energy, my individual desires. Day after day I must sit chained to this chair within these four bare walls while the glorious summer suns were burning in heaven and declaring at the close of every day that the time I was losing would not come again. Stung to the core, I told the children to learn the verse by heart. I left the nursery and slipped down the stairs into the garden.

The dew had not yet dried off the park. Trees sheltered it with a mantle of shadow. The river was shooting through it like a silver arrow. I found a shady anonymity in the fern garden where the peace was disturbed only by the humming of insects on the wing.

Another sound intruded. It was the murmur of voices. A glance confirmed that they belonged to Mrs Cornhill and her eldest son. I perfected my concealment behind a well-dressed foliage. The strollers came within my range.

'And why is she locked away all the time?' young Mr Cornhill asked. 'What offence has she committed?'

I wondered who the criminal was. The lady supplied the answer. 'Miss Cooke renders the service for which she is paid. She is not a member of the household.'

'Nor is she the mother of the baby brats,' the son argued: 'yet she takes all her meals with them. I wonder why?'

Mrs Cornhill urged her firstborn not to be tiresome. 'There is a great difference between people like ourselves and Isabel.'

'I do not see it,' he said. 'Are you afraid she will sing bawdy songs at table or take her tea from a saucer?'

'She is a person of the working classes.' Mrs Cornhill lowered her tone for delicacy. 'Her sole duty in life will be to God and to her family, whereas ours is to society.'

'As society is composed of families and their God, it seems to me that there is no difference at all,' the young man said; 'yet anyone can see that there is a very great difference between an intelligent young woman and the two mites with whom she is engaged all day and night. I feel sure she would welcome some adult conversation as much as I would welcome fresh company at our table.'

The shorter of the strollers paused. Her silken skirts agitatedly rustled. 'You think yourself high-minded. Are you sure that you have not merely allowed your head to be turned by a pretty face? I did not notice such concern for Miss Hubbard when she was in the house. Could that have been because she was over forty and had whiskers on her chin?'

'I was a child then. It is a child's business to obey his parents. I am a man now and it is a man's business to follow his principles, although I will readily assent that Miss Cooke is agreeable.'

'When you are head of your own household,' Mrs Cornhill's voice was ice, 'you may use it to overthrow the social order, although I pray you will find a wife who can make you see sense.'

'You will have Miss Cooke join us for Sunday luncheon.' The young man's intonation matched his mother's for arrogance. 'I doubt the breach will topple the social order.'

No mention was made of this discourse (which much surprised me) but a short time afterwards Mrs Cornhill said she had decided that the children were now of age to dine with their parents at weekends and I might accompany them.

I suppose the Cornhills were no worse than many of their class. They believed that status and refinement had been bestowed on them by God through mercenary worth. The poor were mere livestock, a resource to be exploited. Other than that they were to be ignored. I, in my turn, learnt not to judge my employers but to view them as productions of their system who knew no other way to be. Yet I began to perceive Finch Cornhill as a different kind of person. When Sunday came I found myself too tongue-tied from long months of solitude to contribute but was well content to listen while he held forth on worldly matters of which I had no knowledge and in which his parents had little interest.

He spoke of the exploitation of small children in mills and mines, of people of the colonies sold into slavery. When he introduced these unwelcome elements of the outside world the children looked enchanted, Mrs Cornhill appeared mortified and her whiskered spouse seemed thoroughly confused by the intrusion of plain conversation upon the business of dining. I wanted to applaud. Bravo! I thought. There is a rebel under this self-satisfied roof.

Afterwards, to the ire of his mother, he invited me to walk in the garden.

'Isa must attend to the children,' Mrs Cornhill warned.

'And so she shall,' he promised. 'I see little enough of my small brother and sister. They will come as chaperons.'

The children were awed by their important title and behaved with exemplary reserve.

'I owe you an apology,' the young man said. 'I am sorry if I appeared abrupt.'

'Mr Cornhill,' I replied, 'you did not seem abrupt. You were abrupt. Indeed, in that modest social sphere from which I spring, behaviour such as yours would be deemed uncivil.'

He paused to give me surprised scrutiny. 'If I am to be deemed wanting in cordiality, you may be found lacking in humility.' He looked pleased rather than irked by this discovery.

'Would you like me to bend my knee and curtsy, sir?' I placed ironic emphasis on the final word.

'Very much I should like it,' he said, and he gave a surprising laugh. 'For then I could look down on you. You are too tall either for humility or for any man to admire you to advantage.'

'You have a strange way of displaying admiration,' said I.

'I meant my barbs for my mother and not for you. Alas, for all her porcelain complexion, she has the hide of a rhinoceros.'

Now that I no longer feared him and understood the nature of his mother I was able to laugh and was rewarded with one of his own rare but delightful smiles.

'Yet I must confess,' he grew serious again, 'I was testing you too. I had thought a female so pretty must also be vain and shallow. I was mistaken. I see in you a young woman more curious about the world than about her reflection in the mirror, one with a fine quick brain and a delicate sensibility. I believe it is I who should bow to you.'

He did so, causing an explosion of giggles among the children.

'Can we be friends now?' he questioned, as he arose.

'I place little value on declarations of friendship,' said I. 'Friendship is as friendship does. We shall see how we proceed.'

'May we start, then, by addressing one another as friends? You must call me Finch.'

'It would be a breach of social order,' I pointed out.

'Good. Let us breach it! Let you and I wage war on artifice and snobbery.'

34

It was not long before I came to esteem this eldest son of the house whose idealistic nature was a worrying puzzle to those who had bred him to be their replica, whose rationed smiles and brief outbursts of mirth were as sunshine in a cold climate. I began to look forward with all my heart to the family meal on Sunday. It was after one of these repasts that he approached me privately. 'I worry about you,' he said. 'I fear you must be lonely.'

'Less so with Sundays to look forward to,' I assured him.

'It grieves me that because you are not rich, you are condemned to spend your time with two spoilt infants.'

'I could find worse company,' I said.

He laughed. 'I am sure you could find better too. I am here too rarely to help your situation but I have thought of a way to leave you good companions.' And he thrust into my hand a bundle of books. I turned over the spines to discover the names of those who were to join me in exile: Byron, Campbell, Wordsworth. They sounded stout fellows. I could not have envisaged what friendships we would make in silence, what journeys pursue, what philosophic puzzles resolve, what romances initiate.

Thus began my real education and, with it, a deeper acquaintance with my benefactor. His own fine mind I imbibed with Boswell, Hume and Moore. An insight into his heart was discovered via Shakespeare, Milton, Pope; and by a more direct route on the day I encountered, tucked inside the pages of a volume of Goldsmith, Finch's hand-written note. 'I envy this genius, for I know how much you will like him.' With considerable daring, I returned it with my own memorandum. 'I like the sender even better for he has dispatched kindness along with genius.'

Now every volume brought its bulletin. A life that had been bleak and empty became rich in friendship, lacking only the flesh-and-blood dimension of that precious boon. It was strange but pleasant to discover that I soon missed this earnest young man almost as much as my own parents. In our struggle to survive I had had no expectation of romantic love. I had envisaged only a practical and useful life. Yet on the rare occasions when I stood close to Finch I experienced all manner of feelings jumbled in together. I felt weak in his company and, at the same time, immensely strengthened by his connection to me. I thought that with such a presence by my side I could work to improve the world. There was nothing false or foolish in him. I knew he would not waste time with me if he did not care for me.

One day I was surprised to find in my reading parcel a copy of the Bible. Finch must have known I was well acquainted with its content. I opened it and found fresh revelation. A hand-penned note prefaced the sacred scripture. 'Upon this good book,' Finch had written, 'I swear that my affection is yours only and for ever.' What feelings I experienced I need not describe. Those who have known love's requital will recollect the light that illumines the deepest chambers of the soul, the sense of humility that almost overwhelms surprise, the desire for worthiness and goodness upon which new generations are founded. To those not yet thus blessed, I shall not demean such solemn joy with a summary. I merely wish you the reality – and soon. Yes, I felt joy and relief too, and gratitude, but soon composed myself and went about my work. I had no need for giddy celebration or sentimental reassurance. Finch was offering me no less than his very self. As my heart was already in his keeping I perceived no barrier to our being together for life.

Oh, how unhusked and innocent are the young. Finch was but eighteen. He had no expectation of any money until he was twenty-one. He warned me – unnecessarily – that his parents would not approve of our alliance. They would be ambitious for a match that carried both social and financial advantage. They would almost as soon see their eldest son dead as married to the daughter of a poor tailor.

He vowed to do all in his power to evade his mother's matrimonial schemes until he was independent. In the meantime, we agreed to say nothing of our feelings and to show as little of them as possible so as not to arouse suspicion. Impossible, though, to fully mask the joy that had entered my soul and sustained me through the many trials in that superficial household. There was even the pleasure of a shared secret in the formality of our meetings. Any private rendezvous we rationed to a pauper's portion. Only once a month or so would we permit ourselves an 'accidental' encounter. Our conversation then came out in a great flood of passion concerning books or causes, yet lit by a different, underlying passion, never yet exposed.

On the day he kissed me I was in the garden with the children, planting spring bulbs. The enterprise left them muddy and I sent them to wash before lunch while I completed the task alone. After they had gone I savoured a moment alone in the sunshine with my eyes closed. I was thinking of Finch (in private moments I rarely thought of anything else) when he came upon me by chance, sat quietly on the grass beside me, and kissed me. It was the barest benediction yet brought me more pleasure than any touch in my whole life. We did not prolong the kiss. I opened my eyes and we laughed – both at his audacity and my surprise – and then he squeezed my hand and went indoors.

'Finch kissed Isa,' little Dorothy proclaimed, with importance, over lunch.

The servant's timid ministrations made a clamour in contrast to the silence that prevailed. Mrs Cornhill seemed to turn to stone although the eye that fixed upon me was full of lively rage.

'Don't tease, Dot,' Finch said gently. 'Others at table may not share your sense of humour and I am sure Miss Cooke taught you not to lie.'

'I'm not lying!' The little girl's tone rose in piercing self-righteousness. 'I saw you. Isa sent us in to wash but I forgot my doll and came back. You were on the grass. Her eyes were closed.'

I waited for an almighty row. I was confident I had earned one. Mrs Cornhill remained monstrously gracious. The rich feel no need to express their fury. They are fully aware of their power and know how to use it. She severed her meat, she sipped her wine. She observed, in pleasant conversational tone, 'I should think, Finch, that Miss Cooke is perhaps not the one to teach Dorothy about honesty.'

You may imagine the agony that followed. Naturally, I was unable to eat but was obliged to remain at table and make a pretence of doing so, while conscious of the huge orbs of my little charges fixed upon me with burning curiosity. I then had to take them for their Sunday walk. When we returned I could find no trace of Finch. Mrs Cornhill was waiting and ushered me into her parlour. She looked me over once then turned her back on me and I endeavoured to fix my attention on the pretty room with its oyster-coloured walls and pale gold curtains, its long mirrors that held, like watery vessels, great bunches of water and greenery from the outside. 'My son,' said she, in very controlled tones, 'has expressed his regard for you.'

I hung my head and said nothing. I felt immensely blessed that he had had the courage to stand up to her, yet I was afraid.

'You will understand, of course,' she turned to me with a sneer, 'that this is absurd. You are a tailor's daughter. Such events may occur in penny romances but never, ever in real life.'

I glanced beyond her to the racing river and tranquil garden, honeyed by afternoon light, where I had had my first kiss. I would fix my thoughts there and resist any urge to defend myself lest she succeed in snaring me into me into unwise admission.

'He says,' her chin rose in a challenging fashion but her voice remained soft, 'that he means to marry you; that he will defy Mr Cornhill and myself in order to do so.'

I had begun to tremble. Somehow, her control made me feel the full force of her antagonism more than if she had raised her voice. She walked up and down, then paused and looked me over. Her wordless judgement of my plain working-woman's dress was more humiliating than any expressed insult. No matter that my grey gown had been cut with much pride by my father and was better stitched than any of her finery, her glance expressed its plainness and unsuitability for her parlour and her company as painfully as if she had stripped me of all my clothing.

'Have you nothing to say?' she demanded.

'No, ma'am.' I knew her strength now and was so terrified that I could barely whisper. My only comfort was that she must soon dismiss me and then my ordeal would be over. I would work with my parents until Finch was in a position to make me his wife.

'There, Miss Cooke!' She gave a little laugh, which startled me. 'There is no need to look so much the guilty party. I attach no blame to you. I would not expect judgement from a girl of your class. It is my son who has had the advantages. It is he who must take responsibility for this foolishness. It is he,' she added in a tone that was almost playful, 'who must be protected.'

I made a small curtsy but trembled so much I almost fell over. 'I shall leave Happen Heath at once.'

'Indeed you will not,' she said sharply. 'To do so would be to compound one irresponsibility with another. I will not have you inconvenience me more than you have already done. You will remain in this house until you can demonstrate yourself a sober and unexpectant young woman.'

'Very well, ma'am,' I agreed, although I secretly vowed that I would write to my parents and ask to go home. In that moment my longing for home and for my parents and sisters was almost too intense to bear.

'And you will not see Finch.'

Some flash of defiance must have lit my eyes, for Mrs Cornhill gave her mirthless laugh again. 'Sadly, none of us will be seeing much of my boy in the next few years in consequence of this misfortune. Finch is to be removed from university. Mr Cornhill and I have agreed that he has had too much exposure to liberal influences. Mr Cornhill has kindly agreed to purchase him a commission.'

'A commission?' I thought I understood but preferred to believe in any other possibility.

'He is to go into the army. I am sorry we did not take this action sooner. Indeed, Mr Cornhill urged it, being a military man, but I allowed myself to be swayed by my son's preference.'

'How long?' I whispered.

'I do not see that it is any of your business. Naturally, we hope it will be for a lifetime career but in any case for seven years.'

It was a disillusion to discover that the power of love is no power at all compared to that of superior wealth and years. My eyes filled with tears and without meaning to do so I raised them to my employer in appeal. The look she gave me then caused me swiftly to revoke any entreaty. It was a look of triumph.

'Mr Cornhill has expressed a preference for my son to serve abroad,' she revealed. 'We are both agreed on it. Finch has a restless nature and, sadly, a romantic one. It would be better if it were out of his system before he finally settles down to marry.' She gave a sentimental smile to this idea and her expression then sharpened again. 'Do not think yourself hard done by,' she said. 'You imagine you have been deprived of happiness. In fact, I am sparing you disappointment and humiliation. My son and you are matched only in youthful appetite. In a very little time he would come to despise you for what you are – a common creature of flesh and blood – whereas he is high-born and high-minded. Get along now. We have wasted half the day over this nonsense. Please return to the children and their prayers. I do not wish them to turn out as foolish as their brother.'

I crept away to my upstairs quarter where the children awaited me full of guilt and interest concerning the explosion they had unwittingly triggered. I tried to envisage a pearl stitched on my hem but felt mainly as if some small but vital scrap of my body's machinery had been torn away, leaving a wound that bled only a little, but if unattended would surely, in due course, prove fatal.

Yet I did not despair. I would find out where Finch was stationed, write to him very plainly (merely to state that he should do as his parents wished and I would wait for him as long as was necessary) for the pretty ornament our romance had been owned no place in the present circumstance. All that remained was the plain contingency of our being together. Not for an instant was I swayed by Mrs Cornhill's version of events. I was confident that in all the world I would find no companion more sympathetic to my nature. Young and powerless I might be but I had on my side the virtues of patience and perseverance, and I believed that these would see me through.

As soon as an opportunity presented itself I composed a long letter to my father. I was about to post it when Mrs Cornhill appeared with a quantity of lace she wanted attached to one of Dorothy's dresses. She showed a manner no different from usual. She sighted my correspondence and said that Martha, the serving maid, was going for a walk and would take it to the post. To tell the truth I was glad of the extra labour for it left me less time to fret about my fate or that of Finch and it was some comfort that Mrs Cornhill had chosen not to punish me further. Perhaps she judged me sufficiently chastised.

It was a week before I was to learn the full nature of my employer's reprisal. It was more devious, more odious, than anything I could have envisaged. I had just made a mild reprimand to little Dorothy for eating jam from a spoon when she turned to me with a sly look. 'I scarcely judge you in a position to correct *me*, Isa, for you are so very common.'

In that moment I was too shocked to respond but I was soon to learn that this was not an aberration but a campaign. Mrs Cornhill had taught her children to revile me. The little ones, whose instruction had been my sole pleasure, now became my tormentors. They mocked my accent and my unfashionable attire. When I corrected their manners they would jeer at my own.

I could not doubt who had done this. There was an air of mischievous collusion about the dame and her brood. It seemed beyond belief that a mother would corrupt her children in order to castigate an enemy but I recognized her tone in every utterance from their baby mouths. One day I took Dorothy on my knee and said, 'You have always been my friend. Why do you now wish to hurt me?'

She hastily abandoned her perch and pouted. 'Finch was sent away because he was your friend. If Freddie and I are your friends, we will be sent away.'

42

I had lost my only remaining allies at Happen Heath. I passed a dismal and impatient time awaiting my post.

About a week after this Mrs Cornhill came to my room, her well-worn artificial smile pinned upon her porcelain features. 'You look sad, my dear,' she said. 'This should cheer you.' And she handed me a letter. Emotion blurred my vision to see that dear, familiar handwriting. The script was not that of my father, whose writing skills were sufficient only to his business needs, but of my sister, Sally, next in years to me, who transcribed Father's correspondence in my absence. That rounded, hopeful, youthful hand seemed extended to me in love.

'I am going home,' I said to my visitor.

'Won't you read your letter?' She spoke softly. Although I did not choose to have her share that small portion of my happiness I could wait no longer and tore the seal on the precious missive.

My dearest daughter, we are so happy that all goes so well with you.

My heart missed a beat. Had he not paid attention to what I had written? It was a moment before I could concentrate on the words again.

We miss your bright smile but are greatly heartened by your success. The money you send home is helping to make ends meet. Take care of yourself. Poor Mama has been unwell, but, as usual, continues to work and care for the family. Be happy, child, and know we share that happiness. There can be no greater pleasure in life for any parent than to have a child who shows them well in the outside world. With love from all and in particular from your proud Papa.

Mrs Cornhill placed a hand upon my shoulder. 'You wrote hastily, child. I knew you would regret it. It would have been selfish to distress your poor parents with your little lapse. I thought it best to place some hopeful words upon the page. I copied your hand as best I could. There, now! Aren't you glad to have made your papa proud?'

She quitted the room softly and left me to my misery. Although the brass catch rested loosely in its lock, that door might have been bound by chain and padlock. I was in a trap and I had fashioned it myself. In spite of the fact that she hated me she would not let me go. I had made myself too useful.

I have already recounted how my father kept us buoyant by reminding us, in times of adversity, to consider someone worse off than ourselves. In that moment, I could not have envisaged anyone more cruelly disadvantaged than myself. In that time, I had no acquaintance with the child known as Matilda Fitzgibbon.

CHAPTER FOUR

─────◦◦◦◦◦─────

She sat now in a corner of Mabel Wilcox's parlour. She was still pale from her collapse of the previous day and seemed at a remove from reality. Mr Ellin had hoped to make himself her ally but although she gave him a brief look of gratitude when he asked Miss Wilcox to depart, after that she withdrew into herself, her plain little brow crowned with a frown.

He pulled his chair up close and made himself as genial as possible. 'Now, who are you, little girl?' He spoke softly so as not to startle her. 'You do not seem like the child of a pauper. Your accent, when you can be induced to speak, is refined enough.'

On this occasion she, apparently, felt no such inducement. She kept her silence with the slightly ruffled preoccupation of a bird on a windswept rock at sea.

'All you have to do is tell me of your life before you came here. For instance, what is your real address?'

The girl said nothing. Mr Ellin was disappointed that, in spite of his goodwill, she wore her customary sullen expression. She was still beautifully attired but today her hair had not been dressed in ringlets and instead was pulled back severely from her face. 'Matilda!' he entreated. She responded with a puzzled look, a frown, the smallest flicker that came close to, yet did not signify, recognition. So, perhaps Matilda was not her name. It was a start. He stood up and paced the room to escape the rebuke of her unyielding inattention, taking covert glances at her on each turn. He thought she bore her finery like a bride who is being married against her will. He considered that her unflattering hairstyle suited her.

'That man who brought you here, who styled himself as Mr Fitzgibbon, was he really your father, or perhaps a guardian? You were surely not delivered by a stranger?'

Just for an instant, she raised her eyes to him. It was an oddly old-fashioned look, disconcerting in a girl who could be no more than twelve or thirteen.

'Do you not trust me?' he appealed.

When at last she spoke it was in a voice as quiet and controlled as any adult. 'Why should I trust you?'

Mr Ellin felt indignant. 'Who else is there to take your part? What do you suppose would have happened had I not taken pity on you?'

The lass looked away, not abashed, as one might expect, but to conceal an expression of rebellion.

Her interviewer felt aroused to vexation himself. 'You do nothing to improve your situation. Whatever misfortune has befallen you, it is surely not the fault of myself or Miss Wilcox? Poor Miss Wilcox went to particular lengths to be civil to you and you repaid her benevolence with indifference. Could you not have made some small effort to respond?'

For the first time the mysterious young person looked at him squarely and he saw that the look he had taken for sullenness was, at least in part, exhaustion. He observed as well that although her skin was sallow her eyes were pretty — a smoky shade of grey that wistfully complemented the dark shadows underneath. To engage with that gaze was a disconcerting experience. He had an odd sensation, of sighting in a jeweller's window a gem stolen from oneself.

'How should I have responded?' In spite of her weariness the girl spoke with spirit. 'Had I answered her flattery I would have been party to a fraud. If I told the truth about myself, I would at once have rendered myself homeless. As to Miss Wilcox's kindness, it was as this room is today – all brightness and no warmth.'

Mr Ellin almost smiled. While he paced he had been rubbing his hands together. Miss Wilcox had not troubled to furnish the parlour with a fire for this appointment. And yet he had not been wholly conscious of discomfort, perhaps because his companion provided spark enough to compensate. 'Have you not been taught,' said he, 'that a lady ought to use her sense to listen gracefully and hold her tongue intelligently?'

'It would appear, then,' she rejoined, 'that I am not a lady.'

It struck him that it was a long time since he had shared such intelligent female company. Pity it came in such a package! 'You can tell the truth to me,' he assured her. 'I mean you no harm.'

'I don't suppose you do,' she said. 'No more do storm and fire unless I cross their paths unwisely, and yet I do not trust them. Why should I you, sir?'

'Because you have little to lose,' he suggested.

'You are wrong, sir. I would lose my secrecy. It has stood me in good stead for some time. Do you yourself not value a safekeeping for your secrets?'

Again he had to smile. The mite had seen through him at once. 'I do not deny it. But I am a man of independent means, reliant on no one. There would be little advantage in boring everyone with details of my past. Whereas you—'

'You know nothing of my past,' she interrupted him. 'It may be that its disclosure will only bring further disadvantage.'

'Where, then, do we stand?'

'Why, sir, trust should be a mutual thing. Perhaps it would make a good start if you were to tell me something of your life.'

He could not help laughing. What a queer little thing she was. In spite of all her disadvantage, she was so much in possession of herself that he expected her at any moment to ring for tea. 'I am a bachelor,' he said. 'I am thirty-five years of age. I pass a pleasant existence with enough and not too much money to live on.'

'Are you immune to feelings?' she pursued. 'Do you not have some consuming interest in life that you long to share with everyone you meet?'

'As a matter of fact I am keen on outdoor sports. I like to fish and shoot.'

'What do you shoot?' Her eyes grew wide and he laughed.

'Not young ladies. Game, mainly.'

'No game, sir, nor sport,' said she, 'for birds possess no weapon to contest your skill. They are entirely defenceless.' Her slight frame trembled as it did under interview by Miss Wilcox.

'They are well matched to man's limited dexterity,' he answered mildly. 'They have the gift of flight.'

'Which was given to them by God to be taken away by all-powerful mortals.'

'I detect a hint of irony, miss, but was not man given dominion over the beasts?'

Her small hands gripped the edges of her chair and indignation blanched her knuckles. 'Did not the Lord forbid us to put asunder what he had put together?'

48

'Ah – he was speaking of matrimony, a subject dear, I believe, to most young ladies.'

'And perhaps of the more enduring marriage between man and nature, which even death cannot end.' The child ignored his coy remark.

'Are you always so snappish, miss, or have I hit upon some nerve-ending?'

'I had a pet hawk.' She frowned as she said it. 'I tamed him myself.'

'So, then, not a city miss,' he breathed, and she looked at him in a baffled way as if he had somehow contrived to trip her up.

'And what of your other accomplishments?' Mr Ellin spoke lightly to hide his discomfiture. 'Are you, perhaps, a master of the pianoforte? I have noticed that the Misses Wilcox take pride in their kittens' skill upon the keys.'

'Indeed, no, sir.' For the first time she had the manners to look abashed.

'How then do you pass your leisure hours?'

'I think.' She frowned.

'Do you, now? And what, pray, does that achieve? I see little encouragement of the accomplishment in this establishment.'

Her look again grew subdued. 'It makes me dizzy. Sometimes it causes me to faint.'

He realized at once that he had hit upon some crucial clue. Her homely face grew soulful and stubborn and she seemed to sink in upon herself. He thought very quickly. The mood had passed where they might spar with one another on an intellectual level. 'I have known strong feelings,' he said.

She lifted her eyes at once and he saw the soulful intelligence that was there. What a curious little creature she was. At one moment when he looked he saw a plain and stubborn infant, pathetic but empty of appeal. In another, he beheld a striking and individualistic female of gravity and even stature. One thing he could adduce: she was neither used to nor suited to the feminine frippery in which she had been attired. He tried to picture her in plain brown, but there was an anarchy that underran her repressed exterior, a wild gypsy soul that bespoke neither modesty nor submissiveness. Who are you, little girl? he wondered silently. Whoever she was, small-talk would find no audience. To capture her attention one must speak directly to that soul.

'I was, perhaps, ten years older than you are now and ten years younger than I am at present. I had recently completed my studies in law and had, so my employers kindly told me, the prospects of an excellent career. And then . . . I fell in love.'

'I congratulate you, sir. It sounds like a very fine start in life.'

Mr Ellin sighed. 'No, child. Not fine.' Again he had the disconcerting illusion that he was in adult company but then he saw that her feet did not quite touch the ground from the seat on which she sat. 'I can merely say that I put both love and the law behind me for once and all, for both had found my weakest spots and discovered me to be as poor in judgement as in moral fortitude. I was, perhaps, fortunate in having a small independent income.'

He felt foolish suddenly in having spoken such intimacies to a mere infant but when he caught her glance he saw a look of understanding and of sympathy. 'It is perhaps better, sir, to have known love of any kind than never to have had acquaintance with it at all.'

'Dear child,' said he, 'you must talk to me.'

She gazed at him intently. 'Believe me, sir, that I must not.'

'If we could assure Miss Wilcox of some other person's interest, or some financial security . . . Have you another relative? Your mother?'

At this last question she looked so forlorn that he became concerned. 'What is it, child?'

She watched him patiently. 'I feel unwell, sir.'

He wanted to comfort her but he could tell from the containment of her body that she was in a place where no comfort was. He clapped his hands together in a manner that seemed false to himself. 'Young girls are often prone to fainting fits. I am certain you just need a tonic for your blood. I shall get Miss Wilcox to call the doctor.'

The girl smiled faintly to herself and he realized how foolishly he spoke. Doctors cost money. Miss Wilcox was already intent on recovering her unpaid fees. There was little prospect of her investing further in her unprofitable pupil. The young female who sat so composedly before him apparently had no one in the world to look out for her. If he took an interest in her, he must also take responsibility.

She may have noticed his thoughtful look. 'Please do not concern yourself, sir. I do not care what happens to me now.'

Mr Ellin, who had long surrendered to a half-life, was disturbed to see such resignation in one so young. 'You know not whereof you speak. You have your life before you, and all that is lovely on this earth.'

'As to that, sir,' she said, 'few people seem ever to notice what is lovely on the earth. They are intent on other things. Do you not think, sir, that God must find them ungrateful?'

'I had not thought,' he answered.

'But imagine, if a gentleman were to invite guests to dinner, and they scarcely noticed the feast he set before them, but sat about demanding other things and fighting among themselves.'

He was amused that the clever little creature had once more succeeded in diverting from what she did not wish to discuss.

'And suppose,' said he, returning to his point by the route of her own diversion, 'that upon that table was a dish called hope.

Do you not consider that in dismissing this delicacy you would be turning away from the most sublime of God's offerings?'

'I do not find it on any table I can reach,' she said.

He sensed that those small shoulders carried some very large burden and against all his commonsense instincts he longed to help her bear it.

'Then Mr Fitzgibbon is not your father?'

'No, sir.'

'Who, then? Who is he?'

Mr Ellin's urgent tone startled the girl, whose face, when she looked up, was the very picture of misery and confusion.

'Did some stranger simply call to your door and dress you in frills and carry you off to this place? Did he further take the trouble to twice correspond with your tutors?'

In his eagerness to garner some usable information he allowed impatience to enter his tone. He cursed himself at once for the child went very white and gripped the edges of her chair.

'Let me call Miss Wilcox,' said he. 'I shall ask her to fetch you some water.'

'No, sir,' she said.

'I will get it, then.'

'No, please stay, sir.'

'I wish that you would give me your trust,' he urged.

She looked earnestly into his eyes. She said nothing but he understood. In engaging in debate rather than maintaining her customary mute stance, she had bestowed on him some measure of that precious commodity.

'Let me get you pen and paper,' he said gently. 'Perhaps it might come easier on paper.'

He placed a table before her. Reluctantly she accepted a writing implement from his hand. 'First, sir,' she said, 'you must promise to pass on nothing I have said or am about to say.'

'But I must tell Miss Wilcox.'

'Particularly not her.'

'But why, child?'

'Because,' she replied softly and solemnly, 'my past is something little and frail. But it is mine. Let Miss Wilcox get her hands on it and she will worry and tear at it until it is frayed to nothing.'

Mr Ellin had to hide a smile at the image this presented, of Miss Wilcox as a red-headed dog with a scrap of silk in its teeth.

'Swear it, sir.'

'Very well,' he said.

She swayed and her lips went pale. Then she scratched determinedly and briefly at the paper. When she was done she looked utterly weary and allowed her eyes to close. Mr Ellin seized the paper eagerly. He felt his blood chill as he read her words.

I was sold like a farmyard creature. No one wants me. Only God may help me now.

CHAPTER FIVE

Now that Mathilda was deprived of her prospects, Miss Wilcox saw what a very ordinary child she was. Common, even. A pale, undistinguished face, narrow limbs, hair that was no particular colour, and a donkeyish shade of that. No wonder someone had almost stifled her in frills to pass her off as pleasing. It irked Miss Wilcox that she had shown eagerness for a gift that was only wrapping. Worse, she was now expected to pay for it. The more she considered her situation the more she pitied herself. She had allowed her trusting nature to be taken advantage of, first by the swindler who delivered the child, then by the little fraud herself, and finally by Mr Ellin, who had made her agree against her principle to keep the wretch under her roof. Bad enough he had requested that of her but to insist also that she ask no questions!

When his interview was at an end Mr Ellin had gone directly to her and said in an offhand way, 'Put her to bed.'

Miss Wilcox was piqued by his dismissive tone, as if he somehow considered her to be the servant of the misrepresented minor. 'Tell me what you have discovered,' said she.

'I cannot,' he answered.

'I wonder why?' She tried to hold vexation at a minimum.

'Because she confided in me.'

'There may be a legal matter here,' she challenged. 'I am owed money. Perhaps Miss Fitzgibbon would prefer I called in the police to interview her.'

If she sought to dismay that gentleman she had little understanding of his nature. He gave a narrow smile and said she must not put herself to trouble that would undoubtedly affect the reputation of her academy. 'I can tell you this. The child has been through some crisis. As yet I have no understanding of its nature. But reassure yourself, I intend to find out.'

Miss Wilcox felt his rebuke. She also understood that her most reliable accomplice had now allied himself to her adversary, although she was at a loss to imagine why a bachelor would make a child the object of his interest. 'I think you ought to give me more information. After all, I am the one with experience of girls. Has it not occurred to you that I may be in a position to help the child?'

'No,' he said mildly.

'Allow me to be the judge of that.'

He reiterated the negative. 'Miss Fitzgibbon's confession is meaningless without facts. Furthermore I must insist you do not interview the girl yourself.'

'What am I to do, then?' She was both petulant and unnerved.

'You will care for her until my return. I intend to carry out further researches.'

'You are very sure I will do as you say. I see no reason why.'

'I can only rely on your kind heart,' said he, with a wry look. 'Naturally I will reimburse you for her accommodation. Do I have your word that you will not try to question her?'

'I suppose, if you insist, but I do not see why I should not try to be useful.'

'You can. See to the child.' He spoke in a tone that could only just be termed civil. He allowed his lips to touch her glove before he departed. 'Oh, and a very merry Christmas.'

As he took his maleness from the room (and its accompanying aggravation and reassurance) at first she felt bereft. She had no one now to lean on. Her position in the world was too harsh. But then in a moment her spirits improved as her own independence of will was restored to her.

What, after all, did she owe Mr Ellin? She frequently felt that she was more agreeable than she ought to be because of the rumour, which was agreed by everyone, that he meant to marry her. Yet he had given no real intimation of his intentions or his assets. After all, she knew little more about him than about her unwelcome guest in the parlour.

She went directly to the room where that irritation was slumped in a cold sleep. Miss Wilcox paused from glaring at the girl to consider where her true loyalty lay. Since her conscience was bright with good housekeeping, the answer came at once. Of course it lay with the parents who had intrusted their children to her, and who paid their fees. Was she not betraying their faith by allowing the other pupils to keep company with a waif who came from who knew where? The reputation of her academy rested on turning out young ladies of social grace and accomplishment. It was clear to anyone that parents of good standing would have produced a better-looking and better-mannered girl. But she must and would know what devils had attempted to pass her off in society.

The Misses Wilcox had themselves once had ambitions for an outing in society. They each remembered, as if it were yesterday, a time when they were like the young ladies in their care: one moment in raptures over a verse of poetry, the next, in high excitement imagining the kinds of lovers they might have; when they were limp with crushes over Lord Byron or a schoolmate, then saintly with the notion of submitting to a Higher Nobility – a husband.

To be honest, the husbands had never had any kind of precise outline, for the young Misses Wilcox had found it hard to extend their imagination beyond themselves. They envisioned vague, brooding male presences, well endowed with large estates and incomes. The striking young sisters, Mabel, Lucy and Adelaide, were more concerned with the important details of dance steps and ball gowns; and wedding gowns. The copper-framed trio was confident that having acquired degrees in manners and fashion each would take London by storm.

They came from a household whose reputation derived more from the good name of the father than from any social distinction. Mr Wilcox was a physician, not famous or fashionable, but dedicated and good. There was money enough to send the girls abroad to 'finish' and a little left over to launch them in a modest way, but their mother was ambitious. She wanted, in particular, for her daughters to fare better in matrimony than she had. To this end she goaded her husband to improve his medical practice, to sell his offices in a poor part of town and set up a fashionable clinic among the wealthy. It was while the sisters were in Paris that their father died. The worse tragedy, which they were to discover on their return, was that his death had been brought on by a failure of his practice as well as his heart. He did not have the cajoling manner favoured by the rich. He neglected his most important clients to see to those more deserving. His wealthy patients began to murmur that he would bring fever with him from the destitute. Soon his expensive waiting rooms were empty. To tide him over until things improved he used up his savings and borrowed more. In short, the young ladies returned home to discover that they were fatherless and penniless.

But poverty is not short. It is long. It is the slow realization that the cheese and bacon in the larder know no way of replacing themselves, that the shoes and gowns of which the wearer is already tiring must resign themselves to active service into old age; it is the dreary dawning upon three elegant young ladies that their personages, once so winsome that each was scarcely jealous of the other, must now commence a long and lonely and unlovely withering – for they lacked that asset essential to the flowering of romance: a good fortune.

It was, ultimately, the knowledge that the very roof over their heads would soon be forfeit that goaded them into earning a living. On the advice of the curate, Mr Cecil, they undertook private tuition. A five-year stint at this saw a narrowing of their lips and several holes in their shoes. When Mr Cecil one day brought his new friend, Mr Ellin, to a meagre tea, that gentleman advised them to set up a school at Fuchsia Lodge. The fees would pay their expenses and enable them to live in modest comfort. Boarding pupils would come from other neighbourhoods and would have no acquaintance with their tutors' pecuniary misfortune. The sisters – hard-headed beneath their frivolous hair – seized upon this paltry providence. Their mother took it worse than themselves, declaring it would be the death of her. She immediately fell ill and collapsed into the arms of a wealthy surgeon. To the astonishment of her daughters, she shortly became Lady Harmon Richardson. As to those chalk-dusted young women, she let them know that a man with a position in society could not possibly clutter up his house with spinsters. She remarked upon their good fortune in having no brother, who would likely sell the house over their heads. After that she took herself off to live with her new husband on the Queen's Crescent in the city of Bath. The girls, having shaken off their dismay, discovered that they had inherited their mother's ambitious temperament and determined to make their school a success. So far it was not in profit but there was money for food and a small amount of coal, and the once-vivacious sisters still contrived to revive their old costumes with ribbons as resplendent as ever brightened the breast of a battle-weary general.

Yet poverty pinches. It pinches the face and the soul and the spirit. Its most venomous nip is that it frequently induces those it visits to despise others who wear the same affliction. The Misses Wilcox had recovered their pride in some measure by garnishing their home with agreeable and aspiring young ladies. To wield influence over such ideal females was almost to share in their blessed future. To face the wan and dispossessed stray who sat before Miss Mabel was to gaze into a mirror she had prudently draped. But it was not her mirror. No, hers was tied about with bright bows.

She pulled the child awake. The girl seemed in the grip of a nightmare for she shielded her hands with her face. 'No, Mama,' she mumbled. Upon waking properly she opened her eyes wide and said, in surprise, 'Oh, Miss Wilcox, it's you.'

'You played Mr Ellin for a fool. You need attempt no such tactics with me.'

'Mr Ellin was kind to me.' Matilda rubbed her eyes wearily and adjusted to her inhospitable surroundings. 'It is a long time since anyone has been kind to me.'

'Insolent child!' Miss Wilcox's hand itched to slap her. 'No one could have been kinder to you than myself. I was even accused of partiality by another far more deserving than yourself.'

The child's head nodded slowly, a gesture that made her seem infinitely old. 'You pretended, as I did.'

'So you do know!' Miss Wilcox pounced in triumph. 'I suspected it all along. Now we shall make some progress or you will use your independence to find yourself another sponsor. Is Matilda your real name?'

'No, ma'am.' The child frowned and seemed to concentrate, and then she sighed. 'It seems familiar but it is not mine.'

'I want your name – your full name, if you please?' This time she stepped forward, seized the girl by the shoulders and shook her. The victim neither trembled nor quailed. She seemed to have passed beyond that.

'Have you no idea what is for your good?' Matilda apathetically shrugged. Miss Wilcox dropped her. 'I will deal with you. Make no mistake of that.'

Yet she had no notion how to deal with her. She had not to date encountered any opponent who resisted her with such vigorous indifference. 'Who is your father?' she demanded. 'Do not bother to suggest it was the fraud who delivered you here.'

'No, ma'am.' Matilda noted that anger tinted the schoolmistress's complexion to a shade of red that argued with her hair and bow. 'As to the identity of my father, in truth, I do not know.'

It was too much for Miss Wilcox. 'Have you no shame?' she demanded.

'Why, yes,' the young person said; 'but in matters for which I am responsible.'

'Have you no fear, then?'

'I am no longer afraid,' the girl said; 'not since I talked with Mr Ellin.'

'Mr Ellin cannot help you.'

'I know it, ma'am. I told him so.'

Miss Wilcox began almost to fear the stoic she confronted. 'Why, then, do you persist in your intransigence?'

'I came to see that what happens matters not at all. I have nothing more to lose.'

'We shall see about that,' Miss Wilcox said. 'Stay there. Do not move. I shall return.'

CHAPTER SIX

She went to her sisters. The three women, who might have diverged into separate entities upon the influence of husbands or children, had instead been soldered by their pecuniary secret. Disappointment and fear formed a bond deeper than affection or mutual interest. They had no means to bring any enriching elements to their alliance. In old age, if fate did not adjust its steering, bitterness and jealousy would be conscripted to add a little substance to a thin, sisterly soup. In the meantime, they offered a united front to the world and were ready in an instant to condemn any who discommoded one of their company.

'Have some tea.' Miss Lucy was a bright bustling stalk of solicitude and curiosity. 'Come and get warm.' For this room was soft and merry with firelight.

'What news, sister?' Miss Adelaide fitted herself snugly to her sibling on the sofa. 'What did Mr Ellin report of the sham?'

'That he wishes us to keep her over Christmas.' Miss Mabel spoke in French for discretion, in case of any eavesdropping *enfants*. 'He has gone once more in pursuit of her past.'

'He has not found one already?' Miss Adelaide spoke sharply. 'He was with her half an hour.'

'He declined to say.' Her narrow lips grew thinner still. 'He offered to pay for her keep.'

'How much?' demanded Miss Adelaide.

In truth, the shillings and pence of it were not a necessary part of the negotiation. They knew Mr Ellin. He would pay exactly what was right, no more, no less. They also realized that that measured sum would, in their circumstance, make the difference between a merry Christmas and a straitened one. It affronted their sense of justice that the price of their festive dinner was the soulful enigma who loitered in the chill parlour.

'Mr Ellin is taking our good nature for granted,' Miss Lucy pronounced.

'Yes, indeed,' Miss Adelaide supplemented. 'Whatever he means to offer will be too little to cover the risk of harbouring – what? After all, we still know nothing about her.'

'But I do know something.' Miss Mabel produced at last, from her leg-o'-mutton, her card. 'After Mr Ellin's departure I spoke to her myself.'

'And found what?'

'That she confesses to a masquerade. That she never knew her father.'

The other two sisters drew back and then forward, as a charmed snake does.

'And furthermore she accepts no shame in this.'

'Infamous!' Miss Adelaide's hiss augmented the reptilian comparison. 'You know, I was never quite taken in by her. Her hair is cut far too short for fashion.'

'Yes, and there is nothing of girlish simplicity to her. She is insolently grown-up for her size. I suspect the influence of unsupervised reading.'

'We cannot have nice children exposed to her.'

'We will go to the authorities,' Miss Lucy concluded. 'Let madam see how she will like spending Christmas in Balk Hill.' (It was the workhouse to which she referred.)

They took satisfaction in a picture of the pampered young person waiting in rags for her gruel until the image was replaced by one of themselves celebrating the festival with a shoulder of pork and a jug of water. 'But if you have already given a promise to Mr Ellin to care for the child – unwisely, of course – then your honour is staked on it,' Miss Lucy said.

'He got that promise from me,' Miss Mabel complained.

'We must make the best of it.' Miss Lucy sighed. They had a long career in making the best of things.

'I see no reason why we should not be able to find advantage in the situation if we put our heads together,' Miss Adelaide added.

Those three heads, not unprepossessing in themselves, presented a peculiarly wintry prospect as they sought to summon some boon. But do not underestimate them! Their accomplishments come from the school of adversity, which breeds keener students than any other. It was not very long before Miss Mabel said, 'Who will pack Miss Fitzgibbon's trunk and bring it down to me?'

Adelaide went. The trunk was fetched and opened on the floor of Mabel's room. The pretty garments were retrieved from Mabel's chest. There was an interlude of whispering, though Adelaide's lips were firmly compressed. The sound was that of gorgeous fabrics being sifted by rueful fingers: the Genoa velvets, the glacé silks, the spotted muslins, the French organdies. She almost moaned as she picked up a dress of antique watered silk, the bodice covered in Alençon print and the skirt ornamented with flounces of English lace. Into her clutches then came a gown of damask satinated Pekin taffeta in the new shade of garnet china rose. This was stuff in which to glide through the world; the sheen and pile of it a calling card for admiration. The garments were an education for any handsome young lady. In them she would learn to walk and sit, to adorn. Thus festooned, she would begin to exploit her charms. She thought of the paltry scrap who had inhabited them. To drape a dullard thus was worse than tragedy. As well to dress up a rat or a donkey.

Miss Adelaide held to her throat a little dress embellished with French lace. Youth rushed back into her countenance to soothe her. She would have it. She would have that lace and remake it for a fichu. For a feminine woman to be denied nice clothes is for a traveller to be deprived of water in a desert. She smiled to see herself in her new lace collar, perhaps with a pin in it to make the lace spring out around it. She fetched the ornamental object. Yes! Just like that!

She heard her name called out sharply by her sister. Hastily she packed the trunk and dragged it down the stairs.

'But why did you want her clothes?' Miss Lucy was asking. 'You mean to turn her over after all?'

'Indeed not, sister.' Miss Mabel smiled coldly. 'A promise is a promise. If it comes to it, a bargain is a bargain. Is it not right and fair, then, that having been duped into making a pet of that young person without a penny's recompense, we should now be entitled to profit by what is clearly more ours by right than hers?'

'I cannot quite see how we would profit from possession of her wardrobe – yet I agree we are entitled to it.' Miss Adelaide tried to sound indifferent although her mind was with the lace. 'I suppose we could cut it up for fresh trimmings.'

'I think not!' Miss Mabel removed the trunk from her grasp. 'All of these garments are quite new. We will sell them as they are. Do you have any idea what a Russian sable muff such as this costs?'

She had to revise her hopes upon discovering that some of the fine garments already showed signs of wear. 'Careless child! She has walked through a hem.'

'Oh, Mabel,' begged Miss Adelaide, 'may we not make over for ourselves those clothes that she has damaged?'

'It would not look well to be seen in the cast-off garments of our pupil,' Miss Mabel reproached. 'I had another scheme in mind. There is a widow living above this town who occupies her spare time with charitable work. I believe she would be happy to undertake the repair of the damaged garments and pass them on to some properly deserving young person.'

Miss Adelaide knew from long experience that there was no arguing with her sister. The trunk was firmly shut. She put her hand to her throat and felt it naked and ageing.

'What of Matilda?' Miss Lucy wondered. 'You mean to deprive the child of all her clothing?'

'I am her guardian twice appointed,' Miss Mabel pointed out. 'I cannot support her in a lie. I shall find some suitable attire.'

When the Misses Wilcox parleyed their predicament in French it bypassed their limited imaginations that this would not protect them from undersized eavesdroppers for it was a particular boast that French was taught in the school. Soon it was the property of all three fee-paying pupils that Miss Fitzgibbon was a fraud. The little deputation at once presented itself to the disgraced schoolgirl.

'Why did you not tell us?' the doughty Diana demanded. 'No matter how bad the truth we might have preferred it to the overdressed prig you represented.'

Matilda shook her head. 'You would not say that if you knew the truth.'

'What? Are you a criminal? A murderess?' Mary Franks pressed with interest.

Matilda murmured miserably, 'I don't know what I am.'

'Oh, pooh!' Jessy Newton scoffed. 'Now that the precious heiress has been unmasked she is still trying to make herself a mystery. Let us leave her to her imagination.'

'Yes, leave me,' Matilda begged. 'There is nothing to be said. It is all lost.'

'What is lost?' Diana questioned, more gently. 'Your fortune?'

'My past,' Matilda whispered.

'She is far too young to have a past,' Mary Franks declared. 'She only claims it to give herself airs.'

'If you have anything to say then you had better say it,' Jessy added. 'Miss Adelaide plans to send you to an orphanage.'

'Wait!' Diana said. 'Perhaps we have been unfair to her. It may be that she has been ill-used. I think we ought to give her a chance.'

The chance was to be denied, for at that moment the children heard a determined footstep and those who were free to make their escape did so with haste.

Miss Wilcox had returned and suitably equipped. 'Undress!' she commanded the girl.

'What – here?' Matilda looked around the cold reception-room.

'Anywhere. I doubt anyone cares to look at you. Put on this.' She laid before her a drab work-dress, stained and worn. It had belonged to a little between-maid called Bessie, who had been let go as an economy.

Miss Wilcox stared moodily out of the window while the child struggled to retain her modesty. When the stilled rustle of fabrics signalled the end of the task Miss Wilcox turned round. It would be unkind to say she gained satisfaction from what she saw but she believed a debt of honour due her for the hoax she had endured and this went some way to paying it off.

'Look at you!' she declared. 'You have faded away to a scrap of dust. You scarcely exist at all.'

'I do exist,' Matilda protested, but her voice, too, was dulled to dust. 'My soul exists. Does not scripture say that all else is vanity?'

'How dare you talk to me of vanity?' Miss Wilcox said; 'you who dressed like a princess with no pretension to the title!'

'If those clothes did not make me a princess then these will not make me a beggar,' Matilda whispered, with weary defiance.

'Do you not care that I have stripped you of all that gave you significance?' Miss Wilcox spoke almost in wonder.

'Not unless I believe significance to be rolled up in a bale of cloth.'

'You have the devil in you,' Miss Wilcox declared. She marched the child to the fireplace so that she could see herself in the overmantel. 'Now how do you like yourself?'

Matilda gazed with interest. Her pale face showed no perceptible change of expression but her eyes were keen and she looked over her reflection as if inspecting a stranger.

'Do you realize,' said Miss Wilcox, 'that if I put you outside the door at this moment you would be just another urchin in the street?'

'I would be free,' Matilda breathed.

Miss Wilcox could not understand why her contest with so slight an opponent left her exhausted. She did not consider herself a cruel person and believed she had acted justly. The problem, she decided, lay in the fact that the child had no nature. 'You are not affectionate or afraid or ashamed. You are not even pleasant to behold. Oh, I cannot bear to look at you.'

'Where are you taking me?' Matilda said, as she was dragged from the room.

'To where you may repent at leisure.' Miss Wilcox held her at arm's length as she drew her up the stairs, past the first floor where the pupils had their cots and curl-papers and hid their dolls, to another level where Matilda had shared a room with her tutor, and then up a narrow ladder to a landing that had neither light nor paint. 'You are to remain alone until you have acquired a proper attitude. You will be let out when you decide to tell me the truth. And believe me, young miss, ere long you will be very glad to speak.'

Miss Wilcox opened up a dark room. She thrust the child inside and closed the door.

'Miss Wilcox!' came Matilda's bleak, bewildered cry.

No sound followed save the turning of a key in the lock.

Those who considered themselves well acquainted with Fuchsia Lodge would have been surprised by the quarter in which the girl now found herself. She stood quite still until her eyes adjusted to a strange artificial night and gradually made her inventory. Where bright curtains snugly guarded the windows of the public rooms, here were only dark cobwebs. The small attic quarter had neither chintz nor hearth. There was a narrow bed – bare of all but a rough blanket. An intimidating colony of oddments of furniture, including a vast wardrobe, blocked most of the small window.

The room, like Matilda's new attire, had belonged to the little maid, Bessie. Now it housed pieces put to store when the residence was adapted to a schoolhouse. Now its only occupant was a chill that felt like an actual pinching presence. No one had thought to leave candle or lamp, so that darkness played with shapes on the gloomy walls.

What can Miss Wilcox have been thinking of – a woman – to cast a child into such a place? Why, she thought nothing at all, except that an irritation had temporarily been removed

68

from her presence. She judged that she had scored a minor victory, both over the irritating pupil and the vexing Mr Ellin, for although she had given a promise to keep Matilda under her roof she had made no undertaking to keep her in her sight.

And what of the girl? How did she feel when cast into this claustrophobic space, cut off from all her kind?

She felt relief. Now, at last, she was free to think, to be herself, whatever self that was. When she heard the scrape of the key, she did not feel imprisoned. It was as if that implement had undone the shackles that confined her. At last she breathed. In the past months she had had no time to herself, not even at night when she had to share a room with Miss Wilcox. She had had no opportunity to take a long walk, which might have cleared her mind. Even the very clothes she wore were a bondage.

For a long time she stood in the cluttered space, letting shadows gather round her. At length she moved to the window. Her footsteps made a timid knocking on the bare wood floor. She peered past the wardrobe at fields glittering with frost. Little creatures would go hungry with the ground so hard, she thought. In the distance a village had the cosy glow of Christmas: the smoke of extra fires, the light of rooms prepared for visitors. The village was only a walk away yet it might be a foreign country. She knew nothing of it, except that from it sprang, at intervals, Mr Cecil and Mr Ellin.

She wondered about Mr Ellin. He was the first person who had shown her kindness, the first to consider what manner of human might be concealed beneath the frilled exterior. There was a certain sympathy between them. They were both people who hid their intelligence, and more besides. Yet at the very moment when she had felt inclined to trust him, something within her signalled a warning. Perhaps it was because he could value the death of a bird over its life.

A hawk? Why had she said she had tamed a hawk? She saw, for a moment, a merciless, luminous eye fixed on her in complicity; taloned claws that sat as satisfyingly on her wrist as a silver bangle. Had she known someone who owned a hawk? Had she read it in a book and fancied herself the proprietor of such a handsome predator? Or had she merely wished to equip herself with a worthy adversary for the sporting Mr Ellin? As usual, when she tried to think, her head began to ache. She made a braille crossing around the furniture to the bed, and found she had wasted a journey. Both mattress and blanket were damp. She felt very cold and lonely now, and hungry, for no one had troubled to bring her food; and tired, tired enough, almost, to die. Perhaps she had only to lie on the dismal, narrow bed and wait for consciousness to fade. She was interested to find that this notion did not appeal. Miserable or not, she would have her life. She would not allow the Misses Wilcox the satisfaction of having their problem so neatly erased.

Negotiating the furniture, she explored various cupboards to see if any might contain warm clothing. There was a trunk such as might be used to store blankets. She lifted the heavy lid and was disappointed to find only a large supply of old papers. She felt her way back to the wardrobe by the window. The big doors groaned as she prised them apart. She fumbled inside and came upon a large quilt, folded in quarters. She climbed into the wardrobe, pulled the quilt all around her and lay down as best she could. In this confined, camphor-smelling space she at last felt warm and safe and private. A voice inside her head whispered softly: 'Go to sleep, little Emma.' Who was little Emma? She had no idea, but she must be someone loved. She found this a comfort and kept repeating it as she fell asleep. After that she slumbered through the night with no disturbance, except to those occupants of the room below who heard her shouting in her sleep to her mother. It was a chilling sound for it was not a cry of appeal but of dread.

Early in the morning a certain party entered the room and, finding it empty of all but furniture, called Matilda's name.

The child in the wardrobe woke. Let her come and find me, she thought.

'Matilda? Are you there? I don't know where you are but I've searched every room.'

It could not be Miss Wilcox, for Miss Wilcox knew very well where she was, having placed her there herself. She opened the wardrobe a crack and saw a diminutive vision in a large white nightgown. She crept out, stiff and disconcerted, and inquired of this visitation its business.

'How cold this room is,' Diana exclaimed. 'I've brought you food.' Into her hands she thrust bread and cheese and a mug of milk. 'Miss Wilcox must be very wicked to leave you here. I shall tell my father.'

Matilda ate. She thanked this erstwhile opponent who had braved Miss Wilcox's wrath to aid her. 'You are brave and kind. I wish we had been friends.'

'Then we shall be.'

The child gave a great sigh that touched the tender heart of the other young girl. 'It would be impossible for one such as me to be friends with such as you.'

'I will decide that,' Diana said. 'I choose my own friends. They need not be rich or pretty. The only thing I cannot abide is artifice.'

Warily, Matilda placed her cold hand into Diana's warm one. 'You will find it difficult to believe but we are of a mind on that. I prefer this ragged gown I am wearing to those in which I arrived.'

'Then why?'

'I wore the garments that were given me as every child does. I came here because I was brought here. Would you yourself not have elected to study in an academy with different values?'

Diana squeezed Matilda's fingers. 'I liked my other school and fared well there. I don't know why I was sent here. But never mind about me. We must concentrate on your situation, and quickly, before Miss Wilcox comes. My father is a busy man but he is kind. Whatever your trouble, I am sure he can help.'

'No, it's impossible.' Matilda shook her head and got her old desolate look.

'We shall see,' Diana persisted. 'Come home with me for Christmas. I have no siblings and it is lonely since my mother died. You may share my clothes. We are near in size and I have sufficient to spare. Well? Will you come?'

Before Matilda had time to answer the door burst open. A very flustered and displeased Miss Wilcox presented herself. 'Diana – leave here,' she said tersely. 'You know you are not allowed in the private quarters of the house. Matilda! What have you got there? Have you been stealing food?'

'I took it.' Diana faced the accuser. 'I would deem it a lesser crime than that of attempting to starve one of your pupils. So, I should think, will my father when I inform him.'

'Matilda is no longer a pupil,' the voice of authority established. 'There are institutions charged with the feeding of the destitute. And when do you propose to speak with your father?'

'At Christmas,' Diana said.

'Did I not tell you?' Miss Wilcox mused. 'I have had rather a lot on my mind. You are to remain here for the holiday. Your father and step-mother are to spend the festival abroad.'

Diana seemed to dull like a lamp extinguished.

'If you wish to know the whole truth, my dear – and I tell this only for your own good – your step-mother finds you rather a trial. She says that no pleasant existence is possible in your company as you refuse to engage in conversation as a civilized art but turn every subject into an argument.'

'It's not true,' Diana said, but her voice was already broken down by defeat. 'My step-mother is a snob and a hypocrite.'

'It was your outspokenness that had you removed from your last school.'

'I don't believe you,' Diana wept. 'Miss Sterling always encouraged us to speak up for what is right.'

'I do not doubt it,' Miss Wilcox said; 'as a result of which your step-mother feared you would turn out an unmarriageable termagant and persuaded your father to remove you to an academy dedicated to the refinement of young women. Now, go to the classroom and read Mrs Chapone's *Letters on the Improvement of the Mind*. Be glad you are not like poor Miss Fitzgibbon who belongs to no one and has nowhere to go.'

CHAPTER SEVEN

There must have been those other than Miss Wilcox who wondered at Mr Ellin's concern for an unknown child. Men at liberty rarely respond to childhood (perhaps themselves being bound to that state by a want of responsibility). Yet this bachelor did not run wholly to type. For reasons of his own he was sensitive to the sufferings of the young. For the same reasons, he had a suspicion as to the true circumstances surrounding Miss Fitzgibbon.

He did not at once set out on his journey. He had a number of seasonal engagements to fulfil. Besides, he was not a man given to urgency (and, of course, he was short a compass and a guiding star). For a long time he sat at his desk and gazed out the window. The season's mood had grown subdued. The sky had put out its dirty linen. Bright capes and bonnets showed luminous against their winter background and Miss Wilcox, bustling in her blue merino dress and cape with a little hamper on a charitable errand, made a peacock daub on a drab canvas.

Mr Ellin was not as idle as his critics might have judged him. He had that inward-outward gaze that marks the thinker.

When Miss Wilcox brightened his vision, he perceived a bright and busy insect. If he had been brusque with her, it was for the sake of the child and not out of ill feeling. Miss Wilcox was as she had been made. Although she believed otherwise, she exactly filled and fitted her role in society. She was a make-doer. If she swept from her path all that was obstructive to her goal it was only from loyalty to her nature. He did not dislike her. Rather, he admired her as he would a valiant insect. Reduced to poverty, she would neither look for pity nor sink to despair. He had no doubt that out of the scraps at her disposal she would make a serviceable quilt.

When he tired of the external view he returned his attention to his study. This room was as different from the quarter he had recently quitted as might be imagined. That the walls wore an indifferent coat of buff paint mattered little since most of their space was filled with shelves, and these covered in books and papers. They followed no apparent discipline but were exactly where Mr Ellin liked them and made a martyr-dom for his housekeeper who was forbidden to lay a more aesthetic order upon them. A brown leather chair earned respect from long service rather than good looks. As to the desk it joined, it was impossible to comment on its appearance since it had long since ceased to protest its identity from under a clutter of valued items – maps and magazines, newspapers, letters. Brown velvet curtains divided this cerebral world from the natural one beyond. The glow from a brass lamp made a romance of so much masculinity and, in the midst of it, Mr Ellin was as contented as a cat at a stove.

Having efficiently excavated the clutter on his desk he cleared a space and spread out the objects of his immediate attention; to wit, a map, a magnifying glass and some paper. He opened out his map, lit his pipe and wet his pen. 'Matilda,' he set down in his careful script. 'Conway', 'Fitzgibbon', 'May

Park'. 'Midland County'. Somewhere in the existing misinformation was the clue that would lead to her true identity.

He began to make notes on paper. She was a rich little girl grown poor. She laid no claim to either mother or father yet had not about her the air of a poorhouse girl. No, she was too self-possessed for that. So, she was not brought up to servility. Who had been the source of this upbringing?

Mr Ellin paused to ply his pipe with fresh tobacco – an activity to which he frequently resorted when his brain required a private moment for its deliberations. As he got a comfortable smoke going in its bowl he had a vision of Miss Matilda's woebegone countenance when he tried to win her trust, and the absurd slight he had felt when she asked why she should trust him. Such bankruptcy of faith suggested a betrayal by those she most trusted. Her mother or her father?

He spread before him the pathetic little note the girl had scratched out before she fainted. A shudder ran through him as he reacquainted himself with her words. *I was sold like a farmyard creature. No one wants me. Only God may help me now.*

To tame those phrases into some form amenable to logic he had to banish that desolate child's face from his mind and try to view the words as symbols untouched by emotion. 'Sold' was a florid expression, which might possibly be informed by some strong female sentiment. How might a young woman be sold? Into marriage? Not old enough! *No one wants me.* Could it refer to an alliance her mother had made that was unlovely for the child? Was it just a young girl's misery at being sent away from home to a boarding-school and a belief that she was not wanted at home?

He sighed, and decided he was moving a little too swiftly, in danger of heading off the main track and into a siding. It might be unwise to delve too deeply into the riddle of Matilda's disposal before pinning down her origin.

For a young person to spring so mysteriously out of thin air and then for that air around them to grow thinner still made a riddle to confound the most proficient policeman. But Mr Ellin's talent was not a forensic one. His was the skill of the card player. He believed all mystery to be composed of bluff. He further supposed that within even the most elaborate framework of deception exists a code to decrypt for those with time and patience.

It was the gentleman's experience that people cannot fully shed their identity. They can only mask it. There is a conceit in human nature that compels even the most desperate criminal to invest some part of his true designation within his assumed one. Thus he will usurp a name with the same initial as his own, or adopt an anagram of his given appellation, or his wife's or mother's name. Even a false address will bear a fingerprint of home.

Take, for instance, the man who had delivered the child to Fuchsia Lodge – Conway Fitzgibbon. Conway might be his surname and not his Christian name. The address he had given was May Park. It could be that the girl was, in reality, one May Park or Parkes. (But then again, both the name of the house and that of the alleged county began with 'M'. Might there be a scent in that?) He peered at the map with his magnifying glass where a legion of Ms seemed crouched to spring at him like a plague of frogs. He blinked, put down the glass and tried to concentrate again. Fitzgibbon? Fitz came from the French *fils* for 'son', and 'Gibbon'? Well, a gibbon was a monkey.

Mr Ellin stretched and moved to the fire. He placed himself where flames could warm his calves. When they had performed this service he thanked them by turning round and assaulting them with a poker. The hearth responded with a gratifying hiss and a shower of sparks and Mr Ellin was in turn rewarded with a fresh inspiration in the matter of Mr Fitzgibbon.

77

Whoever this monkey's son was he might already be known to the police. Our amateur detective still had contacts within the law. It could be pleasant and profitable, he thought, to join them for a Christmas drink. He considered again. Inviting such interest might only bring retribution on the child's head. (He felt a sudden dismay on remembering how Matilda had clutched her head and cried that it hurt.)

Someone else, then. He considered Mr Cecil. The curate was conservative. Though of the most Christian disposition, he adhered to traditional values. He might deem it best to dispose of Matilda as a charity child. Mr Ellin decided instead to try out the theme on a feminine sensibility, one with no personal interest at stake. He wrote a note for his maid to deliver, inviting himself to tea. Then he made careful records in his notebook of every aspect he could remember concerning Mr Conway Fitzgibbon, for he was convinced that this shadowy gentleman owned the key and the deeds to young Miss Matilda's true history. Only one possibility had escaped Mr Ellin's careful mind – that the gentleman in question might not know his young charge's true history.

CHAPTER EIGHT

Visitors are to be expected at Christmas, but two in a day is a heady number at Fox Clough. I had just received a note from Mr Ellin when my threshold was brightened by another socialite. It was Miss Mabel Wilcox. Her brave colours were a reproach to my winter forest of wood panels and her air of restlessness seemed to chide some suspected idleness on my part. Her chilled cheek met my warm one and her quick eye assessed my assets and my housekeeping. She talked about the season and wondered if I was acquainted with any deserving families in the parish whose numbers included a girl of twelve or thirteen. 'Yes, several,' I told her, and prepared to lose an hour or two to small-talk but she quickly gave me to understand that the head of a school has little time for leisure. She wanted me to pass on some clothing. I wondered why, with leisure at a premium, she had not sent her maid if it was only an errand. I did not then realize that her domestic staff was down to the number of one and that it was this workhorse rather than Miss Wilcox who could not be spared for anything that resembled respite.

She apologized for the poor repair of the garments. 'A very careless little girl.' I stemmed my curiosity as to the origin of such diminutive finery and offered to put my needle to use. I further promised to unite the bounty and the beneficiary in time for Christmas, and duly credit the donor.

'No. Don't mention me. I do not wish for credit.' Miss Wilcox had about her an air at once fevered and furtive.

'What of the young lady who wore them first? Would she wish to be thanked?' My interest began to grow unruly.

'She has no further use for these items. What becomes of them does not concern her.' Miss Wilcox issued an unconvincing invitation to visit her at Christmas and I returned an insincere assurance of intent. She thanked me and departed in such haste that I expected she might ascend into the air in a flap of bright blue wings.

My curiosity increased when I had fully inspected the trousseau. I had not seen such finery for a child since Dorothy Cornhill had been in my charge. The *petite dame* who had damaged and discarded this consignment clearly placed just such a low premium on fine things as my young pupil had then. I fetched my work-box and, as is my habit, prepared to work my way through the tasks, beginning with the most difficult. There was a dress with quite badly torn lace. I pinned the lace to a paper backing, selected some matching silk thread and set to work.

Mending lace is fine work. It holds the eye close to the fabric and makes a fairy marksman of the needleworker. Yet for all that it requires the closest attention, it asks little of the brain but a slow and precarious procession around loop or leaf or spray or bow. Mine, as it followed a pattern of Honiton guipure, found itself on a painful path down Memory Lane.

I recalled an afternoon at Happen Heath long ago when I had finished sewing a quantity of lace in complicated pleats on to a gown for Miss Dorothy. In the space of a month my small charge had altered from a fresh and delightful child to a spiteful miniature woman with all the attendant peevishness and discontent. No one in that house now cared for me and the only one I cared for had vanished, seemingly without trace. My nerves were at breaking point but I determined to keep my temper and my job until presented with some honourable method of removing myself.

'There, Dorothy! I have turned your gown into one fit for a bride,' I said.

The little jade examined my work without any pleasure. 'I wish you would concentrate on your work and stop talking of romance,' she sighed.

My fingers itched to dispense a summary justice but we both of us knew who held superior sway. 'I do concentrate on my work,' said I. 'And I think you will find that I have done fine work here. Won't you try the dress?'

She tugged it on roughly. When one of the delicate lace attachments tore she took the hem in both hands and ripped it further. It was as fine a show of petulance as I have ever seen in any world-weary female. 'Very shabby work, Isa,' she said. 'I can't think how Mama puts up with you.'

At this point I succumbed to bitter tears. Little Dorothy watched me in perplexity. She had no understanding of what was going on or the role she had been schooled to play. On an impulse she came and threw her arms round me. When I returned that friendly touch she struggled free and stamped her foot. 'You do not know your place,' she said, and left the room.

That night I prayed for any kind of deliverance. I was not yet seventeen but felt exhausted by experience. I had known and lost love. I was far from home and among people who hated me. I felt I could take no more of disillusion and disappointment.

It was not long after that that I received another letter from my father. The longed-for release had at last arrived. 'Dear daughter, you must come home. We need you here.' I hugged those words to my heart until I absorbed the full extent of his message and the bitter imperative that underscored its summons. 'Your mother is very ill.'

No one bade me farewell when I left Happen Heath. Mrs Cornhill kept to her bed as if to smile on me one more time would cause a permanent facial affliction. The children watched from a distance with puzzled and woebegone expressions. I waved to them but inside I felt just as they did. How different was my return journey from that which had taken me to my new future. Then I had been innocent. Then I was full of expectation and fear in equal measure. Now I felt I knew all the world had to offer – the best and the worst – and my only hope was to see again some faces I loved.

Yet my education was not quite complete. As the stage-coach returned to H— and left me off at the George Inn, a gentleman (a stranger) stepped forward. He lifted his hat, relieved me of my bag and helped me from the carriage. None had aided me on my outward journey, nor paid me attention. Had some invisible transformation occurred in my term at Happen Heath? Had I, without permission, absorbed some of the rarefied atmosphere that signifies privilege? Perhaps it was merely that my hair was better dressed or my bodice improved by a needle jealously attentive to the fashionable detail beloved of my employer. At any rate it was a small satisfaction to discover that I had acquired some advantage from that daunting sojourn.

There were no such advantages for poor Mama. It was a shock to find her altered and wasted by sickness. As usual, she made no complaint but did her best to be up and cheerful. I urged her to return to bed and held her hand until she slept.

That rough and wasted limb seemed more noble and beautiful by far than the blanched tapers of my former employer. My mother smiled at me with such affection that I had a difficulty keeping tears in check. She apologized for having taken me from my bright new life. Mercifully, in the light of what was to come, I did not tell her the real truth but merely said that I had missed my family and was glad to be back. After she slept, I had to indulge the younger children, who were at a high pitch of excitement. All the while, I was aware of Father's anxious look and I knew he was eager to speak with me. I was no less impatient to have a time with him. I prepared the children's supper and promised a cake on the morrow if they would make an early night of it. At last they went to bed and Father and I were alone in the little room that served as kitchen and dining-room and work-room; where every item of furniture had served its time and borne the brunt of family life. No gracious chamber could have been more appealing, nor any company more soothing than that in which I found myself. My father looked me over in the gentle light of the fire. 'Do you know,' said he, 'your mother was once as lovely as you are now?'

'She is lovely still,' I responded, with feeling. 'There never was a better woman.'

'Yes, and now you are a woman too. But, you know, she was fair – as fair as you are. She sacrificed all for her family. I wonder how many would do as much?'

I shook my head. On recent experience, I doubted there were any.

'Are you, I wonder, as like your mother as you seem?'

His voice had an edge of sadness and I thought carefully before I replied: 'Yes, I think I would sacrifice everything for someone I loved.'

He frowned and then went on quickly: 'I have no wish to intervene in your life, but I can see no alternative.'

'Do not fret on that account,' I said. 'My life at Happen Heath was not as you imagine. I am very glad to be home.'

'Were you not happy there?'

'I knew both happiness and unhappiness in great measure, but the first was short and the second long.'

'Ah, child,' he said. 'You do not realize it yet. I wish you never needed to know. But that is the way of life.'

'It matters not, Father.' I smiled. 'All is well now that I am home. May I tell you my story?'

Again he hesitated. He studied my face with a wistful look. He took my hand and squeezed it. 'Yes, tell me everything. But first I think you ought to hear what I have to say. As you can see, your mother is very ill. The treatment she requires will be expensive. That is why you are needed.'

'What can I do?' I wondered. 'I will do anything – and gladly. I will take care of the house and do all the sewing but surely even the meagre pay I sent from Happen Heath was more than I might earn by needlework.'

His gaze then was the most rueful I have ever seen on that kindly countenance. His fingers touched my cheek. 'You are but a child still, after all. You do not yet know how most women earn their keep.'

'Most women do not earn their keep.' I spoke with an indignant memory of Mrs Cornhill. 'They are kept by rich husbands as pampered pets. Only poor women earn their keep.'

'Yes,' he said; 'women who have no dowry. But if a girl is fair to look at, that can sometimes be her dowry.'

I frowned into the firelight. 'To trade looks for marriage would seem a shallow bargain for both parties. Is not that institution based on a mutuality of the heart and soul rather than the superficial attractions of money and appearance?'

He looked away. 'Some might say that all the attractions on which marriages are founded – aye, even the best of them – are superficial to begin. The deeper qualities grow with the years, through respect and kindness and care for children.'

'I do not like this conversation, Father,' I said uneasily. 'I do not approve of it. I wonder why we are having it. I never heard you talk in this manner before.'

He put his face in his hands a moment and I saw the utter weariness that had overtaken him. I wanted to reassure him but understood that we were both in the midst of some ordeal that must be undergone comfortless. When he lifted his head it was to look at me in appeal. 'It is for she who sleeps next door.'

'What, Father?'

'There is a gentleman whose suits I tailor. He has been coming to me many years. He remembers you as a child, and later as a young woman. He was always impressed by your manner, but in recent years by your appearance too.'

'I know no gentleman.' I was unaccountably afraid. The sense of safety I had felt upon arriving home was now less absolute.

'He would like to know you.'

'I did not come back to court,' I protested. 'I came home to care for my family.'

And then in a voice so faint and tired that it would barely carry he added: 'He would like to marry you.'

I could not suppress a cry of dismay. I was certain that if I could not be wed to Finch then I would marry no one. I rose from the chair where I had felt so comforted. I retreated to the furthest corner of the room. 'What? Is he rich? You mean to marry me off to some rich man?'

Father sighed. 'No, not rich. He does well enough. He has promised to take care of any expenses in this house — both those concerning Mother's medical care and the education of the children.'

I understood now what was being asked of me. The whole future of my beloved family depended on me. How slight a thing seemed a new romance between two strangers compared with the well-being of a household. In my youthful idealism I had spoken out against shallow bargains. Superficial indeed must our untried sentiment show beside my parents' enduring love. Only I knew it was no trifling thing. Finch and I cared about the sufferings of others. We believed that together we could work to change their conditions. Yet what was being asked of me now but a sacrifice that would relieve the sufferings of those I had loved all my life?

While I made my miserable deliberation Father came and took me in his arms. 'My dear daughter,' he said, 'I should not have asked this of you. You are young. You have your life before you. I feel there is already someone else in your heart. Forget all I said to you. We will manage somehow. Now, come and sit by the fire again and tell me your story.'

So this is adult life, I thought, as I let myself be led back to the warmth. It is the understanding that every gain comes burdened with its opposite. If I decline this unwelcome offer I do so in the knowledge that I may never see Finch again and yet will have dashed the hopes of my family. If I accept, then no matter how the marriage turns out or how little I care for the man, I am obliged to cast all notions of Finch from my heart.

I felt not sixteen but seventy as I huddled close to the fire and put out my hands for comfort. 'You are right,' I told my father. 'I did meet someone.' I turned my face to him and forced a semblance of a smile. 'But he was not of my class and there was never any prospect of a future. He has now gone abroad. He will marry some rich girl chosen by Mama. Now, what of your gentleman? If not rich, is he pleasant?'

CHAPTER NINE

When Mr Ellin came to see me in the afternoon he found me a little raw around the eyes, partly from attention to fine work, but also, I confess, from a little self-indulgent homily to reverie. He did not comment on my mawkish appearance, neither to offer sympathy nor to make me feel self-conscious. He settled to the fire and gave every appearance of happiness at having achieved one of his favoured perches. I was greatly relieved to be returned to the uneventful present and looked forward to a village news report from my sociable guest. I liked Mr Ellin's company for our relationship was free of the undertones that can burden friendship with expectation and judgement. I was not in search of another husband and was confident he sought no other prospect in myself than that of tea and muffins. Both arrived promptly and we settled ourselves in very agreeably against the winter afternoon. He was a good story-teller and could always be relied upon to transform the mildest gossip into a gripping serial.

'Mrs Chalfont.' He stirred his tea and put butter on a scone, watching with patient approval as it melted. 'I have a strange story to relate. I am hoping your female intuition may throw some fresh light on it.'

'I am anxious to hear your tale and loath to dash your hopes, but I have always relied in life upon my practical nature rather than intuition,' said I.

'So much the better,' he smiled, 'for the tale itself is so fanciful that it may need to be anchored by practical deliberation.'

Thus I was introduced to Matilda Fitzgibbon. Mr Ellin told the story in his customary leisurely fashion, beginning with his own first encounter with the child. As he spoke I sewed, for I aimed to complete my needlework that afternoon. The tale, which took my interest from the first, did not progress very far before it was interrupted. 'Great heavens!' exclaimed Mr Ellin with a start. 'Where did you get that cloak?'

It was a very particular garment – a silk pelisse edged with fur and lined in scarlet velvet. When I told him how it came into my possession he expressed a degree of emotion uncommon in one so phlegmatic. I understood why when he had recounted the whole of his story.

'It is an unhappy tale,' I remarked, 'and you are kind to make it your concern.'

'I once had acquaintance with another such.' His light and pleasant tone masked a sombre depth. 'This child seems to walk a familiar Calvary.'

'And now she is not only nameless, penniless and parentless, but without clothing as well,' I summed it up.

'Were she not so much a child and so unprotected, I should derive fascination from the elaborate vanishing act of her past, but there is too much that is pathetic. Something in particular puzzles me. She is so eloquent in her misery that although she articulates little she expresses much. I cannot explain it. Her eyes seem to speak to me as of old acquaintance. In one way she makes me feel uncomfortable yet in another, I am at ease in her company.'

'Her case is pitiful to be sure.' I opened my button box to seek a match for an absent fastening. 'Yet why would anyone have taken such trouble to establish her only then to abandon her?'

'My first instinct was that a guardian meant to rid himself of a wearisome responsibility.' Mr Ellin glanced at the little discs of bone as I emptied them into my hand. With an eye uncanny in a man he reached out to select a perfect pairing. 'As she bore no resemblance to her handsome custodian, I was confident she bore no direct relationship to him. She was the plain child of poor but loving parents who had been so inconsiderate as to depart this life without providing her with a fortune.'

'Yes, but surely he would take pity on her even if he did not love her,' I said.

Mr Ellin's changeable orbs took on a hue of slate. 'Certain natures are entirely without pity, especially when something voiceless and defenceless is placed within their range.'

I was surprised by the sudden change in my companion. 'Yes, but even still – although a plain niece might fetter a handsome man at liberty, in the ordinary way he need not involve himself with her. He would simply employ some plain woman to see to her education and instruct them both to keep out of his sight.'

'Quite right, Mrs Chalfont!' Mr Ellin brightened and was his familiar self again. 'It was the same realization that obliged me to revise my original construction. After several days of deliberation I came up with another theory. Matilda Fitzgibbon was not the plain daughter of poor deceased parents. She was the plain daughter of rich deceased parents. She was, in fact, precisely what her fake pater had alleged – a little heiress. The only deception was that she was not *his* heiress.

My conviction now is that Conway Fitzgibbon – whoever he may really be – is, in fact, the poor relation. Fitzgibbon might have accumulated debts that required immediate repayment. If he could dispose of his defenceless little relative his problem would be resolved.'

'He meant to kill her? Oh, surely not, Mr Ellin!'

'I did not say so. Even a cold-hearted scoundrel might balk at murder. There are other ways to rid oneself of an inconvenience. For instance, he might lodge her in an obscure institution, then make himself undiscoverable. Of course he would need a corpse and a funeral before he could benefit from Matilda's fortune. Yet children come at a low premium. With the right contacts the corpse of a minor can be readily purchased for a moderate sum. An unscrupulous medic might be persuaded to sign a death certificate for a child he had not known or examined. To avoid questions, the new heir might go abroad for several years. As to what became of the child, if she died, it would almost make an honest man of him. Should she survive, she might expect as good a life as God intended for plain females already stamped with the disdain of their Creator.'

I felt quite shaken by this grim picture until a more hopeful one presented itself. 'Why do we not stay the hand of this inconsiderate Creator? I could pay the school fees.'

'So could I, Mrs Chalfont, and I have thought of it, yet in so doing I would abet the devil's work and become accomplice to her abandonment. The simple answer will not suffice. Whoever has deprived Matilda of her rightful legacy must be punished – and severely. I shall find the villain and bring him to account. But where to start? Stick a pin in a map and set out in quest of a plain and unwanted little girl? I could find a thousand in a week and very likely keep them if I wished. I need some other lead. If only I had a clue.'

'Well, then, that is where my practical nature comes in. I have two,' I told him.

'How can you?' he said. 'You have only just heard the tale.'

'First, it goes without saying that she did not originate in these parts.'

'How, so?'

'The shoes are too dainty for Deerfield's hills or Rooksbury's hollows.'

'Where, then?'

I held out the garment on which I had just completed my repair. 'This elegant little piece bears its own identity. If the scoundrel who delivered the girl sought to cover his tracks, he ought to have removed the labels.' I showed him the small embroidered tag, bearing the grandiose appellation of some high-fashion seamstress who had concocted the apparel.

'And the other garments?' Mr Ellin quizzed eagerly. 'Are they thus identified?' We examined them one by one. Although some came from other sources, all were from the one town. This was a long way from Midland County.

'Well done,' Mr Ellin said, with feeling. 'Now I have a starting point. I have respect for your sleuthing powers and will appoint you my assistant. You said you had a second clue.'

I did not own up to Mr Ellin but my observation was not entirely reliant upon my investigatory skills. In truth, the name of the town where the pretty garments were fashioned drew my eye because I had once had a connection close by. My second indicator was less impressive.

'This is nothing, really, but a personal deduction. All of the garments are in good taste – not just in terms of fashion but there is a genuine elegance of style. It suggests that the purchaser has a close acquaintance with refinement and is not just some jumped-up individual with more money than sense.'

'So! Perhaps a genuine aristocrat?'

'Infer what you will, Mr Ellin,' said I. 'I can only state that the man has taste.'

Mr Ellin appropriated the last muffin and stood to leave. 'You will forgive me, dear lady. I am eager to be about this business.'

I acquitted him without delay. Although I did not doubt his commitment to the cause in hand, I had a feeling he had other business to pursue. An agreeable bachelor is much in demand at Christmas, and not merely in houses with marriageable damsels. Married ladies, too, like the company of a congenial unwed male. In the eyes of a man who views them as more than the source of dinner and fresh linen, they may catch a glimpse of their own former fair, unfettered selves (and women need to view themselves as attractive much more than they need any other to see them so). Mr Ellin was even liked by husbands. He gave them no cause to be jealous for he never exerted himself to a pitch of flirtation. He merely paid attention to the female sex, a skill deficient in most of his gender. Indeed, far from imposing any tensions on the matrimonial table, he brought to it a bounty. He took up the slack in marriage. He wove an entertaining narrative between womanly gossip and manly discourse so that both husband and wife could view one another's opinions as being more interesting than they usually were. He had the added advantage of being of no distinct class. His accent was elusive, his charm unquestionable. Amusing as his stories were, he made it a cardinal rule never to sacrifice a previous host to his narrative, so he was as much in demand in the best houses as in more moderate dwellings such as my own. And Mr Ellin enjoyed his itinerant social life. Perhaps its most pressing privilege was that he had not to lift a finger. He did not need to burden himself or others with gifts, he was not required to reveal his true personality or motives; he had no obligation to return the hospitality (for how could a poor bachelor with only one servant provide a dinner?). He had only to be. There is no equivalent for this in the female sex, except in a small and charming child.

The little girl described by Mr Ellin did not appear to enjoy this natural advantage. Still, I thought I should have liked to meet her.

'About Matilda!' Mr Ellin paused at the door. 'Although I am anxious to try to resolve her past yet I am reluctant to leave her. I no longer care to intrust her to the schoolmistress sisters.'

'Send her to me.' I spoke without hesitation. 'I shall be alone at Christmas. I would be happy to have a child for company.'

Gladly, he accepted my offer. 'But I must warn you. This is no ordinary child.'

The little creature who was delivered to me had about her the air of an elf; not just unworldly but other-worldly. A ragged housemaid's dress augmented an already poignant vision. Her pale face was haunted by shadows and her dark hair had not been dressed to flatter. On being delivered to her new address she showed no more interest than a parcel passed from one destination to another. I invited her to make herself at home and she perched on the edge of a chair and directed her eyes out of range of human contact. She seemed resigned to her new situation but registered neither surprise nor pleasure. Although I have in my lifetime encountered other children in low situations, this one seemed the most abused.

Mr Ellin made the necessary introductions and then he took his leave. As he departed, the child turned to him with a quick look of appeal or regret. I accompanied him to the door and he lingered a moment to address me privately: 'Things are worse than I imagined. Miss Wilcox sold her remaining apparel to make good the losses she incurred.'

'I have not yet delivered the garments I repaired. I shall restore them to her,' I said.

'Leave me one,' Mr Ellin said. 'It may be useful for identification.' He set off and I returned to the forlorn object in my care.

'I have some of your dresses.' I spoke lightly. 'Miss Wilcox asked me to mend them. Would you like to put them on?'

Her small face showed some fire and she shook her head.

'You don't want them? They are yours.'

'They are not mine,' she said. 'Nothing is mine.' But then she bunched a piece of her rough gown in her fist and said: 'This is mine. It was given to me.'

I bent down to make our faces level. 'Have you really nothing? No souvenir of childhood? No doll or toy given by someone who cared for you?'

Interrogation seemed to frighten her. She drew in her breath and cast her eyes away. 'I had a ring.'

'Why do you not wear it?'

She risked a swift glance at me, considering how much to reveal. 'It would have been taken from me. I have hidden it.'

'Tell me where and we shall retrieve it.'

'It is too late. I have lodged it where none shall ever find it.'

Although she seemed in control of herself I could feel the disquiet in her and sat close to her until it was stilled. 'Let me make a dress for you,' I said. 'It would give me pleasure. I will give it to you and then it will be yours.'

She watched me warily as I went to fetch some fabrics. I had purchased them for my own winter wardrobe but I deemed myself better equipped than my visitor. As I am no longer young my tastes are somewhat sober. I laid out for her inspection a dark green alpaca, a dove-grey merino-cashmere and a

94

Scotch plaid cloth. To my relief she began to pay some attention. I got the feeling her tastes were on a par with my own. After a time a timid finger pointed to the green. 'And how would you like it trimmed?' said I; 'lace or ribbon?'

Again she shook her head.

'You may choose anything you want,' I said gently.

Her voice when she spoke was ghostly. 'A dress I can move around in,' she said. 'One in which I could run and not feel fettered. One where I can pass almost invisible.'

I had the sense not to try to argue or to flatter her. 'I will put a very narrow binding of russet velvet,' I said. 'You will look just like the leaves on the trees.'

When I had measured her (she was painfully thin) I spread the fabric on a table and considered how to cut it. It suited me to have an occupation. All attempts at conversation had failed. I wanted to keep the child company yet not to oppress her with my attention. If she chose not to talk, I saw no reason why she should. Conversation need not be a two-way exchange. It can also supply the art of the story-teller. Mindful of what Mr Ellin had told me, I would try out no fairy-tales on this juvenile. No. I would endeavour to engage her with a narrative that was realistic, original and close to my heart. In short, I decided to tell her my own history. Having briefly journeyed to that site where my youth was laid, it was still dominant in my mind and I was glad of undemanding company on a return excursion.

'I married when I was not a great deal older than you are now – just a month short of my seventeenth birthday.' The pale face was drawn to me with curiosity. 'His name was Albert Chalfont. I knew him no better then than I know you.'

I saw questions gather on her small brow. Weariness rested there too and I paused to put a rug round her shoulders and a stool beneath her feet before returning to my work table.

95

'Mr Chalfont was two and forty years of age. He was short and stout. He had a pink face and a brief quantity of hair in a fading shade of ginger. He owned a small shop and a small store of conventional opinions, which he was content to make last a lifetime. He was proud of the fact that he had made every penny he owned and had never read a book in his life.'

I had my audience now, albeit one with sceptically raised eyebrow.

'Was I in love? Oh, yes! As much as any girl ever has been. But not, alas, with the one elected for my life's partner.'

Matilda looked at me sharply. She opened her mouth as if to object, yet no utterance was expressed.

'Young girls do not own their own lives.' I answered her silent query. 'They have a will and a soul and a brain as men do, yet they cannot govern their destiny. You will understand, Matilda, I was not forced to marry by my parents. It was those capricious elements – Fate and Fortune – that dictated I should. If it appears strange to you that I should have volunteered to make myself the wife of this solid burgher, well, as I tell it now, it seems strange even to me. And yet at the time I saw no other path on which to place my feet.'

Her look changed now. There was a glance of sympathy and understanding.

'I was introduced to the man who was to be my husband. To tell the truth I cared not one whit for his appearance or his opinions. The single thing that concerned me was that he was not the man I loved. I felt some law of nature and of heaven was transgressed in uniting me with any man other than Finch Cornhill. Yet as I watched my poor sick mother daily weakening, it gave me strength to see through what had begun. I asked Mr Chalfont if he meant to offer financial assistance to my family and he agreed that he would. I, in turn, consented to be his wife. It was done. It was as simple as that.'

What is simple on the outside (what is achieved by resolution and not desire) makes felt its true impact on the subterranean pathways of the senses. My tortured mind cast about for ways to help Finch understand the step I was about to take. Yet if I could find him what should I say? That I was to marry another man? No justification would make that right in his eyes or lessen the hurt. But if I told him I still loved only him? No! I had forfeited the right to that love. In affirming it, I would betray the man to whom I had promised myself.

I did nothing. I said nothing. Like many a young woman I allowed marriage plans to heap up around me so that soon I seemed to blend with them. Father made me a handsome gown. Albert bought me a showy ring and in a short time I found myself like a sleepwalker in the church vowing to love and honour until death a man with whom I would not, in any ordinary way, have passed five minutes in conversation.

He lived at a distance of eight or so miles. I had anticipated that this remove from my urban environment would take me to the kind of pastoral setting that used to fill my gaze upon coming out of H— Church. Far from it: the busy market town of Rooksbury had so much smoke from its competing mills that we lived in a permanent haze of fog. Slum houses abounded around its many mills, and the pavements were black with soot, which on wet days turned to an oily, clinging sludge and did grievous damage to hems. Although Rooksbury's church was of a most handsome design, its outstanding feature was not the view but the odour, for it was situated right by the railway goods yard where the night-soil wagons were kept, and these were removed but once a week. What with the soot and the smell and the commerce and the poverty it was small wonder that the bells of Rooksbury's church were used to ring out the devil each Christmas Eve.

Marriage surprised me. Ensconced in four stuffy rooms above my husband's shop (furnished by his late mother), equipped with a small quantity of wedding linen and a duster, I was expected to don my new status and grow into it at once.

So let us tackle this matter of marriage, this regulator of passions and property and population. For men, it may be a mere framework for their lives but for women it is the space within the frame that must be filled. Without children, without any useful employment, this is akin to filling a leaky vessel with water. I was not in love with my husband and therefore suspect that I was in the generality of women rather than the exception. I had not anticipated happiness, in consequence of which no disappointment lay in store. It was not the quality of marriage that dismayed me but the quantity of it. Confined in close proximity to the plump and whiskery personage who considered me as much his property and as much for his usage as if I were his pipe or slippers, I had need to remind myself that this shackling was not for a week or a year, nor for the number of years to which a criminal might be sentenced to bondage, but until one of us ran out of breath.

My husband was as eager in application of his marital obligations as in his business activities and I had to get used to his attentions. Discomfort seems to be the general lot of women so I made my adjustments as best I could. Worst for me (and for many women, I suspect) was the lack of privacy for my head. As it had not occurred to my spouse that it currently owned any content, he took it upon himself to fill it all day and half the night with his own theories and opinions. In bed he snored into my ear and by day he talked into it.

But all of that is commonplace, if generally unspoken. So where lay the surprise? The surprise was that in spite of such and so much strangeness, I remained unchanged. I had imagined that I might grow settled and subdued, yet the alienation only served to cement my identity. My affections still rested where I had lodged them. My restlessness persisted. Even my hopes continued to disturb my circulation like fresh, disquieting breezes.

If I may put in a good word for Mr Chalfont it is this: Albert was so delighted with his life that it almost compensated for my waning enthusiasm regarding my own. He was delighted with his business. His person and appearance afforded him no end of enchantment. And now, on top of everything, he had a wife who was young and strong and considered fair to look at, and he was enraptured with his acquisition. He never asked me for affectionate reassurance. If I had questioned him about his feelings he would have been as perplexed as if I had elicited his view on the latest French novels. Appearances were what counted. It was one of his opinions and he used it well.

I must have fallen into a silent reflection for the length of green fabric lay before me as dark and virgin as a forest and beside it my scissors with silver beak awaiting its prey. And in her corner by the hearth Miss Fitzgibbon was curled up, fast asleep.

I carried her to bed (she weighed no more than a child of ten or eleven), returned to the chair she had warmed and sat there an hour or more, staring at the fire until its dragon forces subsided into rosy dust.

It took me the princely space of a week to get to know my husband, for he was a man of habit, a sheet of paper with well-spaced writing on one side only. He rose early, breakfasted at the same hour every day, dined each evening on tea and bread and butter and mutton. At meal-times he liked to entertain me with tales of the grocery trade. It is a testimony to their poor entertainment value that he frequently fell asleep while thus engaged. Once or twice as I gazed upon this portly statue, emitting snores as peaceful as a kettle on a hob, I thought, He has never bared his heart to me, nor shown anger, nor spoken of childhood slights, yet were I to sit an examination paper on any aspect of Mr Albert Chalfont, I would come out with flying colours. And I have known him but a month and been married a week.

A considerably longer time elapsed before I fully knew myself as Mrs Albert Chalfont. It was odd to find myself addressed as madam when I had not fully shed my childhood; to discover myself (at a certain level) a figure of authority while having mislaid my independence. I even forfeited my given name, for Albert declined to call me Isabel or Isa. In his household I was Belle. Belle Chalfont! It was a name for a plump, youngish but settled matron. This was not the reflection my mirror threw back at me. In it I saw a face and figure not yet fully formed, a life not wholly shaped, hopes not yet entirely crushed.

In the space of a year I had known three separate addresses. I had the vaguely weary and impotent feeling of a traveller still in transit on an arduous journey. As my husband was older than me it was natural to be obedient to his will (and he was not a harsh master), but although my lips and moving parts gave service, my heart and soul declined to submit. Daily, as I went about the business of a faithful wife, I became more and more the ardent lover of another. I could not forget him (I know not if I sincerely tried). I could not crave a dishonourable resolution. And so I prayed. I prayed for Finch's safety and his understanding. I stormed heaven that one day, in some manner, the unbreakable connection between us would have its fulfilment.

Naturally, my husband saw nothing suspicious in this activity. He liked to see me on my knees. He considered it a fitting occupation for a wife. 'Good girl, Belle.' He would pat my head discreetly as I knelt to present my begging bowl to my

Creator. 'That's women's business, praying is. I'm not a religious man but I still feel the better for seeing an angel at her prayers.'

Sometimes he felt so much the better for this hypocritical vision that he fell to kissing me, and all that accompanies this activity in marriage, and I then considered it a judgement upon the unsuitable content of my supplications.

In the meantime, there was one attraction in my new life. It was my husband's grocery shop. It was a dear little corner shop, situated in the busy market-place, rather dim within, and with a great many shelves in the dark wood he favoured. On these were arrayed, in higgledy-piggledy fashion, every manner of garden produce. Mr Chalfont was an industrious man. He rose each day at dawn to drive his cart to his suppliers. His vegetables were fresh and sweet. Yet the premises most avowedly lacked the touch of a woman. A lacklustre youth (in slapdash overall) served as his assistant. The shelves were not polished nor the rosy cheeks of apples shown to advantage. The long wooden floor rasped underfoot with traces of dust and straw. All in all it showed a manly sort of housekeeping – the kind that gets things into a generally tidy shape but without exploiting them to benefit. This privilege, I decided, would fall to me. I looked forward to composing a handsome display of fruit and vegetables in wicker baskets outside the shop, which would make better space for customers within. I envisaged the wooden shelves polished to a high degree and boasting row after row of glass jars with jams and preserves, which I would make at home. Potatoes would be in wooden barrels instead of sacks. On the counter I would keep a jar containing small pieces of confectionery to reward the children of customers. Most of all, I confess, I looked forward to adorning this unpretentious premises with myself.

Until this time I had thought neither to admire nor despise those who made their living in trade. Now it seemed an attractive employment. There is no snobbery or cruelty in an onion or a pound of tea. Their purveyor provides a useful and honourable service. I knew Albert to be ambitious and was convinced that I could assist in his objectives. My parents had always worked side by side. I am sure this co-operation played no small part in their devotion to one another. At last I could see some promise in my connection to Mr Chalfont. With a common purpose we might make a fair union. I perceived it as an antidote and a balm to my soul's unrest.

I am no stranger to hard work and now I could not wait to seize a broom and take my place at my husband's side as the grocer's wife. On a fine March morning when the lambs signalled their happy arrival on distant moors I put on my pinafore, pinned back my hair and prepared for my new career. It was a morning to spring-clean the mind of morbid reflection. The small market street with its cluster of shops and vista of mills and hills seemed an invitation to enterprise. There are those who view toil as a punishment devised by God to chastise our sinful state and others who consider it as one of the many gifts he lavished upon his creatures. I have always belonged in the latter category. To feel useful (and, if possible, appreciated) is one of the greatest pleasures on this earth. Now that I had acted upon my resolve I felt my sluggish heart begin to beat with some measure of its former zeal. I presented myself for industry.

Albert was delighted to see me. 'Why, the spring morning has stepped through my door. Dear Belle! Did you come because you missed me?'

When I told Mr Chalfont that I was ready to commence employment he looked perplexed. 'Not you! If I'd wanted a shop girl I'd have found one plainer and stronger.'

I took this for indulgence and assured him that it was my wish to work.

'And so you shall, wife.' He handed me a large head of cabbage. 'Take this home with you and prepare it for my supper.'

'I will do that and gladly, sir,' said I; 'yet it has always been my intention to work alongside my husband.'

His jovial expression altered and he gave a warning glance in the direction of the assistant. 'Not in the shop.' He spoke in a whisper now. 'You'll not work in a shop. 'Twould shame me. Go home now and we will speak of this later.'

We did not address the subject until he had tackled his mutton and tea and the supplementary cabbage, after which he announced: 'I meant what I said, Belle. If I'd wanted a drudge I could have married a dozen girls – aye, and had a dowry too. I am an ambitious man, madam. I sought a wife who will be a credit to me when I am successful. I waited a long time, and when I saw you, I would have no other.'

'What? An object, then?' I spoke out in dismay; 'an ornament, without a role to play.'

'Oh, never fear, madam. You will have your role to play.'

'What, then, is my role to be?'

'Why, that of my wife,' he explained, as if it was the simplest matter in the world.

I have always despised that species of female who keeps her hands and her mind soft while others toil. 'That is not employment,' I protested. 'How can there be shame in honest labour? We are, as I understand, of limited means.'

'Now, that is not entirely accurate.' He rinsed his mouth with tea, patted his belly and permitted his digestion a muted expression of content. I sighed, preparing to learn that I had, after all, married a rich man and was to be his unproductive adornment.

'The truth of the matter,' he beamed, 'is that I have not a brass farthing to my name.'

Now it was my turn to feel betrayed. If a cheap bargain had been struck to make us man and wife, then with the lowest possible expectation, I might suppose he would keep to the letter of that contract.

'As you are my wife you may as well have the whole truth. I am up to my hocks in debt.'

I was forced all at once to comprehend the full gravity of what I had done. I had married a man under false pretences – false on his part and false on mine. I had signed away both life and love for a debtor's promissory.

'You have tricked me,' said I. 'You led myself and my father to understand that you would undertake his expenses.'

'Aye, lass,' he said calmly. 'So I shall.'

'I have had enough of idle promises,' I coldly rejoined. 'The fact of the matter is that we are poor.'

'No doubt, my dear, but that is an intimate fact, of concern only to you and I as a married couple. What matters to the outside world is appearances. Now, although it is true that my business is small and I am in debt to the bank, if you are to be seen behind my shop window, lank-haired and red in the face from exertion, then the whole world will at once be privy to this information. If, on the other hand, you are only to be found in your own home with servants in attendance, then I shall already have the trappings of success.'

'Servants?' The notion alarmed me more than I can say. I envisaged us accumulating a whole horde of dependants whom we would be unable to support.

'Aye, madam. They will be yours to choose and yours to command. It will be your privilege to make their lives a merry hell, if you so decide. Trust me, my dear. I have a nose for commerce. If we can present the right appearance to the world and entertain important people in our home, our credit will be increased and I shall expand.' As if to demonstrate this point he placed his hands at a distance from his already swelling waist.

'You cannot go on endlessly acquiring things on credit,' I objected. My own father had never borrowed in his life and my husband's scheme seemed to me deceitful and perilous.

He laughed again. I could not be comfortable with the sound for it lacked the solace of shared humour. 'I got you on tick, my beauty,' said he.

CHAPTER TEN

On my way to bed I remembered to look in on my visitor. She was asleep yet not at peace. She had the look of one caught in a storm. Her face was pale and strained and she moaned faintly in her dreams. I smoothed her blankets and touched her forehead, and for a moment her eyes opened in panic then closed again, after which she seemed to sleep a little sounder. As I put myself and my thoughts to bed I deemed it a strange coincidence that she and I were powerless females both, who had been unwitting parties to a sham. Each of us had been set up to play a decorative role for which we had no appetite. Perhaps it was God's providence that had led her to me. I hoped it was so. But my practical nature suggested the more likely explanation that she and I shared a disposal common to members numberless of our sex.

On the morrow I arose early and applied myself diligently to the abandoned stretch of green fabric. My guest would be dressed today. So engaged was I in cutting a heart pelisse that I failed to discern an elf's footstep on the stair and it was not until I sensed a humid breath upon my neck that I realized I was being attended. Matilda stood very close by and watched my work with interest. I broke off to join her for breakfast. I had asked Mary, my servant, to use the best linen, china and silver, to forfeit the few surviving blooms from the garden, to put out several preserves and some sweet rolls, for I wished to make a merry start to the sad little maiden's sojourn.

My breakfast parlour is of itself an antidote to winter, being the one chamber where I have violated my husband's manly panels with paint the colour of a summer sky. At the windows are short curtains of thick French lace. The effect is that of a little ship at sea. Matilda studied the room with her usual gravity before taking her place at table. She did not make much progress with her meal but continued to absorb every aspect of the scene. We supped our tea and worried about the weather, as quiet and comfortable together as two old maids. I, at any rate, was comfortable and she less uneasy than before. 'Do you think it will rain?' said I.

'Not yet,' she reflected; 'but I do so wish the sun would shine.'

'Why? Do you desire a walk?'

'No, thank you. But I seem to have had so little sunshine in my life,' she oddly responded. 'And it would look pretty on the silver tableware.'

'I am sure you are no stranger to silver,' said I.

She gave me a reproving look, which suggested I had breached some etiquette with this sly line of conversation. I took my reprimand with due contrition and swiftly amended my discourse. 'All lights have their own beauty. Imagine if this white tablecloth were a plain of snow. See how the winter light mitigates its harshness, putting planes of soft grey to lull us for the hibernating season.'

I made no mention of the added bonus that, when I composed this picture of our breakfast setting, Matilda's grey eyes shone with the full register of greys of the sea.

She has her own beauty, I thought. It is not to be interfered with by any superficial values of fashion.

When I resumed my needlework I invited her to occupy herself as she might and to consider the house and its contents her own. She took her time inspecting my handiwork, which adorned most visible surfaces – the feather flowers, wax fruit, embroidered cushions, shell work and seaweed pictures. These curiosities, like a traveller's trophies brought back from his voyages of discovery, charted the course and distance of my youth.

'Do you like them?' I asked her.

'It is fine work,' she diplomatically replied.

'Work for idle hands,' I replied. 'Take anything you like for your room.'

'It is not my room.' She carefully restored a sampler to its setting. 'Soon I shall be gone.'

I considered how to answer this melancholy reminder. Already I had made up my mind to ask Mr Ellin if I might care for the child until the matter of her future was resolved. Yet at this moment I had no authority and she was not to be cajoled with insincere assurances. 'From now on, Matilda,' I promised, 'it shall be deemed your room. It shall be so whether you are in it or not. If you pick an object and place it there, then there it shall stay. And wherever you are, you will know that this souvenir and your room remain unchanged and await your presence.'

She chose a frame of pearly seashells inside which sat a rather doleful likeness of my youthful self. Although she did not smile I had the notion my proposal pleased her and it gladdened me that some modest purpose might at last be served by those emblems of my inactivity.

It is said that every picture tells a story. Matilda inquired if there was one attached to her chosen object. There was, and she settled by my side to hear it – a situation that afforded us both serenity and made redundant the harassment of the winter winds outside.

Mr Chalfont remained adamant on the subject of wifely propriety. I was to be his peacock on the lawn, a decoy set up to advertise our imaginary status. My single task was to exhibit my indolence for the purpose of enticing rich and influential people. The notion enraged my sense of decency. I implored my husband to allow me some occupation that would at least be honest. 'I have a brain,' said I.

'Then I wish you would use it,' he answered, with uncharacteristic gruffness.

'I thought to make improvements to the shop.' I imparted my plans for displaying the fruit and vegetables to advantage and lining the shelves with home-made preserves and pickles.

'There!' He brightened. 'That's honest industry. You boil up your preserves at home and I'll line the shelves with 'em. As to your suggestions, I will follow them and gladly. It is for this purpose that I married a young lady of taste.'

A parade of domestics was brought to the house for my inspection. At first I sent them all away and tried to reason with my lavish spouse. 'But Mr Chalfont, it is generally considered that one needs an income of one hundred and fifty pounds a year to employ a single servant and five hundred pounds to pay for three. Do we belong in either category?'

'Not precisely,' he admitted. 'The outgoings in a business – and especially a developing one – are such that it is difficult to define in any given year what might be accounted as profit. Then again, servants form the purchasing power in a household. If our housekeeper became friendly with another, we would soon have orders from that other household. Why, we would have to expand to make good the orders. Stop worrying, my little princess. Can't you occupy yourself as other wives do – choose new fabrics for the home?'

'But money, sir! What's to pay for them?' I begged.

He laughed and congratulated himself on his impeccable taste in having selected such a spouse. 'If you were like me, Belle, we would no doubt end up in the debtors' prison. If I were like you, we would break even but always be poor. But as I am reckless and you are thrifty, I shall run like a racehorse and you shall keep tight the reins. We will be a power in the land. Oh, madam, was there ever such a team?'

My arms felt too slender to hold back such a horse. I agreed, in the end, to one servant. I had no idea how to choose a worker and decided that honesty must be the qualification. On this basis I selected Mary Oldroyd, for her advertisement was the humble embodiment of that quality: 'A girl of unremarkable character seeks a situation in a household.' So there I was at seventeen, mistress of my own household (or house of cards, as it seemed to me), with unremarkable spouse and servant and with nothing to do. I applied to Mr Chalfont to let me visit my family at weekends. To my surprise he made no objection. In his eyes a dutiful daughter was almost on a par for excellence with a dutiful wife. Thus appeared a measure of air in my stifling existence. My mother rested better for my presence. Father allowed the furrows on his brow to ease. The children alighted upon me like an excited flock of birds. As for me, I cannot express the relief I felt in returning to a house where the residents kept both feet upon the ground at the one time and where I could engage in plain labour and plain talk.

It was natural for Father, as I worked by his side, to inquire how I fared in my married state.

'Mr Chalfont is kind,' I truthfully replied.

'And are you happy?' he pursued.

'Happy to be here with you.' I concentrated on threading a row of needles.

He gave me a sad, searching look. 'Are you not content in your marriage?'

'It is not as I expected,' I responded, as circumspectly as possible.

A look of amusement softened his weary countenance. 'And what, pray, does a young lady of seventeen expect of matrimony?'

I had not intended to encumber him with my anxieties but something of his paternal condescension unleashed my indignation. 'I anticipated honesty,' I said. 'I expected that we would build our home slowly but surely by hard work and mutual endeavour.'

'Is he not a hard worker?' Father said in alarm. 'Is he a gambler? Does he drink to excess?'

'No, Father. He is very hard worker. But he does not wish me to work at all.'

Father looked at me intently, as though trying to impart some of his own forbearing disposition. 'I know you for a diligent young woman. It is how you were raised. But I will tell you this. I am glad your husband has seen fit to protect you from the rigours of labour. It would grieve me to see you worn out by hard work as your mother has been. In due course you will find some worthwhile outlet for your natural industry. You must be patient and trust your husband's judgement. He is your master now.'

'I cannot trust him,' I protested. 'He got me under false pretences. I married him so that he would assist my own dear family but he has as good as admitted to me that we are penniless.'

Father was shocked. 'Do not cast doubts on Mr Chalfont's honour. He has been the very soul of kindness. He has already undertaken all our bills and more.'

This surprising revelation stemmed my tide of protest. Where on earth had the money come from? I murmured my thanks to Father but perplexity must have lain heavy on my brow for later as I sat with my mother she took my hand and spoke to me with infinite kindness. 'Marriage is always difficult at first for young women. When you have children it will make sense.'

So great was my innocence, so large my disconcertion at finding myself married to an unchosen and incompatible mate that it had not crossed my mind that this unnatural bonding might yield so natural an outcome.

'A child?' I said. 'I had not thought of that.'

'Think of it,' she said; 'and pray for it too. But you must play your own part. Be happy and open up your heart. Eldest daughters always grow up responsible, but you, dear child, seem to carry the burden of the whole world upon your shoulders. Take the gifts your husband has to offer and stop wishing for different ones.'

It was typical of my mother to ask no prying questions but only offer sage counsel. I vowed to follow her advice, and when Easter came and Mr Chalfont proposed a trip to the sea, I readily assented. I had always wanted to visit the sea and had an instinct that the sharp winds and the salt smell might blow away some of the confusion and anxiety that burdened me. I asked if I might bring two of the younger children with me. In his usual easy-going fashion, he agreed. We went to Barlington, travelling first by train and then in a little open fly that introduced to us the bracing salt air.

A bank of cliffs had been set down by nature to stop the might of the ocean bursting over the town. I was overcome both by the power of the sea and its delicacy, the drama and the subtlety of its colours. At one point it was dark green and blue and white. At another, it had woven strands of sun into its fabric and spread out its lace upon the sand. So overcome with feeling was I that I had to ask my husband to walk on with the children. I could not join them until I had shed some tears. After I had lightened the pressure of emotion my spirits began to rise.

I set foot upon the beach and entered a fabulous, insubstantial world that seemed some leagues above our earthly one: the soft sand that crumbled beneath the foot, the vast force of the ocean, which expired with a muffled crush upon the shore and was reborn on the waves; the fierce, joyful, metallic praise of birds overhead. Even the air was served as a rare delicacy for it was of a remarkable purity yet seasoned with levity. One felt one could take off like a kite and fly into the sky. Indeed, the children almost did so, running close to the water with shrieks of delight. I caught up with Albert and we followed at a more sedate pace.

When we had paraded the length of the beach we rested on a rock while the children made a whole city out of sand. As they decorated their architecture with stones and shells Albert could not resist making his mark upon their empire. He rolled up his cuffs and bent down to compose a mighty monument. I could not but be amused by his childish and affable nature. I was touched to see how readily the children responded to him and began to think that a cherub replica of my guileless spouse might not be hard to like. We could be children together, bar the door to passion and make innocence our muse. I had sojourned briefly in the adult world and made acquaintance with its baits and traps. Now I could return to the pleasant garden of childhood, which I had so recently forsaken. I clambered down from my rock and crouched to collect as many pearly shells as I could carry. I could be useful in my way – a good daughter to my parents, a protective sister to my siblings, an obedient wife to my spouse and a loving mother to my children. In that moment, on that day, it seemed a recipe for contentment and I embraced it.

No infant came to sweeten our household. We slung our disappointment between us and shouldered it in silence as couples do. Albert continued to live upon his anticipations and to celebrate his future at an alarming pitch. My mother, after a brave struggle, yielded to God's call. This blow was bitter indeed. To have saved her life would have justified my own. Now I was bound for life to a hot-air balloon that kept me fettered yet adrift.

Mr Chalfont believed there was a practical solution to all ills, and when he noted my despondent state he prescribed the remedy of a party. 'I am now acquainted with some significant townsfolk. It would be no end of a benefit to let them see how well we do for ourselves.'

He composed the menu himself, copied from a society report. For a man who dined daily on mutton, tea and bread and butter, it was to be a considerable affair: clear soup, then brill with lobster sauce. This would be followed by oyster patties, mutton with artichokes and, at last, a caramel pudding with whipped cream. There were, in addition, grapes, walnuts and pears. Enthusiastic as he was for his menu, Mr Chalfont was more excited yet by his assembly of guests. He had snared a barrister, a council member, a mill owner, a man of the cloth and someone distantly related to a duke. These and their marriage partners made up our table.

A cook and butler were hired for the evening. My regular staff, to the number of one, professed itself astonished by the quantity of food with which significant townsfolk were prepared to furnish their stomach. I would hazard that some of the guests found the feast no less excessive. Nevertheless it was elaborately admired, as were our living quarters and even myself. Having done justice to these mighty topics the company fell to the kind of discourse that, apparently, is the currency of significant townsfolk. Mrs Wainright, wife of the mill owner, commented on the shabby dress of a particular young curate and hazarded that it would improve when he had a wife. At this point, Mrs Hargrave, the vicar's wife, interjected to say that he had a sister whose duty it was to see to his presentation.

'Yes, because he is a man of the cloth,' agreed Mr Hargrave.

'No – because she is a woman and he is a man,' said Mrs Hargrave vehemently. 'No woman should allow her brother to put on linen in a state of dilapidation. No woman in the enjoyment of her health should allow her brother to do anything that is woman's work.'

Other variations then arose on the theme of a woman's place. Mr Reuben Greenwood, the barrister, revealed a shocking truth that there were women who were endeavouring to enter his profession.

I said I did not see why they should not, if they had an aptitude for the law and sufficient funds for its study, unless in doing so they would use up the situations needed by men with families.

'Precisely so,' said Mrs Wainright. 'And such indulgence is the fancy of single women with nothing to occupy them but selfishness.'

'Yes, but single women must have some means to support themselves,' I reasoned. 'The kind of positions which are presently open to them pay barely enough to keep body and soul together.'

'"Man for the field and woman for the hearth. Man for the sword, and for the needle she. All else confusion,"' recited Mr Hargrave, in a voice that throbbed with emotion, adding – lest he be guilty of claiming too much credit for wisdom – that these were the words of the poet Lord Tennyson.

This seemed to dispose of the female sex for once and all, yet it left an opening for my nearest companion Mrs Schofield to disclose that she had travelled a great deal and stayed in the best houses. Her conversation was a list of capital cities and country seats. As she bore no interruption I found her company to my taste until she chanced to mention Happen Heath. I kept silent but Mr Chalfont's ear had been melodiously struck by mention of my prestigious erstwhile address and he could not hold his tongue. 'Happen Heath? Belle lived there,' he said.

The woman looked surprised but contented herself with making a dome of one eyebrow. 'And were you acquainted with the son of the house?' said she.

Futile to bar the door to passion when passion dwells within the walls. At the mention of Finch my whole being was thrown into confusion. I could not speak and merely nodded.

'And had you lately had news of him?' Mrs Schofield — intrigued, no doubt, by whatever expression she had planted on my face — kept her excited eye on me.

'No. Please tell me.' I spoke as quietly and calmly as my overwrought nerves would permit.

My companion and her speech seemed to move into slow motion, which made me want to shake her. 'It is too dreadful.' She looked away as if she could no longer bear what was in my eyes. 'A fever. The family is distraught.'

'What? Is he ill?' I whispered.

'My dear Mrs Chalfont,' the wayfarer now looked at me directly, 'he is no more.'

I felt every eye upon my face. How should one react to the news of a death? How respond when the light of one's soul has been snuffed, when all is darkness save that rank of well-lit orbs perceiving the meat of drama? Why, in the commonplace, of course.

'In which part of the world did he die?' I asked.

'Well, in England,' said Mrs Schofield, distinctly disappointed by my reaction.

How long had be been in England? I had been married a little over a year and had achieved the ripe old age of eighteen. The measure of resignation I had accorded myself I now perceived as complacency. Had I truly loved him I would have walked through fire to find him and that love would have kept him alive.

I sat through several more courses of the interminable meal, bade my guests good night and bore half an hour of Albert's rejoicing on the success of our swindle. 'What an elegant air of boredom you essayed,' he gloated. 'They will all believe you are used to better company. And so you are, Mrs Chalfont – late of Happen Heath.' He had to seize me by the waist and waltz me around to express his glee. It seemed an eternity before I could achieve the luxury of solitude. I did not go to bed that night but waited until Albert's snoring drilled the darkness and then I gave myself up to my grief. By morning I had consumed suffering to excess. Albert observed that I looked pale and suggested that I had a tendency to exert my brain too much. He counselled me to strive less and said he believed there was no end of elegant arts for ladies with which I might acquaint myself.

That morning I retrieved the shells I had collected from the shore at Barlington and, arranging them meticulously into suitable patterns, pasted them on to a bare wooden picture frame. I had then to think of some dear memento to preserve in its square. I had no image of my mother, none of Finch, so I fashioned a portrait of one more who was lost to me. Seated at the same mirror where I had passed my nocturnal vigil, I drew a portrait of myself. I was bidding farewell to my youthful self. The half-wed and half-hopeful girl was gone for ever. I was a married woman now.

CHAPTER ELEVEN

A meagre snowfall made lace of the land, and birds in their branches kept mute vigil. Nature, half in mourning, wore a grey mantle and sighed in the trees. In a garden a surviving rose turned its defenceless countenance to a blustery jury and bravely faced its death.

The loudest noise was the importunate cough and rattle of trains, their warrior howl. Like gods, they owned direct access through river, cliff and hill. They sliced into towns and cities, charged immovable mountains. As the ribbon of iron advanced across the land, isolation grew less a difficulty and solitude less a possibility.

Aboard one of these wonders was Mr Ellin. Unlike the other passengers who were bedecked with parcels and bubbling with high spirits, he bore no gifts and carried but a modest valise, which contained (along with his favourite pipe, his current reading and some unremarkable changes of clothing) the surprise of a small item of female apparel. Contrary to the merrymaking home-comers, he was heading away from hearth. He was decidedly pleased with this situation. He had enjoyed several exceedingly pleasant and sociable days and could now escape what he considered to be the most boring day of the year. As a man who had long severed all close ties, Christmas owned no lien on his affections. Moreover, he relished the anonymity afforded by so much coming and going on the part of other travellers.

I am as undistinguished as a moth, he thought with satisfaction. Neither exceptionally handsome nor especially ugly, neither ostentatiously rich nor emphatically poor. No one is dependent on me and I am answerable to none. I have that fortunate personality that can conceal absolutely its true temperament. What debts or treasures of the heart I possess none can even guess, for man is so cunningly fashioned that no one can see into his soul.'

Having thus made his gratifying inventory he reached into his case for his novel in order to while away an hour until luncheon. As he did so, his hand made voluptuous contact with a scrap of velvet. This unlikely junction was as disturbing as a touch of fire and he had to look before he could realize that it was only the garment mentioned before, the velvet-lined pelisse worn by Miss Matilda Fitzgibbon. He hoped to introduce himself to its maker and identify its purchaser.

He smiled as his eye caught sight of the dressmaker's label. 'Madame Lucille'. He wondered what doughty English dame had helped herself to a pert French appellation. Well, he looked forward to making her acquaintance. It would be yet another small and undemanding adventure in his measured existence. He suspected she was one of those females who express a secret life through their work, for although she was undoubtedly industrious and probably dull, the little cape was an exercise in theatre. His own view was that such fashions were not suitable for juveniles. Children, like men, should be allowed a camouflage of dullness in order to enjoy the freedom of their status. Women, of course, were required to draw attention to their appearance, and he supposed they enjoyed it.

Or did they? Certain birds must rue the exotic plumage that betrayed their cover. Were there women who considered their visibility an affront to a modest or independent spirit? As had become customary, his thoughts returned to Miss Fitzgibbon. She, of course, was but a child, yet he could not imagine her transformed by a few years into a frivolous peacock. Would life process her with unassuming anonymity? He did not think so. A depth of passion underran that insignificant exterior.

He pulled himself up short at the realization that he had permitted himself to wander into her future when his single commission was to retrieve her missing past. He was considering, yet again, the oddity of her situation when a strange thought occurred to him. *We have most of us mislaid our past, although some of us have done so on purpose.* His own history was as well sunk as a galleon run aground on rocks. The Misses Wilcox had buried their unwanted prologue as daintily as any mother cat her kittens' messes. Even his equable friend Mrs Chalfont, he suspected, had severed connection with a former, less tranquil self. Do we thus sell ourselves short? he wondered; acting out assorted selves instead of becoming the sum of our parts?

Yet too much reality might make us mad or unruly. Society demands civilization. Untamed things are considered dangerous and are generally sacrificed. Glancing idly out of the window he saw, through a veil of winter, a boy trudge over a patchwork of frozen fields. It was a peasant lad, but as he looked the figure altered. Mr Ellin saw a different boy. He pictured now a slight and fair youth of some ten years whose bowed gait and slow but steady pace bespoke both suffering and endurance. He seemed a gentlemanly little fellow. His features were sensitive, his expression anxious and sad. From time to time he paused to wipe blood from his face; blood but no tears. Stoicism might have been in his nature or have grown from the knowledge that those who would feel for him existed no more. Yet his suffering had finally outrun his endurance. Mr Ellin felt his pain and suffered with him, but he was powerless to act now as he had been powerless to act then: the boy existed no more. Poor fellow! He could not hope to escape his tormentor. The latter had three times his years and weight. Mr Ellin rubbed his hands over his face. When he looked again the scene was bare once more. Then his eye was caught by the lightning arc of a hawk on the bleak landscape. The bird might expect to dine well on such a day. Small creatures would be rashly abroad in a search for food. He felt a raw stab of pity as the bird swooped. Still, this predator killed only to feed itself or its young. It did not torture for sport.

The train divided the thinking man and the aerial huntress. Mr Ellin took out his watch. It was time to visit the dining car and he had not absorbed a word of his novel. And it is all your fault, waspish Miss Matilda, he accused. The mere fact that your puny form once inhabited an item in my care has disturbed my tranquil brain.

Yet he did not feel discomfited. He took a strange solace from the small and unlikely garment in his custody. Although of itself a homage to artifice it seemed, by association with its wearer, a talisman to truth. Impossible to recall that grave countenance and avoid one's heart and conscience.

It was evening when he reached M—, a town modestly perched upon the foot of the Pennines yet boastful of its lace. He lodged his bag at a convenient inn, banked his fire and put his nose in at the bar. This chamber contained as much celebration as would have been occasioned by the Queen's birthday. Mr Ellin sought a relatively unfevered site and ordered ale. Upon tipping the steward he asked if he might be directed to the residence of the seamstress known as Madame Lucille.

He found his destination in a small but prosperous terrace. He could judge from the freshness of her paint, the thickness of her curtains and the shine on her brasses that the lady did not undercharge for her services and wanted not for clients. He could also discern from the overall darkness of the place that there was no one at home. Looking closer he observed, tucked into one of the shining panes, a small white card: '*Madame Lucille est en vacances – 20ième dec au 1 jan.*'

Our sleuth was not unduly discomposed. His nature was such that obstacles merely added texture to his pursuits. So, Madame was French after all! No doubt she had her own story to tell. He did not immediately return to base but passed another half an hour in patrolling the town until he had made a fair acquaintance with its bricks and byways and shaken the staleness of travel from his limbs. On regaining the inn he pitched himself in among the celebrants and ordered drinks for all. His objective – to obtain information about the Frenchwoman.

'My sister is a gloveress for Madame – God help her!' offered one very miserable and down-at-heel little fellow. Mr Ellin was at a loss to know if it was the glove-maker or the dress-maker who needed God's clemency, but that would soon be revealed.

If the gentleman had considered himself acquainted with the town consequent upon his evening ramble, he had not yet encountered Bett's Lane. In this extremity of the borough's body the grand plans of architecture and drainage had run to grief. The houses seemed to have been thrown together from the planks and rubble of other wrecks. Sagging building leant towards its like, one stitched to another by flimsy lines of washing. Barefoot children played in a reeking stream that no amount of cold, fresh air could sanitize. Yet Winter had got inside the buildings. She lodged in the houses with her ugly sister, Damp, and lay in wait for such victims as were born weak or grown so through age or infirmity.

He found his contact along with half a dozen other women in an attic room bare of furniture except the benches on which they sat and a long table where they stitched with furious haste at a variety of garments. Six such abject females he had never encountered. Thin and dishevelled, worn before their time, they neither raised their eyes nor greeted him. The gloveress he could identify at once, both by the nature of her work and the fact that she wept softly and continuously, pausing now and then only to blow her nose and wipe her face, then inspect her fingers to make sure that they had not been contaminated by her grief.

'Sarah Ellis?' he called softly.

She looked up, the picture of guilt and misery.

'May I speak with you? My name is William Ellin.'

An anxious glance directed at her work suggested that moments to spare were few. Yet she was used to obedience. She rose swiftly and motioned him towards the window where they might stand, for there was no other chair.

'I seek information concerning a client of Madame Lucille. I shall pay you for it,' he said.

At the mention of money she wept even harder.

'Whatever is the matter?' said he. He noted that crystals of ice had formed inside the window and that the young woman's fingers were blue as woad. At a distance he had judged her to be about five and thirty but close up he saw that she was a decade younger.

She told him she had taken home a pair of gloves to finish them but the baby had laid hold of a glove and chewed it.

'But why are you working when your employer is on holiday?' he wondered.

'Madame has orders for the New Year ball.' A hasty operation with damp handkerchief effected some repair upon her face. 'She left instruction for delivery before Christmas.'

'But don't cry,' said he. 'One damaged glove does not merit such mourning.'

'You do not understand!' She undid the good work on her complexion with a fresh downpour. 'I'm paid two shillings and sixpence to sew a dozen pairs of gloves, but if one gets damaged I have to pay the full price of a pair, which is three shillings and sixpence.'

Mr Ellin looked at his hands, comfortably sheltered in kid. He inspected this protection, observing all its narrow pathways and minute but durable linkage. Never had a pair of gloves been invested with such significance for the gentleman. He asked if he might see the coverings in question. She docilely presented him with a pair of objects in pale blue kid, one of which had several fingers slightly limp and sticky, due, no doubt, to the application of the teething infant. Gloves such as this would have begun to weather within five minutes of usage, yet a slightly damaged pair could not be sold at reduced price. No, the unfortunate genius that constructed them would have to pay the full, fantastic cost.

'My aunt had a pair of gloves the very same as these,' he remarked mildly. 'She lost one and has been unable to locate its like. They were her favourites. You would assist me greatly if you would allow me to buy her this duplicate for Christmas.'

The gloveress sniffed back her tears. She gave him an old-fashioned look through her grief. She had seen through his charitable ruse. 'They will find no other wearer,' said she. 'Take them.'

'Then I must be permitted to pay the full price as you would have done.' He carefully counted out three and sixpence. 'Oh, by the way, I wonder if you have ever seen this before?' He produced from his case the pelisse.

For a time Sarah Ellis seemed in a trance. The shock of having her debt erased was almost as great as its burden. Upon recovery she said, 'I do recall this piece. Such a pretty thing for a little girl!'

'Do you, by chance, know who ordered the garment made?'

She thought again. 'Oh, I remember. There was a fuss because Madame didn't want to make for a child and the customer said that one item of female apparel was no different from another, and one dressmaker no different from another, and if she did not want his money he would take it elsewhere. Madame likes money, she does. She did not care to have him take it elsewhere. And he seemed to have such a lot of it. He never argued the sum she asked, just told her to make a whole wardrobe of clothes for the child.'

'Did you see this gentleman?' Mr Ellin inquired.

'Yes, sir. I sewed the child's gloves. I remember he was in a hurry and I had to deliver them to Madame's house. Tiny things, they were! I thought it a waste, for any normal child would have ruined them in a minute's play.'

Not this one, thought Mr Ellin.

'And what did that gentleman look like?' he asked. 'Did he make conversation with you?'

'He was well-made but stern, sir; of a pale complexion, but his hair was dark. He made me afraid. He did say something to me. He directed a very fierce gaze at me and inquired about my children.'

'What did he ask?'

'He wanted to know if they went to school. I said they did, for I feared I might be sent to prison for neglect, but what use is it to go to school when they have neither clothes nor food?'

He was at a loss to answer but wondered what use it was to have them at home, gnawing on their mother's labour. 'What is it that they do, then, if they do not go to school?' he gently pursued.

'Why, they work, sir,' she said. 'One minds the baby and the other's a little doffer in the mill. That's how life is for children such as mine. If they can walk they work, and if they can't they beg.'

So deeply was the present inquisitor affected by her plainness and her bluntness that he almost forgot his line of questioning and would have been pleased to leave, but for the fact that there was another child at the mercy of a cruel world.

'Do you know if Madame was paid for her work? Did the gentleman have an account? Might he have left an address?'

'He paid her straight in cash.' The gloveress's pale eyes were wide with the memory of it. 'On the very day I brought the little mitts. I never did see so much money. Such a quantity came from out his breast that I thought he must be stuffed with it like a scarecrow.'

'Can you remember anything else?'

'Why, yes, sir. It's coming back. It's when I mentioned "scarecrow". Although he spoke like a gentleman and had the manner of one, he did not look like one. He had a careless way with his appearance – good apparel, but worn too casual.'

He pressed a guinea into her hand. Although she tried politely to decline, the other seamstresses raised their eyes and lamped her bright and stern as cats, and the coin was put away. 'I am grateful to you, Sarah,' he said. 'You have been helpful.'

'I only wish I had, sir,' said she. 'But I know little of the gentleman.'

'You have given me some useful insights into Mr Conway Fitzgibbon.'

'Oh, but, sir,' said she, 'that was not his name.'

He felt a thrill as when the line tautens underwater or the finger bids the trigger break a wild bird's flight.

'What was he called, Sarah?'

'I do not know, sir. I can tell you fair what he was not called, but not at all what he was.'

CHAPTER TWELVE

On Christmas morn I told Matilda we were to have an outing in society.

'If you wish it,' she replied.

'Which is to say that you do not.'

'No, ma'am.'

When I asked for her reason she replied that she had had enough of society. Her answer might have seemed precocious to any who did not observe the cloud of despondency that accompanied it. Thus far we had got along well. To say she had settled would be to claim too much. Her nights were passed in the twitchy, vigilant slumber of a hunted animal. In her waking hours she seemed to derive contentment from her room. She carried books from the downstairs shelves and arranged them near the bed. Numerous small objects she selected – cameos, ornaments, craft-work – to give her quarter character and history. She even rearranged the bed, exchanging her pale blue quilt for one embroidered by myself. She liked to perch in this nest and read a book. Sometimes she would sit at her toilet table gazing at her image, not with girlish vanity nor even girlish insecurity, but simply as if asking the very question others asked of her: 'Who are you?'

We had thus far undertaken one excursion to the outside world. We had travelled to Rooksbury where I had shown her the shop once owned by my husband. She seemed disappointed not to find the name of Chalfont on the door, but it is the thriving business of a different grocer now. In other establishments, small gifts were purchased for various friends, and necessary extra fabric for my guest and a strong pair of boots suitable for our hilly terrain. Although she demurred at first she proved a decisive and careful shopper. She liked fine materials in subdued colours. I applauded her choice and said she now looked much more herself. She replied that if the self could be located in a set of garments then we ought to say our prayers in a wardrobe. We had progressed to conversations and although they were more of a philosophical than a practical nature and their paths were thick with signs marked 'Trespass!' we found ourselves of a mind on many subjects.

'Do not imagine you have yet exhausted the whole of society.' I spoke lightly, for I knew by now that she must manage her melancholy moods on her own. 'You may discover there are yet some mortals that bear acquaintance. Come. Put on your bonnet. We will first pay a visit to church and pray that the ordeal will not be excessive.'

On emerging from the house of worship several of my neighbours paused to greet me but none offered compliments on my companion. Although bedecked in her new cape and bonnet the impact was too discreet to amaze the public. The only ones to pay attention were the Misses Wilcox. They said nothing but their eyes were riveted to the small, nondescript girl. This so discomposed her that she all but hid in my skirts. I returned stare for stare and they unhinged their gaze and gave bright attention to some other acquaintance.

Whether their interest derived from conscience or resentment I neither knew nor cared, for my rootless sprite, with her sombre woodland colours, thoughtfully knitted brow and apprehensive fingers latched into mine, pleased me well. I had begun to feel as any mother might, an easy complacency in the attachment of my young and a pride sufficient to disregard the views of others.

I must confess here to a small defeat. In spite of my efforts I had failed to raise Matilda's mood or her appetite. She still picked at her food. When I tried to tempt her with dainty dishes she always said the one thing: that she had a little ache and would dine when it abated. She was less uneasy in my company than hitherto and seemed to like my house, yet her child's body was built around a core of isolation. There was a sense of something terrible that nearly crushed her. I had told her as much as possible of my own life to encourage her to reveal something of her own, but although she now almost clung to me, still she could not trust me.

Yet I myself was more content than I had been in years. Strange that such consolation should come when no longer sought. I sometimes thought that if Matilda's thirteen or so years could have been stitched backwards over mine then her young shoulders might not have been weighted by oppression, and the loneliness that had filled my cup might have tilted clear away. I remembered to give thanks for this change in my fortune before quitting the house of God.

Our next stop had, it must be said, only a modicum of either godliness or cleanliness. At the outskirts of a village close to ours, called Battle Ing, there used to be a weaving mill with basic cottages built for labourers. My late husband was much impressed by the owner of this establishment but when the miller died the works fell to disrepair, as did most of the weavers' cottages. Some lie abandoned. Others house, in considerable discomfort, those too vulnerable to find more fruitful pastures.

Matilda's sea-deep eyes searched mine as we arrived at this unlikely social setting. The cottage we entered was in such a low state that no amount of scrubbing would have rendered it habitable and its occupants were, in any case, too weary with working for others to care much about their own surroundings.

A widow by the name of Leah Sykes, lived there with her children, a girl of eleven called Jess and two infants. Jess had been in service since her eighth birthday. I once asked her if she believed in God and she said she did for she saw how He helped the rich, but she could not think Him kindly for He left the poor to help themselves. They were indeed very poor, for although mother and daughter worked all the hours God sent, their income was such as would barely sustain life.

On this occasion they had made some domestic effort. A good fire burned in the grate (using, I dare say, a week's ration of coal). There was a cloth on the table and plates laid out, for they were expecting me and knew I would not be empty-handed. I introduced Matilda, feeling uncomfortable when the child exhibited her usual public manner – a lifeless handshake followed by a swift retreat to the furthest corner – for Jess and her mother would surely judge her a little snob. To cover any awkwardness I proceeded to unpack from my basket a cake, some fruit, a cooked ham, a bottle of port. There were sugar confections for the younger children, a train for the boy, a doll for the girl. Thus far nothing had been given to Jess, and she was entirely without expectation but gazed indulgently on the infants' pleasure.

'I have something for you, Jess,' I said. She made a clumsy bob and said I ought not to have put myself to expense.

'I did not,' I assured her. 'Your gift comes via another and at second hand.'

Jess removed a covering from the other basket to reveal, freshly pressed and fully mended, my portion of Matilda's erstwhile wardrobe. Her hands flew to the garments, then withdrew in a dither and hid behind her back in case they were dirty. 'Oh, Mother!' she cried. 'Oh, look! They're lovely.'

The widow looked uncomfortable. 'Bless you, ma'am,' she thanked me. 'They're not for the likes of our Jess. Jess is a working girl. They're too dainty. They'd not last a day.'

'For a day, then, Jess shall wear them,' said I. 'She is more deserving than any other girl I know.'

'May I, Ma?' Jess wheedled.

The mother looked at me. I nodded firmly.

'Well, it's a queer thing for one of our station to come by such style,' she said. 'But, then, life has turned up so many cruel surprises that maybe there should be some kindly ones. Try them on now, Jess.'

To my surprise Matilda spoke out: 'Let me help. I shall dress your hair.'

She took the ribbon from her own locks for this purpose. The two children disappeared into a corner and there was much to-do. Jess was very thin and wiry but she had big, raw hands. The dress she put on was no more suited to her than to its original wearer. She had a kind of bonniness but her features were too rough and her hair too coarse, and her feet were shod in clogs. Yet the biggest difference between her and Matilda was that, while the latter had cowered within her finery, Jess rejoiced in her bedecked appearance. I had a compliment ready but before I could offer it the widow clapped her hands to her face and cried: 'Oh, Jess! My little Jess, a beauty! Isn't she just a picture, ma'am? Any prince would marry her now.'

Few princes, I thought, would win as fine a wife as that young girl, and if the elegant garment did not endow her with beauty, it furnished her with confidence. Work-worn little Jess flowered. 'I shall wear those pretty clothes just the once and then I'll put them by. But they shall have their use. I'll keep them to show my children. I don't suppose I'll ever go to a ball or a dinner but I'll get a husband, for most women do, and then I'll have children and they'll know that Jess Sykes did have her day.'

The vexing garments had earned their keep. Matilda and I returned home well satisfied with our morning's work. Only one wish remained to me – that on the day Jess chose to wear her frippery the Misses Wilcox would chance to be passing by.

An agreeable mood persisted through the day. I had elected a quiet holiday for fear of startling my little bird. As I had given my maid the day off we cooked our meal together, making a great ceremony of it. Matilda even ate a morsel to please me. Afterwards we entertained ourselves with board games, followed by a brief, impromptu and badly executed concert.

I had planned the day carefully and it had passed well. By eight o'clock we were yawning, ready for a light supper and a sound sleep.

There is a natural temptation to revisit our sites of victory and thus it was, as we ended our pleasant festival, that I happened to comment upon the morning's work. 'Don't you think that Jess looked splendid in her finery?' said I. 'And what is better, she never doubted that she was suited – or entitled – to it.'

At this the girl seemed to revert to melancholy. 'She has as much a right to it as I,' she murmured.

'Or I, if it comes to the matter,' I reminded her. 'Remember, I grew up in a house not unlike hers. In any case no woman has a right to ornamental apparel. It is in every instance an artifice. And as for you – it was merely that you did not care for it, not that you did not merit it.'

To my dismay she sank her head into her hands and began to sob. I at once laid an arm on her shoulder. I assumed the excitement of the day had been too much for her. 'Oh, ma'am, you know nothing of me,' she moaned. 'I am all pretence.'

'Who you are matters not to me. I am glad of your company.'

'I am the basest creature that ever lived.' She shuddered. 'I am from the gutter. No one could care for me. Not even my own mother.'

'Dear child!' I cupped her face. 'You are wrong. And yet you are right not to try to hold such thoughts to yourself. Speak them out and we shall make little of them.'

'I cannot!' She sobbed until she was almost in hysterics. 'It is too terrible to talk of it.'

The child achieved such a state of distress that I doubted my competency to deal with it. She seemed like one who had been borne along by a flood but was now entangled in branches that held her fast yet exposed her to the brunt of the torrent.

'Tell me what is on your mind,' I coaxed. 'I am sure that you may safely speak to me on any subject. I will either forget it or act as you prefer. But if talking seems impossible now, try to lift your thoughts. Lodge them elsewhere.'

She listened. I believed for a moment that she would follow my prescription. Then her face went blank and in another instant she was seized by blind panic. I saw it happen and I could not help. Her vacant eyes stared and her whole self seemed stricken. 'Emma,' she murmured. She looked then straight into my eyes and cried out, 'Emma!'

In another moment merciful nature rescued that small frame from its ordeal. She moaned and her hands went to her head. Her face then went very white and her form became limp.

It gave me little satisfaction to have one more piece to add to Mr Ellin's puzzle. I felt sure the girl had lost her memory.

In the morning I summoned a physician. He administered a spirit of vinegar followed by a sedative, and I offered him a brief account of the preceding events. He strongly advised admission to an institution where her condition could be investigated under proper supervision.

'I would prefer not,' I said. Having seen the panic in her childish eyes I was resolved to keep her within my own care.

'She cannot be left in this no man's land where she currently dwells,' the doctor advised. 'She believes it to be a hiding-place yet it is fraught with horror. Her mind will be weakened by terror and confusion. Someone must lead her to safety.'

'I will try,' I vowed.

'If you fail,' he warned, 'she may be forced back instead of forward. I have seen people retreat into themselves so that they ceased to communicate with the outward world entirely.'

With this heavy charge upon my mind I sat by the girl's bed. When she opened her eyes I read to her. As soon as she sat up I fetched her milk with honey. After a time she struggled to get out of bed but I detained her. 'Rest, Matilda! Let me look after you.'

A look of confusion came over her face. She stared at me, seeming not to see me, and I suffered a deep anxiety. Her brow then cleared and she looked at me explicitly and said, in surprise, 'My name is Emma!'

'Not Matilda? How do you know?'

'I heard someone speak to me by name. She said but a single word, "Emma". There was no one there yet I knew myself to be addressed by someone dear and familiar.'

'Who called you Matilda?' I spoke as circumspectly as I could.

'He did!' Her face acquired an anxious aspect again and I quickly hushed her.

'Your father?'

'He was not my father.'

'What of your mother? Is she alive or dead?'

She shook her head as if at an invisible horror. Her eyes were fixed upon some dark point. 'I expect she still goes on.'

I contemplated what the doctor had said. *She must either retreat into herself or be led to safety.*

'We shall find her. Whatever has passed between you and her, a mother will always forgive her child.'

She looked at me with a kind of pity, lay down again and cried herself to sleep. I passed the day pacing by her bed. Free her from this prison I must and would.

At one point I fell asleep myself. I awoke to find her gazing at me intently. 'I know where to look for my mother,' she said.

'Good.' I spoke in a practical fashion. 'Then you must go there.'

The child looked so alarmed that I hastened to assure her the journey would not be undertaken alone. 'I shall be with you. Together we will confront your past. Whatever is revealed, whatever comes to pass, I will not leave you.'

'Are you not apprehensive?'

'Yes, but my foreboding is of a different order from yours. My concern is that when your mother once more lays eyes upon her little girl she will want to take her away from me.'

'Oh, no!' cried Emma, in such dread that I wondered indeed what this lady had inflicted upon her young.

'Do not fret,' I urged. 'For the moment let us concentrate on recovering your strength.'

The following day she announced a desire to get up and go for a walk. I deemed it wisest to let her have her way. We dressed in all manner of warm clothes and set out for the cemetery. If this sounds a morbid aim then you do not know our graveyard. It is a place of great tranquillity and beauty, overlooked by a fine old Norman church and offering a view to a distance of six or seven miles across the valleys known as Colne and Calder. Its only disturbing aspect is a stocks placed directly outside it so that poor wretches must augment their humiliation by contemplating their eternity. Within the burial ground itself, the atmosphere is one of intimacy and even affability. Children always like to come here for there is a dear little miniature house that was once a schoolhouse (and now looks as if it might house fairies) and they like to read the poignant homilies inscribed on the stones, often, alas, to other little lost souls. Emma and I passed a pleasant half-hour speculating on the slumbering citizens of this prime site and then we walked home through the woods. When we came to a hill, Emma hitched her skirts and laboured to the top. She remained there, quite still except for the wind that buffeted her, for a space of some twenty minutes. At length I summoned her back, for it was very cold.

'What did you see there?' I asked her.

'I saw a world such as has been denied to me for so long that I had all but forgotten how to breathe. And I heard the wind. The wind spoke to me.'

'And what did it say?'

'My name. Emma: the two syllables sighed into the trees. I am not entirely the nonentity I imagined myself to be. I am known to the wind.'

When she had done she leant against a tree and I was pleased to see a natural colour in her cheeks. The process of healing is begun, I thought with relief. We shall see you through this ordeal and let you commence the freshest part of your existence unburdened.

As an antidote to the trial to come I decided to put her to a small but difficult test. I mentioned in an offhand manner that I had a message for her to deliver on the morrow. She took the package obediently and only added as an afterthought, 'To whom?'

'To the Misses Wilcox.'

She gave me one bright, hurt glance and promptly withdrew into herself.

'What do you suppose is in the message?' I asked her.

'You are sending me back to them,' she said dully.

'Anything but that.' I spoke from my heart. 'The package contains payment in full for your school fees. You shall not carry a debt for which you are not responsible.'

Although in Mr Ellin's view, I would now be abetting Lucifer's work, I was almost prepared to risk my soul rather than Emma's sanity.

Later, when I came to her room to bid her good night, she was at her prayers: 'God bless Mrs Chalfont.' Her eyes were shut tight, her concentration fierce. 'Keep her safe and grant that she may never know the real truth about me.'

CHAPTER THIRTEEN

Mr Ellin passed the festive eve alone at M—. He ordered a chop sent to his room and as he chewed absentmindedly on that rugged rib he scratched away minutely with his pen in his black-bound notebook.

(1) He is a gentleman but has not the look of one, which means that (a) he is an imposter of his class or (b) a renegade to his class.

(2) He was acting in haste and in stealth. Had he come from near or far?

Not far, Mr Ellin reckoned, as he was in a hurry, yet he deemed him to be not of this immediate town (he might not wish to be recognized).

As the man's aristocratic impersonation had managed to pass muster under the shrewd eyes of both Miss Mabel Wilcox and Madame Lucille, Mr Ellin decided to accord it some legitimacy. His first task must be to locate all the large houses within a radius of twenty miles. Then he would try to pin down those that had a nominal association with the false address given by Mr Fitzgibbon. May Park? It could be June Court or April Arbour.

Now, how to inquire? He could not go around questioning people about a Mr Conway Fitzgibbon, since such a party did not exist. Who was liable to know all that was good and bad in a neighbourhood and the true hearts of its residents? Who understood its motivation and kept its secrets? None but God, he decided. Who, then, might be next in command to that wise but oft-inaccessible administrator? Why, the rector, of course.

Clergymen come in three varieties. There is the hell-fire type, who has great entertainment value but is so consumed with sin and self-worth that he is of little practical use; there is the conscientious and caring kind, who is generally poor and shabby and modest and whose lights are seen only by those in need; then there is the self-styled prince of the Church, who likes to mould that title in the temporal cast; who makes himself the lackey of his social superiors, toadying to every lord and lady in order to gain entry to their houses, attending to the poor only to remind them to be useful and repentant. Mr Dolland was of the latter ilk.

Mr Ellin apprehended him at his place of business after morning service. Mr Dolland did not like to be delayed. He was on his way to visit one of the privileged gentlemen whom his visitor sought. Mr Ellin explained that he needed to speak with him on an urgent matter and would detain him but briefly.

'I cannot offer you hospitality,' Mr Dolland warned. 'My maid is at liberty and I am to dine with Lord and Lady Eldred.'

'I require only that service for which you yourself are employed,' Mr Ellin assured him.

'Someone's dying, I suppose.' Mr Dolland sighed.

'Not dying.' Mr Ellin relented. 'In danger – a child who may have a connection to this parish.' He did not tell the full story at once, but only said that, through unknown circumstances, a young girl had been separated from her family.

'Can it not wait until the morrow?' Mr Dolland asked.

'If you consider it acceptable for a young person to remain in peril another day, then it can,' Mr Ellin amiably agreed.

Mr Dolland had no acquaintance with humour or irony, and intimations of either always made him feel accused. With some reluctance he led Mr Ellin to his very comfortable ivy-clad residence. The latter allowed him to suffer a while as he lowered himself into an accommodating green sofa while the other gentleman stole an agonized glance at his watch. 'I wonder how I may help you?' he peevishly inquired.

'Well, it is simple. It would appear that this girl – about thirteen years of age – was presented at her school by a gentleman, who if not of this parish was at least of the vicinity. It would have been a gentleman of good address. I considered you the most likely to be acquainted with such a person.'

Mr Dolland almost forgot about the hour. He seemed in raptures, holding forth about 'the quality'. He even volunteered some refreshment – a choice of tonic or potass waters. Mr Ellin scarcely had to ask a question but only to write as fast as his wrist would follow to keep up with the flow of names and acres, attendant gracious wives and beautiful children. Fourteen families and four bachelors were listed and a full dossier supplied with each. Mr Ellin made due note of the unwed males.

'Do you think you recognize your gentleman there?' the rector wondered. 'Would you like me to introduce you? I had not known that any of my dear neighbours had lost a child, but if that is the case, then I would be happy to assist in reuniting them.'

Now that Mr Ellin had what information the clergyman could yield he was able to tell the full story. At once his host's attitude changed. 'You seek a villain?' said he.

'As I mentioned, I am not in full possession of the facts, but it begins to look that way.'

'You'll not find one in my parish or in the next. All our gentlemen are of the highest probity. However, if you are looking for a miscreant, I can point you to one at once.'

'I wonder who you have in mind?' Mr Ellin said.

'It is this girl of whom you speak – she and her accomplice; no gentleman, I assure you! Why, sir, it is the oldest trick in the world. A man dresses up an urchin to pass her off in society. She remains where she is lodged long enough to ascertain what is of value and then the wretch returns to complete the burglary. Lady Carrol had a girl employed who let a man in to steal the meat. It may be the very one of whom you speak. No, that child would be in prison still.'

'The girl in question has done no wrong,' Mr Ellin said. 'Her situation is pitiful. I have a note from her. She asked me to show it to no one, but as you are unacquainted with her, this won't be a break of trust.' He handed over the faintly scrawled message which he carried with him everywhere.

'"I was sold like a farmyard creature. No one wants me."' Mr Dolland read it aloud, scowling in consideration. To Mr Ellin's astonishment he then burst out laughing. 'She's theatrical, I'll grant you that. The little d——l would not have fooled me. Sold out, she means. Her scheme has gone awry. Her partner has absconded and she is left alone to face the music.'

'Yes, but why would he have troubled to furnish her with a wardrobe that was assuredly of more value than anything in the schoolhouse?'

'You are making the naïve assumption, sir, that the wardrobe was paid for. I would be willing to wager that every stitch on that young person's undeserving form was stolen.'

'Mr Dolland, this is uncharitable!' Yet Mr Ellin felt unaccountably uneasy. He had no evidence that the man who had presented his overdressed charge at Fuchsia Lodge was the same one who had paid for the garments. 'Besides, it is scarcely relevant. The school, though of good repute, is run by three sisters in reduced circumstances. There could be no possible advantage in it for a thief. It simply makes no sense.'

'On the contrary! It begins to make perfect sense.' Mr Dolland was warming to his theme. 'The perfidious pair have been involved in some unscrupulous but unsuccessful scheme. Both are now sought by the law. They are on the run. If they move together, the man's flight will be hampered by the slower movements of the female. Moreover, they will be easier to track down as a pair. So! The man – I should think he is probably her father after all – will likely go abroad. Now, how best to conceal a young female? Why, in a ladies' academy! It is indeed the perfect deceit. Who would think of raiding a respectable girls' school for a criminal? And who would even consider casting an eye in the direction of one so modest as you describe? You know, I applaud the fellow, although I abhor him. It is a great pity that some of the best brains in contemporary society are bent to crime instead of business. Indeed, I often think my own wits are not best extended in the service of the Lord. Not, my dear fellow, I assure you, that I have the least appetite for villainy. No, I meant I ought to have been a detective.' He laughed with childish glee. 'I think, after all, I am in the wrong business.'

'Indeed,' said Mr Ellin, with a sarcasm that was undetected. 'I think so too.'

CHAPTER FOURTEEN

Although I had asked Emma to deliver the message, I did not intend to leave her to the tender mercies of the Misses Wilcox. My plan was to follow at a safe distance and to present myself like a second surprise package at the moment the consignees opened the dispatch and discovered its content. It was a devious design, to be sure, but there were advantages in it for all. The Misses Wilcox would have their payment. Emma would have her acquittal and I would be granted the trivial satisfaction of perhaps witnessing a bloom of embarrassment on those cheeks that nature did not regularly favour with blushes.

When this was out of the way I meant to take Emma for a holiday. I thought we would travel to Barlington where I had first encountered the ocean in the company of Mr Chalfont. I believed it would afford her as much delight as it did myself and the sea air would restore her strength.

In optimistic mood I presented myself and a tray of breakfast at Miss Emma's chamber. I knocked, entered, and was confronted with an empty bed. Stealthy sprite! She had stolen a march and was up before me.

I sought her in the house. I put on my shawl and braved the garden. No little girl was to be found. Then I had a notion. I went back inside and searched the mantelpiece upon which the message had been perched. The package was missing. So! She had foxed me. She had decided to brave the Gorgons on her own. I graciously accepted defeat. She was cleverer than I and certainly more courageous. If we were to make our way together I need expect no dearth of challenge. The young miss was as independent as an island.

Breakfast having been rendered redundant, I put on some coffee, cut a slice of Christmas fruit cake to go with it, and made ready to present it to her as a victory laurel upon her return. I knew not the time of her departure but the Misses Wilcox's residence was less than an hour from my own and I doubted they would detain their guest for longer than it took to relieve her of her burden. I picked up a piece of work and stitched at in a distracted manner.

The coffee grew cold. The clock struck a second hour. I chided myself for my apprehension. She was not an infant. If she chose to take a stroll round the town, then that was her privilege. Perhaps she had met some schoolfellows. Good sense did not allay my fears but only argued my excuses out of existence. Emma did not yet like to go anywhere without me. When lunchtime came I set out for Fuchsia Lodge. Miss Mabel greeted me frostily.

'Has the child been here?' I asked at once.

'If you mean who I assume you mean, she has not,' she answered. 'That young person would scarcely dare to show her face under the prevailing circumstances.'

'Never mind that now,' said I. 'She has gone missing. I sent her here this morning with a message. Do you have any notion where she might have gone?'

'What message?' Miss Mabel's consideration was instantly attendant upon her own loss rather than that of my charge.

'If you must know, it was a clearance of all her obligation. I undertook to pay her school fees.'

The schoolmistress's normally inexpressive face was animated by a rare register of emotions. Interest quickened and was relieved by pique. Fury and disappointment then gathered her sharp features into a premature ageing. Several times in the space of a week she had seen recompense wing its way towards her, hover wonderfully near and then renew its flight. 'Are you sure she has gone?' she said. 'Have you checked for her possessions?'

'She has none,' I replied. 'You made sure of that.'

My neighbour awarded me a none-too-hospitable glare. She seemed to boil down to a veritable stew of resentments until brightened by yet another aspect – that of vindication. 'So! She is a thief too! She has made off with your money – or mine.'

This assertion stung me to the quick. In all my concerns, that specific one had not presented itself. It grieved me now, both in its particular and that others should think it of her.

'I wonder,' said Miss Wilcox, 'that you had so little sense as to intrust a proven fraud with anything of value.'

'I wonder,' returned I, 'that you have so little sensibility regarding the safety of a young person lately in your care.'

'Do not fear for her safety, dear Mrs Chalfont. Undoubtedly she has returned to whatever den sprang her upon us. Believe me, you are better rid of her, and sooner rather than later. There is no nature in the child. She is an actress and a criminal. If I were you, I would count my blessings at being rid of a pest – and count my silver too.'

'She could have my silver and welcome,' said I, 'if it would in any manner ease her existence. I care only for her welfare. What should I do? Should I notify the police?'

'Why not? Undoubtedly she has a string of misdemeanours to her name. You may well bring recompense to other victims.'

After this exchange of bonhomie I returned to my home. That comfortable refuge where I had made a truce with loneliness and learnt to make light of solitude seemed furnished in every corner with memories of its transient lodger. Here she had nestled with a book, there stood on a chair to arrange branches of spruce on the mantelpiece; in this spot, she had, with the solemnity of an angel (though without the voice of one), frailly voiced a ballad and moved me to tears.

Perhaps Miss Wilcox was right – not in her judgement of the child, which seemed at odds with all that was obvious in her character, but in her blunt assertion that I was best to lose her sooner rather than later. I had grown too attached to her. My custody was never to be more than temporary. It was agreed with Mr Ellin that as soon as her source was located she would be returned to it. But I had accepted that in word only. In my heart she was my companion. In private I had viewed myself as the one who would guide her to womanhood. The mind travels swiftly on the wings of hope. Sometimes I even pictured at my hearth figures smaller yet than my slender damsel: her own children brought back for their portion of my affection.

Why did I attach such a freight of emotion to a child whom others considered unlovable? Well, I have my reasons. You shall hear of them soon.

She was gone. No note was left, no farewell uttered. I blamed myself. I had pushed her too radically, had chipped the fragile assurance painstakingly established. She no longer felt secure with me, preferring instead the cold and unsafe world.

Yet although she was gone, she was not gone. I could not sit by the fire without thinking of Emma abroad on the freezing day with no food – not even breakfast – and no single possession in the world. I could not lie down without wondering where she would lay her head that night. So far as I could tell, she had no friend and knew as much of the world as any anchorite. The money she had taken would last but a little while.

What could I do? If I notified the police and she was, as Miss Wilcox suggested, in some sort of trouble, then I would endanger her further. I did what women do. I sat by the window and envisaged every sort of menace and peril. I suffered my imagination to conjure them up and vividly to animate them and then to pitch among them a child whose sensibilities I wore as my own. In short, I endured the helpless anguish of every mother whose child has quitted home too soon and too unready.

CHAPTER FIFTEEN

I said that Mr Chalfont and I had no child. That is the truth, yet not the whole truth. About a year after the death of my mother I found myself visited by the happy malady that is the hope of every married woman. No sooner than predicted, the child assumed a full set of characteristics in my mind. I was confident that she would be a girl — not the winsome, golden-ringleted type that most parents seem to covet, but a solemn, sensitive, intelligent little person, who would be both pupil and tutor to me. Looking back, I suppose it is true to say that my projected infant owed more in the way of heredity to Finch Cornhill than to myself or Mr Chalfont, but in fact heredity formed no part of my consideration. Not only was my child as visible to me as if her portrait had been painted and hung about my heart, but I felt her as a long-lost companion with whom I was soon to be reunited. From my present lofty site of maturity, I perceive it as the reaction of a passionate and immature young woman who liked to lodge her emotions whole and, having lost one safe-keeping, invested the entirety of her sentimental hunger in the only one whom she might freely and innocently love.

Albert entertained no such complicated notions. He cared not if it be boy or girl, fair or dark, sensitive or merry. He wanted to be a family man. As for me, he indulged my every whim and treated me as if I were a precious heirloom rather than the bearer of the heir. When my lack of appetite persisted he suggested a holiday and some mountain air. Remembering my mother's wise words I made no protest, and we consigned our responsibilities to the timid servant and the slovenly grocery assistant, and were on our way.

We departed on one of those sultry days whose air emanates from the death-chamber of summer and reached our destination in time for the start of a storm. The inn — allegedly the highest in England — was small and characterful and had put on a few airs and added these to its prices. Under different circumstances I might have protested at the expense, but I arrived in need of rest and at once took to my chamber, while Albert (having hovered solicitously as I attempted to eat some soup) retired to the bar to find convivial company.

It was not until the following morning that I could justify the little inn's conceit. It was a fine day (the first of autumn) with that low sunlight that gilds all it touches. The inn looked out over majestic mountain peaks. Small clouds brushed the mountains with a dramatic sweep of darkness, then lifted to exhibit the season's soft colours. I felt well that morning. I was eager to be out. Albert (in whose solid make-up impulsiveness did not feature) declared we would make a good breakfast, then address ourselves to the day. I was pleased with myself for I was able to eat a little and earned much praise on this account.

It was Albert's plan that we should rent a carriage to take us for a leisurely drive and stop off for lunch at the next town before returning to the inn.

'Oh, let us walk,' I pleaded. 'I wish to be in the open air.'

The innkeeper told us that the most common way of viewing the sights was on horseback. 'You ride through the Buttertubs Pass and then come upon a panorama of particular beauty,' he elaborated.

'Is it safe?' Albert worried. 'We are neither of us accustomed to horseback riding.'

'Oh, very safe,' the innkeeper assured us. 'John Keel is an experienced guide and his horses as steady and slow as turtles.'

After the undignified business of being hoisted on to a large and patient mount, we began a sedate progress up a narrow mountain trail.

'Such a sheer drop!' Albert exclaimed. 'Is this not hazardous?'

'No, not at all,' Mr Keel assured us. 'The animals do not mind the height, and we can trust in them. Horses have very good instincts.'

'All the same, I shall be glad when we are in the pass with solid rock to both sides of us,' my husband murmured.

'Oddly, the horses do not like the pass,' their owner observed. 'I always ask folk to dismount as we go through it, for it has a strange effect on the creatures.'

I, myself, had been too taken with the view to consider its potential hazard (my mount set down its heavy feet slowly enough for me to count every stone and fern). Far below, the river poured between boulders with a whispering energy and brewed up a creamy foam where it eddied into rock pools. High above, the hills beguiled us with their changing light and colour. It was exhilarating beyond all imagining. I could hold but a single thought: I was to bring a new being into this beautiful world.

So absorbed was I in the scene aloft and underneath that I failed to notice it was about to be erased. Quite without warning (it seemed) we were plunged into the blackest darkness. We had entered the mountain pass. I was visited by a suffocating sense of horror as we were sandwiched between high, closely packed vertical stone stacks. Thus might one feel in the mouth of some prehistoric beast. There was something else in there. It was as though the very teeth of the cliffs oozed despair. When the guide asked me to dismount, his voice was smothered. Sound could not live there, and yet there seemed to issue from those stone cliffs a vague, yet persistent ringing moan.

Of a sudden, I felt faint and panic-stricken. Albert descended from his horse and held out a hand for me. I knew I could not step down for my legs would not support me. The tunnel was quite short and I resolved to say nothing and glue myself to the horse's back until we attained the light again. I shook my head at John Keel's sharp command to me to dismount. I know not if my unease communicated itself to the poor dumb beast or if it, too, sensed something infernal in the place, but without warning it emitted a shrill whinny of pure terror, rose on its hind legs and waved its forelegs as if to fend off the evil. In an instant, I was hurled to the ground. The terrified creature then pranced in violent apprehension and I felt the full force of his hoof make contact with my body and slam me into those dreadful fangs of stone.

When I awoke I thought I was still in the pass, for the faint moaning sound persisted. I realized then that it was coming from myself. I looked around in fright, and found myself gazing at the reassuring countenance of my husband and at another gentleman who was a stranger. Both regarded me with the utmost compassion and I was soon to find out why.

My baby was no more. The horse's hoof, the evil mountain pass, had claimed that little life. The stranger, who proved to be a physic, explained that the injury I had sustained would make it impossible for me to bear another child.

I was given a draught to let me sleep again. When I awoke the sun was shining and the curtain had been drawn back to give me the full glory of the view. Yet I saw it not. I dwelt now in the dark place where my best hope had been shattered. My whole world was the black chill of that mountain pass.

I have come to believe that each person has a site of desolation. Those who have sojourned at this spot know its stark climate and pitiless wastes. There is neither light nor growth. All human company is obscured by shadow. No rest is possible, for the atmosphere is full of demons that agitate the nerves to a pitch of frenzy; no calm, for the air is rent with a howling that comes from the very centre of oneself.

How does one escape that place? There is no escape. Why did I not die of grief? Why does not everyone who comes to this region? I did as all creatures do, compelled to live in inhospitable climes: I placed foot after weary foot, determined to go on until I found once more the light. And yet the barren landscape persisted. In due course I built a nest for myself. With pleasant thoughts and good deeds, with books and friends, with hearth and garden, I endeavoured to fashion a shelter for the soul.

I am bound to confess that I did not accomplish this – could not have done so – on my own. About a three-month had passed and we were back in our abode above the shop (which seemed to me as bleak as any other place) when Albert came up with a prescription for my recovery. 'It's time you had your own home, Belle. I'll build you a house where you'll be happy again. I've found a perfect site for us. It's a mile or two out of town with trees to shelter it and a beck to water it, if you care to make a garden.'

I told him bluntly that an increase of debt was scarcely likely to buoy my spirits.

'No debt, Belle.' He spoke gently. 'The fact of the matter is that we are in profit. We have done rather well this past year. We have money in the bank.'

This news was so surprising that it almost roused me from my inertia. 'Why did you not tell me? You know I worry about money.'

I saw from his expression how deeply he carried his own sorrow. 'It seemed unimportant for a time. We had so much the better wealth.' He covered my hand with his. 'Yet money can help. You shall see, my dear.'

I imagine Albert's new project was conceived in part to aid his own recovery. At any rate he plunged himself into it with the enthusiasm he had brought to all his ventures, and I admired this stoic male capacity to overcome adversity. At first I could scarcely interest myself to visit the site, yet when I did, I own I liked it. The situation was a patch of gold on Deerfield Moor. A part of it was warmed with sunshine, another part soothed with shade. There were old trees to break the winds. Yet it was the view that won my heart. It was the same vista with which God had rewarded my childhood visits to church at H——, clear across to Castle Hill, and with Black Hill thrown in for good measure.

As yet our only neighbours were a family of foxes, in whose honour I named our new establishment Fox Clough (a clough being the name hereabouts for a valley). In regard to the house, Albert said I could have any design I liked, yet his own ideas were so clear they brooked no argument, and in any case I cared little. Upon a particular point I did make my feelings known. 'Six bedrooms are surely a superfluity for one married couple and a single servant.'

'Yes, but think how it will appear to my associates and competitors. Appearances, Belle! Who but a successful man would live in such an establishment? People will be queuing up to offer me business.'

I no longer had the strength to argue and in any case there appeared to be some veracity to his stubborn and specious logic.

Within a six-month the house had been completed, its leaded windows and bricks of millstone grit making it seem a sturdy, long-term tenant of the moor (but for the untamed earth that yet surrounded it). Our new situation gave my husband a drive of four miles daily to his work, but his optimistic nature turned this to advantage, for he saw it as a means of acquainting himself with new suppliers and customers. The lodgings above the shop were converted into storerooms to enable expansion of his business, and I became the mistress of a large (and largely empty) house.

At first my new home did nothing to raise my mood. The dark wood panels were oppressive. The house was gaunt and empty and I had neither heart to fill it nor energy to care for it.

'Get another servant,' Albert said; 'two if you like. We can afford 'em.'

A housekeeper and cook in due course joined us. The servants scuttled nervously about. Cook presented daunting feasts for which I had no appetite. 'Find some activity, Belle,' Albert urged. 'Furnish the house. Fill it with what you like.'

'So large a house should be filled with children,' I said.

'Well, do so, wife,' he said.

'Oh, Albert, don't be cruel. Where am I to find them?'

He sighed with impatience. 'Have you not three young siblings? Would they not care to join you in so fine a residence?'

I gazed at him in astonishment. 'You would be prepared to take on all my family?'

Mr Chalfont shook his head. 'Dearest wife, I have already done so. It would come as a great relief – an economy too – to have 'em all under the one roof. Go along now, child. Write to your father. Tell him we have a home for one and all.'

What expression he found on my face then I know not but it made him laugh. 'Belle, dear, for a moment there, I could almost have sworn you liked me.'

'Of course, sir,' I mumbled in confusion.

'Now, don't "of course" me. I know right well I weren't what you had in mind for a husband. You'd have wanted someone young and handsome and fanciful. Yet any lass who's treated right will grow to like her master. Stands to reason! I made a promise to your father that I would make myself worthy of your affection. I know I haven't much to offer, but such as there is, it is for you.'

I had to turn away to hide my tears. I had never yet considered my husband in any light other than that of practical (or impractical) provider. Yet his wholehearted kindness touched me deeply.

That large house gladly absorbed its quota. Although I still pined for my lost little child, I had to shed my all-absorbing self-concern. My own sisters were motherless waifs. My father was a tired and broken man. From the moment of their arrival my life was committed to them. Albert displayed no jealousy of this dedication. He accepted the children as his own and they adored him. He was always ready for play and made no protest as muddy boots and sticky hands applied themselves to his expensive wood and handsome furniture. My father had always liked him as a simple, honest man, and they spent many happy hours exchanging tales of business.

In due course I made a most contented and affectionate wife to the creature I had taken for my worse half. I became indulgent of all his little follies and foibles (especially as he had sufficient sense to allow me to guide him in important matters). As time went on his appearance was no more to me than that of a favourite and comfortable pair of shoes. His harmless chatter was the soothing babble of a stream. I came to believe that many of those worldly precepts whose seeming coldness shock and repel us in youth are founded in wisdom. I grew to respect Albert. In matters of commerce he proved to have no equal.

As to that strange alliance of opposites known as marriage, I eventually believed myself, as most women do, an expert on the subject. Habit and kindness and constancy, I concluded, formed its strong weave. Passion and intellect were but embroidery on the fabric. As it required a strong degree of common sense, a wealth of organizational skill and sufficient mettle to sustain it under siege, a deepening fondness might likely endure better than a grand passion.

Perhaps marriage prospered best in equable climes and could suffocate in a tropical heat. The passion that fuses two hearts into one might dim that organ's capacity to extend its affections to the many friends and relatives, the weeping children, lame dogs and stray cats that enter its fold to warm themselves at its glowing hearth.

As to intense passion, had not experience taught me that it burned more than it warmed? How often did it meet with a requital? Did Finch ever love me as I loved him? I had to ask myself why he had not tried to find me. And for those happy souls whose declarations of undying love were echoed in the voice of the beloved, how long did such feelings persist? Could they last unto death as marriage does? And what might replace them? Disgust? Indifference? Certainly I would have begged leave to doubt that they lasted on the man's part; and on the woman's – God help her, if she was left to love passionately and alone.

Do I convince you? Did I seem too eager to persuade myself? We shall check for revisions in due course.

From the moment of my family's arrival, I no longer had time for sentimental reverie or mawkish self-pity. Now that I had a proper home to run I cast myself into it, heart and soul. In due course, I could look out from my manufactured refuge and rejoice that it extended as far as the eye could see. My house was warm and safe, my garden a soft and sheltered place.

Granted, I never ventured far from it, but I came at last to a frame of contentment where I could aver – and believe it – that I was tranquil.

Yet our sorrows live on with us. They lie in hiding until the living have departed and then they shyly show themselves. My sisters, having been very well educated at the expense of Mr Chalfont, in due course married and moved away. My father lived on but a decade, and five years after that my husband was taken from me.

Yes, Albert died. He died upon a good deed. A bleak winter night brought a neighbour with a sick child. My husband was himself in bed, enjoying a comfortable flu. As was his disposition, he insisted on taking the infant to hospital in his trap. Pneumonia repaid his kindness. Albert was always hale as well as hearty. I felt confident he would find the simple answer to this setback: a dinner for twenty, a visit to the Lake District. Yet he now faced a most unsparing creditor: this one, who exacted his very breath. In a startlingly short space that bank ran dry. He gave a small sigh, patted my hand. He had no breath to say goodbye. I held his hand until that limb grew chill. I could not quite believe some puffs of snow had turned a sturdy grocer into a pale monument and myself into a solitary.

But let us look upon this thing dispassionately. A lifetime contract entered in revolt was nulled by heaven's intervention. The anchor on my dreams was raised. Although my youthful hope had been dashed by news of Finch's death, still, I might (after a proper period of mourning) envisage a bright future. There was but one brake upon the enterprise. To those not familiar with this restraint, it is known as grief.

Albert and I had built our nest and raised our young, had taught and learnt from one another. We had comforted each other in sorrow. I had been loved patiently and abundantly.

The master I once dismissed as unremarkable I now knew for that most uncommon of God's creatures. He was a contented man; and contentment has a sweet contagion. Many a poor soul stopped me in the street to tell me how, when times were hard, he dismissed their debts. For years I searched the house for his benign assurance and found that my best support had been removed. If it took me a long time to know myself as wife, a more daunting stretch elapsed before I could accept myself as widow.

Now I had an empty house again. All my sorrows came to live with me. Perhaps the most poignant of these was the child I should have shared with Albert.

You may understand from this with what shining hopes I invested a brief visit from that strange and solemn waif who came to me out of – and vanished into – the thin, cold air.

CHAPTER SIXTEEN

Yet thin air does not absorb solid matter. A robin's-eye view might have shown a frail young girl resolutely trudge the distance to Fuchsia Lodge. It might have marked her pause for prayer when she came to the church, and afterwards her entry to the cemetery, there to make her way to a certain grave for a private conversation with its occupant. 'You were a plain man, Albert Chalfont. Perhaps I might have spoken with you. You were a father to those not your children. You might have been a father to me.' For in spite of her very particular circumstance, she wanted what all children want, a mother and father, a home, a secure base to set her roots. If her object had replied, he might have said: 'Go home, lass. Get your feet in a mustard bath.' Or: 'The longest journey begins with a single step.' With or without this advice she proceeded. When she reached the schoolhouse she lingered with hand upon gate. If only the small dispatch she bore could absolve her past. Her witness might have focused on her troubled countenance and measured the depth of her sigh as she turned away and began to pace this way and that before slowly turning on the path that led from town.

From its lofty perch a winged spectator might barely have distinguished her from her winter surroundings: a modest scrap of brown and green, a winter leaf, blown by the wind. No other footstep offered friendly echo. No cartwheel made its creak on the descent. All humankind was indoors, enjoying the leisure and fellowship of the season. Even nature seemed an outcast. The beck was petrified in icy silence. The very fields seemed shamed by their nakedness and turned bristled backs to the road. Only a few sheep complained of their lot. Yet even they belonged to someone and could look forward to a renewal in the spring. Where was she to find regeneration? With every step her sense of loss advanced. She was a child still. She wanted a mother's kindness and a father's guidance. She felt too young and weak for this unwanted independence. A kind word, a warm touch, would have seemed the very breath of heaven to her. The only air that touched her was the grating wind. She was so overwrought her legs trembled as she walked. Yet foot succeeded foot, and she made herself walk as briskly as the elements permitted. She did not know what distance lay between her and the railway. She had no idea of railway timetables but thought only of achieving the shelter of the station's waiting room. Almost as soon as she had begun her great voyage the sky furrowed its brow into drab folds and sent out its armies with arrows of hail. It peppered her face with painful shot and burrowed in under her collar.

To avoid the worst of the climate she sought the shelter of the woods. She kept her path parallel to the road and tried to marshal those facts that were in her keeping. Before coming to Deerfield she remembered driving through the busy streets of a city. She had asked its name and was duly informed. The carriage (a closed one, of a type used only by wealthy passengers) rolled through a narrow and dirty lane on the corner of which stood two young women in ragged dancing clothes. 'Poor girls, they must be cold,' she had murmured, and her companion replied that they had more, poor wretches, than cold to bear. She wondered why no one tried to help them.

Her head began to ache with the effort of remembering. The woods were very dark and she decided to return to the road. Her heart made frail protestations as she ran in one direction, then another, emitting little gasping sobs as her garments caught in dense growth. An hour or more passed before she found herself on the road again, which was now obscured by a running torrent of mud.

She had completed not much more than half her journey when faintness and the weight of her rain-sodden cloak felled her and she landed heavily in the wet. She must find rest. She toiled on until at last she perceived the welcome shape of a cottage. This hovel belonged to a recluse called Eli Hirst, who made his livelihood by poaching with the aid of a fearsome hound called Demon. At first the only feature Emma could discern was the decaying hovel and a puny thread of smoke that issued from its chimney. They must be poor, thought she. I shall not ask for bread, but only for refuge. The restless shadows in a gloomy interior suggested a sluggish fire and no auxiliary light. She was trying to make use of the glimmer to distinguish what manner of human dwelt within when her vision was filled by a frightful sight – a red open jaw inches from her face, a set of slavering teeth, the snapping of which was accompanied by a low menacing growl. She saw small fierce eyes in a hungry face and this framed by a mass of shaggy hair. She cried out in alarm and stepped back. The hound – for it was the poacher's dog – came no further and she perceived that it was attached to a stout chain that allowed it to keep intruders at bay but gave it no liberty. As her fear diminished she felt a pang of pity for the beast for she saw that it was kept half-starved to encourage savagery. The dog sustained a high-pitched bark and leapt on its chain, which clanked and rattled. Above this din she perceived a sound even more chilling to the blood. It was a dry rasp of human laughter. What manner of person could be amused by her disconcertion and the frustration of the poor hungry creature? Peering into the dark she saw that a man had emerged from the cottage and was pointing at her a shotgun.

'Looks like you'll not get your supper yet, Demon,' the man laughed again, 'not unless I shoots her for you. You'd make short work of that bag of bones.'

'Sir!' Emma tried to make her voice firm. 'I did not mean to trespass. I merely sought shelter from the weather. May I rest awhile and then be on my way?'

'To be sure, miss.' He lowered his shotgun and emitted once more the weary cackle that passed for mirth. She took a step or two and the weapon was pointed at her again. 'But if you proceed this way you'll rest for all eternity.'

'I come as a friend.'

'I never knew a friend,' he said. 'I've lived this long by recognizing every creature as my enemy – and that includes the dog. I'll give you ten seconds and then I'll shoot. I'd like to see you spring in the air like a rabbit before you go down.'

There was a coolness in his tone. It was his very indifference that convinced her. She turned and ran. She could no longer clearly see the path and before she reached the bottom she tripped and fell. For a few moments she lay where she was and then she looked up. The cottage was in darkness now. Even the dismal fire seemed to have gone out. Of the householder there was no sign. It rained as hard as ever and if there was any other house on the horizon, darkness obscured it. Cautiously she crept up by the side of the building. She could discern very little now and was feeling her way warily when the dog came upon her like a train from a tunnel. She felt the hot breath upon her face, almost she felt the fangs on her features. She glanced quickly at the dwelling but the marksman had likely gone back to his pot. This time Emma did not retreat. For some reason she felt no dread. She stayed where she was and whispered into that hot red jaw, 'Do not be afraid, little brother. I am only a friendless being, as you are.' The dog's ears went back a bit and it growled half-heartedly. Emma risked her hand upon the wild animal's mane.

To her surprise the beast whimpered and bowed its head. She patted it until it ceased to shiver and then she buried her face in its ragged fur. What solace there was in that heavy-breathing bulk. The animal sighed and lay down against the wall of the cottage and Emma curled up against its warmth. Why had she called the dog 'little brother'? Why was she not afraid? Anyone else would be. Some forgotten part of herself knew the nature of dogs and trusted them beyond any human. It interested her to think that this part of her was not lost along with her memory but was free to advance, independent of her present limited and mistrustful mental kit. In due course the rain ceased and she drew comfort from the great-hearted animal. She even slept. In the morning she woke to find her head beneath the comfortable weight of the dog's shaggy muzzle. She sat up and stroked its fur and it licked her face. Perhaps this is the first time that either of us has known the balm of closeness to another living creature, she thought. We are both tamed by it.

She heard a noise from the house and concealed herself behind the wall. The man emerged with a bowl of meagre scraps for the dog. 'Here's your dinner, Demon.' The poacher laughed. He rattled the bowl, making the dog lunge on its chain, and then he placed it just out of reach of the animal, which whimpered pitifully. When he tired of this mindless entertainment, he stumbled back indoors.

Emma crept from her hiding-place and brought the food to the hungry beast. The animal did not at once eat but hung back and watched Emma soulfully. 'Eat, my friend.' Emma patted its head to encourage it. 'Don't be afraid.'

The dog inclined its muzzle to the food, then raised its eyes as if to form a question. 'Oh, you dear!' she cried. 'You want me to eat first. But hungry as I am I have not as much need as you. I have money in my pocket. I have my liberty. This food is barely enough to keep you alive, but you shall have it.'

All the while she spoke she stroked the animal to soothe it. She thought the creature craved this affection even more than food for it was only when she moved away that it crouched down and devoured the meal in several gulps.

As she resumed her journey she felt more optimistic. The sun was shining, though weakly. 'I have money in my pocket. I have my liberty,' she repeated to herself, as she paid the fee to pass through a toll-gate.

A mile further she came in sight of an inn called the Three Sisters. She brushed herself off as best she could and ordered breakfast. After several cups of strong tea she set out once more. Another mile brought her to the railway, where she purchased a single ticket and sat by the fire to dry her clothes, and await the train.

CHAPTER SEVENTEEN

Christmas passed; its wrappings vanished into drawers and fires; its gifts into use or storage. The shops withdrew enticement and resumed supply. Hospitality and house-keeping were modified for everyday use. The Misses Wilcox reopened their doors and two little girls were returned for improvement (the third having passed a dreary festival in confinement). Mr Ellin came back from M—. For once his chameleon presence brought me no pleasure for I had the disagreeable task of informing him that I had mislaid the precious object intrusted to my care. I told the story, apportioning to myself the entirety of the blame. 'Given her distress and the delicate state of her nerves, I ought not to have tested her.'

He looked thoughtful. 'But she took your money.' A reflect-ive silence ensued – then: 'We must go to the police.'

'Oh, why?' I was surprised and dismayed by his response. 'Because of the money?'

'Of course not. She may be in any sort of peril. The time has come to stop playing amateur detective.'

Although I bowed to his judgement I had to wonder if I detected some minute shift in partiality.

We went to make our report. Yet what precisely to report? Emma had neither a whole name nor any address. Her appearance, unremarkable in itself, had been a manufactured thing. There was no fixed image of the young person, no painted locket or daguerreotype.

Besides, as the uniformed enforcer kindly informed us, her whereabouts were none of our business. The girl was not of our flesh. She was old enough to work and likely old enough to marry. Furthermore he could not imagine why respectable folk would want a little wretch already sought by the law.

'What do you mean?' My heart missed a beat.

'A charge of theft has been placed against a young girl of the same description.'

'By whom?'

He named accuser and accused. 'They called her Matilda Fitzgibbon but warned it was a deception. It's the same young ruffian, right enough.'

This cost Mr Ellin some of his customary sanguinary disposition. 'You say she is a criminal. Why, then, won't you find this dangerous malefactor?'

The constable shrugged. 'The nation teems with villainous urchins. They are as numerous and elusive as a plague of rats. But find them? Why, only death can find them. A haystack would as likely yield a whole embroidery kit as this great nation cough up one half-grown foundling.'

We called upon the injured parties. All three spoke together at a high pitch until we felt like herrings scavenged by seabirds.

'A star-shaped brooch, quite unusual, you know.'

'And valuable! Shall I tell you what it was worth?'

'No need to tell *her*. You may be sure *she* knew well enough.'

Mr Ellin implored the Misses Wilcox to forsake the harmonies and confine the narrative to a solo.

Miss Mabel recounted how on New Year's Eve they were to visit a Mr Glover, a merchant, who had four daughters. It was hoped to persuade from him the eldest two for enrolment in Fuchsia Lodge. The Wilcox sisters meant to make a good display of themselves, to dress their best and play the piano and garnish their conversation with phrases in French; in short, to demonstrate what an excellent finished product they would make of the young Misses Glover. Miss Lucy and Miss Adelaide donned their brightest winter gowns. Miss Mabel selected a more demure shade, a claret velvet worn to display to advantage the one piece of jewellery the three possessed, a star-shaped brooch with ruby centre and small pearls and diamonds in its rays. It was a very pretty piece that had belonged to their grandmother and had been left to the ladies to wear in turn.

The schoolmistresses had been upgrading their everyday outfits by adding bows and detaching sleeves when Miss Mabel made a discovery. She was at her dressing-table with a small black box in her hand. That box was the general resting place of the star-shaped brooch. It was now empty.

They searched high and low but they knew it was gone for it was never out of its casket. Worse, they knew who had taken it.

The day was a disaster. They arrived at Mr Glover's establishment in such distress that he considered them a miserable, neurotic trio and pledged to send his daughters to a school run by married ladies. The following day, the three sisters, still in tears, presented themselves to the constabulary and reported the theft.

'What do you think, Mr Ellin?' We reviewed the situation as the gentleman returned me to my dwelling.

Usually he contrived to make an entertainment of all events (and the evening had not been without dramatic possibility) yet he remained subdued. 'Mrs Chalfont, the girl has twice taken items to which she had no entitlement – first the brooch, then the money. The very clothes she wore may also have been the objects of a theft.'

He told me here of his own investigation and of the strong opinion of the clergyman, Mr Dolland.

'You are surely not influenced by the views of a close-minded stranger?'

Mr Ellin sighed. 'It is difficult to ignore facts. A charge has been laid against her. She is wanted by the police.'

'What of your own judgement? You met her. You liked her.'

'In matters of the female sex my judgement has not always been flawless.' This statement was delivered with a levity that belied his rueful expression.

'Are you so ready to forsake your earlier theory – that she was the innocent victim of an unscrupulous guardian?'

'By no means,' he assured me. 'My investigations proceed. In truth, I suppose I wanted her better than others believed her. She is beginning to seem far too human for a sprite.'

'I would rather her human than sprite,' I said.

'Will you at least review your possessions to see if anything is missing?' he countered. I did so, though in a half-hearted manner. Sadly, I was compelled to report a positive reply. 'This house has lost the only thing it contained that was of value – the little maid herself.'

CHAPTER EIGHTEEN

Emma had scarcely boarded the train when a fellow-passenger attempted to engage her in conversation. She had been occupied in counting her money. She was alarmed at the rate at which it had diminished. Rail travel had proved to be costly. Having set out with a guinea and a crown she now found herself with only a five-shilling coin and a handful of change.

'How much money is there clasped in that little hand?' the speaker said. 'Show me.'

'I will not, sir.' She gazed out of the window, which altered its scenery with indifferent dispatch.

'Very wise. Show no one your money.' He had a peculiar accent, which gave the words a loose, rubbery quality in his mouth and made him difficult to understand. 'You might prove a great attraction to persons of low morals.'

This assertion so startled her that she turned to her unwanted companion and found a small man with an exceedingly large suitcase. She thought, He will be quiet now he has seen me, for she had learnt that her habitual expression, caught between apprehension and suspicion, was a deterrent to social intercourse.

To her surprise the individual smiled and held out a hand half shrunk into his sleeve. 'Arthur Curran,' he presented. 'Put away your money now. Hide it while I'm watching.'

Emma could not help smiling. 'That, sir, is a ridiculous suggestion.'

'And that, miss,' said he, without rancour, 'is an impertinent assertion. Well, if you won't show me your possessions, would you care to see mine?'

'I am weary, sir,' she pleaded. 'I should like to be alone.'

'What do you suppose I have in this suitcase?'

It made her shudder to think that the suitcase was quite commodious enough to carry a corpse. 'I do not think I care to know.'

'Ah, you do!' With a flourish he unlocked the case and flung it open. 'Now, what do you think of that?'

Emma did not know what to think. Clearly she was in the company of a madman who imagined his trunk to contain all manner of wonderful things. 'It is empty,' she declared.

'Exactly so!' he agreed in triumph. 'And do you know why?'

'Indeed not.'

'For the reason that I sold every blessed thing. I am a packman. I buys and sells – ribbons, buttons, corsets, caps, dresses, dress fabrics, boots, umbrellas. Housemaids is mad for fancy umbrellas. I buys in London and sells in rural parts. Betimes, I buys in the country and sells in the city. But chiefly I sells in the country. Do you know, little lady, why I have sold out all I carried?'

She shook her head.

'Because of Christmas. Folks will buy anything at Christmas. They would buy a rat with a cap and bells on. Would you like to share me dinner?' He took from his pocket a bottle of beer and a packet of bread and cheese. 'How's that, now? Fit for a king! Do you know what I'm going to tell you? This is a great oul' nation, for all that me countrymen held it hostile. Here's me, arrived over here with nothing but the rags I stood up in. And where do you think I ended up?'

He looked so eager that she expected he might say he was a footman in Buckingham Palace. 'The workhouse!' he supplied in jubilation.

'The workhouse? But is that not to be dreaded above all?'

'There is folks that would rather die than go to the work-house, but as for me, I would rather go to the workhouse than die. You are given a bed and a morsel to eat. You can build up your strength and go on from there.'

'With nothing to start, how could you proceed?' Emma wondered. 'You must have had something.'

'A modest sum, yes.'

'And how, sir, did you acquire that modest sum?'

'Well, how do you think?' He shook his head in impatience. 'I stole it, of course.'

'You are a thief!' she exclaimed. 'You dared ask me to show you my money. You should not boast of your dishonour!'

'Were I not dishonoured I should be dead. If I were a corpse I should be modest indeed, and not boast of it.'

'Some might prefer death to dishonour,' Emma proposed.

'There is little honour in a starving man.' His face grew melancholy and he fell briefly silent. 'Base living extinguishes the spirit.' He began to sing a sad song. His voice, which had seemed uncomfortable with words, had a sweet mastery of tune. 'Did you like that, now?' he said. 'Would you like another?' The wizened head looked as if it might contain an endless store of songs so she shut her eyes to deter him.

Arthur Curran's narrative grew stranger and stranger. For a time she listened but then she slept. When she awoke the carriage was empty. Her first feeling was of regret, for time had passed swiftly in the company of the eccentric foreigner. This was followed by a disagreeable impulse of alarm and she had to search her pockets to make sure her money was still there.

As she stepped on to the platform the first thing to strike her was the smell. It was of oil and iron, a drab stench of unhygienic humanity, a surprising savoury aroma of cooking. She was still considering how to manage her breathing in such an atmosphere when she was assailed by the noise. The grind and whistle of the trains, the cries of porters met with further-off trumpetings of vendors and the high-pitched whine of beggars. The station itself surprised her with its grandeur. Within it everyone had business and was urgently about it. She was all but paralysed by indecision. She would have liked to summon a cab and ask the driver to take her to a lodging-house. How far would he travel? How much would it cost? If the driver wanted all of her money she would be in no position to argue. Her head swam, as it always did when challenged with deliberation. She looked around for some respectable person. Yet who in that bustling throng would notice such as she? To her surprise she saw that someone watched her – a kindly looking woman, of sober but refined dress.

And then: 'Little lady!' Arthur Curran called out. 'Have you no one to meet you? I'll take you in hand.' She felt relief on seeing that friendly, withered young face. Then she remembered his strange stories. He had told her he meant to make his fortune at an exhibition of all the world's wealth and industry, which was to be displayed in a glasshouse. When she asked who would be so foolish as to place treasures in a house of glass to which every thief would have access, he answered that it was the scheme of a foreign gentleman married to a rich little

173

woman who wore her diamonds on her head. He claimed that he had recently come from a country where millions died because there were no potatoes for them to eat. Undoubtedly his head had been afflicted by a shortage or surfeit of potatoes. She must trust no one, and especially not a thieving Irish vagrant. She moved away, pursued by the Irishman. 'Little lady! Should you find yourself short of a crust, go to Petticoat Lane. The Jews there are kindly and will give you the bread their children do not eat.'

'Thank you,' she said. 'I am not alone.'

'Ah, you are! Now, should you end up in the poorhouse, go in with the Irish. They are sometimes bad with the head lice but are less inclined to depravity than the English.'

Emma escaped and presented herself to the lady, who had kept her in her gaze and who now held out a gloved hand. 'Marjorie Hammond,' she introduced. 'I was watching you. I thought you looked solitary.'

Emma had resolved to act independently yet she was too fearful and exhausted to carry on and this kind woman had surely been sent by God to aid her. 'Thank you,' she murmured. 'I need lodgings.'

'Have no fear.' The lady's voice was gentle and low. 'I am from a Christian society. My work is to meet young girls who travel alone. Have you no luggage?'

'No, nothing.'

'Poor child. You are friendless and have no place to lay your head. Who knows that you are here?' Her clement voice was a balm.

'No one.'

Very gladly she allowed herself to be led away through an exit of Doric-pillared splendour. They came out into the New Road, which had been built to accommodate the procession of poor beasts for slaughter on their way from Uxbridge to

174

Smithfield Market. The street existed in a permanent mire from its terrified traffic. A sinister smell of death and decay emanated from the adjacent cats' meat and horseflesh market. Despite this odd air of corruption Emma could not suppress a gasp of wonder. Although it was night, the street existed in a strange sort of daylight. Despite a noisy rush of rail passengers clamouring for cabs, the gas lights made the street a place of softness and mystery, with pools of light fringed by blackness and silence.

To either side of the elegant station were new and respectable-looking hotels. She need not have worried, after all. Yet her companion hurried her by. 'They would charge you five shillings for bed and breakfast only.'

She was grateful for the warning. She might need four or five nights for her search.

They turned on to Gower Street, with its neat lodging signs in tidy terraced houses. The thought of a bed made her yawn sleepily. She was hungry too. Foolishly, perhaps, she had rejected Arthur Curran's offer of bread and cheese. In the morning she would make a good breakfast and begin her inquiries. If all went well, she might be back in Deerfield by the start of the new year. But Gower Street did not suit her saviour any better. Miss Hammond's only comment was upon an imposing entrance with a fine building within: 'It is the godless college.'

'Might we not take lodgings hereabout?' Emma implored. 'I am very weary.'

'Since the railway opened, unscrupulous innkeepers have set up close to the station to lure the innocent traveller. Their rates are infamous. Many are dens of thieves. We must walk awhile yet.'

Dwellings thinned out. After several turns they approached a broad commercial street, which was bathed in such a lurid light it seemed the whole of the thoroughfare had been set on fire. As they drew closer it could be seen that the flares came from the stalls of numerous street-sellers. Candles had been stuck into large turnips or bundles of firewood. Fire glowed through holes beneath baked-chestnut stoves or leapt from flares of thickly rolled brown paper. There were old-fashioned grease lamps, with smoky red flame, and white light from the new gas lamps. Vendors bawled their wares: 'Fried fish, hot eels, pickled whelks, sheeps' trotters, meat puddings, hot green peas, cough drops, tea, coffee, ginger-beer, hot wine, new milk from the cow.' At intervals the light showed up dismal alleys that ran off the street, teeming with poor people. The eerie glimmer seemed also to illuminate some dark alley of her mind. A voice spoke softly to her. 'We are in the city now. Soon we shall have rest and food.' She looked thankfully to her rescuer but Miss Hammond had not spoken. What ghost had addressed her? She scoured her memory and was rewarded with the usual agonizing rebuke from her brain. She must lie down. Shortly after they had passed the market she sighted a tavern called the Marquis of Granby. 'Most unsuitable for a young girl!' Miss Hammond pronounced, and Emma bore down upon a dejected sigh.

On they walked. How long the distance she did not know. In her depleted state it seemed very long. They came by a handsome church behind which hid a hideous slum, and shortly after that a square well populated by merrymakers.

'They are speaking in French,' Emma said, in amazement. Had they, on this long night, passed out of England altogether?

'We are in Soho,' Miss Hammond said. 'It is where the French people live.'

At last they arrived at a tall, dignified building, which bore a sign: 'House of St Silas, Refuge for Homeless Women'.

This must be the place, she thought. How wise of Miss Hammond, for I am both homeless and in need of refuge. Yet still they did not linger. In due course they departed the main thoroughfares and entered a mean street where the glass of the gas lamp had been broken and the flickering flame cast a fitful gleam upon scenes of poverty and wretchedness. What had become of the gardens after which this dismal alley was named? Terraces of tumbledown houses were so crammed with people that they poured from every doorway and window like an infestation of rats. Dirty washing hung on poles. The noise and the smell were indescribable. Shuffling figures in rags gaped as they passed. Weary as she was, Emma thought she would be glad to quit this neighbourhood. To her dismay Miss Hammond had stopped. She turned to the child with a reassuring smile. With a shock of recognition and dismay Emma thought, I am home.

CHAPTER NINETEEN

At Fox Clough I spring-cleaned my house a season early. I pruned my roses until they looked like shorn convicts. I set sufficient seedlings in my glasshouse to plant the Himalayas. When this was done I commenced on a design for a most complicated quilt. None could call me idle. I was busy as the day is long, albeit that January days are, by general agreement, abbreviated ones. Yet although I darted this way and that to evade him, my specific suitor lay in wait. No mortal he – my dark prince was called Despondency. By day I bustled, by night I worried and sometimes I wept. For although not idle I was not useful. Although not infirm, I was helpless.

Mr Ellin, meanwhile, was engaged upon a calmer course. He had written to legal friends in London to ask if they might advise him on a missing girl. They advised him to come at once to London, to spend some days, to eat some dinners. He next communicated with the members of the gentry listed by the clergyman, Mr Dolland, concentrating on its bachelor core, asking each of those if he might call upon them, which scheme being set in train, he looked forward to the season's sport and sociability.

I was left alone to ponder my ineffectuality. If Emma had depended upon me, I had let her down. It seemed to me now that I had failed all those I loved. I was the cause of Finch's exile. My only child owed her death to me, because I had stubbornly wanted to take the air instead of travelling in a carriage. Pride had prevented me being sufficiently grateful for a good husband. The same defect had assured me that I could aid Emma's recovery better than any qualified medical man. Why? Because I considered myself to possess a superior brain to those who would advise me. Far from being the brains of the house, I had proved myself, in every instance, a total booby.

The new year brought days of icy sparkle and made a dandy of modest Mr Ellin. As he set forth for his outing in society he was equipped with new riding habit, boots and stock. To each of the elegant addresses, he brought with him his usual air of mystery. In every house he received (and accepted) invitation to stay.

The duration that followed was so pleasant that he had to ask himself, as weeks went by, if he really wished his mission to conclude. What if he discovered an unpleasant truth about Emma? The puzzle that had sat so appealingly upon the poignant young person was now muddied by unsavoury elements that might not bear better acquaintance.

For Mr Ellin was the sort of gentleman who liked his females exemplary. This derived in part from the death of his mother when he was very young and his instinctive elevation of her departed soul to sainthood. He was lazy about his own soul. He said his prayers, he believed in a divine justice. He considered himself to be not too bad (though not too good) and viewed spiritual housekeeping as woman's work. If ever he encountered a woman who was perfectly good, he might work hard enough to make himself appeal to her, then let her take over the infinitely more strenuous labour of improving him.

Emma, of course, was but a child, yet in their first meeting she had pulled him up so short that he had almost felt himself bettered by it. Now he was compelled to view her in a different light. Now he wondered if there was not something cold and knowing in her manner. Clever she might be, yet perhaps too mature for her years. One had to wonder where she had acquired such knowledge of the world and if she had not been tainted by it. He felt confused and confounded by the girl. He chided himself for immaturity in attaching such standards to a juvenile yet overall blamed not himself but his trusting nature. Once before he had committed his confidence to a female and had found out that the angel in whom he had lodged the keeping of his better self was rotten to the core.

Such deliberations were deferred. He had visited three houses and his inquiries had yet yielded no significant outcome. His hosts gossiped wonderfully about their neighbours (Mr Dolland would have been surprised by the frolics of some of his most cherished flock) and loaned him their sisters or female cousins to decorative effect at dinner. Contemplating those among them who were unwed and not unattractive, he had to own that the view was enhanced by a shadowy backdrop of fine estate with a stretch of fishing water and a stable of horses, for these girls all shone with the outer light of a handsome fortune.

Now may be revealed the secondary impediment to Mr Ellin's attaining the married state. He had a love of easy living that ran a little beyond his ability to support it. He liked a gentleman's life.

To be fair, William Ellin was not a fortune-hunter. He would never pursue a well-off quarry. Without the routine requirements of mutual sympathy and sensibility, he would be quite content to retain his bachelor status. But given that Cupid might strike his wary heart, and that he would bring patience, charm and an outstanding forbearance of small-talk to the ensuing union, might not the recipient of his commitment furnish him with a little material comfort? No active campaign was ever engaged upon, yet he sometimes day-dreamed on the agreeable prospect of love and land in a combined package.

Yet there was a further obstacle upon the aisle. Mr Ellin had once known love. It was so long ago he scarcely counted it. You will have noticed, reader: the manly heart tends to cancel what it cannot conquer or accommodate. But that time comes in each man's life when memory overtakes ambition and Past assumes a brighter shade than Present.

On the day he had met Teresa Welles neither love nor marriage was on his mind. How could they when he was only ten years of age? Besides, his first sighting of her had shown none of the promise that was later to be fulfilled. To his childish eye, she was a disappointing visitor – a girl too old to play with, too abject to address. What had become of her? No, he would not think of it. He was pledged never to think of it.

He had one more house to visit. He rode out on a morning when the cosmos held her breath and captured his in a cloud. The sun was a pearl on a cloak of grey fleece. Nature, this day, was an enchanting artifice, a woman dressed to woo. The horse's hoofs hammered a drum-beat and knocked silver sparks from the frozen earth. It was good to be a man upon this scene, a thing of living blood and sense, to make a first print upon the silence.

He had reason to be excited about his final destination. None of the other house-holders was well acquainted with its owner but they claimed he was often absent and neglected his fine estate. They also said that he was guardian to a little girl.

The veiled sun slipped behind a cloud. The cumulus became a glassy cluster, swollen with light. The planet then emerged in a blaze of splendour. Colours slid around one another, their brilliance defiant of man's weak vision. Mr Ellin felt that Nature made sport with him. She blinded him, contesting him for mastery. He ceded her victory and took a woodland path. Playfully she pursued him. Ribbons of pink light dappled his eyelids as the sun peeped between the trees. A beam touched the dead ferns and they rose in a golden tide. It warmed the air and damped the icy floor to diamonds.

The thoughts that had lately pestered him were put to rest. In this surrounding, solitude was noble. Creation has the power to heal all, he thought. And it is democratic. Such treasures as now endowed him were showered upon poor as well as rich. Another sound then burst upon the silence. It was the agonized cry of a creature caught in a trap. It subdued his exuberant mood. Suffering creatures were all at a remove from joy or beauty.

He found the creature and released it – alas, too badly injured to run. With a sick feeling, he put it out of its misery. It made no struggle but watched him patiently, its timid face puzzled and submissive. The rabbit's meek acceptance of its fate brought unwanted to his mind another little creature. It was the boy, Willie, the fair, suffering youth whose image he had projected on to a frozen field as he gazed out of the window of the train to M——. This little ghost, so long cast in shadow, now crept out into the sunlight and begged of his flesh and blood his debt of recognition. In horror and in pity Mr Ellin looked upon the stoic scrap. This time he did not turn away from the memory of his childhood self.

Upon the death of his mother Willie Ellin had become an orphan and was removed from the place of his birth to a strange and unlovely establishment called Golpit in the care of his half-brother, Edward. His brother did not like him for he had hated and resented Willie's mother, who was his father's second wife. In the custody of Edward and his wife, beatings were the boy's daily lot. He could endure them for they must surely pass with manhood. Far more he dreaded his brother's threat to send him to a trade, which would deprive him of his one remaining privilege – his birthright as a gentleman. Once, when he could bear no more, he ran away to his old home. Within a day, Edward had found him. Only the presence of a gentleman with whom he had mercantile relations – a Mr Bosas – prevented him venting his fury. With a warning from this person for restraint, the man returned the boy to the site of his misery.

The lad had a small room he called his own. It was only a kind of garret, and contained but a crib and a stool. Yet, such as it was, he preferred it before the smart drawing-room, two floors below. If his poor tossed life numbered any peaceful associations, they were all connected with this cold, narrow nest under the slates. Hither he retired early, on the night after Bosas' departure – rather wondering to himself that nothing had yet befallen him, even dimly conceiving a hope that perhaps his brother had for once sincerely pardoned. It was half past eight of a summer evening, not yet dusk; consequently Willie had brought a book with him and, sitting near the little window, he could read. A year ago some love of reading had dawned on his mind. The taste had not been much cultivated, but it throve on scant diet full as much as was healthful. At present he liked *Robinson Crusoe* as well as any other book in the world. *Robinson Crusoe* was his present study.

His thoughts were all in the desolate island when he heard a step mounting the ladder staircase to his room. It pressed almost the last round ere any more disturbing idea struck him than that it must be wearing late, as the maids – who also lodged in the attics – were coming to bed. Suddenly he felt a weight in the tread that forbade the supposition of a female foot. The wooden steps shook, his door shook too; it opened, and a shape six feet high, broad and rather corpulent, entered.

Willie had never, till now, seen his brother enter his chamber alone by night. In all his trials he had never been visited thus in darkness, and in secret. I should not, perhaps, say in darkness, for the hour was shared between two gleams – twilight and moonlight. It was a very pleasant night, quite calm and warm, and only a few faint clouds, gilded and lightly electric, curled mellow round the moon. The door was shut, the thin child sat on his stool, the giant man stood over him.

'I have you safe at last, and I'll very nearly finish you now,' were the first words spoken in rough adult tones. None must expect qualified language or measured action from Mr Edward Ellin. He stood there strong, brutal, and ungovernable, and as an ungoverned brute he meant to behave.

The boy pleaded only once.

'Wait till tomorrow,' said he. 'Don't flog me here, and in the night-time. Do it tomorrow in the counting house.'

But his half-brother answered by turning up the cuff of his coat, showing a thick wrist not soon to be wearied. He had brought with him the gig whip. He lifted and flourished it on high. This was the rejoinder.

'Stop,' said the expectant victim earnestly – so very earnestly that the executioner did stop, demanding, however, 'What am I to stop for? It's no use whining – sooner or later you shall have your deserts. You ran away and you shall pay for it.'

'But mind how you pay, Edward. A grown-up man like you should be reasonable. That whip is heavy, and I am only moderately strong. If you strike me in anger you may cut deeper than you think.'

'What then? Who cares?'

'If I were to be hurt more than you think of? If you had to be taken before a magistrate and pay a fine or be transported?' suggested Willie.

The idea was an unlucky one. The whole bearing of the boy was antipathetic because incomprehensible to the gross nature under influence. Edward Ellin growled fury in his throat. 'Insolent beggar!' said he; 'so you threaten me with fines and magistrates? Take that! and that! – &c.'

He had fallen to work. It seemed he liked his business, for he continued at his exercise what seemed a long, a very long time. The worst of it was, Willie would not scream, he would not cry. A few loud shrieks, a combative struggle, a lusty roar, might probably have done wonders in abridging Mr Ellin's pleasure; but nothing in the present case interrupted or checked him, and he indulged freely. At last there came a gasp – the child sunk quite down – the man stopped. Through the silence breathed some utterance of pain – a moan or two – the slightest sound to which suffering Nature could be restricted; but in its repression only too significant. It induced Mr Ellin to say, 'I hope you have had enough now.'

He was not answered.

'Let me see you play truant again, or wheedle Bosas, and I'll double the dose.'

No reply – and no sob – perhaps no tear.

'Will you speak?' The flogger seemed half frightened, for Willie's exhausted attitude proved that he had indeed received enough; possibly he might have swooned, which would be troublesome.

But this was not the case. He spoke as soon as the severe pain of the last cut permitted him. 'I cannot bear any more tonight,' said he.

Ellin believed him – told him to go to bed now or to — another place, whistled, and walked off.

By and by, after Willie was left alone, he gathered himself up. It would have been sad to watch him undress and creep painfully to his crib, and sadder to read his thoughts. Scarce an interjection and not a word passed his lips; for some time, scarce a tear wet his eyelashes. He had lain sleepless and suffering for over an hour ere there came any gush that could relieve; but at last the water sprang, the sobs thickened, his little handkerchief was drawn from under his pillow. He wept into it freely – then he murmured something about his life being very, very hard and difficult to bear. At last, after a long pause, he slowly got on his knees – he seemed to be praying, though there were neither lifted eyes nor clasped hands nor audible words to denote supplication, nothing indeed but the attitude and a concentrated, abstracted expression of countenance, denoting a mind withdrawn into an unseen sphere, preoccupied with viewless intercourse. As he returned to earth, his eyes, hitherto closed, slowly opened. He lay down, probably he believed his petition heard; composure breathed rest upon him; he slumbered.

Willie cannot rank as a saint: his patience was constitutional, as his religion was instinctive. Temperance in his expression of suffering was with him an idiosyncrasy. Prayer was a need of his almost hopeless circumstances. Oppressed by man, Nature whispered to him, 'Appeal to God,' and he obeyed. Some think prayers are rarely answered; and yet there have been penetrating prayers that have seemed to pass unchallenged all gates and hosts and pierced at once the veil.

Willie was left kneeling at his cribside, his face and hands pressed against the mattress. He had been severely flogged, and for a time felt sick, but he was not maimed or dangerously hurt – not corporeally maimed. How his heart fared is another question.

It might seem that the watchful care of God had temporarily been withdrawn from this orphan, as he shrank powerless to resist under a tyrannic hand — as he afterwards moaned alone, pale, faint, miserably though not passionately weeping, compelling himself, according to the bent of his idiosyncrasy, to a sort of heroic temperance of expression, even in extremity of grief. In man's judgement it might be deemed that this child was forgotten even where the fledgling dropped from the nest is remembered. Willie himself feared as much. There was great darkness over his eyes, and a terrible ice chilled his hopes — his very hearing was suspended. He did not now catch an ascending step on the ladder, nor notice the door once more opening. It required the near glare of candle-light to snatch him even transiently from himself and his anguish.

The hand that brought the candle placed it on the narrow window-sill. Someone then approached Willie, sat down beside him on the edge of the crib; an arm passed round him, another drew him towards a warm shoulder, lips kissed his forehead, and eyes wept on his neck.

'Poor boy! Poor wronged child!'

The voice uttering these words belonged to an age not many years beyond Willie's own: the speaker seemed a girl of seventeen, blooming, and with features that, if they borrowed at this moment interest of pity, gave back in return beauty distinct, undoubted, undenied. Fine indeed were the eyes that dropped tears on Willie and all lovely the arms, the hands, the lips by which he was protected and soothed.

'I heard what has happened — heard it from my room below. I fear you are terribly hurt?' said she.

'I don't care for the pain — my mind suffers the most,' the boy declared, with a groan. This sudden transfer from terror to tenderness relaxed for one instant the power of self-control.

'Hush, my love, my child! Hush, Willie, forget him: he shall never hurt you more,' said the young comforter, rocking the sufferer in her arms and cradling him on her breast.

187

Softened even while relieved, Willie wept fast and free and very soon easier. By gentle hands he was helped to bed, he was lovingly watched till he slept, he was kissed in his slumbers; and then the guardian withdrew, only to think of him through the night, to listen against molestation, and to be prepared at one menacing symptom to come out resolved to defend.

CHAPTER TWENTY

Mr Ellin laid down the little dead animal. He remounted the chestnut mare and rode hard out of the forest. Upon a rise, his destination came into view. He slowed his mount on the ascent. What had been park was now a wilderness of overgrown grass and neglected trees. As he reached the end of a long line of limes that bordered the drive, he came upon the estate's secret. It whispered and went on its way. The house had a despondent look – not uncared-for yet unappreciated. He thought it must be empty. Something else then caught his eye. It was a scrap of blue, larger than a bird yet smaller than a man. Despite his equivocation regarding his errand, his breath almost stopped when he saw that it was a small girl, exquisitely dressed, who made a listless promenade before the mansion. He spurred his horse. The child looked up and ran away.

A housekeeper answered his knock. He asked to see the master of the house. She told him tersely that there was only herself and the girl. He greatly desired admission, yet there was a closed look to both the house and the servant that told him neither was interested in visitors.

'I am related to the girl,' he said quickly. 'I have come a long way. She would be disappointed not to see her uncle.'

'Well, poor little thing. I'm supposed to let no one in, but I feel sorry for her.'

As he followed the woman into the house, his eye was drawn to lovely rooms closed up, their furnishings draped in dust sheets. 'Has the house been empty long?' he asked.

Again he received her shuttered look, a warning not to pry. 'The house is not empty. I told you. There's me and the girl.'

'Why is she not at school?' He tried to bring sufficient command to his voice to elicit a response.

'She was at school.' The woman brought him to a small parlour, which was not closed yet did not look quite open.

'What happened?' he asked.

'Let her answer your questions if she will.'

He longed to say, 'What is her name?' yet he must not betray himself. An uncle would know the name of his niece. In any case the servant had now departed to fetch his imaginary relative.

He was inspecting the room for traces of its occupancy when he heard a cry of 'Uncle! Uncle!' This girlish treble had the less ladylike accompaniment of footwear thudding on the stair.

The door opened. A female face appeared round it, took in the company, then decidedly fell. 'You are not who I expected,' said she.

'To tell the truth, you are not who I expected either,' he responded, for this was a very coquettish little person with huge blue eyes and fat gold curls, which she brandished to dizzying effect. 'Shall we call it quits and I'll take my leave?'

'No,' she said petulantly. 'Stay and talk to me.'

'Very well, then. Tell me where your father is.'

'He is dead. He died in India. He was eaten by a Bengal tiger.'

'Oh, and when did this disaster occur?'

'Eight years ago. I was but a little thing.'

Although he doubted the specific nature of her father's death, he could at least eliminate him from his inquiries. 'I have made a mistake,' he said. 'I am at the wrong address. I ought to go.'

She shut the door behind her and blocked it with her diminutive frame. 'If you leave I shall inform Mrs Haddon that you lied to her and are a robber come to steal the silver. Likely she will call the police.'

Likely she will, thought he. 'Very well,' he yielded. 'We shall have a visit. What is your name?'

'I am Vanessa. Who are you, sir?'

'I am William, and as I am now your guest I am obedient to your command. What shall we do?'

She looked nonplussed for a moment and then said, very decisively, 'We shall take tea. I will fetch it.'

'Won't Mrs Haddon make us tea?' he queried.

'She might, but it would make her peevish,' Vanessa said.

She left the room and reappeared very quickly, bearing a tray with some pretty cups but no teapot. From a cabinet she fetched a decanter of brandy and liberally filled a cup, which she handed to him. 'Mama says that gentlemen never really like tea. They only take it to be polite.'

'I hope you do not intend to partake of this brew.'

'Of course not, but I do not like tea either.'

'Why are you not at school, Vanessa?' he said. 'Where is your mama?'

'Mama is in Switzerland for the good of her health. I thought school a dreadful place. I had to sleep in a room with other girls. There is a governess coming to teach me. I expect she will be a beast.' As she spoke she moved around the room and occasionally executed little ballet steps, rather stiffly.

When she completed a turn he almost expected to see a key in her back. 'Now, you answer my question,' she demanded. 'Why, upon seeing me, did you deem it a mistake? Most people are pleased to make my acquaintance.'

'I am certain of it.' In the odd situation in which he found himself, Mr Ellin rather felt the need of his unusual refreshment. 'I was not referring to you. I came to see the gentleman of the house. I did not know he was dead.'

'Nor is he,' Vanessa said.

'What? Not eaten by a Bengal tiger?'

'Oh, yes, my father was, but he did not own this house. The house belongs to my uncle – my real uncle.'

'And where, pray, is he?' said Mr Ellin.

'He is away. He keeps a house in London for himself and he travels often.'

'May I contact him?'

'No. He is a spy on a secret mission for the government. No one may contact him.'

'So you are all alone in this big house. Are you not lonely?'

'Not I!' She shook her curls. 'I have all manner of things to do. I have a great many dresses to try on. Do you like this one? I chose it to match the ceiling, which in my view is the only object in the room *quite* as radiant as it ought to be. Don't you think I am very pretty?' (Another turn was executed.) 'Some say I am almost as beautiful as Mama. Do you not think I am tall for my age? I am only ten but my uncle says I could pass for twelve or thirteen.'

'Do you like your uncle?' Mr Ellin asked. 'Is he kind to you?'

She sighed. 'He is kind enough, but he is not very merry. Right now I do not think I like him well at all.'

'Why not?'

'He bought me a present but then he took it away.'

'I expect you were naughty.'

'I am never naughty. I eat custard and cabbage and everything that is disgusting, for Mama has taught me that ladies must not draw attention to their appetites, either by being too greedy or too particular.'

'Your mama has trained you well,' Mr Ellin complimented. Yet although she was the very model of what is deemed ideal in her gender – a winsome little blue-eyed beauty, so schooled in artifice that it had overtaken all reality – it was easy to imagine why the absent uncle might run short of patience.

'I must take my leave,' he said. 'I am engaged for dinner.'

'It was a most beautiful present,' she wheedled. 'Don't you long to hear about it?'

'Not yet, for my unsatisfied curiosity will give me an excuse to call again.'

Her huge eyes showed a hint of uncertainty, of pride – not quite wounded – but impinged.

'Thank you for the tea.' He bowed.

'It has been a pleasure, sir.' She dropped a beguiling curtsy. 'Next time, perhaps there will be cake.'

As he departed he felt a pang for the poor decorative and discarded little doll but then he shook himself very thoroughly. Had he not encountered her kind in the adult form? Was he not best placed to know that, sooner or later, the pretty kitten becomes a full-grown cat and avenges her wasted life on any vulnerable male? Had he himself not been eaten by a Bengal tiger?

On his way out he looked back at the house. Murders were committed to protect such sites, he reflected, yet others had not a roof to put above their heads and those privileged to own fine estates often could not be troubled to occupy them. It was a queer sort of justice that a monument to man's greatness should become at last a cage for one lonely little girl.

This little girl was watching at the window. She was thinking sadly that he had not noticed her. She was regretting her wasted narrative. Mama had taught her always to make her conversation interesting, especially where gentlemen were concerned, and she had done her utmost to add interest at all points. She had also been instructed to save some arresting snippets to the last so that the same audience would be left with a memory of a female who was fascinating as well as captivating. But how did one get a gentleman to stay long enough to listen? She felt certain he would have liked the story of her present. How many girls of her age are sent to order a whole wardrobe of clothes for themselves? How many are brought to visit their mama's grown-up seamstress to pick out the finest silks and laces and have them made up in any style they choose, only then to be told they may not keep them after all?

CHAPTER TWENTY-ONE

A very different establishment marked the first night in London of the counterfeit Matilda Fitzgibbon.

The house where that Christian lady, Miss Marjorie Hammond, brought her waif was a tall and narrow wreck. It sagged on its joists. It dribbled from its drainpipes. It seemed almost derelict, but for a crudely written sign in one window: 'Lodgings for travellers – 3d a night. Boiling water always ready.' Some of the windows contained no glass, the gaps being covered over with planks of wood and, in one instance, paper. Although Emma had asserted that she would prefer modest surroundings, modesty here was multiplied to the point of meanness. Miss Hammond knocked on the door and in due course it was opened by a thickset and dirty-looking man.

'Good evening, John.' Miss Hammond spoke with her usual gentleness. 'I have a little girl for you. I want you to take good care of her.'

'Are you going to leave me here?' Emma addressed her guardian angel fearfully.

'Of course, my dear,' Miss Hammond said. 'I have my work. I shall return in the morning.'

Emma peered inside the house, which surged with life, as if all the dregs of humanity had gathered for a mêlée. 'Who are these people?' she whispered in fright.

'They are poor friendless souls such as yourself,' Miss Hammond said. 'Do not despise them.'

The lady went away, and the girl was brought into the house where, by dim candle-light, she could perceive that all the chambers, apart from one set aside as a kitchen, were in use as dormitories. Flock beds, supplied with an ill-assortment of coverings, filled every inch of space. Most were already occupied. Some contained three or four people huddled together.

'Is there a quarter for children?' Emma wondered.

'Yes, miss,' said the unsavoury-looking host. 'In with the women. As you are one of Miss Hammond's girls, you shall have a bed all to yourself. But you'll take a little supper first.'

He brought her into the filthy kitchen where grease and flies made company for one another. A few individuals were cooking their supper, but some had settled to sleeping on the floor.

'Is there not a bed for these people?' she asked.

'If they want it, but they prefer the floor for that way they save a penny,' she was told.

The man brought her bread and tea, and one of the creatures at the fire offered to cook her a herring for a penny. She was hungry, but the look of the saleswoman made her disinclined to accept. The tea was exceedingly strong and sweet and the vessel in which it was served was cracked and stained but she forced herself to drink some of the hot beverage and eat a little of the bread. I cannot sleep here, she decided. I shall just have my bread and tea and rest at the table. At least I have shelter. To her surprise she was instantly overcome with drowsiness. To keep awake she decided to finish the tea but her fingers refused to grasp the cup and the nightmarish scene vanished from her vision.

She was woken towards dawn by the feeling of hands lightly touching her body. She sat up with a start, which action made her head ache and swim. To her dismay, she found herself in bed in one of the overcrowded dormitories. It was too dark to see distinctly but various coughs and snores and groans assured her of her company. Of her imagined contact there was no sign. All around, the overabundance of humanity slept soundly and the air was choked with the smell of unwashed bodies. Emma became aware of a sensation of extreme irritation. She felt as if a small army marched over her body and attacked her with miniature weapons. She tried to adjust the bundle that passed for a pillow for better comfort, then emitted a cry of revulsion as she saw that insects were creeping across it. A volley of curses from the sleeping bundles close by her urged her back to sleep. She felt so faint that she almost lay down again. But no! She was in a verminous bed and was suddenly assailed by the sinister conviction that she had been given an opiate in her tea.

She got out of bed as quietly as possible and made dazed progress to the kitchen. It was in darkness and she did not like to light a candle for fear of disturbing the sleeping bodies on the floor. She sat at the table, trembling. She would keep a vigil there till morn. She would focus on the following day, a new day in which she would take herself to a bath-house, find a decent lodging, sleep in a clean bed and then commence her researches. For reassurance she put a hand in her pocket to make contact with her wealth. Her fingers there met the cool lining of her pocket and nothing more. A frantic search of her other pockets brought her the realization that she had not a penny nor a farthing in the world.

At about nine o'clock Miss Hammond returned. She found the object of her mercy slumped across the kitchen table fast asleep. 'Wake, Emma.' She shook her gently.

When Emma saw who was there she flung her arms around her and sobbed uncontrollably. 'Oh, Miss Hammond. I have been robbed of all I possess. I was drugged last night.'

'Who can have done this to you?' Miss Hammond demanded.

When Emma detached herself she saw that this person had entered the room. 'It was him!' She pointed out John, the innkeeper. 'He gave me supper. He put something in my tea that rendered me insensible.'

The kitchen was now deserted but for her rescuer and the innkeeper, all other residents having left at eight o'clock in accordance with the regulations of the house. A rough sort of tidiness had been imposed upon the room, a fire was lit and it looked homely if shabby. It did not seem half so terrible as the night before.

'Well, John?' Miss Hammond demanded.

'It's sometimes hard for young ladies to sleep here,' he said. 'I put a sleeping draught in her tea from compassion. Then I put her to bed. I swear I never touched her money. I meant well. I am sorry if I did wrong.'

'Did he do wrong, Emma?' Miss Hammond inquired.

'My money was stolen. I am now destitute,' Emma said.

Miss Hammond took her hand. 'Do not be downcast. I have very good news. I have found work for you. You will have fresh clothing, good food – a warm place to stay.'

Emma kissed that other party's hand. 'You have been sent by heaven. Hot water and soap is my most immediate requirement.'

'Where we are bound, my child, the baths are both plentiful and perfumed.' Miss Hammond smiled.

'What is the nature of the work?' Emma asked, in surprise.

'You will be among young women such as yourself. The work is light. You will dress in fine clothes. All that is required is that you be pleasant and obedient.'

'If I am to be useful I ought be clad in serviceable apparel.' Emma spoke with an uneasy memory of her ornate school dresses. 'I would prefer it.'

'Do not frown, dear,' Miss Hammond said. 'You are not pretty, yet your intensity has an appeal except when it is disapproving.'

Emma fixed that intensity upon her saviour. The unease that had been gathering in her had now grown to alarm. Miss Hammond exchanged a glance with the innkeeper. 'I know what you are about,' Emma breathed. 'You are both in this together.'

'There's gratitude!' The innkeeper turned away to conceal an insolent smile.

Miss Hammond held out her arms to Emma. 'Poor child, you are worn out and confused. Come and see your new abode. You will feel very different when you have had a warm bath and a change of clothes.'

Greatly did Emma long to respond to those arms yet she had mislaid all trust now. 'I will not come.' She wept.

'Be sensible, child,' Miss Hammond said. 'You cannot remain here without the price of your lodgings. This city is inhospitable to those without resources.'

Something in her tone had changed and it convinced Emma of what had hitherto only been suspicion. 'You placed me where you knew I would be robbed and left destitute,' she said. 'You have done this to other young girls. You shall not do it to me. I shall find some respectable situation.'

Miss Hammond smoothed her hair under her hat and pulled on her gloves. 'Although you are upset you ought not to say things you will later regret. I shall leave you alone awhile. Think very carefully about your situation – and think of this! Every person in this city profits by the disadvantage of some other. You will not twice encounter benevolence such as mine.'

As she exited in her powder-blue skirt and cloak, Emma felt herself a pathetic and ridiculous figure, attempting to stand on her dignity while her skin still itched under her clothing and her face was haggard and tear-stained. All her courage was gone. She felt cold and cowardly. Perhaps she had misjudged Miss Hammond. Was she not wicked to assume the very worst of one who by her manner seemed to signify all that was best? Tears fell down her weary face. I can't help it, she thought. I know things that other young girls do not know.

CHAPTER TWENTY-TWO

It had been her design first to find her bearings and then go in search of her mother. Yet no sooner had she left the lodging-house than she found herself at a seething junction where seven different roads converged and each of these a heaving stew of humanity. On one street an astonishing array of odd-ments of old and soiled clothing was on offer. In truth, the display was more museum than market, for some of the gar-ments were of such antiquity as to represent a bygone era, with old top hats forced into company with servants' under-garments and fur capes flat with grease. Another alley purveyed battered boots and shoes, the majority of these being ranked around cellar holes in the pavement from which pro-truded lively and tousled human heads. A third route sold nothing but food, raw and cooked and in varying condition. Vendors shouted out their wares and neighbours roared at one another across the narrow streets. The noise and the stench were such that her first instinct was to turn and run back whence she had come. Yet she had travelled such a long way that the elegant railway station seemed but a mirage.

And she had no money. Why had she not had the foresight to purchase an outward-return ticket?

She tried to recall the advice Arthur Curran had given her. In her weakened and confused condition she could think of nothing save the variety of food being sold from stalls and tents and carts at a street market to her right. Her nostrils were assailed by the varying odours of boiled meat puddings, meat pies, baked potatoes, tea and coffee. From the ranks of beggars that wistfully and miserably surveyed the scene she ascertained that these items cost money and served no function in the lives of the impecunious except to torment them with hunger pangs. She remembered Arthur Curran's terrible story about the starving people of Ireland. Was this how she would meet her end? She wished she had taken his advice about concealing her resources. If she had hidden some coins in boot or bodice she would have woken fully before anyone could have taken them from her. She sighed woefully. She ought not to have been so judgemental of the eccentric Irishman. After all, who was she to judge him? She, too, was a common thief. And he had been kind enough to offer her bread and cheese.

The memory of this humble meal fuelled her appetite. She stumbled on to where she saw people gathered around a baked potato stall. A breath of comfort emanated from this homely nourishment and she stood warming herself until the sweet earthy scent brought her close to fainting. 'Please, sir!' She clung to the stall for support.

The stall-holder held out one of his productions, which looked hot and wholesome. 'That will be a halfpenny,' he said. 'Three farthings if you want butter and salt.'

'I have no money,' she said, 'but I am very hungry.'

The vendor indignantly withdrew his ware. 'Them as eats 'em pays for 'em.'

'How am I to pay?'

'By honest labour,' he indifferently replied. 'Find yourself work.'

She wanted to say, 'I am but a child.' Yet all around she saw children far younger than herself, their infant features bent to the single task of earning a penny or two to stay alive for one more day. One of these presently forsook her custody of a cage of bedraggled birds, darted out swift as a cat, and snatched from the cobbles a damaged apple. As quick as seen, she was gone. Now Emma watched as other scraps of nourishment spilled over into the dirt. When no one noticed she dived upon some blemished fruit and began to gnaw on it hungrily. In an instant a frightful creature seized her, a woman with muscles big as a man's and a face blackened with bruises and dirt. With a cry of dismay Emma squirmed from her grasp and fled. She took the road to the left, it being the only one that was not solidly crammed with murderous merchants, their customers and their wares.

After several turns she found herself on a long avenue of two connected streets with high titles, yet Crown Street and Castle Street had nothing of grandeur except their names, being dismal and featureless and backed by wretched rents. The novelty or pathos of the streets ceased to affect her. A numb exhaustion overtook her and she seemed to be in a waking dream. She felt some echo or shadow follow her, as though this experience was eclipsed by an earlier one. The odd thought ran through her mind, *It is as before*. A bolt of pain seemed to sunder her head. The scene before her began to swim. 'Please help me,' she whispered urgently to a passer-by. The pedestrian took no more notice than as if she was invisible air. People hurried by on all sides. There must be one among them who would show concern. 'Help me,' she sobbed.

No one did, but by and by a girl of about fourteen, wearing a patched shawl over a conglomeration of cast-offs, walked up to her and struck her in the face.

'Why did you do that?' Emma touched her cheek in astonishment.

'Leave the streets to them as needs 'em.'

Emma burst into tears. 'I have eaten nothing today and scarcely anything yesterday.'

'If you want food, sell that fine cloak and bonnet and buy it.'

'I have no other clothes,' Emma said. 'What should I wear? Even now I am cold.'

'You would dress in rags as all beggars do,' the girl declared indignantly, as though Emma, by improper attire, had brought disgrace on a noble calling.

The lure of soap made her follow a sign for the Orange Street baths but the price of cleanliness proved to be a penny and she had not one such in the world. Presently she came to a great square with two fountains. A swarm of mendicants was scattered about Trafalgar Square like a dusty sack of potatoes. She picked a path through them to refresh herself at the fountain but someone warned her that the water was tainted. Night came. It marked a margin on the endless day and brought the instinctive supposition that she might now rest. Yet the air grew even colder and the dark brought fresh terrors. She was perched on the steps by the square when a savage creature, reeking of drink, swooped upon her, caught her by the hair and hissed in her ear, 'Give me what money you have or I will cut your throat.'

'I have nothing,' she gasped.

His wild eye gazed into hers and saw the abjection there. Still holding her hair he thrust her to the ground. 'I will not waste my blade. You're a puny thing. The d——l will take you anyway.'

She crept into a house of worship with a tall steeple balanced atop a portico but as she rested in a pew the warden told her he must lock up for the night. Without hope or aim she wandered on. To her relief she came upon a very respectable thorough-fare. Surely decent people will pity me, she thought. I shall knock at a door and ask for help. This enterprise left her at the mercy of an ill-tempered servant, who shoved her back with a broom.

The lamps now illuminated a scene of imposing grandeur yet paupers still loitered at their base and Emma no longer had any expectation of kindness. She approached a shabby young woman with a baby at her breast.

'Where do poor people such as you go at night?' she asked.

'To the river, miss,' the girl whispered.

Miserably she went on until she came to a great bridge. Ships bleached their linen by moonlight and ragged people huddled on steps leading down to the water. She sat as close to them as she dared and folded her arms against the cold. The full realization of her plight now assailed her. In the space of a day she had cut herself off entirely from society. Without money, she could not return whence she had come. She could not wash or feed herself. She had not the price of paper and stamp to contact those who might aid her. Out in the open in the bitter cold, she would most likely die, as her attacker had predicted. Piece by piece, like a mist in the sun, she was disappearing – first her past, then her sponsor, her clothes, her money and now, soon, her very existence. Who she was, who she had been, what she had done would no longer matter. She had heard that to die of cold was not so bad. Several times this pleasant death seemed to hover near but was fended off by troublesome thoughts. One of these was that death would not erase her sin: she must still face God's judgement. 'For what I have done,' she prayed, 'God forgive me. To those who have been kind to me, bring comfort.' After this the cold seemed less to penetrate her full sensibility and she noticed not when the water dripping from the bridge froze and frost formed upon her bonnet.

She was woken by a rough voice in her ear. 'I'm your mother!'

Alarm surfaced first, followed by reluctant consciousness. 'Mother!' She forced herself to face the ill-smelling creature who had claimed a portion of her space. Relief and disappointment mingled when she inspected the coarse countenance. 'I don't know you,' she said. 'You're not my mother.'

'No, but say I am,' the woman whispered. 'See over there — those men? They have been watching you. I know them for ruffians.'

'What would they do to me?'

The woman shrugged. 'Buying and selling. Buying and selling. That's all there is in the city. A lump of coal or a lump of flesh — all merchandise. Do you take a drink?'

'I should like some water,' Emma said.

The woman produced from her rags a stone flask. 'Try this. Well, you ought. It will keep you warm. It will keep you from death.'

Emma forced herself to take a mouthful. That frightful refreshment, which threatened to prise the flesh from her mouth, did, a little, ease the cold. This was the very worst part of the night. The chill cut her like blades. Her face and her teeth ached with it and all her limbs felt heavy, yet her brain seemed to bob lightly at a distance from her head.

'Why are you kind to me?' she asked the old woman.

'I thought we might go into business together. You are a naturally miserable-looking child. It is an asset that could be put to good account.'

'Tell me how?'

'We might design a tragedy to accompany your looks — a tale to render folks so uneasy as to empty their pockets.'

Emma shivered yet felt too lethargic to make any effort to warm herself. 'It sounds a crooked design.'

The crone regarded her balefully. 'There is no straight road for a woman. For all that folks talk of honour and virtue, it's only theatricals for the female of the sex. Be she bride or beggar, she must bite her lip and hide her feelings and put on a very grand show for such as will offer her charity.'

Emma wanted to argue, although her teeth chattered so that she could scarcely speak. She had seen for herself how young girls of good family were schooled to duplicity. Yet if women accepted it so, then were they not party to the conspiracy? There must be some who would strike out, whatever the cost.

'You've gone very queer and silent,' the old lady complained. 'Not dead, are you?'

'No.' Emma watched as a great barge folded its sails to pass under the bridge. She was wondering how long honour could contest cold and privation. She had known but a day of want and already her individuality was shrinking to insignifance in the face of so much anonymous misery – human souls crushed to the bottom of society in a stinking sediment. No one loved or pitied them. None seemed to care how they lived or died. Who would write their history?

'Were you married?' she asked the old woman. 'Had you children?'

'I was married to a man, but he were more use with his fists than his hands. I had a little boy – dearest little fellow in all the world. He died.'

They sat in a melancholy silence until Emma at last perceived a little natural light in the sky. Morning was coming. She felt astonished and relieved to have survived the night.

'Would we try some tricks?' the beggar woman said at last.

'I came to the city for a purpose.' Emma declined. 'I must try to see it through.'

'I'll be on my way so. But you must not stay here, miss. You must find some hiding-place where you will be safe.'

'But where?'

'Oh, everywhere. I'll show you if you like.'

The old woman creakily arose. Emma endeavoured to follow her but found she could not move. The cold of the night had robbed both arms and legs of all capacity to move. She struggled to bring some life to her limbs but almost fell down the steps into the river. Her ragged companion dragged her back to the bridge but instantly she collapsed again. Upon seeing this the old woman looked around, then clapped hands to face and let out a frightful shriek. 'My little girl! She is crippled – my only one! Her that I begged and stole for to keep her decent so that by and by she could keep me.'

At this point, a gentleman, attempting to look in any other direction, crossed her path. He moved a little unsteadily and his face was flushed from a night's celebration. The old dame seized his cape and clung to it. 'For pity, sir, please help or we are done for!'

The man irritably tried to cast her off. When she clung on tighter he struck at her lightly with his cane. With a loud moan she fell to the ground. Hating her, hating himself, he flung down some change and hastened away to summon a cab. When he was gone the old cadger calmly gathered the coins from the pavement, picked herself up and went to assist Emma. 'Sleeping out will do that,' she sympathized. 'I've sometimes had to crawl on hands and knees after a night in the cold.' She helped Emma back to her feet. 'Take your time and try to move your limbs gradual.'

In due course her blood began to circulate. Yet when she did walk, her limbs pained her as if she, and not her companion, was the ancient one. Pins and needles then shot through her arms and legs and this, with her light-headedness, made her feel altogether odd and insubstantial. Sorry as she was for herself, she felt more pity for her aged companion. 'It must be hard to have to live out of doors at your age,' she ventured.

The old woman shrugged. 'You gets used to it. You gets so you'd feel smothered indoors.'

'Yes, but to end up old and all alone,' Emma pitied.

'I's always been a loner,' the old woman said. 'Never could stand folks for long – neither men, women, dogs nor children. Especially children.'

'But you said you had a little boy.'

The old thing cackled. 'And so it seemed, as I said it. I gets up to so many dodges I sometimes confounds myself.'

They came to a tunnel running underneath a street, its cobbles so slimy they looked like a close-packed colony of frogs. The old lady declared that she had reached her address. Before they parted she handed Emma a coin.

At first Emma demurred, for she did not wish to take money from a poor person.

'It is your earnings. You shall have it.'

Gratefully Emma accepted. This time, she would make something of the day. She went directly to a coffee stall. She purchased hot coffee and drank it down quickly. There was change of her coin and she asked for a ham sandwich. As she bit into it a bitter taste arose in her throat and she could not swallow. To her disappointment, she felt too ill to eat.

Beads of perspiration had broken out on her face. Now she burned with heat so that she wanted to tear off her cape and bonnet. A moment later she began to shiver violently. If I could sit awhile, she thought. There must be somewhere I can rest. She remembered then a premises she had passed on her long journey with Miss Hammond – the House of St Silas. A plate on the door had declared it a refuge for homeless women. I shall go there, she resolved. Oh, why did I not think of it yesterday? Now, it is so far away. Yet once arrived she would surely be safe. It must be done. She was too cold and exhausted now for tears or sighs. She merely placed foot after foot on the hard cobbles, jostled by crowds of strangers and terrified by a choking tangle of horse traffic. Several times she lost her way and had to ask directions. Sometimes she stumbled and was obliged to cling to railings for support. It was noon by the time she came to the address she sought and she had barely strength to press upon the bell. A lady answered. 'Dear child!' she said.

Intimation of kindness covered Emma's face in tears. 'I am homeless.' She wept. 'I am without family or friends.'

'Yes, and you are but a child.' The other gave worried assessment. 'We cannot accommodate children here. Come in awhile. There are institutions for such as you. I will help you if I can.'

All of her will impelled her towards the warmth and order that lay across the threshold. Yet instinct warned her that the offer, though kindly meant, was no better than that proposed by Miss Wilcox. In such a foundation she would lose all independence. She would be set steadily upon the treadmill that is a lifetime's path for the poor. She would forfeit any opportunity to resolve her past.

'Thank you,' she said. 'I know where to go.' Yet she could travel no further. When the warm breath of the house was sealed off she felt as if her own last sigh had been stolen from her. Only by a great effort did she drag herself into an adjacent church. It was a strange, eerie establishment, with statues on pedestals hovering like pallid ghosts and coffin-like boxes ranked upon the walls. She recognized it as a papist place of worship. She had been warned against such by the Misses Wilcox for its dangerous superstitions, yet at this moment it seemed less hazardous than any alternative. She looked about for somewhere to hide and saw that the wardrobe-like structures on the walls had doors to either side. It must be wonderfully dark and safe inside. When no one was looking she slipped into one of these. The accommodation lacked a seat and she had to crouch with her arms upon a ledge and her head resting on them. It was cramped and uncomfortable yet, like a bird on a branch, she slept.

She dreamed a man was asking her about her sins. This was repeated more urgently until it appeared to be a reality: 'How have you sinned, my child?'

The voice was coming through a little grille before her face. 'Who are you?' she said. Her own voice sounded cracked and faint and strange. 'Why do you wish to know?'

'I am your confessor,' imparted the doleful disembodiment. 'Repent of your sins and I will make you clean.'

Her first thought was of clean clothing, a clean bed with clean sheets, and she was overwhelmed with drowsy longing. It must be true what Arthur Curran had said, that base living extinguished the spirit, for these material assets had assumed a paramount importance. Very quickly, though, she recollected the intolerable burden carried by her soul. 'I do repent of my sins,' she said.

'Then confess them,' he urged, 'and by God's power, I will absolve them.'

'Such things as I have done, I have done,' she breathed. She was overtaken then by a fit of shivering and had to yield to it before she could speak again. 'Yet speak them I cannot – especially to a holy person.'

'God knows the secrets of every man's heart, child.' The unseen speaker grew intent. 'Whatever troubles you, He knows it. It is His business, not mine, to judge.'

'Terrible things,' she said. 'I could not put words to them.'

'Let me help you.' He spoke more gently. 'I will ask you questions and you will answer them.'

All at once she was seized with yearning to be rid of the secret that tormented her. She knew the man would revile her, yet she need not witness his abhorrence for she could not see him. She was still subject to alarming alternate waves of heat and cold and her consciousness seemed such a slender state that she was not wholly certain if she slept or woke.

'I would confess,' her voice was a mere weary croak, 'but I do not think I can form the words.'

'Let us begin with the Ten Commandments,' said the priest. 'I will recite them and you may stop me if you recognize where you have erred.'

Why, she thought; there are scholars in everything. This man is a scholar of sin.

'Now I will repeat the seven deadly sins,' he offered, when he had completed the other litany. 'We may hope to find something here.'

As he enunciated a particular temptation a cry of dismay escaped her lips. The clergyman sighed. 'You see how sin burdens the soul. Man was not made for wickedness but for good. His soul despairs when the body condemns it to corruption.'

'I know it,' the penitent sobbed. 'I must be very wicked.'

'You sound like a child,' he said.

'Please do not look at me,' she begged.

'Do not be alarmed,' he said. 'I only mention it for this reason. Wicked deeds alone do not constitute sin. There must be free consent and full knowledge. Did you know what you were doing, my child? Did you freely consent to it?'

'I cannot answer,' she replied.

'Think,' he said. 'Think very hard. It is of the utmost importance.'

She shut tight her eyes and tried to penetrate the dark recesses of her memory. This brought its usual result. A pain, more piercing than any she had yet experienced, seemed to cleave her brain in two. In that instant, it felt like a shaft of judgement sent to impale her for ever in that spot. With a sharp cry and clutching her head, she scrambled from the confessional. Those who had come into the church for morning prayer looked round to see a small figure, wild with distress and very flushed in the face, stumble into the church aisle, stand panting a moment, then raise her eyes to heaven and drop heavily to the floor.

'Has she fainted?' a hushed voice whispered.

'Her eyes are open, yet how still she is. Can you hear us, child? Can you speak?'

Emma could hear the voices and her own rough breathing, yet neither sound nor movement could she execute.

'Loosen her cloak! Good heavens! Her clothing is soaked through with perspiration. Her forehead is on fire.'

'Don't touch her! She may be contagious.'

'What shall we do with her?'

'She looks respectable. Perhaps she has a family?'

'No, her clothes are dirty. She must be a street child.'

'She is so still. Is it a fit or a fever?'

'See how she perspires. It must be a fever. We must get her to the workhouse infirmary.'

CHAPTER TWENTY-THREE

For those with the good sense to be born to the right parents on the appropriate side of the city, London presents a pleasant prospect as winter plays out its spectacle and spring waits in the wings. Mr Ellin met his friends at the Wig and Pen club in the Strand. Although it would be generally agreed that the air of the metropolis was not so pure as at his permanent address, there was a sense in which one could breathe more freely. The great sweep and scale of the city, the beauty of the buildings, elevated and ennobled man. And man responded to it. In the club, no one spoke of indigestion or toothache. The good ales and wines, the plentiful and wholesome food and the lack of any female company to impose small-talk or temperance made it easy for an Englishman to feel a chosen race and gender.

Mr Ellin had observed a great number of changes since his last visit to the city. Many concerned the preparation for a specific event and it was this that dominated the conversation of his old colleagues. 'An industrial exhibition in the heart of Belgravia to enable foreigners to rob us of our honour!' Thus spake Sir Robert Walbrook, a judge.

'The whole of Hyde Park and very likely the whole of Kensington Gardens will be turned into a bivouac of all the vagabonds in London!' Mr Thomas Mallord, a barrister, expressed himself.

'The great elm trees of Hyde Park are to be cut down for one of the greatest humbugs, the greatest frauds, the greatest absurdities ever known!' A solicitor, Mr Titus Bentley.

'I would advise people residing near the park to keep a sharp lookout for their knives and spoons and serving maids!' Here was the judge again.

Mr Ellin had already been to view the giant glass construction that was to house the Great Exhibition. It was an astonishing undertaking. It covered twenty acres that had previously belonged to nature. The trees had not, after all, been cut down. Instead the design was adapted with a curved transept to enclose the soaring boughs. It looked as fragile as a cake but its strength had been tested by three hundred soldiers of the Royal Sappers and Miners running and keeping time in unison. The curiosity and fear and wonder that surrounded this vast curiosity shop was not really to do with its sturdiness or size or location. It was to do with its universality. The horse-riders on Rotten Row now picked their dainty path past an Arab camp, complete with tents and palings, which Tunisians had set up to guard their exhibits. Giant steam-ships arrived daily into London port, from Portugal, India, Turkey, France. The roads to Hyde Park were crammed with heavy vans piled high with exotic imports, pulled by long teams of horses. Fez caps of scarlet cloth and navy pantaloons enlivened the sober-suited city crowds. Outside the Crystal Palace long queues of wagons waited to unload the prizes of excavation and industry and invention. Mr Ellin guessed (and a great many others feared) that London would never be the same again. The marvel of the exhibition was not that it would display the productions and oddities and treasures of the whole Empire and beyond, but that it would mingle the tongues and colours and customs of the world in a city much occupied with its own nationhood.

'*Punch* magazine has called it the "Crystal Palace". I like the name,' he ventured.

'That artist fellow Ruskin has the right of it. He refers to it as a "cucumber frame between two chimneys",' grumbled the judge.

He waited until his fellow-members had exhausted their jaws upon the juicy bone of Prince Albert's pet project before introducing his own subject – that of a lost girl. His friends were imbued with the probing minds of their profession in which empathy played a second to inquiry.

'My dear fellow, the question you must ask yourself is, did the young lady flee in order to engage with her past or with her future?'

'It seems to me,' said Mr Ellin, 'that in her case, the one might be contingent upon the other.'

'Not necessarily. Could there, for instance, have been a young gentleman? Young women are very prone to run off at the call of Cupid.'

'Oh, rubbish,' said Mr Ellin. 'She is but a child – and a plain one. She knows no one.'

'She knew you. She knew Mrs Chalfont. By your own admission both had offered her friendship and protection. She must be a devious and wilful young person to have departed with no word and a sum of money not rightfully hers.'

So, the old ground was covered again, the old doubts reintroduced. It was Mr Ellin's strongest instinct to turn away from what caused him pain. He had done so before and would like to do so again, to return to the comfortable and impersonal controversy of the Exhibition. Yet he had given an undertaking and was bound by it.

'Once she is found, then she may be judged,' he said.

'Ah, but finding her – that's no simple matter. Do you have any idea where in this great nation she was headed?'

'None,' Mr Ellin confirmed.

'Well, let us assume it to be a city. One large city is much the same as another. Possibly she has found employment, in which case she will have gone to reside with a family. But to get work without a letter of reference – that's unlikely.'

'And if she has not found work?'

'Then it's the streets or the workhouse. If she did go to the workhouse, as she is over twelve, she would have been sent out to some menial work and put to board with a family. That's a possibility. The workhouses would have records. What is she called?'

'Emma.'

'Her second name?'

'Don't know.'

'How long has she been gone?'

Mr Ellin counted off the weeks and the days. His old colleagues were shocked. 'Dear fellow, forget about her. Children do not last long in the streets. Might she have come to London?'

'I have no reason to think so. I only know that she has disappeared. Yet she cannot just have disappeared,' he argued with himself, thinking of the strong individuality of that lost little person.

'She can,' interjected a quiet voice from behind a newspaper. The journal being lowered, the voice was revealed as that of Mr Arnold Siddons, another legal gentleman. 'Young girls disappear in the streets of London every day – literally, they vanish and are not seen again. Some are girls from the country. Others are servants out on an errand. One moment they are about their innocent purpose and the next they are no more.'

'What? The London pavements swallow them up? Foreign visitors to the city for the Exhibition should be warned,' Mr Ellin quipped.

Yet Mr Siddons did not smile. 'No, sir. They are abducted and taken to France.'

'But for what purpose?'

'For the worst possible purpose. I need not spell it out.'

An uneasy silence fell over the company. Then a stout member of the judiciary spoke out. 'Rubbish! He is talking about the sensational nonsense that appeared in some gutter journal. Why, it was all found out to be a hoax. The fellow who wrote it was a scoundrel. He went to prison for his pains.'

Mr Ellin had a vague memory of an unsavoury story served up by his London newspaper of a man who had bought a child for a degraded purpose, claiming he had done so only to expose the practice. He had not paid it much attention then, considering it sensationalist, and did not wish to discuss it now. Instead he said, 'Very well, then. If a child were to come to London and did not get snatched from the pavement, is there somewhere else to look?'

'Heavens, man,' said Mr Walbrook. 'Has this strange infant stolen your wallet or your heart? You certainly look at the loss of something of consequence. Well, never mind. If your waif is still walking the streets after her money has run out, her weary foot must sooner or later cross the threshold of the Asylum for the Houseless Poor at Cripplegate.'

'I shall go there at once,' Mr Ellin vowed.

'Check the barometer first,' his informant advised. 'It only opens when the temperature drops below freezing.'

Mr Ellin's erstwhile fellows moved on to the topic of the fire in the clock-tower of the palatial new Houses of Parliament. He left them protesting about the iniquitous taxes on windows and notepaper. He quit the warm lounge of the club with its blazing hearth and aroma of good cigars, with its air of refuge and idle gossip, its colony of pink-faced gentlemen for whom nothing was quite serious except the menu in the dining-room. He kept this picture with him as he walked the distance to the refuge. He had no need to check the barometer. The cobblestones underfoot had a treacherous sparkle.

It was a goodly stretch but he needed the hike and the chill. Engaged with his thoughts he scarcely noticed how soon he left behind familiar London and plunged into a maze of courts and narrow streets at Aldwych. Well-dressed gentlemen frequented such places at their peril. Nightmarish female faces swam up in the lamplight to whisper endearments and brutish men uttered oaths and threats. Shortly after he exited this hell he came upon the Law Institute. With what ambition and pride he had first entered there. Yet the memory now rendered him more melancholy than the miseries of Wild's Rents and Butcher's Row.

By half past four he had presented himself at Cripplegate. A more aptly named site he had never visited. The assembly of ailing humanity included small children and women with babies at the breast. A ragged regiment stretched far down the narrow lane. They stood shivering in the bitter afternoon, their garments hanging in tatters about them. Some had tied string at waist, wrist and ankle in a futile effort to keep out the wind. Some were without shoes and moved from foot to foot, the undefended limbs as raw and red as meat. It was a mute assembly but for the crying of hungry infants and the dull barking of congested lungs.

The doors opened. A fortunate number was admitted. The rest meekly consigned themselves to the cold night. Those who had found refuge warmed themselves at a fierce stove. There was no conversation, just the eager munching of the bread with which they were issued, after which they lay down in their narrow palettes under sheepskin coverings. Aside from the coughs the silence that followed was so complete that one imagined oneself to be in a morgue.

Only one person did not make directly for her rest. It was a young woman, who sat by the stove and kept her eyes fixedly upon this comfort. He inquired if she had seen a girl of Emma's description and she shook her head.

'Have you no need of sleep?' he asked her then.

'I cannot sleep,' she said. 'I dare not sleep. I have been here a week. Tomorrow I must leave.'

'You are a respectable young woman. You will surely find work.'

For a response she slightly lowered from her shoulders her black shawl, revealing a dress so ragged it was falling from her body. 'My clothes are not fit to go into a reputable work-room. There is nothing for me now but the streets.'

When he asked what had brought her to this pass she told him she had been employed as a milliner but had been out of work for three months. 'When my money ran out and I could not pay my rent, my landlady took my clothes. I was forced to leave with only those garments I stood up in. I walked the streets until my shoes let in water and my stockings froze to my feet.' Tears now poured down her cheeks and it was minutes before she could speak for sobbing.

'Have you no family?' Mr Ellin asked. In reply the girl said that her father had deserted her mother when she was a child and that poor woman was now dead.

Mr Ellin was profoundly shocked to see a respectable young woman ruined for want of something to wear. He found himself unable to return to the comfort of the club. Instead his time was spent walking those parts of the city that had hitherto kept themselves secret from his kind – the low lodging-houses, the workhouses, the roofless haunts of the truly derelict. Everywhere he went the crowds pressed upon him, threatening or imploring. Entering through a low black door to a small kitchen where three hideous hags sat by the hearth, he climbed rickety wooden stairs and found, in a filthy bed, a young woman dead with the infant to which she had recently given birth. 'Oh, poor children!' A cry of pity was wrung from him. He tried to pray but could only demand of God what manner of human would surrender a helpless female to such a fate. He closed their eyes and left, his spirit so subdued he scarce observed his abject retinue.

It was almost a relief when he failed to locate Emma. He did not wish to see her as bereft of expectation as these poor people were. He thought of her as he had first encountered her at Fuchsia Lodge, rebellious and disdainful of her ornate trappings. As he came in sight of the great dome of St Paul's his sombre mood had brief reprieve. His runaway valued only her pride and wore it as her single distinction, he lauded. In that instant he became convinced of her innocence. No matter what her past might reveal, she was good because goodness was in her nature. Even as he felt the relief of this instinctive assurance the same phrase seemed to leap back at him and mock him. *She was good because goodness was in her nature.* Suddenly he was overcome with shame. Shame for what? Why, it must be the thought of all the females he had admired because they were handsomely attired. He had not considered that those same garments were wrought by the labour of poor women who had insufficient to feed or cover their own bodies; who might die of want because change of fashion rendered their product unacceptable. Why could God not have equipped us with feathers and fur like the animals? he wondered angrily; rather than with artificial coverings that mark us either for privilege or privation.

CHAPTER TWENTY-FOUR

The day came when little Jess Sykes was to have her turn in fine feathers. Until this date she had not touched (for fear of spoiling them) the contents of the trunk that had been delivered to her on Christmas Day. But every so often she had looked at them. She had taken the basket from under the bed, lifted the lid, witnessed the precious bulk of what was hers and sighed with happiness. When the skin of her hands broke from too much scrubbing or she and her mother were too tired to light a fire, or the woman for whom she worked had vented her temper on her, Jess would rest her mind on the lovely fabrics and feel herself redeemed. It was as if a secret self lived in that trunk – a beautiful, elegant, leisured girl who would one day be released.

It so happened that this occasion arrived just twelve weeks after the precocious little wardrobe. The pleasure-loving Mr Ellin had surprised Mr Cecil by suggesting a small celebration for the poor children of the parish on the first day of spring. This mysterious gentleman of mysterious means had further surprised the clergyman by volunteering to pay for a picnic for the same juveniles and had persuaded his friend, Lord Lovell, to put Lovell Park at their disposal. Mr Cecil had lately observed a change in his comrade. Hard to put a point on it. Was he less cheerful or more thoughtful? He had developed a taste for accompanying the curate on visits to the needy and seemed to enjoy these more than tea with ladies of the parish.

Mr Cecil felt there ought to be some element of work or prayer in the outing to merit the disadvantaged their good fortune, but he did not wish to interfere with his friend's benevolent plan and Mr Ellin was intent on a day of pure pleasure for those who had none in their lives.

If God disapproved He made no outward sign of it, for the sky that day was of the particular blue that bears no comparison, being the blue of a spring sky alone. In mean cottages throughout the village, children were being attacked by their mothers with soap and hairbrush. Some had shoes and some had none, but each had the radiance of eye that gifts a happy child with beauty.

Jess Sykes was finally ready to dress. Thoroughly washed, her hair in papers, she fetched the basket and laid out the clothing on her bed. The blue silk or the pink spotted muslin? Neither! There was a confection smothered in lace and nothing would do her but to present herself in this disguise. She put on the gown, smiled as she saw herself transformed. Then as she ran her rough hands over its soft stuff she felt an obstruction, small and spiky. There was something in the pocket. The discovery did not add to her delight. Rather, it seemed to cause dismay. She brought the object to her mother.

'A little brooch! Well, Jess, perhaps the young lady who wore the dress meant the brooch to go with it. It's probably just a trifle and as we do not know her identity, there's little we can do.'

'But I do know her — the owner of the brooch, that is — for she came to tea at Mrs Corbett's and I saw her wearing it.' She whispered into her mother's ear that it belonged to one of the schoolteacher ladies, the tallest one with the red hair.

'Miss Wilcox?' Her mother looked mystified and a little apprehensive. 'How did her gem come into the gown? Yes, you'd best return it to her.'

'Won't she think I stole it?'

'Never, Jess. Explain how you came by it. She may even give you a reward.'

Like the children, Lord Lovell's park had been dressed in its best. A maypole streamed with bright ribbons. Three boys made music on flute and fiddle. Trestle tables had been covered with cloths and now supported plates of bread, cakes, buns, oranges and cold drinks.

Such a parade of ragged glamour this neighbourhood had never seen. The boys had mainly been deprived of a layer of dirt and their hair raked into submission, but the little girls were a theatre of the exotic. Bows had been cut from other garments. Adult hand-me-downs were adjusted to fit. One might have seen comedy in the scene or pathos, but their own pride in their improvement prevented that. What one saw, mostly, was what these poor creatures might achieve in themselves, given the very least encouragement.

Children differ from adults in that they do not measure happiness against yesterday's portion or tomorrow's. People bring to their grown years a baggage of slights and resentments and fears of the future. When happiness pays a visit they say, 'Pity you left it so late.' When pleasure presents itself they grumble, 'Yes, but tomorrow it's back to the grindstone.' Only children come with a pure heart, ready to be filled up. Their arrival brought new elements to the steady weather at Deerfield: excitement, laughter, rowdy delight. The air trembled with it.

Various ladies of Mr Ellin's acquaintance had been conscripted to pour lemonade, wipe chins and subdue any attempts at violence or piracy. This elect number included myself and, of course, the Misses Wilcox, and I was finally rewarded with the incomparable view of Miss Mabel Wilcox's face as she sighted young Jess Sykes making a stately entrance in the lacy raiment of the erstwhile heiress.

The lady goggled. Her mouth fell. She went pale and then red and turned and muttered to her sisters. The model, seeing herself so conspicuously admired, advanced in confidence and further affronted the ladies by approaching them directly.

'I have nothing for you,' Miss Wilcox said, in a fluster. 'The refreshments are not to be served until eleven.'

'I have something for you, miss.' The child smiled very sunnily, showing teeth already on the road to ruin. She withdrew her hands from behind her back and opened her palm.

Miss Wilcox almost fainted clean away. I have to own, at this point, to an excess of curiosity. I forsook my buns and edged a little closer to the scene. I saw now what the child offered and which was seized with impetuous haste.

'Where did you get it?' Miss Wilcox demanded.

I had to duck behind an oak tree, for the name I heard was my own.

'What? Mrs Chalfont gave you it?' Miss Mabel's glance darted all around, attempting to seek me out and hold me down.

'Yes, but I doubt she knowed it,' Jess endeavoured to vindicate me. 'She gave me some old clothes. I never found it till this morning. I knowed it was yours for I saw it on you once and thought it pretty.'

By now Jess was looking rather downcast at the response. Miss Wilcox regained a measure of her composure, told Jess she was a good child and gave her some pennies. At this the girl skipped away merrily, elbowed her way to a place at the maypole, and began swinging in a way guaranteed to ensure that neither ribbons nor dress would see out the day. I was pleased to witness a young lad gazing at her with the most uncritical admiration.

When the brooch had been restored to the appropriate bosom, Miss Wilcox commenced upon a noisy campaign of self-justification. She complimented herself on having judged well and declared that any of the malnourished infants present would possess a higher degree of morals than the young lady in question. Miss Lucy gave vigorous assent and both were seen to be in their element.

At this point I did present myself for I had observed an aspect of the drama that intrigued me. Only two of the sisters were fully engaged in their victory. The third, Miss Adelaide, had an air of decided unease.

'I see you have had your brooch returned,' I commented.

'Yes, and the thief now caught in all but body.' Miss Mabel's pale blue eye glittered in excitement.

'What do you mean?' said I.

'Why, it is obvious. That Matilda Fitzgibbon – or whatever her name is – stole my brooch and concealed it in her pocket. She meant to keep it.'

'And are you all united upon the point?' I smiled pleasantly at the handsome trio.

'Of course we are. Anyone but a fool could see it,' Miss Lucy snapped.

'Why, then, you must be very well pleased.'

'Thank you, Mrs Chalfont, we are.'

'Yet somehow Miss Adelaide does not quite look it.' I addressed the third sibling directly. 'Surely you are not feeling sorry for the robber?'

A tear escaped her eye.

'Such compassion is touching,' said I. 'Yet I agree with your sisters. If the child stole a valuable piece of jewellery she should be hunted down and punished. Is that not so?'

Miss Adelaide Wilcox turned to her sisters in appeal. 'I swear, I had entirely forgotten until this moment. Events cast it from my mind.'

'Cast what, Ada dear?' the elder sister said sharply.

'I was trying out the brooch on the frock. I meant to make the lace collar over upon my violet wool. You would not let me.' Miss Adelaide's voice emerged as the muffled yaps of a frightened lapdog.

'Control yourself, Ada. Take a deep breath,' Miss Mabel ordered. 'Endeavour to make sense of your explanation.'

A more subdued narrative, still punctuated with sobs, succeeded the breathing. Miss Adelaide recalled the day when Miss Mabel had determined to make a profit from Miss Fitzgibbon's garments and sent her sister to retrieve them. 'Upon seeing the lace, I was inspired to cut it down for a fichu. I had an urge to see how the star-shaped brooch might sit upon it. And then you called me. You called rather loudly, sister, and it alarmed me. I quickly thrust everything into the trunk and brought it down. As I intended to retain the lace, I left the brooch in the pocket for a convenience, but you decided that we should keep none of the garments. That disappointment affected my memory.' Her voice trailed off and she looked miserably at the pitcher of lemonade in front of her.

Such a silence followed that the music and the rowdy laughter on the green seemed to emanate from another sphere. It was Miss Mabel who spoke first. 'Well, then. The matter is ended. No harm is done.'

'I beg your pardon!' I was compelled to speak out. 'The matter is not quite ended.'

'Of course it is. What do you mean?' Miss Lucy demanded.

'You have impugned a reputation. You must go to the police and remove all guilt from the young person you so hastily charged.'

'To be sure,' she said icily.

'I shall check to make sure it is done,' said I.

Such a day of merriment was proceeding all around that I now had to hurry back to my position and commence dispensing buns. How those children fed and how they danced! Little legs malformed from lack of nourishment capered with carefree joy. Children to whom the sound of laughter was as foreign as the music of a string quartet, now made their own mirthful euphony. In the midst of all paraded Mr Ellin, hands behind his back, a senior statesman unused to rowdy youngsters, yet deriving a quiet satisfaction from their delight. I never felt fonder of him than I did on that day.

It was four in the afternoon before the proceedings wound down to a point where I could take any ease. With the other ladies, I packed up the remains of the food for the children to take home to their families. Then I approached their benefactor. 'Mr Ellin, you have done a good deed this day and deserve a reward.'

'That is enigmatic.' He smiled. 'What have you got to improve the lot of an old bachelor?'

'The self-same gift you always bring to me – a story.'

'And shall I have it here or need I sit down?' he inquired.

'You shall have it now for it will wait no longer.' I related the tale of the brooch's return and Miss Adelaide's admission.

'You should have seen her face,' said I. 'I have never observed anything more dismal.' And his face, reader – I only wish you could have witnessed it. Mr Ellin's normally enigmatic expression forsook him. He looked as open and hopeful as a boy. My own countenance, it would appear, had also been affected.

'Contented as a cat!' he pronounced me.

'Not quite correct,' I responded. 'I am near content. All in all it has been a good day's work, but there is still the matter of a missing girl.'

'Ah! I think I am not so much rewarded as reproved.' Mr Ellin bowed his head.

'Not at all,' said I. 'You have gone a great deal out of your way to help that child. If there is any dereliction I blame myself. I own I grew disheartened. Yet this fine day has planted spring in more than those it was designed to profit. I now have the heart to proceed with the search, although I know not how.'

'This is strange.' Mr Ellin took my basket upon one arm and linked my arm with the other as we left the area (earning me a hawk-like stare from Miss Wilcox). 'Whatever spring fever has afflicted you must be infectious, for I feel an absurd bubbling of optimism within my own settled person.'

'Do nothing yet,' I advised. 'Wait until that spring of spring strikes at the brain.'

We walked on a bit and then he stopped. 'Do you know? I have had a notion.'

'Proceed.' I indicated the path to suggest that we might make physical as well as philosophical progress.

'Walk slowly, then, for I must tell another story. Up to this point in my life I believed – and believed it truly – that the answer to a bad deed was to walk away from it. If one found one's foot on treacherous ground, one amended the route and took another path – even if it was longer and less interesting.'

'Is this a story or a riddle?' I inquired.

'Patience, dear friend. Since the year began I have seen much that has influenced my thinking. I have come to believe that the perilous route may be the only way – the one where one engages with one's true self.'

'I have known that path,' I murmured softly.

'Moreover, the idea has come to me that the people we judge unworthy of our company may be victims of the same fears that inhibit our own courage. Indeed, they may be placed on our path not to obstruct our progress but because they need a helping hand in order to move from that place. In short, those we perceive as opponents to our aims may, in a sense, be our necessary allies.'

Although Mr Ellin's strange discourse had now moved from riddle to obscure parable; although I retained a conviction that some people were beyond any redemption; yet, in that moment, I felt a twining of our own paths.

'I wonder what has affected your thinking?' I said softly.

'I saw things in London that I cannot dislodge from my mind. I believed myself to be ill-used as a child but now perceive I have merely dallied like a child in some sheltered playground when I should have acted as a man. I fancied myself an astute judge of human nature. In reality, I have expended my intellectual powers – such as they are – on trivial games.'

'Tell me what you saw in London.'

He shook his head. 'It would not be fitting. I prefer not to burden you.'

'I am not a child,' I assured him.

Mr Ellin came back to my house. That comfortable location, with tea and buttered crumpets, with chairs and tables dressed in velvet, became another place as he described the terrible scenes he had witnessed in the city.

'I imagined my own background to be poor.' I had to pause to wipe a tear from my eye. 'If ignorance is guilt, than I am more guilty than you.'

He shook his head. 'There is more than you know. I carry the burden of a lifetime's judgement.'

'You ought not be so hard on yourself.'

'I don't see why not. God knows, I have been hard enough on another.'

'I have never known you other than kind,' I said.

'Well, then, I will set you right. A long time ago I deserted a lady I professed to love – and one who had afforded me that solace at a time when I most needed it.'

It was thus that I became acquainted with the mystery of William Ellin and the objects that inclined him to a friendless child: to wit, an orphan boy, a harsh guardian and a tender-hearted maid – and the uniting of these by a careless fate which, for good measure, had cast the youth from his very home.

I have observed that men talk about their houses as women talk about their children, with an abstracted and ambitious eye and an urge to impress upon the hearer their singular distinctions. And women react to them as do men to maternal outpourings. Mr Ellin was holding forth about an old stone house called Ellin Balcony and I had to feign affection for this pallid-sounding piece of architecture.

'It was not picturesque,' he scrupulously admitted; 'but its situation was fair. It was on a raised site with an outlook that commanded both sunrise and sunset. On the upper gable there was a balcony of stone – a peculiarity rare in the neighbourhood – and that which gave the house its name. My earliest memory was of being held on high on that balcony in my mother's arms as she told me that I was king of all I surveyed. I believed it. I saw Ellin Balcony as my birthright.'

'Was it yours?' I asked.

'As my father's eldest son, my half-brother Edward inherited Ellin Balcony. You know, I ran away once, back to my old home, but my brother found me. He flogged me until I had to ask for mercy.'

'Was mercy in his nature?'

'He had no nature. Mercy came from another quarter.'

'Did this quarter have a name?'

231

'Teresa.' He fell into a reverie. I judged that he was contemplating the key to some long-locked trunk. He kept his past there. After an interlude of unease he took the key and sank it into its hollow. He gave a deep sigh as he faced his history. From the calm sea of his familiar exterior, it emerged like a cursed haul of sunken treasure. I will tell it to you now as he told it to me.

The young lady called Teresa belonged to a branch of the Ellin family known as 'the American Relations'. For months Golpit had been in a fever due to the impending arrival of these exotics. Carpets were beaten and fresh curtains hung. Lengths of fabric arrived and dressmakers presented themselves to fit Mrs Ellin for new apparel. Why? The legend that preceded the visitors was that they were well-to-do and that the daughter was a beauty. The real reason was that they came from the New World and it was common knowledge that Americans were accustomed to every luxury and convenience. In fact, both parents were English, the mother being a sister of Edward Ellin's wife. Only Teresa Welles had been born in America and although the family had prospered there, the parents hoped she would marry an Englishman. To this end, upon the completion of her education, they planned her first visit to their homeland. To Willie, the event appeared as a beacon in his dim existence. America was a country he knew only from the books he had read. It seemed a brave and exciting place. He made little distinction between native and settled Americans and expected that the girl would look like Pocahontas.

The American niece proved a disappointment. She arrived alone and wrapped in blankets. She was small for her age and looked more ghost than woman, retiring at once to her room where she was attended only by doctors. Why did she weep when no one beat her, the little boy wondered. Where were her parents? These and more questions piled up in his head and when none would answer them, he knocked upon on her door.

'What do you want, little boy?' The girl was now somewhat recovered and he could divine the truth of her rumoured beauty. Pale and shaken still, she had the prettiest features he had ever seen and her eyes were a very haunting shade of grey.

'I would like to know why you are so pale,' he said. 'I expected you would have brown skin and a plait. And I wondered what happened to your parents.'

To his dismay she burst into tears. She told him that the ship *Diamond*, on which they had travelled from New York, had run aground at Cardigan Bay and that most of the hands and the forty passengers, including her parents, their maid and the ship's Captain Macey, had been drowned.

'Then you are an orphan, as I am,' he instructed her. He introduced himself by name and grandly informed her that he was her uncle. 'What will you do now?'

'I shall go home,' she said.

'I wish you would not,' he ventured timidly.

'I must.' Tears washed her lovely face. 'Without my parents I am lonely and homesick.'

'If you were not so old, I would try to comfort you,' he offered.

At this the young girl wiped her eyes and almost smiled. 'I am old, but not very fat, and I should like the solace of a nice little boy. If you put both arms around me at once you will likely succeed in your aim.'

Cautiously he followed her instruction. He first placed his arms apart as if trying to gauge her span, then clamped them awkwardly to her side. To those unaccustomed to contact, the warm human form seems wonderful and fearful. As he touched her, an unbearably poignant memory of his mother assailed him. 'And you must comfort me.' His muffled voice emerged with as much courage as he could muster. 'I am lonely too. No one has ever liked me since my mother died.'

233

Teresa had known the blessing of a happy childhood. It was simple and natural for her to hold the child and stroke his hair. The two orphans clung to one another. Teresa wept but Willie only prayed: Let her stay. Please, God, let her stay.

It was at this moment that Mrs Ellin chose to enter. She plucked Willie from his consoling perch. 'How dare you disturb Miss Welles?'

'He is no disturbance,' Teresa said. 'I was glad of his company.'

'Do not encourage him,' her aunt warned. 'He is a whining wretch.' As she pulled him from the room she promised: 'He will not trouble you further.'

Yet Teresa liked that trouble. Little boys appealed to her, and the kind of games that are to boyish tastes. Despite her gentle look and mien, she had a playful nature. She had grown up in a young country and her own youth shimmered about her like a waking sun. Not yet attuned to English manners (nor thus subdued to womanhood), she made a most beguiling tutor to the lad – in card games, in whistling and (most wonderful of all) in shooting target with a gun.

On an evening when Teresa was out walking and Edward had taken brandy, he summoned Willie and told him it was time for him to commence work in a trade.

'I will not,' Willie demurred. 'I am a gentleman.'

'You are a lazy little layabout. This will sort you.' In threatening fashion his brother lifted up a wooden stool.

'I shall tell Teresa.' The boy tried to hold some ground.

'Oh, will you now? Then you had better be in good voice for she will shortly be back in America.'

'It's a lie!' Willie protested feebly.

Tickets were produced for rail and ship. Willie stared at them dumbly. The date was a week thence.

'Now, what have you to say?' Edward demanded. 'You don't even apologize for calling me a liar. A gentleman would, but as you are clearly not one I must deal with you otherwise.' Even as he spoke he had raised the stool again and struck Willie a heavy blow to the temple. Still the boy did not speak or make a sound. Very quietly he left the room. He placed a foot on the bottom stair and paused to wipe blood from his forehead. His hand trembled as he saw it stained crimson. His very life's blood was as meat to his brother's anger. Upon a timid but insistent impulse he turned and walked out of the door and headed for what had once been home.

It was Willie's intention never to return. But a child of ten has not the means to match his will and within a day he was returned to Golpit. Two days after the departure of Mr Bosas, reprisal came. As usual, Willie took his punishment soundlessly. Yet the flick of the gig whip on flesh and the coarse gloating of its administrator was audible even a floor below. Teresa heard it. She crept up to where the little victim suffered in silence. She comforted him and gave him promise of protection. The day after, she cancelled her passage to America.

Young women in a household are a passing delight, like spring flowers. They do not wither, as flowers do, but are picked and transplanted for a different arrangement – a marital one. Young boys are not privy to such wisdom and Willie Ellin never foresaw a day when he would be without his gentle companion.

Four years passed. A visitor called to the house – a sallow-faced fellow, thin as a whippet, with dark, curling hair and a ready laugh. Felix Osborne was a card-playing friend of Edward. He had come to Golpit to seek the advice of his more hard-headed companion concerning some financial matter. Although he claimed to be beset by worries, these all seemed to evaporate as soon as he set eyes on Teresa. From the day of their introduction he made a campaign of her. Flowers, notes, ribboned caskets of sweets were in daily supply. Teresa's life had been sombre and responsible since her parents' death. The flirtatious young man made her days as exciting and agreeable as they should be for a beautiful young woman of twenty-one; and she, with no experience of the opposite sex, delighted in his merry ways and thought him a very safe kind of man – another little boy, almost, though a more cheerful one than Willie. After all, Felix presented a sharp contrast to the Ellin males: the one whose early woes had made him serious beyond his years; the other, whose self-indulgent tempers were felt even by those at whom he did not direct his wrath. Felix seemed never to know a serious moment. He liked to dance, to play at cards, to pay court. A bare month into their acquaintance he proposed to Teresa and she accepted.

The interlude of safety was ended. The boy's protector was removed and he was once more exposed to tyranny. Yet he was older and stronger now and better able to face his brother. His terror was of a different order – one he could scarcely explain even to himself. On the day of Teresa's wedding Willie found himself in the grip of an agony exceeding any he had endured as a child. He was at that age when shallow emotions live on the surface and deep ones cannot easily find expression, so his misery could only declare itself in callow behaviour. At last Edward seized him and locked him in his room with a promise to deal with him later. Willie vowed that when his brother came to execute that threat, he would kill him. In fact, after he had spent a time alone with his murderous and miserable thoughts, it was a different visitor who sought him out. It was Mr Bosas, the merchant, returned from Portugal for the wedding.

'What do you want, Bosas?'

'To know why you do not behave like a gentleman, when you profess to be one?' the other replied.

'Because I have not been raised to a gentleman's life – and such life as I have I would gladly be rid of.'

'And why is that?'

'I do not know, sir,' the youth exclaimed, in profoundest misery.

Mr Bosas, though English-born, was a Continental by blood. Such people live at a closer remove to the emotions than we do. Almost at once he diagnosed the disorder. 'You are lovesick. You are jealous because that lovely creature who made herself your ally is now at the service of another.'

At this the young boy broke down and could scarcely speak for weeping. 'It makes no sense, sir. I am only fourteen and she a grown woman.'

'Poor fellow,' Mr Bosas sympathized. 'The heart was not constructed for common sense.'

'I cannot be in this house now that she has quit it. I cannot bear it that . . .' He shook his head hopelessly. He did not even know what he could not bear.

'You cannot bear it that she is with another man — that another now receives her comfort and caresses. For the moment you feel it is your lot in life to lose everyone you love. You have had much to endure, yet such trials will build your character. You will grow into a strong oak tree.'

'I do not think so, sir,' Willie complained; 'for melancholy clings about me like a dark ivy and ivy can bring down the oak.'

Mr Bosas did not underestimate the boy's woes. 'I realize that although you are young you speak as a man and that your heart is broken. I could offer to take you back to Portugal with me, but for the present the only work I could offer is as stable-hand.'

'Take me, sir,' the boy begged. 'Take me, or when next you come to England, either I or my brother shall be dead.'

Mr Bosas thought. 'Pack your bags. You will return to Lisbon with me. If you prove diligent and useful I shall teach

237

you to ride and see that you are educated. What you make of the rest of your life will be up to you.'

Edward was glad to be rid of his patrician sibling and liked the idea of him working in a stable. Willie embarked on a long and thrilling sea voyage and arrived in a land flooded with sunshine. In a large house high above the city of Lisbon, young Willie Ellin learnt to work, to ride, to speak another language, to drink wine, to laugh. For company he had Mr Bosas' twelve-year-old daughter, Lucy, who soon persuaded her parents to exchange his sleeping quarters in the stable for a room in the house. From this small chamber he had a distant view of the sea. In an easy-going and affectionate household the trials of his childhood days were forgotten. Teresa kept in touch. She spoke little of her own life, mainly she asked after his welfare. Once she wrote to say that she had had a child. When he remembered he would answer her letters, a youth's carefree scrawled report on weather or sport or the day's ride. He was growing up. He was a young man now and Teresa Welles had become a young matron called Teresa Osborne. When he thought of her it was with gratitude and affection, but mostly he was absorbed with his own pleasant existence.

It is very likely he would have made his home in Lisbon and gone into business with the kindly foreigner but for another communication from Teresa. It contained the news that her husband had died. 'By the kindness of your brother, I am now once more living at Golpit.'

The letter occasioned him considerable unease. Why would she have returned to Golpit when her parents' home was in America? Why call Edward kind? Although he had not been harsh to her, she was fully aware of his capacity for cruelty and he was not a man whom any would designate compassionate. He decided it was time to return to England.

238

From his modest wage William had saved sufficient to pay his passage back. As he rode towards Golpit he steeled himself against the dread that must greet him from the site of his wretched childhood. Yet when he arrived he found it all reduced in power and scale. Golpit was no more a formidable prison but a characterless barracks. He shuddered as he dismounted, not with fear but with a gentleman's aversion to an ill-ordered concern. Then the entrance to that grim estate was opened and the love of his young life was standing at the door.

A shock awaited them both. Three years earlier Teresa had left behind a morose lad of fourteen. There now approached a tall and sun-darkened young man of seventeen. Willie had bidden farewell to a maid of twenty-one. A grave and pale woman greeted him. She looked older by far than her four and twenty years. Her eyes were shadowed with weariness, her black clothing ill-became her and she had about her a pallid and listless air. At first he could not subdue a sense of disappointment. When they embraced, he was unable to return her naturalness. It did not seem fair that this dull matron had replaced his lovely young American girl.

About a week after his arrival he was making plans for an early departure when he came upon her weeping and then he guiltily reproved himself. Of course, she must be grieving for her husband. No woman could look her best when she had just lost the man she loved. He took her in his arms and told her he was sorry.

She withdrew and looked on him fondly and wistfully. 'My dear little friend, I am grateful for your sympathy and much in need of it, but not for the reason you imagine.'

'I am your friend,' Willie said; 'but no longer little.'

'No. And no longer Willie, I am sure. I shall call you William. Well, I am glad you are grown. Now that you are almost a man I can speak to you as one. I cannot grieve for my husband. He never loved me and was never kind to me. Felix married me for my money. He was a gambler and as soon as we were wed he spent what I had. He was a man who lived for pleasure and took it where he wished, even after we were married. He . . .' She hesitated as she saw the wide-eyed youth of her audience. Ah, he was only a boy. She could never divulge to him the details of her humiliation.

'I said that if he could not love me, at least he might respect me. His reply was that I should respect him, for I was a pauper as every married woman was, and if I did not show him deference he would send me to the workhouse. I begged him to let me have the money for my passage and to permit me to return to America. He agreed that I might go but must sell my jewellery to pay my passage. This I did, yet when I got to that dear home, I discovered it was no longer mine and other people were living in it. Felix had sold it. I had nowhere else to go. I was forced to return to him. Once, he locked me in a room for a week with scarcely any food or water. Like a person born without hearing or vision, Felix was born without morals, and yet he continued to borrow and to charm right to the end.'

'How did that end come about?' William Ellin asked then.

'It was dreadful.' She shook out a fan, wept behind it. She set it down, leaving tears to run unchecked. Her gentle face, washed with woe, was a girl's again. 'He was found dead in a house that had been set ablaze. I was summoned to identify the body. He had been burned beyond recognition. I could only recognize him by his gold watch.'

'He left you no money?'

'There was none. Even the house had been mortgaged to a wager. I am as you are, William, an orphan and a dependant.'

Willie sat beside her. He took her hand. Indignation, fired

by a protective ardour, swelled his breast. 'Bad enough that I should have lost everything by my mother's death, but Edward was my father's first son. In your case there was no such contest. You arrived at Golpit as a young woman of means. Surely there is a law to protect the property of a woman from an unscrupulous husband?'

'There is a law,' she answered softly. 'It states that everything a woman owns belongs to her husband. I have since learnt that wise women protect their independence with a marriage agreement, but as my parents were dead there was no one to advise me.'

'My little Teresa! What you have been through!' His voice and look were tender now. 'What will you do?

'I shall remain at Golpit. My aunt has been very ill and Uncle Edward has kindly agreed to let me live here if I undertake her care.' She discussed these arrangements in dazed and unemotive tone.

'That is not kindness!' he protested. 'He is getting the services of a nurse free of charge – the best and kindest in the world. Not for all of that world would I have her at the mercy of a man like Edward.'

'Hush,' she entreated. 'Let old enmities lie. I know Edward treated you unkindly yet he was never cruel to me. I have a child whom I cannot support. At present she is in the care of friends. My aunt is all the family that is left to me. It is God's providence that I should tend to her.'

'Then I shall look after you,' Willie pledged. 'I shall remain here at Golpit to return the service you once rendered to me.'

While Teresa sewed in the evening William read to her. When the weather improved he took her riding and for long walks. It was a source of pride that he was the one to restore her beauty. As months progressed and her youth returned to her he told himself that none would guess the difference in their ages. With his experience of a liberal and sophisticated world, he even felt a year or two her elder. The naturally affectionate relationship that had bound them in childhood now innocently reasserted itself in adulthood. As they walked hand in hand or perched a kiss on one another's cheek he experienced a strong sense of joy in their reunion. They knew one another's innermost hearts and thoughts. They loved each other in the most naïve and natural way. There was no doubt in his mind that he desired – and would have – another kind of love.

The blithe happiness that romance brings must, in a true heart, be counterbalanced by the weightier sense of responsibility. William understood that if he was to afford Teresa any genuine protection he must find some proper way to earn a living. His sense of justice gave him a leaning towards the law. With no sponsor it was an excessive ambition, yet opportunity presented itself via an advertisement in a London newspaper:

> Law – to parents and guardians. A solicitor of good general practice to the city has a vacancy for an articled clerk and would prefer to take as such a young gentleman whose entire charge would devolve on him and whose general education he would willingly direct. His morals will be assiduously attended to.

The inquiries of Messrs Evans and Bateman, Law Stationers, were well satisfied by the gentlemanly youth who came for interview, and his own single query – whether he might in addition study for the law in his own time and at his own expense – received a conditional affirmative: if he proved clever and assiduous in his duties.

By day he worked long hours and by night he studied.

Occasions of leisure were few so his visits to Golpit were rare. He was frequently cold in his modest accommodation, and even hungry. Yet no protest escaped his lips or even entered his mind. He was achieving all that he desired in life. His sense of purpose never wavered. Interesting occupation filled his present, and happy expectation awaited his future.

In due course a telegram informed him that his brother's wife had died. He did not mourn the woman who had denied him her affection, and minded only for Teresa's sake that a burden of work kept him from the funeral. With his customary forbearance, he held his love secret even from its object until the time came when it might seem more than mere romantic fancy. That opportunity arose when he was twenty. In another year he would have attained his majority and qualified in the law. The moment had come to give her intimation of his feelings. A year's engagement would give them time to prepare for the solemn joy that would last a lifetime. To overcome his natural shyness he ordered a modest token that would make his declaration for him, and impatiently anticipated leave.

While he waited, a communication came that was to change his life for ever. It was a letter from Teresa – thoughtful, cheerful, as were all her missives. She often apologized for the dullness of her discourse, explaining that, as nothing ever happened in her days, he would have to make do with the diversions of Nature and the servants. He read with pleasure until she announced that at last she had a piece of news to impart: to wit – she was getting married again.

The dread borne in on him by these words was such that the blood evaporated from his head. For a moment he thought he would faint. He remained like a pallid stone impersonation of himself until his employer found him at his desk. 'Are you ill, Ellin?' he inquired.

William had to fight for speech. 'I have had bad news, sir, from home.'

'Go there now. You have been working too hard.'

Why had he spoken of Golpit as home? That ugly house had never been his home. It was because Teresa was there. Teresa was his home. He went at once. He did not wait to pack. His only thought was first to stop the impending event and then . . . ? He had no money. They would – they must – manage somehow. He would apply to Mr Bosas for help – only a loan, he would pay him back when he was qualified.

As the fever in his brain subsided he wondered, for the first time, who it was that she meant to marry. What prospector had come to claim the treasure intended only for himself?

'Edward!' Teresa told him.

He almost laughed. To him Edward now seemed a wreck of a man. The heavy, sensuous features that had marked the uncontrolled temperament of his youth (and probably made him attractive to a certain type of woman) had run to coarseness. An assiduous application of Grecian Water kept the black in his hair and whiskers but his complexion was red and his figure bulky.

Teresa's expression informed him that it was no joke.

'You cannot marry Edward,' he protested. 'He is more than twice your age.'

'Age does not matter in a man,' she said.

'Do you love him?' he asked.

'Why not? I have no reason to hate him. He has never been cruel to me.'

'Yes, but for the reason that you might already love another.'

'Who, then? How many fine young men do you suppose to have passed through these portals in a year?'

Very shakily he demanded: 'Do you deny that you love me?'

'As soon not breathe as deny my love for you,' she answered promptly.

'And Edward? Has he pledged his love to you?'

'Edward, as you well know, is not of a poetic turn, yet from his looks alone I know well his feelings. You must be old enough to understand that there are different kinds of love. As well as the tender sibling kind, which we have shared, there is the more general kind, based on mutual attraction.'

'Is that attraction mutual?' he almost groaned.

'It doesn't matter,' she said softly. 'I am a dependant. I have no other home. Now that my aunt is dead, I have no purpose here. Edward wants a son. He was disappointed that his first wife could not provide one. As he honours me by offering a home for myself and my child, I have no possible reason to object.'

At this the young man fell to his knees. 'Let me give you reason. If marriage is to be your purpose, marry me.'

Teresa put out her hands and drew him fondly to his feet. 'But you are my darling little cousin and will be so still. You are but a boy. I am seven years your elder.'

She looked so lovely it seemed irrelevant to apply the counting-house skill to her years. 'I am a man, whatever you may think. And in point of fact,' he reminded her, 'I am your uncle. I love you, not only as kin but as a man loves a woman. You make no issue of Edward's age. I would not care if you were seven and a score years my elder. My only desire in life is to be with you and to make you happy. To think of you as Edward's bride – as the mate and companion of a man I hate – is as acid thrown upon an old wound. I shall surely die of pain to see you taken from me twice.'

Teresa turned a deathly pale. She put a hand to her lips as if to stem utterance but it escaped past that ashen gate: 'Darling Will . . .'

William moved to take her in his arms. With an agitated hand she pushed him back. 'Why did you make no mention of your feelings? No word, no kiss, no tender letter?'

'I brought you this.' He offered her the little gift. She unwrapped it. A small exclamation escaped her lips: 'Oh!' It was so dull it might have been an utterance of disappointment.

'I was not in a position to be your suitor,' William said. 'Nor am I still, yet we shall manage and be happy. It is astonishing how contingency augments the practical brain. Already I have worked out a plan for our survival. You will come back with me to London. We will find witnesses and a priest and marry. I shall continue to work and study. We will share a very narrow bed and small rations but we will rest in one another's arms as first we did when I was ten years of age, and know, dear heart, that we have done right the one thing in our lives that really matters.'

Now that he had made this declaration he felt fully confident of his success. Relief surged through him like strong sunshine. Yet she did not look glad. Her face expressed the utmost dismay.

'Do not look like that,' he begged. 'I may be a poor prospect but I will be a good husband and you the best — my only — wife.'

'I cannot,' she breathed.

'If you love me, why not?'

'Because I have already married Edward.'

It is a testimony to William Ellin's stoical nature that he was able to resume, with cool application, both work and study when he returned to London. Those who liked him were concerned for his health for he never seemed to take rest or leisure. Those who had known him in Portugal would scarce have recognized the austere young person whose eyes were shadowed from sleeplessness and book-work. That he suffered, none would know, for none (save Teresa) knew his heart and he did not complain. Teresa did her best to keep a sisterly regard but William had to seal his heart to stop all its substance draining away so he did not answer, or even open, her letters. Had he done so, he would have learnt that Edward was disappointed by her failure to give him a son. Her letters might have yielded intimation that her financial dependence had given her husband a fresh victim for his bullying.

It was at this point that a certain detachment and deliberation entered William Ellin's character. He determined to shut down all intense passions, to express only temperate opinions, to surround himself with companions whose pursuits and thoughts and conversations were inconsequential. Having thus aligned his system for moderation he suffered no strong emotion on learning, after a further four years, of his brother's death. No sense of vindication asserted itself upon the smiting of an old foe; no stirring of optimistic joy at the release of Teresa from a hateful alliance. In regard to Teresa he felt like a man who has recovered from a near fatal fever. To let her enter his mind was to suffer once more the parched mouth, the palsied ague, the horrors of a hallucinating mind.

'Who but a fool would court his own destruction?' had been his summing-up. He had recently qualified as a solicitor and was as over-burdened as any young professional at the start of his career. He did not go home for the funeral.

I was curious to know if he had tried to contact her later.

He shook his head. 'I had come to believe that far from being God's gift to me she was His warning. Any engagement with her could only end in the profoundest disappointment and misery for myself.'

'Except the first one,' I quietly interjected; 'except when she shielded a little orphan boy.'

247

'Yes, except that,' he murmured. 'For that I owed her some-thing – perhaps everything.'

So, the rootless child called Emma, who drifted in and out of our lives, had led us both to our site of desolation. We were silent a long time, each to our own reflections. When I returned to the present, it was to a dark room with a dying fire and a tray of cold tea. I summoned the maid to bring some cheer, and it was only when the lamps had been lit and the fire banked and fresh muffins brought that I remembered how our conversation had commenced. 'I had almost forgotten – this morning as we walked from the village, you said you had a plan.'

'I was in a preaching mood this morning. Now you know me a little better, you might respect my views on the world a little less.'

'On the contrary,' I assured him. 'You have shown yourself to be a resourceful man and a remorseful one. I respect both.'

'Very well. We were speaking, I recall, of obstacles placed on our path. This very day, you stubbed your dainty toe upon a very specific hindrance. To give credit to your spirit, you offered it a hearty kick – and then moved smartly to another path. Can you give a name to that particular rock?'

'Miss Mabel Wilcox!' I answered directly. He said nothing but I deemed his smile quite cunning. 'Mr Ellin,' I pleaded, 'you cannot be suggesting that she and I might find some common ground. That woman represents everything I disap-prove of and she dislikes of me.'

He did not contradict me. 'And yet!' His voice had a ring of its old lazy self. 'Perhaps her feelings towards you are better justified than yours for her.'

'I have always been civil to her,' I objected.

'Yes, and better dressed and better housed. You have passed – according to her vision – a life of idle luxury, while she has had nothing but hard work and futile struggle. You

248

have enjoyed a long marriage while she has been denied that privilege. It would be no great surprise if she viewed your civility as a form of bragging.'

'That is unfair,' I said. 'I never exploited my advantages. Besides, if she feels that way, then why would she wish my friendship?'

'I was thinking of a more practical alliance. You are a fair artist and needlewoman. You have, if I may say, a gift in dealing with children. The Misses Wilcox's little academy is – not to put too fine a point on it – a dismal failure. You are charming, cultivated . . .'

'Do not attempt flattery while manipulating me.'

The path upon which I presently found myself was a thorny one, every gate padlocked.

'For all their faults, the Misses Wilcox are women as you are. Have you never, Mrs Chalfont, felt the disadvantage of your sex, that being born fragile and fair, you were therefore powerless and defenceless?'

A felled tree now appeared on my track. It bore a marked resemblance to Mr Ellin.

'If they are short of money, then I would gladly give them some,' I said. 'Yet what you are suggesting sounds preposterous. Besides, I cannot devote myself to any other object until we have found out the truth about Emma.'

'Naturally!' He looked quite pleased with himself and I felt I had walked right into a poacher's trap. 'And where did that young lady first appear? Where did she lodge and sleep (and talk in her sleep)? Has anyone made a thorough search of that premises? Do we know if she ever spoke to any of the other pupils? As for offering money to the Misses Wilcox, they are too proud for that. They would accept no less a sacrifice than your whole and humble self.'

'They would not want it,' I protested feebly.

'In which case you would be absolved of all further effort,' he graciously allowed.

Thus on a bright, chill March day I presented myself at Fuchsia Lodge. My welcome there was the very opposite of effusive. Miss Mabel, having opened the door a mere crack without inviting me in, announced at once that if I had come about That Young Person, she knew nothing and wished to know nothing.

'No, it's not about her.' I endeavoured to keep my features bright. 'I have a proposal to make – one which might be to your advantage. May I come in and speak with you?'

Grudgingly, she acceded. In the parlour, I noted that the fire was far lower than the season warranted and could not help but observe my hostess's yearning eye upon my Chambord mantle.

'I'll come to the point,' said I. 'I am at a loose end. I would welcome some occupation. I worked as a governess when young and am, as you know, a useful seamstress. Perhaps I could help you teach your girls?'

'Young ladies!' she corrected, and promptly added: 'We do not need any more teachers. We have one master and my sisters and I adequately perform all other functions. We have already let go the sewing mistress.'

'Naturally, I have not so much vanity as to imagine that you might *need* my services.' I swallowed that specific defect as best I could and made my case. 'You would be doing me a good turn in accepting my offer – both offers.'

'You made only one,' Miss Wilcox smartly pointed out.

'The second is merely a repeat of an earlier offering that went astray.' I handed her a small package, which she gingerly undid. Upon seeing its content – the unpaid school fees (with extras) of one Matilda Fitzgibbon – all the starch seemed to evaporate from her fibre. She sank on to a chair. I declare I detected some moisture in her eye. 'It has been a difficult winter,' she murmured.

The last thing I wished to see was that formidable schoolmistress collapse in a heap of emotion. 'It has been a difficult season for me also. Although we may not view one another in the light of natural allies, we might be of service to one another nonetheless.'

'What can you teach besides sewing?' Her eye hardened wonderfully.

'Poetry,' said I. 'I am very fond of verse and believe myself capable of imparting that enjoyment. And I draw tolerably well.'

To my great surprise I enjoyed my new position. Mr Ellin must have been exceedingly pleased with himself for that devious gentleman had massacred a whole flock of birds with one idly flung pebble. He had assured my access to Emma's place of arrival, had swelled the teaching staff at Fuchsia Lodge (but not its expenses) – yet more than that, he had achieved what I now perceived to have been his primary design: he had dealt with my feelings of futility.

I had not come to that small academy to educate. My express purpose was to find even a widow's mite of evidence to Emma's existence. Yet I was aware that I must make myself sufficiently useful to justify my presence. Without my realizing it, the task overtook the intent. I could not but respond to the fresh young minds that absorbed information as a garden does rain.

I visited the school on three afternoons a week to instruct in one of my amateur specialities. Sometimes I brought a morning's baking, which the proprietors, no less than their charges, enjoyed. At home I prepared my lessons to be as entertaining as possible. While I found the values imposed by the Misses Wilcox superficial and even pernicious, the girls were yet unspoilt and eager, and I had to allow that in general subjects they were well tutored. I also had to own that my late husband would have been well pleased with my new situation, for here, more than anywhere, appearances were what counted.

CHAPTER TWENTY-FIVE

Emma woke. She could not breathe. She needed water. She cried out, yet no sound came. An overpowering smell made her choke – a smell of what? Of lye and something else – a sour reek of sickness, thick as fog. Gradually she became aware of the noise, which was akin to a malfunctioning factory. A constant uneven rasping, a fearful juddering as of a mechanism come to grief, a series of ill-matched whines. With difficulty she raised her head to take in the scene. She found herself in a long, darkened room with blue roof trusses embellished, in large red letters, with religious texts. 'God is Truth, God is Holy, God is Just,' she recited to herself. How had she known before she looked? She found herself in a narrow bed in two tightly packed rows of cots whose occupants either lay completely lifeless or struggled furiously, sometimes reaching wasted limbs into the air as if for pity. She knew now what the sound was. It was the chorus of infirmity.

Why is my mouth so dry, and yet my shift is wet with perspiration? she wondered. She slept again.

She dreamed she was in a garden with a fair woman who held out her arms. She was very little and was learning to walk. She laughed as she advanced step by step and the woman laughed too. When she awoke, her face was wet with tears. Yet still her mouth was too dry to cry out.

She began to distinguish the different sounds: the moans, the gasping breaths, the fevered ramblings and the continuous coughing of the wretched inmates. It seemed to pass around the room from one to another, now sharp and hoarse as a bark, then deep and hollow as lowing, or feeble and trembling as a bleat.

The mannish-looking woman in the next bed told her she had been sentenced to fourteen years' transportation in Van Diemen's Land for doing a bit of soft. 'You know what that is?'

She shook her head for still she could not speak. The speaker's narrative was interrupted by a cough that caused her whole frame to convulse. Then she feebly rubbed thumb against forefinger. 'Forgery! After I was sent out I once stole a cup of flour and was given fifty lashes. Any man would have died of it. Not me! I rubbed my back against the wall to open up the wounds. That showed 'em. No cough will carry me off.'

She slept. She woke. Some deft operation was taking place in the next bed. Its occupant was swiftly wound up in her own soiled sheets and carried off by two strong men. She is dead, Emma thought. So that is why I am here. I was brought here to die. No matter. One place is as good as another to die. She slept again.

She awoke. She imagined she heard music. 'Where am I?' she said distinctly. And then, finding that her tongue did not cleave to her parched palate and that it required a reward for this advance, she called loudly: 'Water! I want some water.'

'*Maith an cailín!* Good girl!' someone said.

253

She opened her eyes. She thought she must still be in a dream for there, playing the flute and clad in a hospital night-shift, was a diminutive and familiar figure.

'Arthur!' She sat up. 'Arthur Curran!' It was the eccentric Irishman she had met on the train. 'What are you doing here?'

Guardian angels, reader, come in all shapes and guises and may make their apparitions unaccounted, yet this one gave polite report.

'Bit of an oul' cough.' He thumped his narrow chest. 'I'll be right as rain. I was watching out for you. Do you realize, young lady, that you have been snatched from the jaws of death?'

A tall and soberly dressed gentleman entered the ward. With a stern admonition to Arthur to leave the women's ward and return to bed, he sat by Emma. 'Who are you?' she asked him.

'I am the doctor who snatched you from the jaws of death.' The individual handed her a glass of water and she gulped it thirstily. 'Although I do not claim all credit. You were no willing candidate for the great divide.'

'I thought I was,' said she.

'You should have died. Everyone expected you would. I have rarely seen a better fighter.'

'What of my friend, Mr Curran?'

'Being Irish, he imagines himself to be immortal. If he continues to resist rest, he will shortly discover otherwise.'

'It must be lonely for him so far from home,' she reflected.

'Not at all, for he has brought half his countrymen with him. There has been a great famine in Ireland. Those with the strength and resources sailed for other shores. Our workhouses are now crammed with Irish immigrants. Decent people, and grateful for what they are given.'

'How long have I been here?' she inquired.

'Eight weeks.'

'Can it be so long? I thought it but days. What month is it?'

'March.'

'Is it warmer, then?'

'The nights are cold yet. Where will you go? Have you relatives?'

A weary longing came over her to confide in this sympathetic person but her stubborn nature forbade it. 'I suppose that, like most people, I came equipped with mother and father,' she replied.

Thus, on a foggy March day she found herself – somewhat shakily – out on the street again. The doctor had given her a sixpence to purchase food. Now that she had a second chance she must employ her time and money efficiently. She made two purchases – a visitor's book with a folding map of the city with which to find her way and then a cup of coffee to fortify herself. Of her sixpence she now had twopence. Such wealth as remained could not be squandered solely on food. Yet when lunch-time came she found herself drawn once more to the heat and fragrance of a baked-potato stand. On this occasion, she made no appeal to the vendor but waited until a customer had paid his halfpenny and departed with his purchase and then – neither brazenly nor stealthily – she moved in his wake. After a time this well-dressed gentleman turned and asked her what she was doing.

'I am following you, sir.'

'And why are you?' he demanded.

'So that when the potato upon which you are warming your hands grows too cool to fulfil that purpose, I might have it.'

'The d––l, you will!' He walked on. She silently continued in pursuit. After another half-mile he said, 'It has served its purpose. Have it.' He tossed it and adroitly she caught it.

She was getting wise to the ways of the city, which must, she decided, be akin to the law of the jungle. Mere survival was a form of art that required cunning and vigilance and persistence.

The weather turned to wind and rain. She resolved to put her mind to seeking shelter for the day before the single set of clothing she possessed was destroyed. Her wonderful map denoted, among its other places of interest, the location of the city's churches and she was quickly able to find the nearest one. A grand-looking edifice, with ornate tower and fanciful interior, it was not the sort of place where a poor person might expect refuge but Emma had a better plan. She said a quick prayer for Arthur Curran, then went in search of the rectory.

This establishment reminded her of both a spider and its lair. Narrow black railings guarded a narrow grey residence, with a lattice of leggy black leading on its panes. A singularly underclothed tree showed a web of shuddering branches. Now, who might be the prince of this arachnid palace? A brass plate (not as bright as it ought to be) announced him to be the Reverend Clement Hibble. Boldly she pressed the bell. The noise sounded loudly on the outside, then sank into mournful interior depths. A man appeared, black in all but complexion. His grey face and taut mouth suggested that he was a martyr to the digestion. The sight of a small, cold girl on his doorstep brought no light to that countenance.

'Mr Hibble?' Emma pressed her ebbing courage into service.

He peered down at her but made no sign or gesture, having decided upon the economy of non-commitment.

'Do you have a housekeeper?' she asked.

'What business is it of yours?' said he. 'Indeed, what business, if any, has brought this interruption of my prayer?'

'Then employ me.' She assumed a negative in the absence of any positive response.

'I will not,' he objected. 'What would I do with you?'

'I am a sinner in need of salvation. You would save my soul, sir, which is your concern.'

'You are but a child,' he said.

'I am almost fifteen.' Having no clear knowledge of her years she picked an age likely to advance her employment prospects.

The man looked agitated now. 'The parish has provisions for such as you.'

'Provisions that also cater for every class of degenerate. It is well known that many young females are set upon the path to ruin by acquaintance with such persons.'

He looked around helplessly, as if for any passing member of the constabulary. 'Could you not, by your own efforts, resist temptation?'

'From what I know of my past, it would appear not. Please, sir, allow me in while we converse? I will set your fire and cook your dinner.'

Mr Hibble had recently parted with his housekeeper. This mishap was related in some measure to his reluctance to part with money (although there was another reason). The few females he had interviewed since proved even more mercenary and too old besides. In the meantime, he was having to make do with cold meals and cold fires. He told Emma she could have a slice of bread and butter if she made him a fire and dinner.

Thus she found herself in a house once more – a comfortless one to be sure, hung in every room with tracts concerning the two things most present on her mind – the transience of life and the stronghold of sin. She lit the fire, washed the dishes and searched for food. There was a chop in tolerable condition, the remains of a cold pudding, a piece of cheese. Some instinct told her to let no crumb pass her own lips as she fashioned a repast out of these.

The Reverend Hibble did not immediately sit to eat. Instead, with his customary pinched expression, he inspected the ingredients of his cupboard, carefully opening out each jar and dish and wrapping. Then he wordlessly scraped a shadow of butter on to a wedge of bread and gave her it.

She sat in the kitchen with her meal, he in the dining-room with his. Then he came and looked her over, head to toe, an unflattering critique.

'Shall I go now, sir?' she inquired.

'Out of charity only, I will give you a bed,' said he. 'You may deter Satan by cleaning the house from top to bottom.'

She took the precaution, before accepting this bounty, of reviewing the accommodation. There was a room that had belonged to the previous housekeeper, windowless and without a hearth, but clean and dry. She boldly asked if she might have working clothes to protect her own. He presented her with a dark bundle that had belonged to a large, fat woman. She requested scissors and sewing cotton to make them over.

She cooked and cleaned for him, she laundered and mended his garments, she prayed with him. Out of charity, he suffered her to remain.

She quickly discovered that he was not, as his appearance suggested, a martyr to his digestion. He dined well three times a day and suffered no ill-effects of it. He was a martyr to disapproval. Mr Hibble disapproved of everyone and everything. His grey eye blamed Emma if she cut too many slices of bread, upbraided her if she served too few. Quantities of coal for the fire could never be precisely right. He could find a chore for her at any hour of day or night. The only errand he did not assign to her was shopping. This he undertook himself on the basis that an excursion into the outer world might lead her to temptation. Mr Hibble considered himself an expert on temptation. Whenever Emma undertook some passive task he gave her a lecture on the subject. He informed her that all women were weak, whereas men were divided into two distinct categories: those who would lead women into temptation and those who would save them from it.

Emma believed that Mr Hibble's real purpose in undertaking his own purchasing was to make sure that no money was wasted or stolen and to guarantee that she never had a moment's free time from the house or any other company. Her days passed drearily. There were no visitors, no pleasant company and nothing to read except the most pessimistic pamphlets. He permitted her to walk with him to church on Sunday but immediately put her into the care of a virtuous widow called Mrs Vaughan — a black-clad female of such daunting devotion that prayer leaked from her dry lips in permanent pious incontinence. Only once did she address her charge, to boast that her late husband's family could be traced in a clear line back to the medieval Christian, Mrs Abigail Vaughan, who had left in her will four shillings a year to the Church for the burning of heretics.

Sometimes, peering out of the narrow window, which showed a well-bred avenue cast in mute respectability, she was amazed to think that but a short walk away was all the naked, despairing and colourful humanity of those who made their living by the streets. Although they had no shoes to put upon their feet or bread to put into their mouths, richer by far were they in mind and spirit than this dry bachelor who appeared in every way more God's clerk than cleric. However, there was a certain interest in his discourse. He had made himself a specialist on the infection of sin. It was his contention that the drunkards, the pickpockets, the fallen women, each congregated in specific parts of the city and formed contagious pockets that would gradually spread to corrupt the whole of the population.

On one of the Sundays, Emma was interested to discover that a lecture he had delivered to her as she darned his cassock was now polished for a public outing. She almost took some pride in him for he displayed more fire than she had ever seen in his meagre hearth. His topic today was fallen women. He named particular addresses. He beat his fists on the pulpit as he renounced them for the rotting sores that would eventually make a vast metropolitan chancre. At one point the holy widow at Emma's side gave a sharp intake of breath. She looked about in dismay and then her acid eye fell on her charge. 'I have never seen the Reverend thus!' she uttered. 'He must have come under some excitable influence.'

The Reverend, meanwhile, was sending out a small spray of vehemence as he thundered that no man, under peril of his soul, no matter how urgent his business, must ever set foot in these districts.

A month had passed. As she walked back with Mr Hibble in a blustery April shower, she felt strong and well, having been kept from the weather and regularly fed. In spite of the rain there was a breath of spring in the air and she was as eager as any healthy young animal to be out in it. She was also impatient to resume that express purpose for which she had found herself in the city. Moreover, she now had some useful information from the very last person who might have been expected to supply it.

After she had served him a very good dinner of a roast and apple dumpling (keeping only the most meagre portion for herself, and no pudding) she meekly asked to address him. First she congratulated him on his sermon and thanked him kindly for his protection.

'It was my duty,' he said sourly, and looked at her inquiringly for his coffee.

'I hope I have done mine, sir,' she said.

'Tolerably,' he conceded.

'Yet my position in the house is uncertain,' she persisted.

'I think I have made it very clear.'

'No, sir. If I am your housekeeper, then I ought to have pay for it, and some free time as every servant has.'

'You are not my housekeeper,' he snapped. 'Pray do not give yourself airs. I have no need of a housekeeper.'

'If I am not your housekeeper . . .' She paused and allowed her eyes modestly to inspect the rug.

'Well?'

'Forgive me, sir, but there are wicked people who might speak ill of me for taking residence in the house of a man without a wife.'

'I doubt anyone would waste their time on such speculation,' he declared. 'You are not remarkable.'

'Indeed not, sir. For myself, I care nothing, yet . . .' She risked raising her gaze to take stock of his expression. 'Your own reputation ought not to be subject to the slightest suspicion.'

Some very peculiar shades were animating that drab countenance: first a vermilion outrage at her impertinence, but even as he opened his mouth to denounce her, this was eclipsed by a pale moon of dismay. His open mouth remained unhinged. He looked at Emma. The small, unimposing figure assumed the aspect of a Scheherazade. A dazed panic entered his eye.

'I can see, sir, that I ought to leave.'

He closed his eyes, but even still seemed to observe her departure.

'Wait! I have not dismissed you!'

'I did not wish to interrupt your thoughts,' she said.

'I was not *thinking*!' he indignantly protested. 'I was praying.' (He infused this verb with such passionate tremolo that it sounded more akin to the vocalization of a donkey than of saints.) 'God has granted me an answer.'

'Then I thank you both,' Emma said. 'I would be content with a very modest wage and one afternoon a week off.'

The Reverend Clement Hibble scowled. 'It is not what God proposes.'

'In that case I must take my leave.'

Mr Hibble went to the door. His hands fidgeted and trembled slightly. He shut the door – a move that would have seemed perfectly harmless except that he was still on the inside of that portal, and now he locked it. Emma was very much alarmed. 'If you do not mean to offer me a position, I wish to leave. Please, sir, open the door and let me pass.'

A moment went by in which he did nothing except blink, presumably to free his eyes of the beads of perspiration that gathered on his forehead. 'Sit, Emma. I wish to talk to you. Do not be frightened. I speak with the voice of God.'

She sat. He cautiously appropriated a sofa – a good way off, she was relieved to note. 'You are a plain woman and a good plain worker,' he said.

'Correct in every respect,' she accepted; 'except that I am not quite a woman.'

'You are fifteen,' he said. 'In a year you will be sixteen.'

'That stands to reason,' she agreed.

'A plain, unambitious woman such as you would make a good wife for a clergyman. You are useful and unassuming. You would be neither a distraction to myself nor diverted from your own duties by vanity.'

'When the time comes, I should have no objection to marrying a vicar, were he agreeable to me in his worldly aspect. Yet that is yet too far in the future to contemplate.'

'I do not see why.' He crept round and came to perch on a closer chair. 'Why not decide now upon the course of your life? All your fears will be allayed at once. Your future will be secure and you will have cast Satan from your path for once and all.'

'I will tell you why, sir! Because I do not have any man in mind whom I wish to marry.'

He snatched another chair that had a greater proximity yet. Emma experienced a desire to jump up and run – yet there was nowhere to run. 'You have not understood. In my goodness and mercy I am offering you my very self.'

That gaunt face, which seemed but inches from her own, showed none of the softening of sentiment. She saw the cold light of tyranny in his eyes. 'I do not want it, sir,' she said.

'What?' he said. 'You think yourself too good for me?'

'I believe, rather, that the reverse is true. It is you, sir, who consider yourself too good for me. From the first moment I entered your house, you have shown neither kindness nor approval. We have shared no companionship. You did not ask a single question unconnected to my work in the house. I think, sir, that you do not seek a wife. Rather, you hope to retain the services of a housekeeper without pay.'

It was a measure, she felt, of the man's coldness that he made no effort even to rebuff her claim.

'You are young,' he said; 'yes, too young, perhaps, to realize that the services of a wife are more than those of housekeeper. Yet I have never known a wife to charge for them.'

It took her a moment or two to absorb the full significance of what he had said. 'You do not even like me, sir, nor I you. Can you not just give me a small portion of money for the work I have done and let me go?'

His doleful face with its consistency of wet plaster seemed so singularly lacking in any sort of passion that she thought perhaps it was he who misunderstood what he had just implied. 'No, child, I cannot,' he said. 'You have the taint of sin on you. I fear it has already infected my soul.'

Looking at his long, clamping hand with black hairs on it, as it came to rest upon her knee, Emma was reminded, as when she had first sighted Mr Hibble's house, of a spider. Horrified, she batted that limb away. 'I have done nothing. If there is any wickedness, it is in you.'

He eyed her with lugubrious reproach, then fell heavily to his knees and loudly prayed to God to have pity on a hapless degenerate. Emma had no doubt that it was for her he prayed. Once again his pious cacophony evoked speedy response. He stood up and fussily pulled at his breeches before being seated again. 'For the preservation of both our souls, we shall be married tomorrow by myself,' he declared. 'This will be done with no publicity. For general purposes, I shall announce that you are now hired as my housekeeper. In a year or two – sooner if events render it necessary – I will make it known that you are my wife.'

'You may make away with me first,' she said. 'I would not marry you if an angel appeared in person and demanded it of me.'

'Were you either wife or servant,' he said, 'I would beat you for such insolence. As you are only a poor wretched sinner committed to my care, I shall keep you safe until you have taken to your heart God's calling.' He essayed a self-conscious expression of compassion before quitting the room and locking the door behind him.

'Now I know why you had no housekeeper,' Emma shouted angrily through that partition. 'Other poor women have heard the same speech.' There was a silence outside. He had obviously gone away to sulk. I wonder, thought she; did they exit by the door or – as I shall – by the window?

Relieved of his oppressive presence, she felt quite calm. Although the door was locked she was in a chamber on the ground floor. Aside from a regret that her best dress was in the deal drawers in her attic room her only real apprehension was of being once more homeless and penniless.

First (and with no qualm of conscience) she searched the room to see if there was any money she could take. For a month's hard labour, she was owed whatever she could find. It came as no surprise that the Reverend Clement Hibble did not leave his cash where others might find it. Nevertheless, in a drawer of his desk, she came upon a box with a five-shilling coin and a written message: 'For coal.' She took this and put it away.

Three months ago, she thought, that hypocritical tyrant would have filled me with terror. Now I feel only – what? Pity? Abhorrence? Both – yet some understanding too. I am finding out that what causes most unhappiness in the world is a refusal to acknowledge what one is. Having made this philosophic pronouncement she was dismayed to realize that she herself might be guilty of the charge. From the same desk where she had perpetrated the larceny, she removed a quantity of writing paper, then dipped Mr Hibble's pen into the wet, tenebrous depths of its well. She would do at once what she had intended to do from the very first day of her arrival in London. She would write out all she knew of her history and submit it to whom it concerned.

CHAPTER TWENTY-SIX

I had not been at Fuchsia Lodge a month when one of the pupils asked to speak with me privately. This very singular young maid – my star pupil in all but needlework, which did not interest her – bore a name that suited her valiant nature.

'I wished to inquire about a former pupil, Miss Matilda Fitzgibbon,' Diana said. 'Miss Wilcox will not speak of her. I know she went to stay with you.'

I gave the girl a brief summary of the facts. 'That is all I know, yet I, too, am anxious for information. Can you add anything?'

'No, nothing.' Diana looked thoughtful. 'I spoke with her, you know, the day before she left here. Until then I had deemed her a snobbish and unmannerly girl, yet alone I found her sensitive and sad. I should have liked to be acquainted with her. I know what the Misses Wilcox say about her, yet I believe her to be good.'

I have always trusted the instincts of children more than adults in matters of character and so pleased was I by Diana's judgement that I threw my arms around the surprised school-girl. 'I believe it too. Tell me anything else you remember.'

'When the other girls confronted her about her aloofness, she spoke of having . . . a past. That was the phrase she used. And yet the thing that struck me most was that she seemed so singularly without a past.'

Clever girl, I thought.

Diana went on: 'There is just one other thing. It can scarcely be significant.'

'Tell me anyway.'

'When Matilda first arrived she had a ring. I might have for-gotten this but afterwards I noted a pale circle on one of her fingers. In moments of particular anxiety, she would rub that spot with thumb and forefinger. It struck me as odd that so ornate a person would choose not to wear her single piece of jewellery.'

'Yes. That is odd,' I agreed. 'Indeed, it is strange that one so well supplied with finery would not have had other baubles to augment it.'

Before returning to her class Diana impulsively returned the gesture I had so importunately bestowed. 'Mrs Chalfont,' said she, 'I am glad you are here. We all are. Now we are no longer at the sole mercy of the Misses Wilcox and their notions of proper female behaviour.'

'The Misses Wilcox are your mistresses,' I reminded her; 'and dedicated and skilled ones.'

'Yes, I know, and I ought not to have spoken so, yet I cannot like them and nor, I am sure, can you.'

No. I could not like the Misses Wilcox. Yet a four-week into their acquaintance I esteemed them as more than colour-ful birds of prey. They were women – young and good-looking still – who had striven hard to win their place at the banquet of feminine pleasures only to have it snatched from under their noses and replaced by the bare bones, the bread-and-water soup of mere survival. They were not admirable, yet they contrived not to be pathetic. If they had shed that part of their nature that connects to the affections, they had kept their pride.

A season past, if their school had closed down, I would have said, 'Good! No child should be in such a place.' Had they ended penniless and at the mercy of the parish, I should have thought, Now you know how Matilda Fitzgibbon felt! See how you like the fate you prescribed for her.

What would have become of Emma had she remained at Fuchsia Lodge? I expect the sisters would have sent for Mr Cecil. He might have found some kindly but functional disposal for the girl – caring for young children in a household, perhaps. Very likely both the Wilcox sisters and Mr Cecil would have been altogether more practical and useful than myself.

So if I had not acquired a sympathy for the Misses Wilcox, I had attained a shadow of that sibling virtue, compassion. I wished them success in their venture and meant, in any practical manner I could, to assist that end.

The first thing I did was to inquire about the trinket Diana mentioned. 'Do you remember if Matilda Fitzgibbon wore a ring when first she came here?'

'Mrs Chalfont!' Miss Mabel's breast puffed up in indignation. 'You are surely not accusing us . . . !'

'Indeed not!' I assured her. 'Rings are lost all the time – especially those worn by children.'

'Yes, I remember. She did have a ring,' Miss Lucy supplied. 'There was nothing special to it. It was a commonplace little gold token. She took it off shortly after she arrived. When first she came I remember seeing her sitting in a corner, just staring at it in that abject way she had. To make conversation

I asked her about it, but she merely said it was of no value and she did not remember where it had come from. After that I never saw it again.'

'Did it have an engraving?' I asked.

Miss Lucy frowned. 'I believe it had. Yes, I asked her about it. She responded in her usual insipid manner. She said it had no meaning.'

'Was there a name – or any initials?' I tried to suppress my eagerness.

'No name. It was a sentimental inscription.' She shook her head. 'I can't quite recall. "Two hearts as one" – something of that nature.'

'No initial? Are you sure of it?'

'Yes, quite sure, Mrs Chalfont. At the time we were making great efforts to draw the child out. I would have welcomed an opportunity to add some personnel to her file.'

As the precious indicator faded from significance, I rewarded the sisters' co-operation by applying myself to the success of their academy. Now, three is not a good figure for a roll-call. It draws too much focus on both pupil and teacher. It causes parents to doubt the fertility of this garden of the intellect. It shrinks the profits to a point where bad food and poor heating are the lot of inmates one and all. So, my first objective was to boost the numbers of pupils in attendance.

'By what manner?' The sisters looked bleak and dismal. 'We have not the money to advertise.'

'I have a plan,' I said. 'Parts of it may not appeal, but endeavour to digest the whole before forming an opinion. It seems to me that the first requisite for the success of a school is academic excellence.'

This modest and obvious suggestion provoked a babble of protest. Had they not striven for such? Were they not in themselves examples of it? Their own student achievements were trotted out as *indicia* of their talents &c. 'But how, dear Mrs Chalfont, with only three pupils – two with average application and one very clever – could we achieve what you propose?'

'By attracting to the school more students of exceptional ability.'

A collective and exasperated wail arose. 'How?'

'Quite simply! By offering scholarships.'

I had appealed for patience. I had not quite anticipated it. A fresh bout of objection ensued. 'Give away places? Why, Mrs Chalfont, are you quite mad? You are suggesting that we should take in children and not charge them? Are you attempting to bring us to ruin?'

'*You* will not charge them, yet naturally the fees will be paid.'

'By whom?'

'By myself.'

They looked almost disappointed to see their arguments so thoroughly demolished. 'And how are we to set about attracting these model pupils?' Miss Mabel somehow managed to step above my proposal. 'We could not take in just any intelligent young person.'

'Naturally not!' I managed to conceal my amusement. 'No ragamuffins or hooligans! I had envisaged Mr Cecil as referee. He is in a position to know the circumstances of families in his parish. There must be some with clever daughters whom they cannot afford to educate as they would wish.'

'The term is already half-way through.' Miss Adelaide turned my suggestion over to check the hallmark.

'How many new pupils had you in mind?' Miss Lucy more sensibly counted the knives and forks in the set.

'Three,' I said. 'Six is a far rounder number than three and might even show a little profit in the figures.'

They could not quite be glad of the offer, yet agreed to consider it. When next I came to take a class they presented themselves as a united front and declared that they would consent to my proposal on two conditions: the first, that my offer would be considered only in the nature of a loan, and if profits ensued, all monies would be returned to me. I agreed to this, so long as it cost them no hardship. The second stipulation was not so simple: they would give places to my scholarship girls *if*, and only if, I could also attract the daughter of some titled person to the school. I was amused that they had contrived to interpret my benevolence as a scheme advantageous to myself, which must be countered by reciprocal compensation.

Cash is always at a higher premium than brains in the fair sex, in consequence of which there tends to be a surfeit of the latter. The three gifted girls were swiftly selected. Now the game of hunt-the-duchess began. I enlisted Mr Ellin's help.

'I am in touch with some titled families and they have daughters,' he said. 'I would like to help, but why should they hand their cherished she-cubs over to the Misses Wilcox?'

I thought very hard. 'We must put on the table some dainty morsel irresistible to this pedigree pup,' I concluded.

'Such as?'

'A Spanish dancing master! An Italian singing master – one with oiled hair and narrow hips and polished patent shoes! If at all possible, we should add a name that touches some romantic core in the heart of Mama.'

'He sounds a scoundrel.' Mr Ellin laughed.

'Exactly what a baby duchess craves! Do you know any such scoundrels?'

'Since you mention it, I had heard that Signor Enrico Moffo, the tenor, was giving private lessons. He is everything, I think, that you could wish. He is dissolute, polished, and his looks have survived better than his career. He is, perhaps, a little overweight but we might persuade him into a corset.'

'Capital!' I cried. 'I shall apply to him at once.'

Four new pupils and a singing master soon enhanced the numbers at Fuchsia Lodge. The three scholarship girls were fine, serious young persons and I had great pleasure in helping to shape their minds. The little heiress (a real heiress on this occasion) was a good-natured, excitable, foolish little woman, plump and rather plain but decorated to a high degree. Her simpering manners, her girlish cries and capers, her thin soprano voice brought to the sisters a degree of pleasure bested only by the weekly appearance of Signor Moffo. All their finer (maternal) feelings and all their less fine ones were brought to bear upon her and she rewarded their partiality. She smiled and curtsied, she held forth about her family's estate, her future travels, her fortune. She displayed her modest accomplishments to all and any who would suffer them. This was happiness enough. Yet her presence brought them more than the spontaneous prize.

While the good, intelligent scholarship girls applied themselves diligently to their studies (an application that would take a year or more to bear practical fruit) Lady Millie passed the homework hour in writing letters to her family and friends – letters that glowed with accounts of her new surroundings, the particular attention she received, and, above all, the beautiful, superlative singing master who had improved her voice to the point of professionalism. One of these letters resulted in its recipient – another young lady of title – flinging herself into such an unseemly frenzy of envy that her parents hastily removed her from her current site of learning and consigned her to Fuchsia Lodge.

It takes a long time to attain the wisdom of the world. I had considered myself a tolerable scholar yet was a novice compared to the teaching three. Intellect does attract intellect, but this may be a slow and subtle process. Money invariably (and swiftly) summons its like. They now had two little ladies — undoubtedly the duds of their distinguished families — yet these were the solid bricks on which to build a prestigious and profitable academy.

I owed a point to the Wilcox sisters. They knew a little more than I, but I was indebted further. I now had an interest and fulfilment in my life. I would never end my search for Emma, yet if she was not to be found, at least I had something else to sustain me. The desolation that had bound me was blown away. I went home to enjoy an hour of gardening in the clement spring weather before preparing my next lesson. As I came into the house I saw that there was a letter for me, presumably from one of my sisters. I did not pick it up at once, but called the maid for tea and went to change my clothes.

When I gave my attention to the post I saw that it was not the familiar hand I had anticipated. A fine hand it was, but measured — a child's hand yet well formed. My heart began to beat a little too fast as I saw the name signed to the end.

A note of hope sounded inside me with a clear peal like a bell. Emma! The writing paper was good. There was an address on it. She had clearly found some sheltering harbour. These rational thoughts passed through my mind in a fraction of a second and all the while my less lucid emotional brain was singing: 'Emma is safe!'

I settled by the fire. I poured my tea. I addressed myself to my correspondence. What travels had my half-adopted child to tell? What gossip to relate? As my eyes raced over the page both my tea and myself grew chill. The story she told I cannot repeat. I have not her courage. Here — you shall read it yourself.

CHAPTER TWENTY-SEVEN

I am Emma. It was you, dear Mrs Chalfont, who helped me find this blameless fragment of myself. The rest I must discover for myself.

Everything I know of affection in this world comes from you. I wrap it around me still for warmth, although I may have worn it out. After all your kindness I took your money and left with no word. It must have grieved you and it grieved me too. I had my reasons. I am gone in search of my mother. To do so in your company might be to suffer your rejection and even dislike. I have decided, instead, to commit what I remember to paper and let you read it if you will, and make your judgement in my absence.

Hitherto, you treated me as a tender child. Hereafter, you may choose to view me as something less innocent. As such, you will accept that I can make my own way in life. What course this life may take I do not know, but I have the doubtful advantage of having sunk to depths so low that there can be no lower. I bear the positive advantage of having known the blessing of a true home. Whatever bleak quarters I may henceforth inhabit will be warmed by thoughts of 'my' room.

I begin with my first memory. As the bulk of that commodity has been mislaid, this takes place about six months ago. My initial awareness was of a very dirty room, squalid, dark and cold, which contained the necessities of life, but no comforts. There was a table, chairs with clothes heaped upon them, stove, cupboard and a large bed with myself in it, kept warm by a variety of rags. I became conscious of a foul smell of alcohol and everything that is the opposite of cleanliness, and that this essence came, in part, from a face that was held quite close to mine.

Between it and me, causing sufficient hazard to restore me to life by alerting me to its dangers, was a taper of flame. It was a candle, held hazardously near as if with a wish to burn me, although it was probably to register the strength of my breathing. Its other effect was to cast into startling relief the features of she who held it.

It would be difficult to imagine a less wholesome human countenance. At first I thought her a crone. Her face was a ruin of dirty red skin and wrinkles. Her hair was a ball of bracken, and those few teeth that remained, drab stumps from a bog.

'Who are you?' I inquired.

She answered with another question. 'Who would have sat by your bed while you dallied between life and death? Who would have warmed you with her own body when you were cold as a corpse and soothed you with wet cloths when you burned like Lucifer?'

'My mother?' I said. 'But . . .'

'But? Ain't I good enough for you?' Her eyes were not lit from within as most eyes are. Those brackish pools seemed to borrow their dull gleam from an outward vision of disillusion.

But she was too old for my mother. I gradually perceived that that ravaged countenance had overgrown features not yet middle-aged. Her body and face seemed to have gone through several lifetimes in the space of less than fifty years.

275

'Where am I?' I said then.

'In the bed where I bore you, and where you have dawdled long enough,' was her curt reply. This bed was but a pile of dirty rags and I pitied her.

'Where is my father?' I said.

'Dead and gone to hell, as you well know,' was her strange reply.

I cast about in my brain for what I ought to know but that organ was a jumble of ill-focused pictures, which caused my head to spin and occasioned such pain as made me clutch my head and cry out.

'You're not right in the head,' my mother said. 'You've been ill. You've had the fever.'

Close to death I must have been, for when I returned to the world I could remember nothing. I thought I must have shed my nature in my sleep along with memory for I could find no comfort in the presence of my mother, only a sense of puzzlement and chill. I looked around the room again for some clue. To my disconcertion I saw that one of the piles of clothing perched on a chair was a girl. She sat so inanimate that she could scarcely be identified as a living being. Her dress was ornate but bedraggled and I thought she must be cold in it for she looked very down at heart.

'Are you my sister?' I asked her, for she was of an age with me, perhaps a year my senior, and I thought she might be easier to talk to. The girl turned to me but her face was desolate and she did not speak.

'She is nothing to do with you,' my mother said. 'She's here to work. Now, get up, you lazy wretch. You have been a trouble to me and a great expense, loafing about in bed these past months. Get yourself washed and dressed. I have a job for you to do.'

My first attempt at following her injunction landed me in a heap on the floor for I was still weak and my legs would not support me. After several attempts I made an effort to don the begrimed garments she handed me. These items also had a weary festivity but would have welcomed an introduction to soap and water. While I was at my *toilette* there was a knock on the door and a man came in. I was shocked, because I was not yet fully dressed. He did not trouble to look away but stared at me in a very insolent fashion.

'Not her! The other one,' my mother said. I noted that the girl, who had been seated quite still and mute, began to tremble. My mother handed the man a bottle of some colourless substance and a cloth folded over. 'She's young. Give her this,' she said.

The man took her by the arm and led her from the room into another chamber. As she left she looked back at me and her gaze was like a scouring of the world for pity. I wished someone would smile at her or say something to put her at her ease.

My mother told me to wash and directed me to a dirty bowl of water behind which was propped a cracked and clouded glass. In this I made unrewarding acquaintance with my physical self. Who am I? I wondered, as I smeared the chill water over my face. How can my mother dislike me so? I could only assume (and this proved to be the case) that I had done something to earn her displeasure.

While I was thus engaged there issued from the next room a cry such as almost made my hair stand on end. It was but a faint sound, yet high and hopeless, the last cry of an animal caught in a trap.

'The girl!' I said. 'Something has happened to her.'

My mother looked angry (she seldom looked otherwise) but she made no move. 'D— cur,' she said. 'He did not use the chloroform.'

'What is chloroform?' I inquired.

She replied that it was a new wonder of the medical profession, and added with a sour cackle,' 'They could cut your leg off and you would not notice.'

'What? Is he a surgeon?' I asked.

277

'That's it,' she said. 'But it's all over. Now stop your gabbing and try to look pleasant. There is a gentleman has a job for you.'

By and by the girl and the man returned to the room. The girl trembled more than ever. By an effort she resumed her chair.

Some exchange took place between the man and my mother and she told him he was a heartless brute. 'She's only young. Why couldn't you have used the stuff like I told you?'

The man glanced contemptuously at the patient. 'If I'd wanted a corpse I'd have made one, and there's none would have touched me for ridding the world of the likes of her.'

I went to her and asked if she was cold. For answer she wrapped her arms around her shoulders and rocked herself.

Scarcely had one visitor left than another entered our stately surroundings. This was a man whom nature had created handsome and severity had made fearsome. Scorn competed with aversion in the look he cast around the room and its inhabitants. 'Eliza Brown?' he addressed my mother and then: 'Which one?' with a haughty glance from one convalescent girl to another.

'That's her.' My mother indicated me. 'She's not much but she'll give no trouble.'

'What age is she?'

'She's fourteen,' my mother said.

'She looks younger.'

He walked around me, looking as if he might poke at me with his stick. 'Is she ill? She looks ill.'

'She enjoys the very rudest of health.' My mother sidled to a closet. I saw her furtively withdraw a bottle and tilt it to her lips.

'She'll do.' The man's acceptance seemed overlaid with his distaste. 'How much?'

'She knows some tricks.' My mother wiped her mouth as she returned to our company. 'She's worth a guinea.'

He proffered the money without any argument. 'I'd need a note confirming this agreement.'

278

'You jest, sir,' my mother said, although neither party appeared inclined to humour. 'Put it on paper? Why, this is just a little family matter, not commerce. In any case, I cannot read or write.'

'Can the child read or write?' he queried.

The question seemed to give her reason for pause. 'What's it to you?' she said then. 'You won't be aiming to teach her her letters.'

'Has she brothers or sisters to say goodbye to?'

With a very servile smirk my mother told him that she had not been blessed with further issue.

'Can you part so easily with your one and only?' he asked.

'You're a nosy one,' she said. 'What care you if a widow's old heart is breaking?'

'Pack her things.' The man spoke tersely. 'I shall take her with me.'

Throughout this exchange no one had thought to offer a word or glance to me. The dispirited girl in the lace dress in due course got up from her chair and went to lie on the bed I had recently quitted and cried very quietly. She, at least, could remain in this relative haven. I was to leave my home with a stranger. In spite of my trepidation I was forced to speak. 'Am I to work for you, sir?'

The gentleman cast a questioning look at my mother. 'What have you told her?'

'Will no one speak to me?' I asked again. 'What position am I to fill?'

Something in the looks that passed between them told me that this was to be no ordinary transaction. I glanced from one to the other and saw the conspiracy harden between them. When the man came to claim me I was very much afraid. Having no other means to defend myself I began to scream. The girl in the bed opened her eyes and looked interested.

'You can keep her,' the man said. 'I shall find another. I will have my guinea back.'

My mother appeared greatly disconcerted by this suggestion. 'Leave us a moment, sir,' she appealed. 'Let us make our farewells in private. I can assure you all will be well.'

He stormed out of the room and I did not know if he meant to return or not. At first I prayed that he would not and then when I saw how my mother looked at me and seemed to hate me, I did not know what to hope for. 'Do not think to find mercy under this roof. You have already put yourself beyond any,' she said.

'What have I done?' I begged.

'You brought shame on a decent household. If your father were alive, he would have thrown you out to starve. As it was, your antics killed him and left me a poor helpless widow.'

She proceeded to put words to what I had done. The deeds – nay, even the language – made no clear sense to me. Yet I knew in my heart that I did not feel as a young girl should. I had a burned and wasted sensation, which could not come from fever alone, of having used up all that was worthwhile in life. I wept bitter tears of shame and remorse for whatever I had done. I clung to my mother and implored her forgiveness. 'However wicked I have been, it is all in the past now.'

'You suddenly find yourself too good to do what is nearly every woman's duty. It's a pity you encountered virtue so late. I would not have this fate for any other daughter but you have already made your bed, and none too fussily.'

'Will you not permit me to repent and make my life anew?' I entreated her.

For a response my mother slapped my face. 'There is only one future for you now. You should thank me that I am handing you over to a gentleman and not some drunken brute.'

I broke free from her and ran to the girl in the bed. 'Can you help me? I am very afraid. I do not know what is to become of me.'

The girl lifted her listless face from the filthy pillow. 'Go, you stupid thing,' said she. 'It would be better to be anywhere than here.'

In a dismal trance I went with the stranger. In the carriage he sat as far away from me as possible and kept a window open, despite the cold. I felt myself to be as little to his taste as a diseased mongrel. In due course I worked up the courage to tell him I was hungry. He asked me when I had last eaten and I told him I did not know as I had been ill and unconscious. 'You will eat soon,' he said, and his anger seemed to soften.

I remarked on some poor girls out in the cold and was surprised to detect pity in his response. 'Please, sir.' I tried to take advantage of his lenient mood. 'Where are we?'

He looked upon me strangely. 'Why, in London, of course.'

'Won't you tell me where we are going and why?'

'It is better if you ask no more questions.' He put a rug around my shoulders and told me to try to sleep. In spite of the discomfort of the journey and my general unease, I did.

When I awoke it was to find myself in a very large and grand room and in the arms of a servant who had carried me in. The gentleman was nowhere to be seen. The maid gave me food, after which, without ceremony, she stripped off my clothes and pitched me into a waiting bath. 'What a stink!' she said. 'Don't you never wash?' I was indignant at being thus addressed but could say nothing as my own nose affirmed her accusation. As soon as she had washed me she grew kind. 'Poor little mite,' she said. 'You're thin as a string and your hair looks as if cut in the workhouse.'

As she seemed compassionate I sought a confederate. 'Why am I here?' I said. 'Will you tell me?'

'I can't,' said she. 'Sir has told me not to speak of your visit but what could I say when I know nothing? I can tell you, he's a strange one. He has some pretty peculiar notions for a gentleman.

And what of you?' She wrapped me in a warm towel in kindly fashion. 'I wonder what of your short history?'

She appeared a pleasant and motherly woman and I had an urgent need to rid my head of the hellish images my mother had deposited there. 'May I confide in you?'

'Of course you can. Everyone does.'

I told her what my mother had said and asked if she knew its meaning. Her manner towards me changed distinctly. 'Is it true, what your mother says?'

'I am confused, but it must be. Why else would she have cast me from my home and made me go off with a stranger?'

'Dirty girl!' the maid said, in disgust. 'I did not come to work in a good house to serve such as you.' She turned to leave the room.

'Please don't go!' I appealed. 'Please stay and talk to me.'

'What should I say to the likes of you?'

'Tell me what my mother meant?' I pleaded.

'Aren't you afraid to hear? Any nice girl would be.'

I was very afraid. Yet the thing that frightened me most was my own lack of comprehension. 'Tell me,' I commanded, with as much authority as I could muster.

I cannot but believe that the narrative which followed was influenced by bitterness and spite. She spoke in the manner of a penny novelette. She established a distinct set of characters and related in detail the downfall of each one and their eventual end, through disease and corruption, in dreadful but well-merited death. Bizarre and sensational though it undoubtedly was, I could no longer doubt its meaning.

'There. Now you know.' The maid seemed exhausted by her outburst. 'You knew already, didn't you? Any other young girl would have covered her ears and run from the room.'

With these words she dropped a clean white woman's nightgown over my head and pushed me into a clean bed. This seemed to me the only clemency life had to offer and I tried to keep misery at bay for an hour or two by pretending that I was in a proper home and would wake among people who cared for me.

When I did stir, it was to find another gentleman – one whom I had not seen before – standing by my bed, gazing down at me. He said he was a surgeon and urged me not to be afraid. His look seemed to penetrate me and I was petrified with fear, thinking of what the maid had said. I tried to bid him good night but my lips trembled and no word came. Once more he tried to reassure me. Yet the whole human race wore a different face since my recent education and I knew he intended me grievous harm. When he approached a step closer I fainted clean away.

Later I half woke to hear a murmured conversation. '. . . she will have to be weaned off it gradually. And she has had pneumonia. She should not be moved for some time. Otherwise, all is well.' When I opened my eyes I saw the surgeon in conversation with my purchaser.

I encountered my buyer again in the morning after breakfast. I was still dressed in the outsized nightgown belonging to the servant, having no other apparel except the rags in which I had arrived. I was in a large room, which had a dining-table and chairs, but also armchairs and shelves lined with many books. The apartment was untidy but not unclean and I approved of it. My buyer submitted his commodity to his usual inspection. This time I managed to withstand his unflattering scrutiny. 'You are not a beauty,' he declared at length.

'No, sir,' I agreed. I felt he was already regretting the loss of his guinea.

'Neither nature nor fate has favoured you.'

'I think not,' I agreed.

He gave a mighty sigh and then he said, 'There are many such as you,' as though I might not bother to give myself airs.

He asked my name and I said I could not remember. Once more, and in silence, he sized me up. 'Matilda,' he said. 'Does that sound familiar?' The name evoked some chord of memory – but a distant one – and I said that it would do. He asked me what size I was and I said I did not rightly know. 'I wonder what you do know,' he muttered, and he withdrew.

Later the maid came and measured me with a tape. She did so in a fastidious silence as though loath to make contact with me. When she went away I felt bereft. I was left alone in that large book-lined room, no wiser since yesterday, except as to the depths of human perversion. Having nothing to do and no one to talk to I picked a volume from a shelf. To my surprise and pleasure the symbols on the page became words and the words had meaning. For the rest of the morning I buried myself in the tale of Frankenstein by Mary Shelley.

At lunchtime the gentleman appeared in the doorway. He again bestowed his disconcerting gaze upon me. 'You can read,' said he.

'Yes, sir.'

'Can you also write?'

'I have not recently tried,' I confessed.

'Write this!' He handed me a piece of paper and a pen and recited a verse of poetry. It was an odd sensation hearing it, for it seemed to live in my mind already. I found that I could write ahead of his recitation.

The gentleman's beetling brow was so close upon my page that I could feel his breath and could not help my hand shaking. This, or something else, seemed to anger him further and he paced the room muttering about iniquity.

'Am I iniquitous, sir?' I said. Yet again I got the benefit of his close study. I was becoming used to it by now and trembled only a little.

'I think not,' he said. 'Pray do not think *me* so.'

He quitted the room and I was once more left alone. After a while I heard him leave the house. Perhaps my own wickedness might be measured by the fact that I regretted his departure. All that I knew of civilized exchange in the world (albeit abrupt) came from him. I wept bitterly. The maid came and administered some drops in water. I asked what they were but she only said the master had instructed her to dose me.

Day followed on long and empty day. There was plentiful food, which I could not enjoy for the pains in my stomach. I was possessed of a terrible restlessness and a craving for something, I knew not what. By day I paced the rooms and begged the maid to let me out but she would not. By night I talked and walked in my sleep. The only ease came when the maid gave me my 'medicine'. By now I knew it for an opiate, but I did not care as I hungered for it. Eventually the maid found me some plain clothes to wear and permitted me to patrol the garden but the gate was kept locked at all times. Gradually I regained some calm but I was very miserable. My only company was the servant, who considered me too wicked to speak to. I thought I must be the lowest creature that ever lived for there was no way in which I could please anyone. My sole comfort came from the books in the house and I buried myself in them as determinedly as any despised creature who makes a refuge in mud or sand or straw.

It seemed an eternity before the householder returned, but gauging it now I would deem it to be about a month. He had altered in that space. Whereas he had departed with a modest valise he returned with that same piece of luggage, plus a good-sized trunk. Whereas he had hitherto seemed a disapproving and unemotional statue, he was now in a mood of excitement. He came to see me at once and deposited the trunk before me.

'Well, Matilda! You have made your name. You are quite famous. You are at the centre of a great scandal.'

285

I had no idea of what he meant. How could I, since I remembered nothing of what had passed before I left my house?

'I am very sorry, sir,' was all I could think to say.

To my bewilderment he gave a small smile, although he quickly contained it. 'Even great evil may be used towards the betterment of mankind,' said he.

I was grateful that he tried to comfort me, although I did not believe what he said.

'Well, you have played your part, child,' he said. 'Now let us see how you are suited to another role. Open the trunk.'

I did as I was bade and found myself mired yet deeper in confusion at the sight of what seemed an entire wardrobe of miniature ball gowns, with accompanying shoes and hats and muffs and even weatherproof confections. 'They are beautiful,' I dutifully said, although they were not to my taste.

'They are for you – the very best that money can buy,' said he.

I assumed he had gone to such lengths to try to make me look appealing. 'They won't make me a beauty, sir.' Tears came to my eyes for his waste of effort. 'I am as I am.'

'They will give you some advantage,' he said. 'Go and try them on.'

I sought out the plainest of the garments, but still found myself in a sea of ruffled silk. The gown was uncomfortable to wear. Its adorable hems would have looked well on a porcelain doll but were never made to dust the pavements. As for its pastel colour and lustrous fabric – they enhanced not my appeal but my want of it. Well, there was no help for it. I gathered up the folds of my skirt, stepped into my kid slippers and presented myself.

When I entered the room he made some exclamation; 'By heaven!' or some such. Then he asked me: 'Do you remember your mother?'

'Of course, sir,' I said. 'I have only recently left her.'

'Indeed,' he mused. There followed such prolonged appraisal that I wished to disappear. When, at length, he spoke it was merely to say, 'Well, then – for the present, that will have to do.'

He paced the room several times before turning once more to face me. 'You are to leave here,' he announced.

'What – leave? Are you sending me away?' It was foolish to speak thus since his words were the least confusing I had heard in a month. Why did I not rejoice? I had been a prisoner and now the gaoler's gates were to open. I had been the object of a dissolute bargain and now I might escape its closure. Yet perhaps I am not the only person in the world ever to feel that when one is all alone in it, a familiar evil is more to be desired than a fresh unknown. And I could not believe that on this great planet there was any resting-place for one so undesirable as I. Worth far more than myself was the guinea that had been used to purchase me. And in spite of even greater investment (the trunk of fashions must have cost many guineas) the gentleman who had made that acquisition could find no way to render me acceptable.

'Am I to go home?' I said. For some reason, the notion brought no comfort.

'No, not there,' he said. 'I am sending you away to school. You will be educated among young ladies.'

He must have observed my miserable expression for he queried sharply: 'Don't you deem it a privilege?'

'No, sir, for it will be seen at once that I am not as I appear. Give me back my rags and let me be as I really am.'

At once I regretted having spoken for I brought his anger upon myself. 'Do not speak like that,' he commanded. 'It is by such talk that people allow themselves to be ground down.'

These were almost the last words he addressed to me. We travelled a long way by train and carriage. I wondered why it was necessary to go such a distance when there must be schools close to where he lived.

287

'Because I consider it wise to put as great a distance as possible between us,' he explained. When he saw my woebegone expression he said I ought not to be afraid because there was one of his acquaintance at my destination who would be kind to me. 'Now, please do not ask me any further questions.'

I was delivered to Fuchsia Lodge. Of all the cruel mischief fate has made of my existence, this was the most heartless. To be surrounded by carefree young damsels was to understand the full extent of my alienation. To sense that my very presence was a contamination of their innocence compelled me to shun them. For my companions, I chose only solitude and despair. My temporary benefactor vanished off the face of the earth, leaving yet another blemish on my reputation. I do not know where he imagined kindness lay in that house, for although I encountered every manner of favouritism from the Misses Wilcox, of true benevolence there was none. Yet I have come to believe that there is no den or lair on this earth unknown to God or alien to his touch. Thus it was, when I felt I could take no more, that Mr Ellin came as intervener and I was delivered to your door.

Your fond and thankful Emma

CHAPTER TWENTY-EIGHT

In a lifetime, no normal woman would dream of discourse with such females as Emma now approached. Respectable women did not acknowledge their existence. Without the Reverend Clement Hibble's explicit sermon, Emma would have had no notion where to seek them (and she could not have asked, for even inquiry would give grave offence). Like vampires they destroyed their victims. They vanished in the day as vampires do. By their profession, they outlawed themselves from their sex and forswore its protections and privileges. They had no more hope of happy family life than nuns had, yet nuns had veneration and a clear prospect of Paradise. These creatures were seen as the devil's brigade. They plied their trade under night's dark garb. Pestilence and the poorhouse were the fruits of their service.

No less than any other woman, Emma dreaded what she sought. Yet had not Mr Hibble asserted that there were eighty thousands of such women working in the city? Even the devil could scarcely have so many women in his service.

Her first approach was to Drury Lane where the poorest and shabbiest of Satan's workforce did hard labour. The women in this street were abject, a few of them quite old and ugly and others young and pitiful. One woman had her head bandaged and a severe wound to her hand. When questioned, she said she had murdered a man with a poker and would do the same for Emma if she did not leave them to conduct their business in peace. Very glad was she to do so, yet as she fled this dismal place she made a discovery so strange and disturbing that for a time she was rooted to the spot and unable to quit it. She found that she was back at Short's Gardens, the awful street where she had passed her first night in London. She was surprised beyond measure to think that Miss Hammond had inadvertently led her to the site of her quest. Perhaps, in spite of all, there was some guiding star to steer her course.

This nova presently led her to the dens of Soho where she encountered very strange rouged and whitewashed creatures, with painted lips and eyebrows and a great quantity of false hair. Their provocative clothing made them a parody of their sex and their gaze was as unyielding as that of a man. To Emma they did not seem human at all but like some painted resurrection of the dead. In the cold, hard light of their eyes her courage failed. One of them addressed her in the French language. Their laughter followed her as she ran away.

She went towards Piccadilly where trudged the so-called 'Juliets' named only for their fragile years. Here Emma fitted well enough for all the workforce was under fifteen. Like little ghosts they seemed, thin and hungry and fearful, their darting eyes and anxious faces confirming them as newcomers to their trade. They looked briefly eager to see another girl their age, but none could answer her query since they worked for men who took most of their earnings and beat them if these did not match expectation.

This left her with the address she least wished to visit – the

Haymarket – where women were reputed to introduce their young daughters to the trade.

To bear a child, to nurse it at the breast, then deliver it for violation is more than any normal woman can comprehend. Yet these females were so debased, so addicted to drugs and alcohol, so corrupted in their bodies as well as their souls as to exclude them from their own pathetic livelihood, that they finally parted with the last possession which might earn them a shilling.

It was an infinitely pathetic market, neither mother nor daughter speaking nor looking to one other. The older women – some still in their twenties – appeared ill and haggard, barely conscious of the proceedings. The young girls looked lost and fey. Their spirits were already extinguished; their minds they had absented.

Only the youngest child, about six years of age, still carried any of the light of humanity and she seemed to bear all the anguish the others had subdued. She kept shaking her curly head as if in denial. She spread her hands in a pleading manner, then clutched them to her little breast, which showed bare through her few scant rags. Bruises marked her skin where she had been beaten and she was gaunt and dirty.

It took all of Emma's courage not to run from this place but she must fulfil her mission now or abandon it for ever.

'Does anyone know a woman called Eliza Brown?' she called out, as loudly as her courage would permit.

At first no one took any notice except the youngest girl who, upon hearing a voice, seemed to think herself accused and more violently shook her head. Emma thought she had never seen such a look of distress and hopeless despair on any living face. She could not understand how none of the other females pitied her, but they appeared numb to all feeling. More quietly, she asked her question again. After a time the girl who was nearest turned to look at her. 'Why should we know her?'

'She sold her daughter to a man.'

'More fool her when she could have lived upon her earnings,' one of the older women mumbled.

'I must find her,' Emma insisted. 'I am acquainted with a girl who lived with her.' She neglected to mention that that girl was herself. 'She needs my help.'

'Very likely she is beyond help,' said the first girl.

At this point the girl's mother, a bedraggled slattern who had seemed barely conscious, became aware of the proceedings. 'Everyone knows about Eliza Brown,' she said. 'It seems she lately changed address.'

'Oh,' Emma said, crestfallen. 'I don't suppose you have any idea where?'

'Two bob might remind me.'

Emma handed over the money.

'I heard she had gone to Newgate Prison.'

In a mechanical way Emma thanked the woman and moved away, although her mind was in turmoil. When she came to Trafalgar Square she sat to ponder. What was the nature of her mother's crime? What would she learn if she went to Newgate – that she and her mother were two of a kind? Now that she had at last found her mother she must fulfil her quest. Yet what if revelation proved more than she could bear? She had been made bitterly aware of her low worth yet had managed to accrue a measure of self-esteem. To find herself bankrupt in that account would be intolerable. No, she would not go to Newgate.

She walked away to find herself a bed. When she had had some rest, she would look for work. Yet she did not seek out lodgings. She only walked and walked, not noticing when she passed the Wig and Pen club where Mr Ellin had spoken of her. The nondescript figure was swept aside by elegant ladies whose skirts took up the whole of the pavement. She hurried past the quaint, wood-framed houses. Mr Hibble had talked of harlots and licence and eternal damnation, but the women she had seen were a parade of the earthly damned. No morbid imagination, however dissipated, could summon up such pitiful degradation. And one of them but a babe. Around her were well-dressed pedestrians, bright with purpose. With all her heart she longed to be as any one of them, to forget what she had seen, to wake to a brisk spring morning and commence upon a useful and unassuming life. Yet she could not. By a wispy thread of her own past she was chained to those poor wretches. They were her judgement. Unless she could find some unsullied path to her source, they would forever be her tribe.

Down busy, prosperous Fleet Street her feet took her. As she pressed an apprehensive path through a tumult of traffic on Ludgate Hill, St Paul's Cathedral came in sight. She paused to glance at her map and saw that she had come close to the prison. She sighed and carried on until a gallows, backed by two grim blocks, announced that her guiding star had fetched her to her goal.

The dome of St Paul's rose behind the prison like a hopeful moon, yet its optimistic emblem was denied those within the gaol for the buildings were without windows. A curious odour of dead meat emanated from the nearby cattle market, and the adjoining roads of Newgate Street and Giltspur Street were ominously subdued so that from within that mill of penitence one could perceive the sounds of its industry, indistinct yet persistent enough to hasten the steps of passers-by: the shouts, the mournful cries, the snatches of unnatural laughter.

Cowardice stalled her. She pushed past it and banged upon the door. The keeper opened it a crack and she saw into that dark mansion where criminals were confined.

'This is a hellish place.' Emma shuddered, and stated her business.

'No place for a child,' the wardress agreed. 'Besides, you cannot see her now. Visiting days are Wednesdays and Thursdays. Better yet, why not wait for the hanging? We will make a grand day of it, for she is quite famous.'

'She is to hang?' Emma became very pale. 'What has she done?'

'You do not know? Well, I'll not speak of it to a child. Yet after her arrest the body of a girl no older than yourself was found in the house. She will swing for her murder.'

In spite of her great efforts at self-control this revelation made Emma almost hysterical. 'I must see her,' she cried. 'She is my only living relative.'

'Well, then, God pity you! I will let you have five minutes. I doubt you would wish for more.'

They passed across a prison yard where a swarm of harpies taunted Emma. She threw a few coins and they scrambled like a pack of dogs. Others, who were confined, thrust their hands through iron bars and wailed.

As they re-entered the prison building she felt all around her the locks, the bolts, the chains, the high walls and grated windows of confinement. And this is where my own mother is to end her days, she thought. She had often wondered if her mother might repent of her decision to part with her. Would she in turn find the grace to forgive her? At length they came to a most dark and lonely spot and the guard told her that she might speak with the prisoner. At first she could make out nothing except iron bars set into a thick stone wall and, behind them, the dark gleam of an eye.

'Mother?' she whispered nervously.

The creature snarled. Like a wild beast she seized and tried to shake the bars that divided them.

'We parted six months ago.' Emma endeavoured to keep her voice level but terror constricted her throat. 'You gave me to a gentleman for a guinea.'

'What? Are you still alive?' The woman's voice was hoarse and horrible. 'Has someone not cut your scrawny throat by now to be rid of you?'

'Please, Mother! I have come a long way and at great difficulty to find you.'

'The devil sent you,' the prisoner growled, 'to bring such torment to my old age. First time I laid eyes on you I knew you was bad luck. I should have thrown you in the gutter and left you there.'

In spite of her efforts to remain detached, such bitterness from her own parent affected her and she found it hard to contain her tears. 'Have pity, Mother,' she said. 'I have lost my memory. I know nothing of my past except the terrible things you said on the day we parted. Please tell me anything. Who was my father? What is my age?'

The woman pushed her face close to the bars. Emma's eyes had adjusted to the dark and she could see her now, a grim vision animated only by hate. A dull glitter entered her eyes and she twisted her mouth to a semblance of a smile. 'I will tell you something,' she said. 'What comfort may be had for one in my place will be got from the knowledge that, while you are at liberty and I behind bars, yet you are in prison too. God rot you there!'

She began to laugh. It was an inhuman cackle rising in pitch until it terrified Emma and she got up and ran away. She was bolting down the stone passage when the wardress caught her.

'I told you to have no business with her,' she said. 'When she is hanged the world will be a better place.'

'Don't speak of her so,' Emma wept bitterly. 'She is my mother.'

'You are mistaken,' said she.

She shook her head. 'I was in the very bed where she bore me.'

'Whatever sights that bed has seen it was not the birth of an innocent child.'

'I am her flesh and blood. She told me so.'

'Aye.' The keeper viewed her oddly. 'I would not doubt that she did, having drugged you and separated you from those who might rightly lay claim to you. Come in here, lass. Sit down. I ought to talk to you.'

Emma seemed to move through water more than air as she followed the woman into a small chamber.

'That evil creature sold young women into a life of vice. About a year past her racket was exposed. She claimed she could do as she liked as the girls were her own daughters. Yet upon her arrest she was examined by a surgeon who proved conclusively that the unnatural old hag had never produced any child.'

'Are you sure?' The words fell from Emma's dry lips like chalk.

'I am indeed,' the woman said. 'Are you all right, miss? I am certain you must be relieved. You look pale. Shall I fetch water for you?'

Emma shook her head. 'Thank you. I am well enough. I need air.'

Again she had to face the band of harpies as she crossed the yard. This time she escaped them by running and although the keeper called after her she did not lessen her pace until she had put almost a mile between herself and that dreadful place. She scarcely registered her new surroundings until she saw that her feet were mired almost to the ankles. A fearful din was all around her and she found herself in a running river of blood. As she tried to escape she tripped over entrails that had been flung in the gutter. The foetid air was full of loud moans and cries of terror and the shouts of brutish men. Her terrified eye met the whitened, panic-stricken eye of a bull, which was beaten savagely by a man with a stick. She was in a vast square as big as a park. On every side poor beasts were being pushed and beaten to their death. The stench was such that she almost choked on it, yet when she looked up for a sweeter climate all she saw was a forest of dead animals hanging from iron balustrades and raining down their blood. 'Where am I?' she cried out in dread.

'Smithfield Market,' laughed an unshaven man. 'And you'd best be out of it or they might slit your throat by mistake.' With a murderer's finger he pointed the way and she, as one in a nightmare, pushed past the reek and steam of poor doomed creatures until she found herself in some fresher fog.

She came presently to a handsome shopping street in Cheapside and pretended to admire the window of a linen draper while she stilled her hammering heart. The merchant's glass threw back a blanched and featureless reflection. 'Who am I?' she asked this pallid spectre. She must be relieved. Of course she must. Not to have issued from that perversion of her sex could not be other than a blessing. Yet she found herself, lost and shuddering, in a state of the most intolerable distress. That slender thread – however tainted – which connected her to the earth had been severed. Her guiding star gave one last flicker and expired. She was nothing. There was no one to claim her now. She sank down in the street and wrapped her arms round her head and wept most bitterly. As she sat there, her view was of boots and shoes hurrying busily past. No one stopped to comfort or to query her. Like the child whose natural mother sold her nightly in the street, she was invisible, her suffering no more than that of a half-crushed insect. When she could cry no more she stumbled to her feet and continued to walk. Great buildings soared above her – the Bank of England, the Royal Exchange, the Mansion House. Hours lost their shape and the day began to fade and then to light up again for night. She was hungry, but she did not care to eat, for the strongest human instinct is not to survive but to belong. She came upon a column of stone so tall its gilded summit played with the stars. As she gazed upward a waft of gin touched her cheek and a woman wheezed in her ear, ''Twas built in memory of the great fire which consumed half the city three centuries past, and a quantity of sinners, aye, and likely some saints, for eighty-seven churches burned to the ground.' The woman giggled. ''Tis more than two hundred feet and you can't throw yourself off no more. They railed the top since a poor servant girl cast herself to her doom.'

The speaker slid away into the mist. Yet she had left behind a small, sour glimmer of hope. How great a sin could it be to end what had no beginning? She scarcely even pondered the question. She only wondered where? and how? In a city where the air is made of smoke, its perfumes – foul and fair – draw its map. The mingled aromas of fish and oranges and spices from the market and storage houses and a dark repugnant odour told her she was close to the river. As she took in the smell she found her answer. If none other would claim her, the river would.

In her fevered mind, this dark thought soon took on the shape of bright ambition. No more at the mercy of fate, she would end uncertainty by an act of her own volition. Never again would she be cursed or spurned, never again feel the warmth of human kindness and then the certainty that she did not merit it.

By night the river looked gentle and soft. She walked past poor wretches huddled on narrow stone benches close by London Bridge. The air was poisoned by foul water and the reek from the vinegar and tannery factories, yet she felt at home now. Children such as she owned no place in the world and no pity. By God's mercy she might earn a place in heaven. She climbed down the stone stairs to the water. What strength of mind she possessed would see her through this act.

CHAPTER TWENTY-NINE

In two days I had done nothing save read Emma's letter over and over. My liking of myself grew less each time I saw those words penned in a child's unformed script; to know that a little creature not yet grown to womanhood had suffered so much and in silence. And why? Because good women like myself were deemed too refined to hear of such things.

The tranquillity with which I had equipped myself I now despised. I no longer wished to protect myself from the harsh realities of life. I scribbled a note to Mr Ellin and gave it to my maid to deliver. That being done, I devoted myself to my most practical ritual of wearing out my late husband's floorboards.

Mr Ellin was not at home. I concentrated on willing his return and was rewarded, within half an hour, by a knock upon the door and an announcement from my maid that there was a gentleman to see me.

'Mr Ellin! Good! Show him in and make us some tea.'

'It's not Mr Ellin!' That bland countenance looked curious and not a little disconcerted.

'Who, then?'

'I never saw him, ma'am, till now.'

'Did he not present his card?'

It was a measure of my quiet life at Fox Clough that my good servant took it on trust that if she was not acquainted with a visitor then I must not be either.

'Show me.' I held out my hand. As though fearing for my safety she first applied her wide-eyed concentration to the card and mouthed strenuously (I had lately been teaching her to read).

'Mary — just give it to me.'

She did so, but before it had time to yield up its science the door opened and the caller strode in.

I could see at once why my servant had been startled. Our guest was particularly striking. He was tall and pale with an intensity of gaze that bordered upon rebuke. He was handsome, to be sure, yet — on this occasion at least — there was little of ease or pleasantry to him.

Why, then, upon encountering this unnerving individual did I suffer an increased heart-rate and feel the blood rush to my face and desert all my extremities so that I was forced, in a fog, to seek the nearest chair? Why was our new arrival so similarly affected that he could only stare and stammer? When he found sufficient voice to utter a single word my consternation was so great that I was very glad of the support of that sturdy piece of furniture.

'Isa?' he breathed.

Faces change yet voices retain the fingerprint of personality. There was no mistaking that tone. Yet I had an urge to touch the form, to see if my fingers would make contact with flesh or air.

'Don't you know me?' he said.

'Are you a ghost?' I gasped.

'A part of me lives.'

The maid looked from one to the other in a fever of perplexity as he and I stepped over several decades and into dazed recognition.

'Finch?'

Reader, you must wonder why I did not instantly recognize the man I had once loved with all my heart. Aside from the fact that the years had wrought great changes, there was another reason, one I instantly laid before him. 'But . . . you are dead!'

'If that is so then no one has informed me of the situation.' He forged a rather grim simulation of a smile.

'Then I wish they had not told me.'

'Who told you?'

'A Mrs Greenwood. A long time ago. I was a new bride.'

A bitter curve came into his mouth. He looked away as if to check it and then he said, 'My brother died – my little brother, whom you tutored. It was scarlatina. It affected the whole family greatly. Poor Mama too has since passed away.'

'I am very sorry to hear it. How did you find me?' I then asked.

That same acid look influenced his expression. 'Do not flatter yourself. I did not come to look for you. I had no idea I would discover *you* here. I knew only that the house was presently owned by a Mrs Chalfont. It was someone else I sought.'

In spite of all the years that had passed, his bitterness was painful. What had I done to earn such hostility? I felt quite crushed by it. 'Well, I am sorry you have had a wasted journey, sir,' I said. 'There has been no other owner. The house was built for me.'

The words he spoke then were so surprising that all earlier shocks were relegated to a minor status. 'I seek a child. She goes by the name of Matilda Fitzgibbon. I brought her to

302

board at Fuchsia Lodge some months ago. The proprietors directed me to this address.'

'Mary, leave us,' I breathed.

'Shall I bring tea, ma'am?' she eagerly inquired.

'No tea. Just go out and close the door.'

When she had departed with a doubtful look at my caller, I asked him, 'How has life dealt with you to make you such a monster?'

He did not look the least bit guilty or ashamed. Instead, he tersely replied, 'The very question I meant to ask you.'

This took me so much by surprise that I was almost at a loss for words. 'What on earth do you mean?'

'You asked me the question first. I think you should explain.'

I silently handed him Emma's letter. He went to the window for light. I watched his shadowed profile and thought he must have looked like this on the day he first brought the child to Fuchsia Lodge. He had left her to stand centre stage and willed himself into the shadows. Old tender emotions battled with the new ones of hurt and anger. I herded them into a fairly disciplined pack at my heels. I would deal with my own feelings later, when I had heard out his explanation.

He read at leisure. He finished the task and folded the paper. Silently he returned it to me and seated himself in an opposite couch. Slowly he looked up at me. 'It is all true,' he said; 'every word.'

'And you were the man of whom she wrote?'

'It was I.'

A moan escaped me. What had become of the youth I once cherished? Had army life extinguished every ounce of his humanity?

'It is all true and yet not one word of it is true,' that same gentleman proclaimed. 'I can explain if you wish.'

'I think you should – but, first, tell me why you abandoned the child to the most intense misery and suspicion.'

'That I deeply regret. Alas, it was unavoidable. I was obliged to conceal my identity. I did not willingly forsake the girl. I was detained in a place where communication was impossible.'

'What? On a desert island?'

'No such luxury. I have been in prison.'

I stood up from my chair. 'Then it is true,' I accused. 'You committed that most terrible crime and were convicted.'

He gave me a look of impatience – almost of aversion. 'Look at you, Isa – every inch the respectable housewife! How well you learnt from Mama, after all. Like all your silly type you love gossip yet fear its contamination. Sit still, if you are able, and you shall have your explanation.'

I sat motionless but for a tremor. He lit his pipe. He gave me a strange, level glance, not compassionate but cool. Apparently not liking what he saw he returned to the window and sat down there. Softly, he began to speak.

'When young I went to serve in the army. I suffered a heart-break, not fatal, yet in consequence of which I decided to give my heart to no single individual but to the world. I became what I was born to be – a campaigner to put right the wrongs of the world. Army life taught me that I was not a company man, so I declined to enter politics or the priesthood. I became instead a journalist.'

There would have been solace in that once: to know he was alive, that his voice was a significant force in the world. Now I wished the story over. I wanted him gone. I could not look at him – and for the very worst reason: the more I grew accustomed to his company, the more I feared my weakness. When my glance strayed in his direction I found myself thinking how tired he looked; how unhappy. His long, restless hands seemed sad. I had an urge to still them with my own. I forced myself to remember that those hands had handed over money for the ruin of a helpless child.

He told me that for fifteen years he had worked for a small but influential magazine, whose mission was to stimulate public awareness and political reform. 'Then, finally, I had to face the greatest evil of our age – the abduction and sale of young girls. Because no one would admit to the existence of such trade, nothing was done to stop it. It has reached a stage where no young girl is safe in the streets of London.'

'But you engaged in this vile trade yourself,' I protested.

'Only to prove it existed.'

'How, then, did you come to learn of it?' I asked.

'Through a society that has long been working for the cause. Years ago I came across a report it produced, which greatly affected me. Since then, I have made many efforts to bring the matter to the attention of the public. No one would take me seriously. At last I decided to produce the evidence in the most sensational manner possible. I would buy a young girl myself, bind witnesses to testify that I had done so, then write about it.'

'And what, afterwards, did you propose to do with her?'

'My initial plan was to return her to her family with a caution. Yet when I encountered the mother, there was something so utterly degenerate about her that my only thought was to keep the child from her clutches. Having placed her in safe-keeping I wrote my story, then tried to lodge her where advantage might find her.'

'At Fuchsia Lodge? There was little advantage for her there, especially after you deserted her. Did you think the Misses Wilcox would open their tender hearts to her?'

'No, Isa.' It was hard to read that face in its silhouette, but the voice sounded melancholy. 'I was thinking of someone else.'

305

'Do you have any idea of the misery to which you surrendered her?'

'I often thought of her. I prayed the world would treat her kindly.'

'I pray your journalistic scheme was more effective.'

'The story received a great deal of attention in London. No one wished to believe it. Those who did descended full of wrath upon Eliza Brown, who had sold the girl to me. She put on a great show of emotion and said she had misunderstood my purpose, that she thought her daughter was to be apprenticed for work and that I had abducted her under false pretences. Without any further ceremony, I was arrested and put into gaol, and those who were to be my witnesses accused of aiding and abetting. They took fright and said they knew nothing of the transaction. God knows what would have happened to me had not some other person come forward and revealed that Eliza Brown had already sold a number of young girls – all of whom appeared to be the same age. Someone else added that they had been acquainted with the same party a long time and had never seen her with an infant or a young child. Her children appeared only as full-grown adolescents. At length she was subjected to a medical examination and it was revealed that she had never borne any child. She merely lured away and sold those borne by others. She was placed under arrest and, in due course, I was released. It was upon the discovery of a young girl's body – greatly abused – on her premises, that she was sentenced to hang for murder.'

'But why should it make a difference that the children were not her own?' I wondered. 'A mother cannot just sell her children.'

He looked at me very gravely. 'As the law stands, a parent can sell a child for any sum of money, for any purpose that may be imagined – so long as the child is above the age of consent.'

The entire tale was so foul and so fantastical that I scarcely knew what to think. It was impossible to accept that such an unnatural practice was commonplace in the great capital. And yet why not? Children had been worked to death in mills and mines and factories until reformers made a stand. I endeavoured to believe in Finch's good intentions, yet another obstacle now presented itself.

'You drugged her. Do you deny it? She says so in her letter.'

'I told you. Everything she claims is true. When the doctor examined her he said she showed signs of opium abuse. She was both restless and lethargic. She talked and walked in her sleep. She was prone to headaches and sudden collapse. He prescribed a limited treatment of the same sedative on a diminishing basis until she was accustomed to do without it.'

'Poor child,' I said. 'She still suffered those symptoms when she came to Fuchsia Lodge. I wonder what other horrors she has endured.'

He fell silent and directed his gaze out the window. I pitied him now. Even when young, he had worn heavily the burdens of the world. I thought I understood his seeming coldness. Having denied himself all comfort, he retained no tolerance for those who sought its buffer. Softly, I crossed the room and went to where he stood. I sought the view upon which his dark eyes brooded. It was a landscape innocent with spring, aloof from the corruption of its human creatures. Gently, I put my arms around him. He whirled round – not, as I first imagined, to respond with like emotion but to thrust me from him, using both his hands to push me away as strongly as possible. 'How dare you?'

I was as dismayed as it is possible to be. 'Because of what I feel for you. Because of what we once meant to one another.'

'You mean to toy with me again?'

'I never toyed with you.'

307

'I risked everything for love of you. I suffered seven years of army life. I would have suffered gladly if we could have been together at the end of it, yet my mother informed me that within a few months you were married to a grocer.'

'Against my will,' I stoutly declared. 'I would have resisted if I could, but it was not possible.'

'Resisted?' He spat out the word with scorn. 'I wonder why women are called the fair sex when the very concept is alien their nature.'

'How can you say such cruel things?'

'You call me cruel — you, who were the very author of that form?'

I was about to protest at the unfairness of this accusation but something in his manner pulled me up short. I had a sudden memory of our first meeting at Happen Heath. His coldly sardonic air then had made me feel all the inadequacy of my class and my years. Perhaps he had not changed at all. This caustic and superior manner was his natural one and the other self, in which I had rejoiced, was but a brief transformation wrought by youthful sentiment, an illusion nurtured into life by my own fancy. I withdrew to the far side of the room.

'Forgive me, sir, for presuming upon the past. Let us lay it to rest and concentrate upon the present. You came in search of the child you called Matilda. Her real name, as you now know from her letter, is Emma. My intention was to protect her, instead of which I exposed her to fresh danger. I know nothing of her present situation except what she set down in her letter. It tells us no more than that she was cruelly ill-used and that she was alive a few days ago when she wrote it.'

'You are wrong, Isa.' Now that I had released my claim he grew civil (although icily remote). 'It tells us several things. It reveals her as a young woman of exceptional resourcefulness. It shows her to be mature beyond her years and of high intelligence. If she has endured thus far, I think we may hope she will survive until we find her.'

'But how to find her?' I appealed. 'A friend of mine, Mr Ellin, has gone to great pains to trace her. He investigated the London underworld. Everywhere, he received the same response. A person with no identity cannot be located as they do not exist.'

'This friend of yours – a Mr Ellin, you say – has taken an interest in the child?'

'Yes. He encountered her first at Fuchsia Lodge. He pitied her.'

'Ah.' A curious little smile found the corner of his mouth.

Was he jealous? I found this phantom from my past a maddening mass of contradictions and soon I wished him gone for all the right reasons. 'We now know how Emma came to be at Fuchsia Lodge.' By an effort of will I managed to devote myself to practicalities. 'We still have no better idea who she is.'

'Perhaps I do know.' He raised an eyebrow. That same look of irony hovered about his lips.

In another moment, I thought, I shall kill him! – but not until I had a response. 'Who? Tell me.'

'I cannot.'

'If you know her identity you must reveal it.'

'I did not say I know who she is. I said I *might* know. There is a difference.'

My pride collided with his obduracy. I would not plead for an answer. 'Well, I congratulate you on whatever progress you have made. How did you find out?'

'It is a journalist's business to discover the truth.'

'Nonetheless, it must have been a daunting task. I should be interested to know how you proceeded.'

At last he relented, and something of genuine amusement entered his expression. 'By the very simplest means. I recognized her – or thought I did.'

'You recognized her? Is she well known? Had you seen her before?'

'The latter – but, remember, it was only a guess.'

'Where did you think you had seen her?'

'On the steps of an assizes courthouse, years ago. I had come as a young journalist to report on a case.'

This was a discouraging revelation. 'Then she has been in trouble with the law?'

'No. She was but four years of age. She was waiting for a relative.'

'But so long ago? Can any true resemblance remain?'

'The little girl in question was not pretty, yet she was singular. She had a particularly haunting expression. She looked desolate and yet enduring. I thought she would make an interesting subject for a painter. She looked, somehow, as if she kept vigil with misfortune.'

'And when you found her again as a young woman, you recognized her at once?'

'At first I saw nothing but a very sickly and dirty waif. I soon suspected she was no offspring of that vile woman from whom I had purchased her. This was a refined and educated child. Yet it was not until the day I brought her to the boarding-school, dressed up and with her hair in ringlets, that I saw a striking resemblance to another unhappy little lady. As you say, it is a long time ago. Without some proof, my guesswork has no value.'

'Who is she?' I petitioned.

'That is what I now mean to establish. If my assumption is correct then this story has its beginnings long before her birth. It is to that point I intend to proceed. If and when I can find any proof, I shall return.'

'I do not think I can stand the waiting.'

Again, the bitter look. 'You never could.'

I tried to overlook this barb. 'I mean, I wish there was something practical I could do.'

'Then find her,' he said harshly. 'You lost her. If she was your own daughter, what would you do? You would search with your bare hands until they bled. In the meantime' — his tone grew moderate again — 'perhaps a little reading would help to pass the time.'

As this suggestion merited no comment, I offered none. He produced from a pocket a pamphlet.

'What is it?' I asked.

'It is such as no nice woman should ever permit to pass her modest eyes,' he said. 'Read it later.'

There was more. Out of his breast pocket came a small leather wallet. It contained a single item — a scrap of faded paper.

'What is this, then?'

'A letter from a loved one.' His face now looked hectic with suppressed anger. 'It was written many years ago. Yet, through all those years I have kept it close to my heart — not for sentiment's sake, but to protect that organ from fresh assaults.'

'Then, for protection's sake, you had better keep it there.'

'Not necessary!' He spoke with a bitterness that was most chilling in its levity of tone. 'For after meeting you again I feel surprisingly immune.'

On this antagonistic note, we parted. It is a paradox of the human heart that, despite the insult and the injury I felt, I was glad he had left something of his own with me, as he had once left his favourite books for my companions. In truth, I almost wished him gone so that I could address myself to the ancient-looking documents he had intrusted to my care. Naturally, I was most concerned with the one he had kept close to his heart, the one that might explain his disillusion. Naturally, being female, I saved this one until last.

The first text was not a letter, but a report. It was headed, 'The Opening Address of the London Society for the Protection of Young Females, and Prevention of Juvenile Prostitution'. It was dated May 1835.

It has been proved that 400 individuals procure a livelihood by trepanning young females from eleven to fifteen years of age for the purposes of prostitution. Every art is practised, every scheme is devised, to effect this object, and when an innocent child appears in the streets without a protector, she is insidiously watched by one of those merciless wretches and decoyed under some plausible pretext to an abode of infamy and degradation. No sooner is the unsuspecting helpless one within their grasp than, by a preconcerted measure, she becomes a victim to their inhuman designs. She is stripped of the apparel with which parental care or friendly solicitude has clothed her, and then, decked with the gaudy trappings of her shame, she is com-pelled to walk the streets, and in her turn, while producing to her master or mistress the wages of her prostitution, becomes the ensnarer of the youth of the other sex. After this it is useless to attempt to return to the path of virtue or honour, for she is then watched with the greatest vigilance, and should she attempt to escape from the clutches of her seducer she is threat-ened with instant punishment, and often barbarously treated. Thus situated she becomes reckless, and careless of her future course. It rarely occurs that one so young escapes contamination; and it is a fact that numbers of these youthful victims imbibe disease within a week or two of their seduction. They are then sent to one of the hospitals under a fictitious name by their keepers, or unfeelingly turned into the streets to perish; and it is not an uncommon circumstance that within the short space of a few weeks the bloom of health, of beauty, and of innocence gives place to the sallow hue of despair, disease and death.

CHAPTER THIRTY

Emma climbed down the steps to the river. The water slapped indifferently against the brick. 'Be done with it,' it seemed to say.

'Yes, be done with it,' she urged herself. Yet how forsaken a sphere she entered. Merely by descending that stair she had cut herself off from all the living world. Far from the clean, anonymous erasure she had craved, the water was heavy with filth and history. It breathed out a deathly stench. Emma feared mainly that if she entered this sodden tomb she would be embraced at once by some other recent corpse. Gazing down into the black and slow-moving depths of the river, where drifted fragments of a broken moon, she caught sight of something else. Another smaller moon kept it company. This one had a tousled halo and large eyes that bored intently into hers.

She looked up. A little girl sat by the water. She seemed about eight years. She had a basket by her side and in her arms a large and life-like doll. Upon her head was a hat of quaint design with shallow brim and some very decrepit flowers on it. Her small feet were cold and bare.

'Are you going to jump?' She gazed at Emma with great violet eyes. She was very pale but with bright, burning patches on either cheek.

'What is it to you?' Emma asked the child.

'Could I have your dress and boots? Mine is all wore out.'

'I cannot remove my clothing here,' Emma protested.

'Now I can't see you.' The little one put her hands over her eyes. 'They'll not keep you warm down there.'

Emma shuddered. She noted that the child's clothes were so ragged that her body showed through. A hand was removed from one eye. 'If I'm going to have your gown when you're dead, I ought to know your name.'

'My name is Emma,' Emma introduced herself.

'Emma what?' the child said. 'Won't you come and talk to me? I'm very lonesome.'

Very glad she was to accept the invitation. She quitted her desolate post and went to join the other child. She was about to say that she was Emma Brown but then she realized she was not. 'I don't know,' she confessed. 'What is your name?'

'Jenny Drew,' the child said. Despite a liberal coating of dirt she had the face of an angel but she spoke with the hoarse and low tones of an old man. The portion of her body that showed beneath her clothing seemed to be no more than skin and bone, and Emma was seized with pity. For consideration of the younger child she decided she must defer her appointment with death.

'Would you like some dinner?' she asked her. 'I have money.'

The little girl glanced with interest at the coins but then looked away. 'I ain't hungry.'

'Come with me and pick what you like. There are stalls selling oysters and meat pies and fried fish and jellied eels.'

The child cocked her head like a bird hearing some half-remembered sound. When the litany of nourishment was ended she merely sighed.

'Have you eaten?' Emma persisted.

'I did eat by and by,' she said distantly. 'I had a bit of old bread that I soaked in water. I've broke the habit of eating.' She was overtaken then by a harsh and violent fit of coughing. When this ended she held the doll tightly to her chest and looked patiently over its solid head.

'You are unwell,' Emma said in concern. 'Let me take you home.'

'What is home?' the child said.

'Where mother and father and brothers and sisters are,' Emma answered.

'I wonder what a home is like,' the little girl said. 'If I was ever in one I could think of it sometimes and it would be like being there, but I never was. Was you ever in a home?'

'I was.' Emma tried to keep herself from crying. She said that a warm fire was there and kindness and good food and a garden where flowers bloomed in summer.

'Tell me more.' The child paid rapt attention. 'Begin with the first light and go on until it is dark.'

Emma sat beside her. It was Fox Clough she described, its ivy and woodwork, its lamps and flowers. She slowly related the ordinary domestic details of a day such as those she had passed there: the housework, the reading, the prayers, the peeling of potatoes for a meal, the stitching and talking, the walking.

As she spoke, Jenny Drew rested against her and began to drowse, but then she sat bolt upright. 'You had your own room? One room, all for yourself?'

'I did, Jenny, but only for a little while.'

'Then it was not your room.'

'It was. It was my room.'

Jenny nestled close to her again. The curly head dropped into Emma's lap. The doll slipped from her arms.

It began to rain. Soft drops soon turned to a heavy, hissing downpour. I cannot leave her here, Emma thought. She is too frail. I must find shelter for us both.

'Come along, Jenny,' she said. 'We shall seek some refuge.'

When the little girl tried to stand it became apparent that one leg was badly twisted. She leant on Emma, her small face screwed up with concentration and with pain. She tried to take a few steps but could do no more than drag her bad leg. She stopped and sighed. 'Damp weather!' she gruffly declared. 'It seizes me. I'd best sit down again.'

'I can help if we could find some nearby place.' Emma looked doubtfully at their dismal surroundings.

'I know a spot,' Jenny said. 'It's not far.'

'Leave that.' Emma indicated the doll. 'I can carry you if it is close by. I shall return for your plaything.'

Under Jenny's direction she located their refuge. It was a run-down warehouse, whose damaged entrance had given access to every manner of vagrant and derelict. Drunken and dissolute people crouched surrounded by their rubbish. On her own she would have fled as far as possible from this hell but she could not carry Jenny Drew any further. She found a corner of the shed with empty barrels and piles of sacking. We will very likely have company here, she thought, both human and vermin, but there is little choice. She spread some sacking in the driest corner and made Jenny as comfortable as she could, then went back for the toy. An awful cry escaped her as she picked up from the pavement that rigid doll. It was the corpse of a human infant.

She did not sleep that night. The cold was too bitter and her grief too raw. For some reason the sight of the lifeless child racked her with anguish. For a very long time she could do nothing but weep. She had imagined herself the most wretched creature on this earth, yet children far younger than herself were left to fend for themselves or starve to death. At length she composed herself sufficiently to wrap herself in sacking and sat up to protect the two children, the one ill – her breath rugged as if dragged over stones – the other passed beyond suffering. The thump of horses' hoofs from the stables below kept her company. A bleary yellow moon, dressed in wisps of fog, lurched out from behind the clouds from time to time to uncover her hiding-place and illuminate a ghastly scene. A rat observed her with a beady glance from its perch atop a barrel. A drunken man staggered over to inspect her. She shook at a pile of rags and said, 'Father, Father, wake quickly!' and the drunk man rambled away.

'This night shall never come again,' she vowed. 'I shall find some means of making my way in the world.'

Towards morning the whole of the squalid scene revealed itself by a vapid light that seemed not to have the energy to raise itself above the colour of muddy water. Emma's little charge slept on. She rose stiffly, stamped her legs to bring life to them and went out to seek some breakfast. She found herself in a strange region of dark lanes and ancient, broken tenements. At street level, a maze of tumbledown stairs, lanes and landing-stages led off the river. Looking up she saw a bustling world above her head. Public houses hung from the perpendicular, seemingly about to topple into the river. Bales of merchandise swung in the air as they were loaded into the massive warehouses. As she passed by London Bridge she saw that the river afforded yet another commotion of activity. The desolation of the night before had been replaced by a veritable forest of sails that stretched far into the distance. The air was full of sights and sounds, the creak of cranes, the rattle of pulleys, the pulsing of steam-ship engines, the hoarse shouts of sailors and loaders. She made her way to Billingsgate Market amid a clamour of church bells that came from all parts of the city. It was a slippery path she trod, the pearly discs of fish scales mingling with a river of mud. Porters in straw hats pushed past men in strange helmets made of hide bearing huge baskets of herrings on their heads. Vats of eels made writhing leaden chains. The salt smell of the fresh catch mingled with the sickly odour of offal. She saw a crowd gathered round a tent, which thawed the cold morning with a breath of sugared steam. The customers were decidedly mixed. There were urchin boys, barefoot and black from head to foot, and elegant gentleman, beautifully attired and considerably merry. She edged her way into the tent and found that it purveyed sugared milk from a great, steaming vat. This delicacy, she discovered, was called saloop and was sold at a penny a bowl. The only paying customers were the gentlemen, who were on their way home from a night of making merry and needed sustenance to steady their legs. The little boys, who were chimney sweeps, could not afford this luxury and were there only to inhale the delicious savour and to warm themselves in the comforting vapour. Emma bought two bowls. One she gave to the chimney sweeps to share among themselves. The other she carried carefully back to where she had passed the night.

Jenny was awake, but only an indifferent ranging of her great violet eyes gave testimony to the fact. She lay where she had slept, her limbs still in a cold and awkward pose, her inward focus on the harsh labour of her breathing. Emma knelt beside her and raised her and settled her against her shoulder. She held the bowl of hot refreshment to her lips. To her relief, the little girl drank. After this she seemed somewhat improved. She sat up properly and began to look around for the infant.

Sooner or later she must tell the child that her brother had died but in the meantime she wanted her to eat some more and needed to distract her.

'You spoke of a great house.' Emma held the bowl to her mouth once more until she swallowed. 'Where was it?'

'Don't you know what the Great House is? 'Tis the workhouse. Was you never in the workhouse?'

'I don't know,' Emma confessed. 'If you were in the workhouse, why are you now on the streets?'

'I ran away,' Jenny said proudly. 'And I'd rather die on the streets than go back there.'

'How do you survive?'

'I earn my living,' the small girl said squarely.

'What can a little one like you do?'

'I ain't little,' Jenny spoke with indignation. 'I been earning my living since I was six. I'm a pure finder.'

Emma had no idea what a pure finder was and did not wish to risk the scorn of this odd little woman by inquiring, but the name suited her unworldly appearance.

'I done all right,' Jenny went on. 'I got my basketful every day and earned my bread – only, on account of the tanning trade, things ain't been so good of late.'

Emma tipped the last of the milk into the child's mouth and politely asked why not.

'Pure finding was always a woman's job. We got along and there was work enough for everyone. Then the tanning trade started using dog dirt as a 'stringent and it was much in demand so that boys and men began collecting it and now there's no work left for the women.'

'But collecting what?' By now Emma was thoroughly confused.

'I told you. Don't you never listen?' Jenny said crossly. 'Dog dirt. That's what pure finders do. They collect dog dirt and they sells it.' Emma sighed and shook her head. This great and grand and evil-smelling city grew stranger by the moment. Jenny had regained some strength and lost patience with conversation.

'Where is he?'

Emma took both her hands. 'Jenny, I have some very sad news to impart. Your little brother has passed away. You must be brave. He has gone to a better place.'

She had anticipated that this news would bring the same anguish to the child that she had experienced, but Jenny Drew merely frowned. 'He ain't my brother.'

'Who, then?' Emma breathed.

'He were nothing to me, although I liked his face.'

'Where did he come from? He looks so newly born.'

'I found him.'

'Where did you find him?' Emma said in dismay. 'How did he die?'

'I found him dead in the gutter,' the child replied.

'Oh, how dreadful! We must tell the police.'

'There's no one cares about a dead baby.' The child spoke almost with a world-weary scorn. 'You can find one any night of the week.'

'But why did you take him and carry him around?'

'For company,' the little girl replied, as if it was the most normal thing in the world.

'Oh, Jenny, Jenny!' Emma shook her head. 'This poor little child must be decently buried. Did you think you could carry him around for ever?'

'Course not,' Jenny answered, in hoarse and elderly tones. 'When they gets to look unnatural I finds myself another.'

'How do you dispose of the poor little corpses?'

'I tosses 'em in the river.'

'Well, not this one,' Emma said firmly. 'This child will be decently buried.'

'Where will you bury him?' Jenny wondered. 'The city is stone to its heart.'

'I'll find somewhere.' Emma wrapped the tiny body in a sack and set out.

Jenny trotted beside her. She could walk better after a night out of the weather. 'We could try St Maggot's. Other folks is buried there. I used to hide there until they found me.'

She led the way to the old church of St Magnus the Martyr, close by London Bridge. There was a graveyard and the remains of a Roman wharf, which used to be Jenny's hiding-place.

'No one hardly comes here, 'cept of a Sunday.' She slipped into the burial ground and, after a pause, Emma followed. She looked around for something with which to turn the hard earth, but there was no loose stone or slate in that well-kept space.

'I've got a little spade,' the surprising Jenny said. 'I use it for my business.' She produced this implement from her basket and in spite of her feebleness, began diligently digging.

'Here, let me. You sit and keep watch,' Emma said.

'I will,' the child said gravely, 'for if they saw you bury a child, no one would likely object, yet if they saw you digging the grass, you'd be sure to go to prison.'

It took an hour of hacking with the miniature spade to make any worthwhile impression. They laid the infant down in the sacking. Emma wept but Jenny seemed to regard it as a solemn but interesting game.

'We must say a prayer above him,' Emma decided.

'I know no prayer,' the other little girl confessed.

'Well, then, I shall say a prayer and you shall name him.'

'Billy,' Jenny decided.

'Just Billy. Is he not to have a second name? How did you get your second name if you were a foundling?'

'In the Great House they asked me who I was,' Jenny said. 'I said that I was me. They seemed not to understand so I asked for pen and paper and drew a picture of myself. They picked it up and studied it and I heard one whisper to another, "Look what Jenny drew." And that is how I learnt my name. Jenny Drew.'

Emma smiled. 'Where did you find this poor infant, Jenny Drew?'

Jenny frowned and thought. 'I think it were near Smithfield.'

Emma said a prayer over the makeshift grave. 'Rest in peace, Billy Smithfield,' she added.

To put some heart into themselves they afterwards went to an inn in Billingsgate for breakfast, which novelty the little girl relished greatly although it was a very dirty place, the tables being stained with old food and the dishes poorly washed and the floor scarcely swept. Emma coaxed the younger girl into taking some gruel. Upon attempting the first mouthful Jenny was overtaken by a fit of coughing. As she struggled for air she fixed her eyes on Emma. 'Are you my mother?'

'No, Jenny.'

'Are you my sister?'

'No, Jenny, I am not.'

'Do you love me, then?'

'I do not know, in truth, if I have ever loved anyone on this earth.'

'Why have you kept me by you?'

'It was not my plan,' Emma said. 'I brought you with me because you were small and ill and alone. My intention was to travel unaccompanied. I came here in search of my past, of which I know but little. I came to find out who I am.'

'But I can tell you who you are. You are Emma. You are a girl. You are as you act and speak and as I see you.'

Emma smiled. 'You are right, Jenny Drew. I am on a quest to restore my honour and if honour there be none, then I shall be penitent and endeavour to improve. Now, try to eat some breakfast.'

Jenny took a spoonful of gruel but that same morsel seemed endlessly to be explored within her mouth without quite passing beyond her throat. When at length she swallowed Emma could tell it caused her some pain.

'When I was in the Great House, I was took to church,' Jenny said, 'and the vicar spake of ones such as you. They walked barefoot and suffered much hardship for the sake of their quest and of doing penance. I thought it would have served them better to do a day's work. I cannot remember the name of them but it were something grim.'

'They are pilgrims.' Emma laughed.

'That's right.' Jenny solemnly nodded. 'I knew it were something grim. Is that is what you are then – a pil-grim?'

When Emma paid for their repast she asked the steward if he could offer her work. 'I'll clean the place and serve the customers. I'm a hard worker.'

The man looked her over angrily. 'Why, you'd scare the customers, you dirty little beggar.'

'So that is what I have become.' She sighed. 'Perhaps it is not surprising when my boots are splashed with blood and I have not seen my reflection in four days nor slept in a bed nor had a proper wash. Still, it is a short time to fall foul of society. If one is seen as destitute then one is almost bound to become so.' She had a small sum of money in her purse. With two mouths to feed it would last but a day or two. She must rely instead on her intellectual resources. As the child at her side began to doze the thought occurred to her that her miserable education at Fuchsia Lodge might, after all, have its uses.

She put a sixpence into the hand of the ill-mannered steward and asked him to care for the smaller child until her return.

'What, are you leaving me?' The little girl woke up and looked alarmed.

'I shall return,' Emma promised. 'When I do, it is to be hoped that we shall have better circumstance.'

'I can think of no better circumstance.' The babe lay down again. 'I have shelter and a companion.'

Emma's first aim was to try to have a thorough wash. She scanned the river to get a sense of her environs. A coal barge was docked at a landing stage and Emma called out to a burly creature with glistening black skin imparted not by race but by labour: 'Do you know the way to the nearest bath-house?'

She was surprised to hear a female voice and a hearty laugh. 'Do I look as if I have acquaintance with baths?'

'I know of one in Orange Street close by Trafalgar Square,' Emma said. 'I think it is far from here.'

'Come aboard and I'll give you a ride to Westminster Bridge,' the woman offered. 'You can cut up meat and vegetables and bread for my dinner in return. 'Twill make a change not to have a black stew.'

A helping hand imparted a ridge of grime yet she did not mind picking up some coal dust on her way. It would all be washed off when she reached her destination.

The coalwoman had taken advantage of her cargo with a brazier burning in a makeshift metal hearth on deck. A bucket suspended over it was her stove. As Emma prepared the food her eyes were drawn in astonishment to the sights around her. The whole of the river seemed akin to a strange insect world, the sails of the boats and barges making white butterflies, the tugs and steamers bobbing like large and small beetles. The side of the river was a city of mud in which pitiful creatures with hungry, hunted eyes and gaunt bodies dangling scraps of rags tried to make their living by scavenging morsels dropped from the trading craft or thrown overboard. Most were boys as young and younger than herself but there were little children, too, and old women, their arms delving in the filth. Sometimes handsome buildings rose behind them, the silt of mud with its bedraggled crop of half-starved humans stretching before them like a hideous garden. As she passed this festering place Westminster Bridge came into view and to its right a most handsome assembly of buildings.

'Houses of Parliament, miss,' the bargeman's wife supplied. 'It's where fine gentlemen makes the laws for more fine gentlemen.'

At the bath-house Emma made very liberal use of soap and water. Her clothing had to content itself with a general dusting off and a wipe where it was stained. She tidied her hair and then had her boots polished by a street entrepreneur. When her makeshift *toilette* was complete she inspected the result in a glass shop-front.

I am still not such as would do credit to the Misses Wilcox's academy, she decided, but, given my natural limitations, I have not done too badly. And now, Miss Mabel! She tied her bonnet tightly beneath her chin and finished with a bow to the side. Having left myself severely in your debt, I must borrow from you once again.

This time she did not return by the river, instead using the road with its busy, respectable houses and shops. The premises on the Strand looked too prosperous and Fleet Street too busy. It was dinner hour by the time her nose led her to small chop-house in Cornhill. She approved the tall, narrow house tidily tucked away from traffic in a quiet alley called Bull Court. Inside, tables set in booths were backed by dim-looking brass rails where diners suspended their coats and hats. Apart from a general disregard for hygiene it was a pleasing sort of establishment. She went in and ordered soup, to be told that gentlemen only were served on the premises.

'I am not surprised,' she modelled her tone closely on that of Miss Wilcox, 'for the whole premises is so dirty that no lady would wish to dine here.'

'I am very sorry, miss,' the man spoke respectfully, 'but we're too busy here to attend to the fine details.'

What a difference a clean appearance makes, and a superior air, even in one so insignificant as I, Emma reflected. 'When my father was alive he spoke well of this house.' She assumed Miss Mabel's accent once again. 'I am surprised to find it shabby. You need a woman to work for you. I will do it, if you like.' She managed to make her voice careless, although she badly wanted the employment.

'I've no money to pay a woman. Any road, you're only a lass and you don't look to me like a working one.'

'We have been in poor circumstance since my father passed away,' she said. 'My mother is in hospital and my sister unwell. You will find me a quick and tidy worker.'

The steward rubbed at his unshaven chin. 'I had not thought to employ another body. What would you be wanting for wages?'

Emma could tell that the man was still undecided and she knew she must in some manner make his mind up for him. 'For a start I shall require no wages, but only board and lodgings for myself and my sister. When a week has passed you may decide if I can pay my way and offer what is fair. I can clean floors and serve at table. I can wash dishes and make beds.'

'And will you mind it if the gentlemen are sometimes a little free and merry?'

'I shall not complain,' she promised.

'Nor shall you,' said he, shortly. 'And if your labour does not suit, you will leave at once and without argument. There is a room. It's not much, but I can put in a mattress and some bedding. When can you start?'

'As soon as you furnish me with pinafore and pail.'

'Start tidying after the customers leave,' said he. 'When you have finished you are free until five o'clock and then we serve again until nine. I will help you wait at table but it will be your task to keep the tables clean.'

'May I sit somewhere until it is time to work?' Emma asked.

'Go to the kitchen and ask the cook to give you soup,' said he. 'Tell him you are the new help. Oh, by the by, I am Jack Whaley. What do they call you?'

'Emma.'

'Emma what?'

Emma was assailed by a melancholy sense of her obscurity but she quickly recalled a little sick child who awaited her and she answered very decidedly, 'Emma Pilgrim.'

In another half-hour Emma Pilgrim stood in the middle of the dirty floor, with a pinafore that had to be folded into the waist to keep it off the ground, and a pail of water, soap and a scrubbing brush. She looked around the now-deserted restaurant and sighed mightily. How on earth did one go about cleaning so disordered a room? She must commence quickly and somehow give the impression of knowing what she was about. The floor was so untidy as to be barely negotiable. Chop bones, cigar ends, bits of paper, made a daunting debris in a sea of sawdust.

It was almost four o'clock by the time she had swept and scrubbed the tables, chairs and floor and polished all the brass rails. Then she had to tackle the spittoons.

CHAPTER THIRTY-ONE

You may remember, reader, that Mr Cornhill left me two pieces of literature for my company. The first was that doleful report on the fate of undefended girls. The second, in its own way, was no less terrible.

It was a farewell letter to a man from a woman. Its tone was both callous and flirtatious. It spoke of the 'exciting time' she had passed with Mr Cornhill and regretted its inevitable end – 'as I will likely not again encounter such ardour, but I am a poor girl and must now bend my pretty head to the practical matter of my future'. In short, she had found someone else to marry. 'Our relationship could never have been viewed by any sensible-minded person as other than a passing fancy and is best consigned at once to the precious trinket-box of youth. There! It is ended. I shall keep as a souvenir our single delicious kiss!'

The letter chilled me, both for its lightness of vein and its odious intent. It bespoke the cheapness of a mercenary female who exploits men for flattery but marries for money. It almost vindicated Mr Cornhill's feelings of misogyny. The sick sensation I experienced upon reading it was intensified by the fact that the signature – the handwriting too – was none other than my own.

It was a month before I would see Mr Cornhill again. A far shorter time elapsed until I resolved the mystery of the letter that I had, and had not, written. It was a counterfeit from an accomplished forger. I had no difficulty in putting a name to that mimic.

Alicia Cornhill would have convinced herself it was for the best. A swift and brutal amputation was (in her estimation) to be preferred to a prolonged and painful festering. Even if the limb might have been saved, it would not have looked as she wished it to look. Having no mirror on the world, save that which showed her own reflection, she was incapable of seeing any point of view that did not serve her own.

When she wanted to stop me leaving Happen Heath, she had forged a letter to my father. Wishing to sever for once and all my connection to her son, she had again copied my hand.

I could picture her addressing her task like a piece of fine needlework, with infinite patience for the precise placing of a dot above an 'i' or the heartfelt sweep for the 'F' of my lover's name. The phrases would have been selected from her personal trinket-box. Likely she had shed an unfit romantic candidate or two in her time. She even sacrificed her love of fine textures to pen the note on the kind of plain writing-paper that would have suited the pocket of a young governess. I well believe she took pleasure in the detail. When the job was done (after several unhurried rehearsals) the blotter would have been applied as tenderly as lips to lips. The raw pain it would bring to her son was no more than that of necessary surgery. That this simple note would brand him with lifelong bitterness would have touched her own heart less than the scorching of a leaf by frost. She had been opposed. She must be appeased.

I had risen above my expectation. I must be set back into my place.

Well, she was dead now. She had been punished most cruelly by the death of her youngest son. I do not doubt she would gladly have seen Finch marry a dozen governesses if she could have had her little boy back. I could not hate or blame her. She had acted, as most do, according to her nature.

All the same, this tawdry revelation gave me pause to wonder. What of my life? How different might it have been? Finch would have come looking for me; of that, I am now convinced. He would have found a married woman. What then?

In spite of the turmoil of my emotions I could not erase my history, nor wish it gone. Even lacking the central ingredient of romantic love, mine had been a happy marriage.

Perhaps that plump hand had not, after all, tampered with the hand of fate but been its instrument. Perhaps it had inadvertently beckoned me to my rightful home and Finch to his true calling.

Oh, I do not know. Whatever the veracity of my retrospective ramblings, one cold truth persisted. For one reason or another all the people I loved were gone from me, and if Mrs Cornhill might be deemed callous, I could be judged for carelessness.

The latter, of course, referred to Emma. Thus, when I had done with speculation and self-pity, I packed up the past with all its regrets and riddles, dusted off my practical self and took a fresh look at possibility. Finch had said he needed evidence. I would find it.

To date my detective role at Fuchsia Lodge had had no notable success. In truth it was rendered all but impossible by the vigilance of the Wilcox sisters. Never underestimate those ladies. They did not take my aid on trust. When enemies are forced into alliance they keep an eye to their own backs and to all possible aspects of the erstwhile foe. It was not that they felt they had anything to hide, rather that I might seek to reinforce my sense of advantage. I had no doubt but that when their present good fortune was fully asserted, they would go to every measure to erase the humiliating indications of their past poverty. They would be reborn as benevolent aristocrats who had eschewed the married state in order to devote their lives to ideal young ladies.

But why, you must wonder, did I not simply state my case – why not say I sought some evidence to vindicate the history of an innocent young person? Ah! The brief episode of Matilda Fitzgibbon sat like a pip in the exquisitely clear jelly of their present picture. To try to fish it out would altogether destroy the moulded perfection. They could only hope it would sink to the bottom and never be seen again.

Thus, if I left my classroom in search of a book or a set of needles they were instantly at my elbow. If I took a turn in the garden, they found themselves urgently in need of air. If I went to fetch a glass of water, they wondered at once and in unison if I might not prefer tea.

Until now I had permitted myself to be herded. Now I determined to pitch my wiles against their cunning. My scheme took several weeks to plan and perfect. First, I prepared a notebook of pretty wild-flower paintings and, as the weather was clement and the meadows prolific, I volunteered to lead the young ladies on a nature ramble. At my own expense I would hire the transport to take us to a noted beauty spot, provide a picnic and all refreshments, then devise a two-mile walk whereon the pupils would identify flowers and paint them if they wished. The idea brought such a chorus of approval from the fun-starved damsels that it was nigh impossible for their guardians to disapprove.

Indeed, the schoolmistresses themselves were quite feverish with excitement at the prospect.

But how, you will ask, did this advance my plan? If I was to lead the expedition, how then conduct a search of the school? My strategy was to absent myself at a point when all other aspects of the treat were too advanced to be cancelled. Still there were obstacles. How would I gain the run of Fuchsia Lodge? What was needed was one indisposed pupil whom I, in a spirit of heroic self-sacrifice, would volunteer to tend.

It might be noted that of all the young persons now enrolled in the academy, only one showed a marked lack of enthusiasm for my excursion. Little Lady Millie hated fresh air or exercise of any kind, except dancing. From the start she had looked exactly as I had hoped – peevish, uncooperative and unwilling. As the great day drew near and interesting hampers arrived at the school, I approached the young nobility and strongly suggested that she looked unwell. I allowed it to sink into her shallow brain that a dangerous influenza was abroad and that, if contracted, it might spoil her travel plans for the summer. The pampered young person grew paler by the second. Before the day of the outing arrived, she even contrived a very solid swoon.

I consigned my flower paintings to Miss Wilcox. I made it known that Lady Millie's health was more precious to me than any picnic. I let it be understood that excursions were unimportant at my time of life, and should be left to fresher females. I even perfected my sacrifice by suggesting that the maid might go in my stead. I helped the lady directresses into their transport and checked the hampers. Then I waved them off. The invalid and I had Fuchsia Lodge to ourselves.

To insure the deceit, Lady Millie had been dispatched to bed. She now struggled to rise. By a bribe of cocoa with cream on the top, I contrived to keep her there another hour. Then I stormed the house from top to bottom. Every cushion was raised; every pot and box checked. I lifted house-plants from their outer casings. I searched under rugs and mattresses. I even managed to find the key to the dismal top room where Emma had been imprisoned. I spent a doleful half-hour there, imagining how this dark incarceration must have affected the nerves of a sick and lonely child. Yet there was nothing to connect me to Emma.

When I came down, dusty and disappointed, Lady Millie was in petulant mood. She had anticipated a full-time attendant. A spark of spite had come into her eye. 'It was kind of you to take a job as nursemaid,' she said. 'I wonder if it is wise for you to assume the burdens of housemaid as well. I cannot think the Misses Wilcox would approve.'

I decided to play her at her own game. 'Well, Lady Millicent,' I said, 'I was brought up to believe that the devil makes work for idle hands. As the day is clement and you seem much recovered, I suggest we might both try our hands at a little useful gardening.'

This recommendation brought an instant relapse and, with an unbecoming curl to her plump lip, she retired to her bed once more. I was then obliged to follow my own prescription. I equipped myself with stout boots, an apron and some gardening gloves, and set forth with pruning shears. Aside from the frustration of having failed in my mission, I cannot proclaim this as hardship. It was a lovely old garden, hedged with fashionable fuchsia, and with a large laburnum that spread its branches over a curved garden bench. The level part of the garden had been consigned to the utility of exercising the young maidens. The rest was left to its own devices. Pretty borders peeped through weeds and on a raised terrace a summerhouse was all but overgrown by a dense tangle of clematis and climbing roses. For the devoted gardener, there is no happier challenge than an untamed enclosure. Here is a ready supply of unclaimed treasure. Here is the best possible exercise in the world. Here is fresh and fragrant air, and God's miracles in abundant supply.

For several hours I sheared, I pruned, I pulled, I dug. The craft and reward were akin to that of restoring old art works. From beneath the bloom of decay a pleasing picture began to emerge. By this stage I myself presented a perfect picture of dirt and disorder. I had, moreover, worked up a very fine appetite for lunch. I felt quite pleased with myself, until I remembered that a person of title had also been left without nourishment a full four hours. I must go indoors at once and save her from starvation.

For a moment, two consciences were at war: that of the good woman who must tend a fractious child, and that of the good gardener who must clear the debris before quitting the task. The gardener won. She needed a wheelbarrow. Finding no shed I set my sights upon the abandoned summerhouse. This pretty ornament indeed proved to be the storage-place and the reason why no one used it. With wheelbarrow in place there was only room for a very slender child to negotiate a way to the seat. A moment after this reflection reached my brain, a second consideration fell into place.

I wrestled the wheelbarrow out into the open and returned to the little house, where rotting timbers gave out the smell of old books and dead leaves made a carpet for the floor. Briars poked inquisitive fingers through broken leaded lights as I sat on the small seat, which brought a view of the river and the surrounding countryside. I thought, This is where Emma came in search of solitude. I could imagine Miss Wilcox's strident voice summoning her; and Emma, with a weary sigh, leaving her refuge to return to the school. Aside from the wheelbarrow there was nothing except several towers of pots stored under the seat.

I crouched down and separated them. Apart from a dried leaf and a dried spider, they were empty of content. As I arose

334

again, I noted that the bench had a hinged lid. I raised it. Inside were some very old seed packs, their painted illustrations faded to ghostly flower suggestions: wallflower, sweetpea, pansy, forget-me-not. Forget-me-not. I prised apart the lips of this last package. There was almost a sense of teasing in the manner in which the small gold ring winked among the tiny seeds. Time was suspended in slow motion as I lifted out the slender jewel and saw the pleasing setting of turquoise and pearl. It was a trinket of no great value yet at this moment the most precious treasure in all the world. I turned it over and saw what had been inscribed on its inside.

At that moment I heard my voice called. It was the sort of peremptory command that must have disturbed Emma as she huddled in her hiding-place. The summons sounded nearer. Its instrument presented itself. Lady Millie looked utterly perplexed and peevish to find me covered in mud and cobwebs when I ought to have been shipshape and in her service. 'Mrs Chalfont!' She spoke in definite reprimand. 'There is a gentleman to see you. Have you entirely forgotten my lunch?'

'Millie,' I apologized. 'I have forgotten myself, my manners and both our lunches. And both must wait a spell longer yet. Tell me who the gentleman is and then please let him know that I shall be along directly I have tidied myself up.'

'I shall not wait,' said Lady Millie; 'and nor shall the gentleman. As to his identity, you can see for yourself as he approaches directly.'

At this she (mercifully) flounced off and the other party came on stage. As one not greatly given to mirth I suppose I ought to add it to his credit that he laughed. 'Mrs Chalfont!' said he. 'I hope I did not catch you at an inopportune moment.'

I contributed some earth to my hair in endeavouring to pat it into place. 'Not at all, Mr Cornhill. I had just done with gardening for the day.'

He looked approvingly around the garden. 'You have done good work.'

'Better even than I hoped.' I took the seed packet from my pocket and emptied its content into his hand.

'Well done!' he exclaimed. 'This is much more like the old Isa. I came here to bring you good news. The puzzle is all falling into place. This may well be the final piece.'

'I'm afraid you will be disappointed. Although the ring is found, it contributes little.'

He lifted the trinket and inspected it. He read the legend that was wrought upon the gold. No name, no initials! The inside of the gold circle had been inscribed with a maudlin phrase: '*WE TWO*'. The words were linked by a graven heart.

'No revelation, sir,' I said. 'Nothing but a commonplace sentiment. It tells us nothing.'

'You are wrong, Isa.' He gave a rather mysterious smile. 'It tells me everything I need to know.'

'Then tell me.'

'Not yet! Have patience a while longer. The truth of the matter is, I came to say something else. I have forgiven you. I made a very bad mistake in carrying that letter close to my heart so many years. It did not protect it. It merely barred the way to any other happiness. It locked me into that dismal time when we were both young and helpless.'

I tried to speak but he put a hand to my mouth.

'Yes, both! I can see now that you were no more culpable than I was. Of course you had to think of your future. At the time I had neither money nor independence. I might have been killed in action. You did the right thing, Isa. The letter seemed heartless but I dare say it served its purpose.'

He was standing too close to me. I found it hard to catch my breath. I had to walk away. I hid in that pretty edifice whose delicate design had been obscured by branch and thorny tangle. Like all of riotous nature my heart felt suffocated by containment and hammered on its fragile frame of ribs. This place was designed for lovers, I thought. Small wonder the Misses Wilcox spurned it. Mr Cornhill came to stand in the doorway. Framed by wild nature and architectural fancy, he looked to me intense and beautiful.

'That letter may have been true to its purpose,' I breathed; 'yet it lied about its agency.'

'Isa, no explanation is necessary.'

'I did not write it,' I stated quickly.

'Isa, don't! There is no need to make excuses. It is all in the past now.'

'I know who did – and not for the first time.'

Now it was his turn to look perplexed.

'The letter was not from myself but from your mother.'

'From Mama? Oh, Isa, don't be absurd. I would have believed Mama capable of almost anything but I know your writing. Don't forget, I had those few brief but precious notes you sent me. The hand was the very same.'

'Long ago your mother stole a letter I had written to my father and used it to copy my hand. She was an apt forger, to be sure. By the same technique, she composed this counterfeit in my name. I swear to you, Finch, I never penned those words. At the same time when you were reading them, my own heart was at the point of breaking. My marriage was arranged by my father, to help pay my mother's medical bills.'

Such a tense silence followed as seemed to prick the air with points of puzzlement. Gradually, his gaze came to rest upon me. It was not the critical scrutiny that had so pained me, but a prolonged dawning of recognition. We travelled within one another's eyes, negotiated all the luggage of our intervening years and, with infinite patience, found at the back of it all the hopeful youth and maid. When Finch finally spoke, it was not with ardour but with infinite regret. 'Oh, Isa.'

'Shall we be friends?' I said. 'We are no longer young and foolish. We have half a lifetime behind us. Yet the sympathies that first bound us may be found to be intact.'

He swooped into the small hut and took my hand. He looked on it in surprise to see it sturdy and mature, not the tender and tentative limb he had first grasped. Slowly, he raised it to his mouth. I tried to stifle my indrawn breath as I felt the warm imprint of his lips. 'No!' He dropped my hand. 'I cannot be your friend. It would be a charade. I wanted you for a part of myself. I could not be content with the fellowship of some other man's wife.'

'My husband is dead,' I said. 'He died many years ago.'

Whatever sympathetic or reasonable discussion might have ensued was disposed of by two warm-fleshed bodies that had been denied their proper meeting. Scorning consultation with the intellect, they sought one another. I cannot remember if he moved towards me or I towards him but only that we were in one another's arms. What sensations did we encounter there? Was there passion? I do not recall. The only clear sensation was that of regaining, after a long absence, the point of belonging. How well God had fashioned us for each other. Height for height, we matched; heartbeat for heartbeat. There no longer seemed any hurry and so it was with infinite leisure that we sought one another's lips.

Fate elected this spectacular moment to re-enter young Lady Millie (her features now such an arrangement of astonishment that I thought her eyebrows would take off in flight) with a second visitor. Given the urgency of his entry, we had no time to rearrange our tableau, and I have to own that even the phlegmatic Mr Ellin suffered a loss of equanimity.

CHAPTER THIRTY-TWO

It had been Emma's intention to acquaint Jenny Drew with soap and water before introducing her to her new lodgings, but the bath-house was too far and the little girl fast asleep so she wiped her face with a handkerchief and wrapped her in her cloak to keep her soiled and ragged clothing out of view.

Their quarter was a small storeroom at the top of the chop-house, which they were to share with some barrels and chests. A small window looked out over the courtyard. A mattress had been laid on the floor and some warm blankets. One chest was left empty to store their possessions and on its surface was a candle and water for washing.

'It is our home,' Emma said to Jenny. 'It is chill but safe and dry. No one will disturb us here.'

'You must be rich and important to get us such a chamber,' Jenny said.

Emma laughed. 'I am the most insignificant creature that ever lived, but I am learning to profit from experience.' She put the child to bed, then yawned and lay down beside her.

'Stay with me,' Jenny said. 'I shall be lonely.'

'I wish I could. Oh, Jenny Drew, I am so weary I think I shall die of it.'

Jenny clapped her hands to Emma's cheeks. 'Don't die, for I would have no one to keep me company.'

'It is said that hard work never killed anyone.' With an effort Emma returned to a standing position. 'So perhaps I shan't die. But I feel I might. Are you hungry?' she asked the little girl.

'I ain't exactly, yet I could chew on a crust,' was the reply.

'If I survive this night, I shall return with a midnight feast.' Emma dropped a swift kiss on the child's grubby brow and went back to work.

The inn was full of the smoke and noise of the evening diners. Now Emma had to face a fresh hazard. As the gentlemen grew genial with food and drink, they became familiar with the only female in the house.

'Would you like to come down the river with me?' A fat red hand trapped her round the waist and a whiskery face was thrust into hers.

She felt so panic-stricken she thought she would faint, but then she summoned Miss Mabel Wilcox to her mind. What would she do in such a situation? In spite of her fright the unlikely prospect almost caused her to smile, but she straightened her spine, tapped the offending arm a little less than lightly with a knife, and spoke in her best Fuchsia Lodge accent: 'Sir, I had taken you for the most gentlemanly person in this establishment. I had made up my mind that if any other person were to speak to me coarsely, I would apply to you for help. I hope I was not mistaken.'

The man look befuddled but he withdrew his hand at once. 'Why, you can certainly count on me. A little joke, that's all. I hope you were not offended. Any other blackguard says a word to you I'll lay him out. Good girl. Here's a sixpence for your trouble.'

A sixpence! She had not only a roof over her head and food to eat but she was earning money as well. She beamed at her persecutor with such open pleasure that that gentleman was sincerely resolved to become her protector.

The thought of sixpence inside her pocket gave Emma fresh energy, and fatigue was dispelled by the pleasant prospect of spending it. What would she purchase? As she carried back and forth dishes piled high with beef and mutton, as she wiped down tables and stacked dishes and fended off well-fed assailants (she said the exact same thing to each one of them and every one was ashamed, although no other gave her a sixpence), she felt as keenly as only women can the pleasure of her own earning power. She decided she would buy herself a second-hand book. But which one? There were so many. Verses or essays? She might choose a novel or a volume describing someone's travels around the world. She felt almost dizzy from choice. That evening everyone thought her a pleasant and willing little worker.

She climbed the stairs around midnight, balancing her candle with a tray of bread and meat and a small pitcher of ale. She had no other thought in mind than to partake of a little nourishment and a very long sleep. At the same time she looked forward to a bed warmed by her small companion.

I wish I had said I loved her, she thought as she paused on the stairs to give such a yawn as almost parted her skull from her jaw, for there is no doubt but that she is lovable.

When she let herself into the dark room, no stir came from the bed. Emma placed the candle and tray on the chest and blew out the light. Not wishing to wake the child, she took a swift draught of ale and a bite of bread and got into bed.

'Jenny!' she called out in alarm, for there was only a cold space in the mattress. She must have gone to the outhouse. I hope she took my cloak to keep her warm, Emma thought. I ought to light the candle for her return. But before she had time to translate this thought into action, she fell asleep.

She woke with the first light. All her bones ached and she felt weary and confused. Glancing around the overcrowded chamber her initial thought was that she was in Fuchsia Lodge in the attic storeroom where Miss Wilcox had confined her.

As her listless brain began to clear she recalled that that was months ago, a lifetime ago, and she was in London in a safe place and all was well. Yet all was not well. She sat up with a start. She was alone in the bed. Jenny Drew was still missing. She pulled on her clothes and made a swift and stealthy exit.

A city in the dawn is like a woman past her prime. Some show up soft and mellow with roses yet in their cheeks. Others display a bleak and mourning destitution of a glory that once was theirs. This one – though still a beauty – had grown stern and mannish and showed the corruption of moral neglect. Where might this great city clutch a small and helpless child to her bosom?

The angular spire of St Edmund the King and the tower of St Michael's, still in their black garb of night, looked down in silent judgement. 'Our great city was built for great people,' they seemed to say. 'Such as you and her have no place in it and ought to make yourselves invisible.' Then, to her relief, she saw that the first of the poor workers had drifted into the street. She approached one and asked how she might find her way to the docks.

After another fifteen minutes she found herself in the same spot where she had made acquaintance with the child. Various derelicts were creeping out from hiding-places, but of Jenny Drew there was no trace. Emma approached a woman with a face as red as meat. 'Have you seen a little girl?'

'I've seen a few,' she said; 'myself included, once upon a time.'

342

'A ragged little girl, but fair. She is lame in one leg and she is a pure finder.'

'Oh, a bunter! I know the one. Jenny Drew.'

'Yes, but have you seen her?'

'I might have done.' The woman eyed her shrewdly.

Reluctantly, Emma handed over her precious sixpence. 'Now can you tell me anything about her?'

The woman examined the coin and slipped it into a pocket. 'She is dead, miss.'

'Oh, what?' A cry was wrung from Emma's heart.

'Must be. She was always hereabouts. A little oddity. Took to collecting dead babies. Tough little perisher, but poorly this long time. We all said she had but a few weeks left to her.'

'Have you seen her dead?' Emma asked.

'Dying's a private business,' the woman said. 'Them as can walk or crawl finds somewhere unfrequented for to give up their breath.'

'I must find her,' Emma said.

'You'll not,' the woman warned. 'That mite will know of places in the city you'd never find in four times her years.'

Emma went back to the warehouse where they had passed the night. Other poor creatures were there, but not Jenny. She gave detailed investigation to sinister alleyways. Various parcels of rags revealed human content, but no curly-headed little girl. Very despondent, she gave up the search and headed back the way she had come. She moved slowly, her arms folded against the cold. She felt inexpressibly weary and thoroughly disinclined to face another day of work. Still, she must keep a roof over her head and put food in her mouth.

A dog trotted by, looking almost as miserable as herself. Poor thing. Likely it belonged to no one. She saw then that it was followed at a distance by a child. Shortly after, a dairy woman came into the street and a small comedy ensued. A cat padded in her wake to catch any drops of milk she spilled from her pails. The dog saw the cat and instantly gave chase, almost tripping up the dairy woman. The child headed off in pursuit of dog and cat, but then she dropped in the street, using the last of her energy to hurl her little basket after the dog, after which she just sat there, sobbing.

'Jenny Drew!' Emma recognized her with relief.

'I followed that dog an hour,' Jenny wailed weakly. 'It wouldn't do nothing.'

'Oh, my poor little friend.' Emma gathered her up. The cold of that small body chilled her to the bone. 'Why did you run away?'

'Run away?' Jenny's huge eyes studied her in perplexity. 'I never did.'

'What made you leave the place where you were warm and safe?'

'I went to earn my living.'

'But I have a job and shelter for us both.' Emma gathered her up and headed back towards that refuge.

'Yes, but you said you might die of it.' Jenny's teeth chattered. 'I feared you might.' She was seized then by a fit of coughing, which remorselessly battered her small frame. Emma staggered onward, until the smaller girl let out a cry of dismay. 'I left my basket!'

'Oh, must we go back?' Emma said.

The great tear-filled violet eyes beseeched her. 'Would you have me waste a night's labour?'

When the child was reunited with her source of livelihood she relaxed in Emma's arms and soon fell asleep and Emma was able to lodge the basket in what she hoped was a safe concealment rather than bring that distinctive cargo back to their place of residence.

The chop-house was filling up with people rested after a night's sleep and hungry for a good breakfast. Emma, who had seen but a few hours' repose, became conscious of her own exhaustion. She laid the sleeping child on the mattress, donned her apron and went to work. A minute passed like a dreary hour; an hour seemed of a week's duration. Her whole body felt leaden and her brain was oppressed and unclear. Depression mocked her. Sounds all seemed strange and harsh to her and her mind was unable to make sense of them. When a gentleman spoke to her kindly to ask if she was not too little for such a burden of work, she burst into tears and fled to the kitchen.

The cook, who worked in a cauldron of steam and a hell of flame, observed the crouched bundle of heartache in his cramped quarter. Pausing briefly in his juggling of pans he picked her up and lifted her on to a stool. Into her hands he placed a cup of hot coffee. 'Drink that,' he said. 'You'll be the better for it.'

The gentle words acted not as a balm but as a needle to a wound and she was unable to take her refreshment for weeping. He paused again, told her to take a very deep breath and drink down the drink. She did as she was bade and her head spun but soon she was able to take possession of herself and return to her station.

At dinnertime she stole away to bring food to Jenny, but the child was deep in sleep, each breath so harsh it seemed to sandpaper her soul. 'She needs a doctor,' Emma sighed. 'But I have no money.'

A dazed afternoon followed the difficult morning. At moments, Emma felt that no one could survive such prolonged endeavour. The shouts of conversation and laughter, the banging of dishes, the heat of the fire passed around her like a hellish torment. When she finally achieved her bed that night she clasped the hot, feverish body of the younger child to her

345

and thought it likely that neither of them would wake to see the morning. This struck her as an idea only. She had passed beyond emotion. She dropped into sleep like a stone into water and dreamed of running through meadows with a little girl who was like Jenny Drew, yet who was not she.

Another cold morning found her. Her bones ached even more. Her companion slept still and was delirious and called out, then laughed in her old man's voice. Emma dragged herself from sleep and cast herself upon the mercy of the day.

To her surprise, this one came easier than the last. She had slept through the night and was refreshed. Now that she had thoroughly cleaned her dining-room it did not take such a deal of scrubbing to set it to rights. Her customers had grown fond of the small diligent creature who brought an agreeable but unnecessary degree of hygiene to their place of sustenance. That day, without making any demands upon her person, another gentleman gave her a sixpence.

After dinner, when business was slack, she asked if she might have time off for an errand.

'Take what time you need,' Jack Whaley said. 'You have earned it – and this too': he gave her a shilling.

A weak sun was shining. The streets seemed less unfamiliar and unforgiving. A few recognizable landmarks greeted her. She was no longer vagrant. She was earning her way and had money in her pocket. She walked until she found a remembered site close by St Paul's where a street vendor made and purveyed his wares. She watched the doll-maker at his work, carving very lifelike wooden puppets.

'Have you got a baby one?' she asked.

'Baby Daniel. My favourite.' He produced a squat little doll in a white dress.

'How much would you sell him for?'

'Sixpence and not a penny less,' he said.

She handed over the money and hurried back. She was pleased to find Jenny sitting up in bed.

'Look what I've brought you.' She dangled the doll on its strings.

Jenny took the toy delightedly. 'What is it?'

'It is a real doll, such as rich children have.'

'Does he have a name?' Jenny wiggled his hinged limbs.

'The man who made him called him Baby Daniel.'

Jenny laughed. 'Well, Baby Daniel, your bones stick out so you'll not be a comfort. But I shall like you anyway.'

'And you'll not be lonely now while I am at work.'

'I've not been lonely.' Jenny smiled. 'Not this day, nor yesterday. That gentleman you sent to talk to me was very kindly.'

'What gentleman?' Emma said in alarm. 'I sent no one.'

'You must have done for I woke to find him sitting by my bed. Bright as a candle, he were, and he liked me. He told me not to be afraid, for he loved little children. I said I loved him too. I don't know why I should have done, for I never afore laid eyes on him, but I felt as if I did, and no one else has ever said they loved me.'

Emma hugged her, but the feeling of unease persisted until she remembered that Jenny had been delirious the day before and had been talking in her sleep. Nonetheless, she took the precaution of locking the door before she returned to her work.

By the end of the first month, Emma found that the hard labour no longer wearied her. She looked with interest upon her raw and toughened hands and realized that, despite the severity of her labour, she had had no fainting fit, no nightmare; not once had she suffered a headache nor felt inclined to wander in her sleep. The food at the inn was plentiful and she had good appetite. In spite of Jenny's worsened cough and fevered ramblings, her caretaker slept the night through.

A season squandered its themes in a grey and watery soup. A silt of waste arose in the streets. It ruined the hems of women good and bad and made heavy weather for the crossing sweepers. The warm and foggy windows of the tavern signalled a welcoming refuge for bedraggled travellers and the small person who ordered their restoration. The regular gentlemen no longer tried to make free with this little woman. One or two of them intimated that they might offer her a less taxing post in their homes, and a room with her own fire. Emma thanked them but declined, for she doubted that the offer extended to Jenny Drew. Besides, she was pleased enough with her present position. A job in a house would likely come with a woman to tell her what to do. She had independence in the tavern and lately money too. Jack Whaley had agreed to give her half a crown a week for her toil and a morning off. She conducted her work as she chose and no one intruded on her free time.

The notion now and then passed through her mind that she had found sufficient activity and purpose for her life. By her own resources she was making a living and she was caring for someone. Far better to earn a menial livelihood than to be a precarious and vulnerable thing, forever ashamed of what one was or was not. No one questioned her about her class or her past. She was self-reliant and appreciated for her labour.

She had also begun to save. She still had her shilling and now a half-crown was added to this. It became quite commonplace for gentlemen, when they were well fed and refreshed with ale, to offer pennies and these she kept in an empty jam pot. Looking at them overlapping at the bottom of the pot, Emma could understand why poor people became misers. The coins spelled security. They promised to shelter the bearer from cold and want and disdain.

The sun became an early riser. Grey skies went into storage and caged birds sang out their yearning from dark chambers. Emma, too, felt the summons of the season. As summer approached she began to explore the city. No longer in pursuit of a crust of bread or a place of rest, a sense of adventure arose in her. In St Paul's churchyard she discovered a great treasure trove of bookshops and at night, by candle-light, she read to Jenny.

As she grew bolder she embarked on longer excursions, travelling on the giant omnibus with its team of horses and layered carriage. At sixpence a mile it was a costly indulgence but she loved to sit on the open deck where, in fine neighbourhoods, the branches of trees brushed her face with blossom. She shared her transport with people of many nationalities gathered in the capital for a great event. In such exotic company, Emma saw herself as others must see her — a workworn female with raw hands and dull hair, still dressed in the cut-down attire of Mr Hibble's housekeeper.

This image reflects a former self, she thought. My present persona merits some more spruce packaging. She counted out her savings, took what might be spared, and from a second-hand stall on Leather Lane furnished herself with an array of apparel. Such items as had, in another time and place, burdened her with misery now afforded her considerable satisfaction. Yet this little wardrobe was the very opposite of showy: a dress in a dark blue check, a light shawl, a plain grey gown with garnet-coloured knots upon the bodice, a bonnet of horsehair with straw plait, a light grey shawl and some summer slippers. The entirety had cost two shillings with a diminutive white frock with a hem of broderie anglaise thrown in for luck for Jenny Drew.

To Emma, the garments signified more than a sudden change of climate that rendered unfashionable last week's boots, umbrellas and heavy capes. She, too, had entered another season. Some inches had been added to her height. Her figure had gained a modest augmentation. She often wondered about her age. When she first had come to Fuchsia Lodge she had been a little girl in adult eyes (though her soul had felt too jaded for that innocent estate). Now, when she donned her grandeur, her reflection showed a grave young woman. The blanched and frightened child was gone. The months that had passed, her education upon the streets and within the pages of books, her working life and the care of a sick child had shaped her. She was not merely a young adult but a capable and thoughtful one.

A strange and encouraging thought presented itself: I set out for London to find my past and myself. The past I sought did not exist, yet that journey made me my real self.

A self without a past or a future, to be sure, yet one who, for the present moment, could judge herself as strong and confident and not entirely the dolt others had once surmised. On this day she even experienced a sensation to which she had hitherto been a stranger. It was a stirring of happiness.

She had made the discovery of green spaces in the city: pampered swathes of nature were set aside as parks where nursemaids sat with prams, people walked their dogs and even made sedate procession upon ponies. Trees and railings sectioned them from the parts of the city where others made their living or sought entertainment or scraped together pennies to see them through another day.

Upon her first encounter with these oases she went at once to tell Jenny. The child was astonished to learn that there was more to the city than the grim sites of her labours. Emma described gardens with green grass and tall trees, where handsome carriages drove about and people walked for pleasure and children played. That little creature who seemed daily to drift at a further distance from life, pulled herself up with a great effort. Her eyes brightened as Emma spoke but then her look grew doubtful. 'Do you think they would let such as me go there – just to look?'

'If I am allowed, then so must you be,' Emma promised.

'Yes, because I am your sister.'

Emma sat on the bed and hugged her close. 'Yes, Jenny Drew,' she said. 'We are all in the world to one another. You are my dear little sister.'

She resolved that she would one day take her little sister to see those green places, but the child was very ill now. She scarcely ate or drank and each breath was a painful exertion.

'Remember the kind gentleman who came to see you?' She spoke gently.

'He still comes,' Jenny said. 'I know who he is now. He says he is my father.'

'I shall send you another kind gentleman,' Emma said. 'A physician who will make you well.'

At this suggestion the child began to tremble all over. 'Oh, please do not. I'll be taken back to the Great House and I shall die there. Such as me is not allowed to die at liberty.'

CHAPTER THIRTY-THREE

We left the scene at Fuchsia Lodge, a frozen diorama of general dismay (myself and Mr Cornhill in compromising proximity; Mr Ellin and the Lady Millie bursting in upon the spectacle). It may relieve you to know that we were not struck for ever in the same tableau. We were rescued, in fact, by Mr Ellin's good manners. Deftly concealing his amazement, he apologized for his hasty entry but excused it on the grounds of important news he had to impart.

'I have just returned from M——! I went to Fox Clough but Mary said I would find you here.'

'What news, Mr Ellin?' I composed myself as best I could (remember that I still wore the household dust and half of the garden).

'I have tracked down the villain who brought Emma here.'

'Indeed.' I glanced at Finch (who had managed to make his face as blank as water) and herded the company towards a less distracting site.

'Allow me a little bragging, if you will.' Mr Ellin's strides were buoyant. 'I have a long-held theory that scoundrels always add a pinch of their true identity to their assumed one. Although I found no reasonable suspicion in any of the estates I visited, yet one address lingered in my mind, both for the beauty of the house and a certain resonance in the title. Does the name Happen Heath remind you of anything, Mrs Chalfont?'

'Why, Mr Ellin! It's remarkable. I had not thought of it. "Happen" could also mean "might" or "may" and a heath would have some kinship to a park. A cunning intellect might consider it to have a similar ring to May Park.'

'Well done! And can you recall the name of the character who introduced Emma to Fuchsia Lodge?'

'Was it not a Mr Conway Fitzgibbon?'

'Allegedly – yet as we both now know that was an imposture. I remained convinced that the man would use the same initials as his own, yet nowhere could I find a suitable candidate with the initials CF. It took me a deal of deliberation to deduce that this clever fellow might have transposed them. His initials were, in fact, FC. Our rogue goes by the name of Finch Cornhill.'

'Excellent conclusion, Mr Ellin,' I congratulated. We arrived at the laburnum tree, under whose gay umbrella the Misses Wilcox kept an eye on their young ladies at play.

'Not bad,' he modestly agreed; 'insofar as it goes, which is not quite far enough. Although I have identified the villain, I have signally failed to track him down. He has been abroad for some time. His little niece will not tell me the truth of it and I can get nothing whatever from his housekeeper. I would advertise but I doubt he would dare to show his face.'

'He is more brazen than you know,' said I; 'for he has already shown it.'

'Now, I beg to doubt that,' Mr Ellin argued. 'If he were to be seen then I should have confronted him.'

'You have,' said I. 'You are.'

I disposed myself upon the bench and allowed the gentlemen to make their own arrangements.

It takes a good deal to discompose Mr Ellin but he now looked thunderstruck. He gaped at me and then at my companion. 'Finch Cornhill?'

The bearer of that name confirmed it.

Mr Ellin's characteristic gentility deserted him. 'What the d—l?'

Finch smiled. 'I am that fiend, sir. I have thrown off my cover. I have disclosed my face. Will you now take my hand?'

Mr Ellin looked from one to other of us in disbelief. 'Mr Cornhill? Finch Cornhill? I will not take your hand. I will take your explanation, sir.'

From this confusion I made my escape. I pleaded a necessity to attend to my appearance and my pupil's lunch, and left Finch to attempt elucidation.

Indoors, I tidied myself as best I could and assuaged the prize pupil with a piece of marzipan cake. I then prepared the placatory repast of tea for my visitors. By the time the two gentlemen arrived indoors, a fairly amicable accord confirmed that Mr Cornhill had managed to fill in my old friend on all the strange, sad story.

'But why did you not take Emma home to Happen Heath?' Mr Ellin was inquiring. 'Why leave her among strangers?'

'For the very good reason that my little niece, Vanessa, has grown to be a merciless snob. She would have made the child's life a misery. I had another purpose. We will talk of it later.'

Mr Ellin nodded. 'I can believe what you say. I met young Vanessa. Still, it is all quite extraordinary – the most remarkable set of coincidences.'

'Not so much as it seems,' Finch said.

'No. I suppose not. I expect you brought Emma to this town because of your old friendship with Mrs Chalfont. You knew of her kind heart.'

Finch cast a wry glance in my direction. 'Not entirely. I did not know her to be here at all. My purpose was quite separate.'

Our detective failed to pick up upon this point. Perhaps he was exhausted by too much discovery. He directed a brooding look at the tea-tray and occupied himself with eating three toasted crumpets in a row.

'But why did you give her false pretences?' I asked. 'Why tell the Misses Wilcox she was an heiress?'

'She ought to have inherited. I only hoped to win her the advantage that was her due.'

'Yet there is another matter for which I would like an explanation directly.' Mr Ellin's legal mind had settled upon a point of contention. 'Although you were confined and unable to make any contact with the child, you sent a gift to the school in her name – a basket of fruit or some such.'

'Not I,' Mr Cornhill answered. 'That was done in my name by a lawyer such as yourself. I asked him to see to the welfare of the child. At the time I had no access to my funds and prevailed on him to use his own money, assuring him I would repay him later. Obviously he had little faith in that eventuality. I assumed he would visit the school, assess the girl's welfare and pay her fees. In reality, the execution of his promise extended no further than that same dispatch.'

'And what of Emma's mother?' I inquired. 'You claimed to know her. May we at last have an end to the suspense?'

'Emma's mother was a fine lady,' Finch said. 'Through no fault of her own, she became connected to a scandal. It made her an outcast. All her friends deserted her.'

Mr Ellin scowled. 'Those friends of hers can have been no true friends.'

355

'I think we are at one on that,' agreed Finch.

'What was the scandal that drove her to such exile?' I wondered.

'She was accused of a violent crime.'

At this Mr Ellin seemed to start as though struck.

'Who was this lady?' My interest was beginning to overtake my patience.

'Perhaps Mr Ellin will tell us.'

Mr Ellin put up his hands. 'My powers of deduction have run dry.'

'This may refresh them.' From his handkerchief, Finch removed the gold ring.

Mr Ellin took the slender object in his hand. I detected a tremor in that sturdy limb. 'I have seen its like before,' he said. 'It is commonplace enough.'

'Read the inscription,' Finch urged.

Mr Ellin did as he was bade. A very peculiar look came over his benign face. His complexion paled visibly. 'Where did you get it?' he demanded.

'Here at Fuchsia Lodge,' I told him. 'It belonged to Emma.'

'Do you recognize it?' Mr Cornhill asked.

'Why should he?' I reasoned.

'The truth of the matter is,' Mr Cornhill spoke to me, 'I brought Emma here because of Mr Ellin. If he is still unable to perceive the reason why, let him read out the initials on the ring.'

There was a side to Finch Cornhill that could never be entirely appealing. In its quest for justice, it was critical and judgemental. I felt compelled to defend my friend. 'They are not initials. It is only a sentimental avowal.'

'"WE," sir,' he persisted: 'whose initials might they be?'

To my great astonishment Mr Ellin replied in a broken tone, 'They are mine.'

'And whose name is represented by the other set?'

356

'Teresa Osborne,' Mr Ellin whispered. 'Teresa Welles Osborne.'

'Emma's mother,' Finch announced. 'A lady you once professed to love – a lady you abandoned to a most lamentable fate.'

'But that cannot be true,' I protested. 'Mr Ellin had made no contact with Teresa since her second marriage.'

'Is that how memory elects to serve you? That is convenient.'

'I remember,' Mr Ellin said.

'Yet you swore never again to see her after she married Edward Ellin.' I was becoming confused.

'I did so vow,' he agreed. 'I meant it too. If I led you to believe that was the end of the story, I apologize. I was not yet ready to face the entirety of the tale. Yet face it I now must.'

William Ellin had not contacted Teresa Osborne. It was she who came to see him after the death of the brother who had taken her from him. At first he did not recognize the ill and miserable-looking woman in black who visited his chambers. When he invited her to be seated she set herself to rest in a cautious manner, as an invalid might, and with pale and narrow hands lifted the veil that covered her face. The visage now revealed was defiant in its despair. 'There! You might as well see the worst,' it seemed to say. Even as he gazed at her, it took him a moment to realize it was Teresa.

'My dear girl!' he exclaimed.

Here was no girl. She was a woman past thirty years in whom beauty had been trampled by circumstance. Teresa had always been one of those females who bloom in happiness and wither in the frosty grip of misery. Now her radiant youth seemed only memory.

In spite of this he felt a tug of tenderness and took one of those cold hands in his to warm it. She did not criticize him for his long absence but merely smiled on him wearily. 'God bless you, little fellow. You have grown into a fine man.'

357

'I am sorry for your husband's death,' he said. 'How did he die?'

'A fall.' She hesitated, as if she found it difficult to speak of. 'He had been drinking.'

'And how do you fare?' he asked her.

She twisted her gloved fingers. 'Not well. I am afraid that Edward's death will once more leave me homeless.'

'Dismiss that fear,' he urged. 'You will surely inherit whatever Edward owned. If you had a son it would be a certainty.'

'I have no son.' She lowered her eyes. 'I have a little girl. I am with child again.'

Poor defenceless creature, he pitied. To be alone at such a time. 'Still, you are his nearest surviving relative. I am confident you shall have your due.'

'But shall I keep it?' She trembled as she spoke. 'A married woman owns nothing.'

'Hush,' he urged. 'Who would take it from you now?'

She glanced all round the room as if fearing that the thing she dreaded might be within its very walls. 'My husband,' she whispered.

'Edward is dead,' William said steadily.

'Yes, Edward is dead,' she agreed.

He began to fear that she had forfeited her reason as well as her looks. 'Then what are you talking about? Who is it that you fear?'

'Felix,' she said.

'Felix Osborne is also dead,' he reminded her. 'You identified the body yourself.'

'I identified a burned-out corpse wearing a watch that belonged to my husband.'

Unfortunate woman, he thought. In her nervous state she had become prey to unreasonable fears. 'You must not allow your mind to feed on morbid fancy,' he told her. 'Come now,

Teresa. You shall see a physic. He will prescribe a sedative. Of course Felix is dead. If he were alive someone would have seen him.'

'They have,' she said. 'I have.'

'You imagine it,' he promised her.

'No.' She had regained command of herself and her voice was steady now. 'Edward saw him too. So did the servants. He was in the house the night of Edward's death.'

'Teresa, no!'

'You must let me talk. Please don't interrupt. Edward had been drinking. You have reason to know what his mood was when he had taken alcohol. When a visitor was announced I thought I would welcome any kind of company. I went out to greet the caller and found on my doorstep – a spectre.

'At first I all but fainted from fright. The thing smiled. It seemed amused by my terror. There was a wild look to him and a pallor to his complexion, and for a time I truly did not know if he was flesh or vision. Then he spoke: "What? No welcome for your old sweetheart?" He even tried to kiss me. I could not move from horror, but Felix merely laughed and went by me into the drawing-room where I heard the laughter of the two men. Dead or alive, Edward welcomed his old gambling companion unreservedly.

'Felix did not trouble to invent any complicated excuse. He said he had been compelled to disappear because of debts. The man I identified was one to whom he had lost his remaining money and his watch in a wager. Felix acquired a new identity and, in due course, a fresh batch of creditors. He and Edward spent the night drinking. It wasn't until Edward was almost in a stupor that the other revealed the true purpose of his resurrection. As if it was a great jest, he pointed out that since he was alive, then Edward was a bigamist. For a large sum, he was ready to forfeit his claim to his wife.'

'How iniquitous!' William exclaimed. 'What did Edward say?'

'At first he was very shocked but then . . . then, he laughed: "Since she cannot produce a son and no longer has either looks or money, you can take her and welcome. I shall not pay a penny."'

'Poor Teresa.' William shook his head. 'It must have made you suffer to hear your own husband speak so.'

'I will not be a hypocrite,' she said. 'I have only ever cared for one man. Very happily would I have forfeited both husbands but for the need of a roof for myself and my child.'

'What did you do while the two men haggled so abominably?'

'I went to bed. I was woken by some commotion in the night. I found Edward at the bottom of the stone stairs. I called out for help. Felix came upon the instant and then one of the servants. They pronounced Edward dead.'

Thus she was released from one unhappy marriage only to be returned to another, and yet it was not the worst of that poor woman's woes.

'As Felix persists in reminding me, I am his wife. Whatever I inherit belongs to him.'

William Ellin understood that the only protection for her lay in Felix Osborne's removal. Naturally, he would only do this within the law. Yet surely the law would do it for him. 'The man is a villain. All we need is clear evidence of it. We shall get that rascal into court.'

The suggestion seemed to distress her. 'Shall I be questioned? Must such private matters be discussed in public?' Poor vulnerable creature, she looked utterly wretched. 'I have done nothing,' she wept, 'yet even to speak of it makes me feel ashamed.'

'Have no fear, little one,' William said. 'I will protect you.' The words came out unbidden. As they emerged, all his

360

self-defensive system came undone for he became aware that his first task was to shelter the one who had made herself his shield. It no longer seemed to matter that she looked ill or old. They had been given by God into one another's care. No true happiness or safety existed for one without the other.

To bring Felix Osborne to justice was satisfying work. If he had been clever in his designs, he had been careless in leaving a veritable battlefield of injured parties, male and female, with hurt pride or wounded pocket. Unlike poor Teresa, they were eager for their day in court. In several identities, he had cheated, misrepresented, misappropriated. There was even a lady who called herself (and fully believed herself to be) Mrs Frederick Osbertson. The latter was one of the sobriquets of the swindler. The nerve of the man! In another of his aliases he had perpetrated the exact crime for which he tried to blackmail a friend. At the expense of this lady's fortune he had supported his reckless lifestyle. The barrister appointed was confident of establishing a file that would see its subject sent for life from his own country.

Yet the wheels of justice move slowly. While the case was yet in preparation William received a message from Teresa: 'I must see you. The very worst has happened.'

There was a sense of quiet hopelessness about her now. It seemed to deaden her gaze and her very voice. Of the vivacious young American girl, no trace remained.

'Oh, I wish I had died instead of Edward,' she moaned. 'It was what they wanted. Now they are attempting to bring that about.'

A cold feeling ran through him. 'What? Has someone threatened you?'

Very still and lifeless, she was. It seemed an effort to answer his question. 'Someone is conspiring to bring about my end.'

'This is monstrous,' he said. 'You must tell me all. Sit down. Start at the beginning.'

Obediently, she sat. 'Do you remember how my husband died?'

'I believe he broke his neck in a fall.'

'Yes, that is what has given him the inspiration for his plot.'

'Who are you talking about? And what? Is someone trying to arrange an accident for you?'

'A very deliberate one.' Quietly, with a pathetic listlessness, she began to weep. Her helplessness, her lack of resistance to those who would harm her were more than he could endure. 'Let me comfort you,' he murmured.

At once the little creature went into his arms. That insubstantial form, with two hearts beating within its fragile cage, filled his arms and his heart to bursting. He cherished the moment, allowing his lips to briefly rest upon the crown of her head. She prolonged the instant until he felt a pact of intimacy between them. Then she raised her wet face to him. 'Protect me from the very law that you are pledged to serve?'

'Darling,' he shook his head, 'you make no sense. Are they trying to do you wrong or to make out that you have done wrong?'

'Both,' she said.

'But what charge could they bring against you that would merit the harming of a hair on your head?' Her sweet, pale lips compressed but no sound came. One day I shall kiss those lips, he thought. One day. 'Say it,' he urged. 'Say it and we shall make light of it.'

She looked around despairingly and expelled the phrase on a doom-laden sigh: 'Murder,' she said.

The ugly word entered Miss Wilcox's well-ordered parlour like a wreckage.

'But who would make such accusation?' I wondered. 'And why?'

'On the word of the worst swindler that ever lived, she was arraigned for the murder of Edward Ellin,' Finch supplied. 'Felix Osborne said he had seen the lady engaged in an altercation with the deceased, then strike him from behind with a heavy object, occasioning his fall.'

'And what of the servant who also came upon the scene?'

'The servant corroborated Osborne's version,' Finch said. 'He must have been paid off by Osborne, or persuaded with a promise of payment. Why? If she was convicted of a capital crime, she would hang – then, even if he served a stretch, he would eventually benefit from her wealth.'

'Surely no one would believe such lies? Naturally, you did not?' I addressed Mr Ellin.

'The very notion seemed preposterous,' he said. 'I thought nothing could ever make me believe it.'

'Yet something did,' Finch interjected.

'But what?' I appealed.

Poor Mr Ellin looked so unhappy I was sorry to have urged an answer, but with a sigh deep as a river he spoke: 'It was Teresa Osborne's lover.'

Several days into the case against Teresa there appeared, as witness for the prosecution, a handsome young man named Harcourt Farrell. He had come to the house to give Mrs Ellin music lessons, and said he soon realized she was unhappy in her marriage. A chill worked its way under William Ellin's sober suiting when the man related how her vulnerable and pathetic air had touched his heart and, without meaning it to happen, his sympathy had turned to passion. He claimed he loved her yet, but when Mrs Ellin found herself with child, he begged her to make amends with her husband and to present the child as his legitimate heir, since he himself had no means to support a family. She declared his scheme futile as relations between herself and her husband were such as to render this deception impossible. She told Mr Farrell she would find a way for them to live together without hardship. 'I neither knew nor wished to know what she meant, for her words troubled me,' Farrell said; 'and more so, the odd, excited manner in which she delivered them. Shortly afterwards, I heard of the death of her husband.'

Teresa continued to protest her innocence and William tried to keep faith in it until a surgeon took the stand. He revealed that Osborne, in addition to the injuries from his fall, had suffered a blow to the back of his head from a heavy object.

'Yet how did this poor broken woman who had lost her looks and confidence attract a young man's interest?' I found myself once more at a loss.

'I had almost forgotten to mention it!' Mr Ellin said. 'Before the trial she looked abject and pitiful, yet in court she was dressed in her best and, although she seemed pale and shaken, she was beautiful again. I gradually began to see how she had duped me – how eager I was to allow her to influence me. She used her tears as hardened men use money – to bribe those who would win her advantage. The gentlemen of the jury would have presented their hearts as a bouquet. After the briefest of deliberations they delivered a verdict of "not guilty".'

'The correct verdict,' Finch interjected quietly.

'What do you know of it?' Mr Ellin said.

'The case interested me so I travelled to the assizes. From the first moment I saw Teresa Osborne I knew she was no murderess. In court she looked petrified and bewildered. Like many women thrust into marriage too young, she knew only the world of her cruel captivity and was as a caged bird released defenceless in the depths of winter. By comparison, the men who claimed to witness her crime looked knowing and greedy – predators waiting to dispose of a poor sparrow.'

'Oh, stop this nonsense,' Mr Ellin begged. 'It was a pitiable business, to be sure, but do you not think, sir, that you and I were the only true innocents in that courtroom? The lady exploited her helplessness to manipulate gullible males such as you and I.'

I interrupted the two sparring males to address Mr Ellin directly. 'You still believe, then, that she was guilty?'

'I do.' He spoke softly. 'Yet not so guilty as I once deemed her; guilty only of ridding the world of a drunken brute. I now accept that I condemned her more for injury to my own dignity than for mortal damage to a human life.'

'Ah, yes! Your dignity!' Mr Cornhill goaded him. 'Tell me, which was the worse offence to your pride – the thought that you had earlier allowed partiality to make you side with a murderess or that that party preferred another man to yourself?'

'Why, sir, your insinuation is offensive!' Mr Ellin protested.

'It is obvious that you are still wary of insults to your male pride,' Mr Cornhill said.

Mr Ellin's fresh objections were soon interrupted by the journalist: 'You forget that I am a man as you are and am subject to the same foibles of my sex. I, too, harboured a lengthy prejudice due to a slight to my vanity. Harcourt Farrell was a good-looking fellow, was he not, sir?'

'As you seem determined to lay bare all my injuries, I might as well unravel my poor bandages. Yes,' Mr Ellin conceded, 'he was one of the finest specimens of manhood I have ever seen.'

'The sort of man who might expect to have a good measure of success with women?'

'I should not doubt that he was quite a prize among the fair sex.'

'And it would come as no great surprise to you that a young lady would choose him instead of a pleasant but unremarkable-looking fellow such as yourself?'

'As you so eloquently put it!' Mr Ellin agreed.

'In short, you ceded to the natural victor. You accepted at once that Harcourt Farrell's claims were true because inevitable.'

'Had you not been called to the fourth estate, you would have made an excellent advocate. Your summing up is flawless,' Mr Ellin somewhat wearily allowed.

'I might have been more thorough than you, sir,' Mr Cornhill ruthlessly suggested; 'but, then, I did not have Cupid in my eye.'

'Cupid at this point made his exit,' Mr Ellin said. 'It was his arrow that was in my eye.'

'Did it make your eyes water? Well, my friend, perhaps they did not water half enough. It interested me that there seemed none other than her barrister who would say a word in the lady's favour. So I went looking – and found someone.'

'Why did you not bring forth this person?' Mr Ellin demanded.

'She was four years of age. My expert was Mrs Osborne's little daughter, who had sat so patiently on the courtroom steps.'

'She was but a babe. What would she know of adult engagements?'

'Little girls are natural witnesses. They hear things not meant for them. I asked little Emma if her mama had had a gentleman friend apart from Papa?'

'And she replied?'

'She spoke very clearly and poignantly for a babe. I remember her words distinctly: "Please can you find him? Mama wants him."'

'Well, there!' Mr Ellin said. 'The infant answered you. Her mother had a lover.'

'Not a lover! I asked if she knew who the gentleman was and again the intelligent little thing said yes, for Mama spoke of him all the time. They had first met when he was a little boy and now he was an important man who worked for the law in London.'

Mr Ellin groaned.

'I inquired if Mama liked Mr Farrell. The child declared that her mother neither liked nor trusted him and had asked her always to stay in the room during the lesson as he had once tried to kiss her.'

'A touching story!' Mr Ellin said. 'A child of four cannot be held accountable.'

'I believed her. Even still, when the case was over, I went to see Harcourt Farrell. The man made no efforts to be likeable now. He had been drinking and boasted of his conquests with other married women. Upon questioning, it became clear that he knew little of Mrs Osborne. He did not know where she had been born or how her parents died. Yet he did have close acquaintance with one of her relations – her husband, Felix Osborne.'

I was curious to know why Finch had gone to such trouble when the lady was already acquitted.

'She asked me to. She had been found innocent yet her name had not been cleared with the one person whose friendship she relied upon. She believed that if he could be convinced of her innocence he would come to her aid. I wrote to that party and tried to arrange a meeting. I received no reply.'

'What was the end?' I wondered. 'Did Felix Osborne stand trial?'

'He did. He was convicted of fraud and transported. I myself believe him to be guilty of Edward Ellin's murder, but no such charge was brought against him.'

'And what of Ellin's estate?'

'The evidence of the court case established that Teresa Osborne had never been the legal wife of Edward Ellin. The house and his money therefore went to his only surviving relative.'

If this conversation sounds a two-sided affair when there were three of us in the room, it is because, for the latter part, Mr Ellin had his head sunk in his hands.

'Do you still believe Mrs Osborne to have been guilty?' I asked him now.

For an answer he raised an anguished face and pleaded with our informant: 'Is there anything I may yet do for her?'

'Pray for her,' Finch Cornhill said gravely.

Mr Ellin's expression was dreadfully dejected. 'What became of her?'

'I kept in touch with her for a while. When she appeared to have nowhere else to go I put her in contact with a kindly old lady who had once been my governess – a Miss Matilda Fitzgibbon. Miss Fitzgibbon was the one who introduced me to books and opened my eyes to the conditions of those without means. She now lived on her own in a cottage and was in poor health. She was very glad to take in the family if Mrs Osborne would look after her. I believe it was a happy arrangement for all concerned. Some years later, I received notice that Miss Fitzgibbon had passed away. As she had only had a living in the cottage I was concerned about the fate of Mrs Osborne. All I could discover was that she and her children were gone away. I do not know what became of them – only that they were homeless and penniless.'

'Then who was the beneficiary of Edward Ellin's estate?' I appealed.

'Myself,' Mr Ellin answered.

'I hope you did some great good with it,' Finch said. 'That

money should rightly have gone to the lady who had served faithfully as Edward Ellin's wife and fully believed herself to be so.'

Mr Ellin shook his head. 'I sold Golpit and used the money to buy back my birthplace, Ellin Balcony. Yet I could not live there. The place seemed to contain some malign and restless spirit. I believed it to be the spirit of my brother, returned to our mutual birthplace to resume a reign of terror. A more literal interpretation might suggest that it was my own conscience denying me rest or peace, yet when I tried to sell the house, others felt this unhappy presence. No buyer came. I returned to Lisbon and worked for Mr Bosas. In due course Ellin Balcony fell victim to the elements. After Mr Bosas' death I chose to settle in England, in a village that neither owned nor knew my history.'

'As you say, Mr Ellin, you have finally tracked down the villain who cast upon the mercy of the world the child known as Matilda Fitzgibbon,' the journalist concluded. 'It was none other than yourself.'

This news struck poor Mr Ellin so bitterly that he succumbed to wretched tears. 'Oh, why must God punish us so? Why must a youthful misjudgement be carved in stone? Why does He give us no second chance?'

'He does,' Finch breathed.

Mr Ellin shuddered but his tears subsided. 'Do you believe she may still be alive?'

'I do not know, yet her daughter lives. Perhaps she is your second chance.'

I was beginning to feel upon my mature sensibilities the impact of that day's cargo of emotion. 'Yes, let us concentrate on Emma,' I said.

'Tomorrow,' Mr Ellin said. 'We shall meet tomorrow. Now, I must take my leave.'

When that unhappy gentleman had departed Finch came and sat by me. 'God does give us second chances,' he murmured.

Yet how had my lover, from a world of separation and an interlude of almost twenty years, been directed to the small village where destiny had so randomly deposited me? To say he had traced Mr Ellin here, that Mr Ellin had led him to me, does not address the mystery. I spoke before of prayers that pass unchallenged all gates. Thus had I prayed as a newly-wed young woman unable to accept separation from my soul's other that one day, in some manner, the unbreakable connection between us would have fulfilment. Thus, by heaven's compass, had he come to me.

I took his hand to halt its progress around my waist. 'Finch, tell me this. Why did you not bring the child to Mr Ellin at once instead of taking her to Fuchsia Lodge?'

He petted my forehead with his lips. 'If Mr Ellin could not forgive the mother, it seemed unlikely he would embrace the daughter. After I traced him to his present address I discovered that he was a frequent visitor to the school and well acquainted with its pupils. I took a gamble upon a particular one winning his sympathy.'

'What, I wonder, of the other child? Emma must have a sibling.'

'I do not know,' he said. 'I never saw the other child. Remember, in the time of my acquaintance with the family, it was not yet born. Perhaps, if we find her, Emma may tell us.'

'She remembers nothing.'

'I believe that when she is safely restored to those who love her, her memory will gradually return. That process may be hastened by some personal reminder. There is still one person who holds a key to her past – her father.'

'Her father?' So strongly had her mother's sad case impressed itself on my mind that I had to think a moment to trace her patrimony and then I gave expression to dismay. 'Felix Osborne! He is her father.'

William Ellin was in the grip of a remorse so harsh he felt that only death would shake it off. His bachelor state, which he had made to seem so congenial, now clung to him like the dust of his ruined birthplace. Teresa Osborne had loved and trusted him, and he had condemned her to penury.

He flung his hat upon the hall table, dislodging a piece of post. A glance at the outside told him there was nothing to interest him; he recognized the writing of a member of his London club. The thought of that glib banter sickened him. In a mood of morbid self-reproach that made him want to destroy all he had so carefully constructed, he seized the harmless piece of correspondence, went to his study and dropped it into the fire. He watched the flimsy paper stretch and sear in the flames. He wished it was his conscience burning there – though, no doubt, in due course it would get its turn in hell. As he stood brooding upon his life and his post a flame illuminated the blackening paper and his eye lighted on a single word: 'Emma.'

Heedless of the fire upon his fingers he snatched the morsel from the blaze. The note was from his friend, Mr Arnold Siddons. 'I believe I have found your little friend. A young girl called Emma works as a serving maid at Jack Whaley's chophouse in Cornhill. She is about fourteen years of age and fits your description of the missing girl.'

CHAPTER THIRTY-FOUR

Spring is generally an optimistic time but at Deerfield this season it excelled itself in promise. Mr Ellin, having had word of Emma, was gone to London to fetch her. Mr Cornhill had taken temporary tenancy of a nearby lodge to renew our acquaintance.

It was a strange thing, at my time of life, to find the mellow chambers of the heart once more flooded with strong sunlight. They say the memory retains only what is useful. Passion, then, must have a poor utility for I had forgotten utterly the ecstatic daze to be found in proximity to an irresistible opposite. He would arrive. My breath would become constricted and my brain delirious. The relief of his touch brought a craving for more. Yet this unruly rapture was but nature's embellishment on a healing landscape. More precious by far were the plain reminders of his presence in my life. I would enter a room, find him intent upon a newspaper and know that I had captured happiness. His restless form, his handsome, careworn face filled my vision and were the very light of my existence. Aside from my anticipation of Emma's return, the whole of the world became an invisible vapour.

Would that I could say that this arrangement afforded me reciprocal concealment. Our little town had too few young people and therefore too little romance. The gossip — who is paying attention to whom; what portion has been settled upon which bride; which young married lady shall shortly have to sacrifice her waistline to Isis — that is the refreshment and connecting stream of every village, had dried to a droughty trickle, until my visitor brought it almost to a rising flood. The arrival of a well-made stranger, his appearance daily at my door had wonderfully infused the populace with new trivia to dissect. It takes no special genius to imagine the general trend of the discourse:

'Well, she's a dark horse! Always played the grieving widow to a turn.'

'At her age!'

'What does he see in her? She must be worth a pretty penny.'

Did such imagined tittle-tattle bother me? In a word, yes.

My life was now divided into two opposing halves: the one a breathless vigil for the object of my desire; the other a regret for the dignity proper to a settled widow. On a particular day when I felt the buzz of speculation rise like flies from a midden as I entered my little classroom, I realized that, like it or not, I must shortly find a point of reconciliation between love and respect.

Finch suffered no such vacillation. What compromises woman merely garlands man with mystery. His attachment to a female made him twice as interesting, whereas my attentions from a man had halved my reputation. Nor did he endure the agonies of indecision that assailed me. A blessed single-mindedness gave him easy answers to every question. When I confided my dilemma he merely laughed: 'Why, we shall settle it. Let us get married. That will give them something to talk about.'

He was surprised when I hesitated. 'Don't you love me? Your lips proclaim that you do.'

'Of course I love you,' I sealed this assertion with another kiss. 'Yet we are not impetuous juveniles now. There are many matters that would have to be discussed.'

'For instance?'

'For instance, where would we live?'

'At Happen Heath, of course. That unhappy establishment will have its true mistress at last.'

'Dorothy lives there.' I spoke with an uneasy memory of the haughty juvenile I had once tutored. 'She would never accept me as mistress of her home.'

'The years have wrought many changes. My younger sister spends most of her time in Europe, evading her maternal duties. Mama is imposing proper standards on heaven now. You are no more a shy young girl. The house will be yours to run as you desire.'

'You are all I desire,' I told him. 'I have no ambition to be mistress of a grand estate.'

'Remember how well you liked it when first you saw it.'

I had thought it, and think it still, the most beautiful house on this earth. Yet Albert had built my house for me. My sisters had grown up in it. My dear father had spent his last happy days there. And Emma's room was in it.

'What of Emma?' I said then.

'Emma will be at school most of the time. In the holidays she will stay with us at Happen Heath if you wish it. I will make sure she is well provided for.'

'As you provide for your little niece, Vanessa?' I was uncomfortably reminded of Mr Ellin's description of that lonely little fantasist.

'Exactly.'

'I mean to adopt Emma if her mother cannot be found,' I

said. 'I mean to bring her up as my child. Would she be yours too?'

Finch left my side to engage in some solitary stalking. His spendthrift strides, which forced a premature return, spoke of limbs born to pace in larger chambers. 'My darling Isa, I shall gladly indulge your every whim. If it pleases you to endow her with my name, then she shall have it, but I cannot make a particular case of her. There are too many children like Emma. I use my pen to fight for justice. If I allowed my heart to become involved the work would end. My heart is for you and only you.'

'Emma is a particular case. You said so yourself. Even as an infant she was stoic and loyal. You would not have remembered her otherwise.'

'Yes, and I remember many other such babes: infant street sellers with bare feet and blue hands and wrinkles where dimples ought to be, little mill workers with limbs deformed from work their undeveloped bodies could not bear. Shall we take them all? How many hundreds can we accommodate?' Then, as if he could no longer stand the separation of a room's length, he came to me and took my hands. 'Remember, dearest, when we were young and swore that together we would change the world? We both believed it then. Do you not believe in it now?'

Youthful fervour generally dies with youth. My own early vision of the world had lost its stark focus. Having judged myself I was less prepared to judge others. I had come to believe that my modest talents were better suited to reassurance than to revolution. Both were surely necessary elements, yet did not travel on the same plane. Once we had truly been twin souls (and being innocent, more soul than body). Were we now mere fortune hunters, raiding sacred ground for treasure?

I contemplated the darling keeper of my past and came to a sad understanding. Because Finch had guarded his heart, had not grown affectionate to human foible through long association with another dear fallible companion, he had not mellowed or matured. Despite his greying hair and gaunt features he was still a passionate and unyielding youth. I did not for a moment doubt that the vast and ruthless world had need of him exactly as he was, but could any mortal woman live up to his great expectations?

'I believe that you could do great good and I could do little kindnesses,' I said at last.

He stepped back from me. For a moment that old wounding curl of contempt came into his mouth. 'Little kindnesses!' he mocked.

'Yes, Finch.' I had to speak quickly, before my courage failed. 'I may be trivial but I must be honest.'

He quickly contained his critical expression and managed a rueful smile. 'Then do me a great kindness and consent to be my wife.'

Why did I falter? To love is to refresh and renew the soul, to explore at tender leisure one's self and another. To marry is to move house — not merely the house of bricks and wood (and I had grown inordinately attached to mine), but that of the emotions. It is to throw out some of the furniture of one's feelings in order to accommodate those of another. Perhaps the sensation of joy seemed yet too precarious to weigh it down with this freight of domesticity. 'Give me time to think about it,' I begged.

He looked so hurt that I almost reassured him with an instant affirmative, but then an odd, cold look came into his face and stopped me speaking. 'You hesitate. You make excuses. I dispose of these and still you cannot answer me. There is only one possible reason why. It is as I suspected at the start. You do not love me.'

'Finch, I do love you,' I protested.

'How much do you love me?'

'With all my heart.'

'And what of the man who owned your body in my absence? Did he also own your heart?'

He spoke so crudely it almost took my breath away. When I failed to answer, he raised his voice. 'Did you love him too?'

I tried to contain my alarm and to speak levelly. 'He was my husband. He was kind to me. A portion of my affection was owed to him.'

'So! I do not have the whole of your heart. A portion of it was owed to your husband — a Shylock's measure to pay off your debts. Tell me now, how large was that allotment? Which part of your heart did you sever in exchange for your keep?'

'The best part!' that organ silently responded, but I knew better than to voice this truth. 'The grateful part,' I said. 'The forbearing part. My husband taught me tolerance and generosity — attributes he owned in great measure. I cannot allow his memory less than that.'

A silence grew between us. I could not penetrate its density. I dared not even look at Finch. It was he, at last, who braved the vacuum. 'Oh, Isa! Dearest Isa! Forgive my selfishness. If you will learn from me then I will learn from you. Let us pledge ourselves to one another and begin to exorcize the past.'

Mercifully, this decision was deferred by the necessity of his making a journey. He had made up his mind to track down Felix Osborne. This distasteful mission he deemed necessary to the welfare of the child for whom he professed not to care.

His plan was to go to London and introduce himself at the notorious Cocoa Tree gaming club in Soho. 'Although Osborne was sent from this country, I'll warrant that if he survived he will have been close to these shores. Gamblers keep track of one another — if only to recover their debts.'

At first I was almost glad to see him go. Those who have been in the grip of passion will know its suffocating strength. It shuts down all the normal senses, occludes judgement, leaves one feeling weak and fevered. I needed time to myself to ponder this great and burdensome gift that had been addressed so unexpectedly to me in middle years. I required a brief reunion with my old composed self – a temporary respite from the role of inamorata and a restoration to my mirror of an ordinary woman's face with its quota of years.

He left. I sat back complacently and awaited a return to equanimity. This trusty comrade chose to leave me in the lurch. Instead of the peace I had expected, I felt panic. Where I had anticipated perspective, I experienced desolation. I could not quite believe what I had wrought by my own fair hand. Having been blessed and then doubly blessed by the same great love, I had set it under my magnifying glass, found a little flaw in it and sent it back. How many women of my years have youthful rapture restored to them, its radiant fabric intact? How many would tug and worry at that lovely substance to test its durability, then try to exchange it for some stouter, duller stuff? Why had I not owned to my inadequacy and begged his guidance? Having wounded him once through no fault of my own I had calculatedly done so again. The noblest being in all the world had bestowed on me the honour of his keeping and I had prevaricated. Once again, I had employed my well-esteemed wits to do damage to someone close to me.

In the days that followed I was subject to the direst self-reproach. When I looked in my mirror, I saw not the serenity I expected but a nervous, ageing, fearful fool. Once released from the mesmerism of romance, he would see the same and be very glad to make his escape. Or, worse, he would take offence (he was ever quick to do so) and choose to make me his enemy again. Speculation heightened as day followed day and no

378

letter came. Then trepidation went up a notch. Suppose something had happened to him. Mercifully, this prospect was easily dismissed. He had survived many more dangerous campaigns and proved well able to take care of himself. Better care, it seemed, than I could lavish on myself. I could not sleep or eat. My limbs felt bereft, my eyes sightless without their chosen object in view.

Do I sound foolish, self-obsessed, unstable? Yes, guilty on all counts, as all lovers are.

I tried to throw myself into my teaching but Fuchsia Lodge had less need of me now and the Wilcox sisters were decreasingly anxious to keep company with one who had known them in adversity. I addressed myself to my garden. A sea of bluebells waved at me. Tight-budded roses made an endearing maternity ward. I salted them with apprehensive tears.

Like water to a desert wanderer, a piece of post arrived. The familiar handwriting declared its identity. 'I believe I have tracked down Felix Osborne to the French port of Marseille. There is no way to verify it but to travel there myself. I sail tomorrow and should be back within two weeks.'

If excessive ardour in the male sometimes effects a cooling of the female passions, it wants only a measure of the opposite to warm them up again. Upon imbibing a liberal dose of Mr Cornhill's detachment, I had need of the strongest self-control to stop myself setting out for France at a gallop, waving a banner with the single word 'Yes!'. The hysteria of infatuation knows but one cure and I would have it at any price. I would sell Fox Clough, move to Happen Heath with Emma under one arm, take the world by the scruff of its neck and improve it. I no longer cared a whit for peace or dignity or for my so-called special talents. I must have Finch by my side. I must call myself Isa Cornhill. It is small wonder the marriage service includes the words 'for better or for worse', for those who have

379

known the full force of the heart's yearning reach at last the point where they no longer care for the consequence of their action, so long as they may breathe by night and day the other's air.

Some prevailing vestige of common sense informed me that this was not the moment for a romantic *dénouement*. Finch's present business sounded both delicate and dangerous. I would keep my answer for his return. However, I could now enjoy a small respite from consternation. What travails might follow our union I must wait and see, but at least my acceptance of it had purchased me a measure of peace of mind.

As soon as I relaxed my vigil upon the post, it came into busy production. In the week after Finch's letter there was a double helping. The first was from the same dear source. It was a small package, neatly tied. I struggled with the sealing wax and impatiently removed the content – a painted miniature, the subject a sprite-like young woman, dark-haired, very fair of face. The features were almost too regular for distinction. Yet one aspect was remarkable. Her ocean-grey eyes were poignant and piercing.

The letter that accompanied this dispatch brought a new kind of joy, of the calmest, most assured kind.

Darling Isa,

This is a portrait of Emma's mother. It was found among the possessions of Felix Osborne – alas, without their owner. That rascal has evaded justice once again, leaving behind a poor woman ill with cholera. She lives in the most abject squalor and poverty. I must remain here until I have seen her safely back to her family. Then the long chain of misery will be ended. Yet one bright feature shines through. It seems to me remarkable that a scoundrel like Osborne should have kept a portrait of his wife. Perhaps that poor lady did almost influence his heart. Perhaps his base soul understood that it had once been touched by something of true worth. One can but pity those who by their own selfish actions deny themselves the redeeming force of love. It has made me repent my own hot-headedness. If I have been too eager with you, then I shall strive for patience. If I have shown jealousy, I apologize for that small-minded failing. If the late Mr Chalfont taught you tolerance, I beg you to employ it with me. I shall not lose you twice. Whatever it takes to keep you by me, I shall make it my mission to achieve. Keep this little portrait safe for Emma and your sweet self safe for me.

    With all my love,
        Finch.

Dear rash, generous man! If I would not give in, then he would. Yet I would show him selflessness too. I had forgotten the hardest and most improving lesson of marriage. The gift of self is not the gift of one's heart or body but of the will.

Two days later there was a letter from another esteemed comrade. The missive bore a London postal mark and the hand of Mr Ellin – a flimsy messenger to bring me news at last of my lost girl. I took this paper angel to the garden and sat with it awhile. It was a day of atmospheric armistice. The sky was a soft, unsullied blue. A host of flowers offered up their fragrance. There was a silence, yet not a dead one. It was a living silence. A lazy mumble issued from hedge and shrub. From high in the trees came the faint, sociable conversation of song. The very air hummed with regeneration. It was the sort of day on which God might have made the first human, in order that he would know the joy of living. What troubles were to come I did not know, but at this moment they were outside my fence. I was in my garden and about to gather in my heart's harvest.

I unwrapped Mr Ellin's news at leisure. It was brief and to the point and not what I anticipated.

I arrived at Jack Whaley's chop-house too late. Emma left yesterday. She took with her her few possessions. No one knows where she has gone. I *shall* find her. As I cannot search the whole world nor even the entirety of the country, I shall go where all the nation and all the world will be convened. Have you drawn a likeness of her? If not, can you do so now? I would be grateful if you would forward it to me at the above address.

After all our waiting, all his searching, by a hair's breadth he had missed her. Why did Mr Ellin ask for a drawing? Was it meant to bring him consolation? Perhaps he merely felt it would console me to bring to life her features.

Possibly he was right. I summoned Mary for pencil and paper. I sat with lead point poised upon the page. I saw Emma now as plainly as when she had sat in my drawing-room. My busy pencil sought out the detail in the blankness. The broad forehead, the fine, expressive eyes, the firm mouth, narrow shoulders, all appeared on the page with a delightful deficit of coyness. Mary came out again and said there was a lady to see me. 'Give me five minutes and then send her to the garden,' I said. I framed the head with hair, and there, I had her to the life, a poignant vision of feminine complexity. I was so absorbed in my composition that I overran my time and failed to notice that my visitor had come out. She made some nervous sound in her throat to catch my attention. I looked up. It was Mrs Farrington, who kept the house where Mr Cornhill stayed. She was ill-at-ease and stood at a distance, tugging the fingers of her gloves.

'Come and sit by me,' I called out. 'I will send for tea.'

She remained where she was and seemed, poor woman, to grow more agitated by the moment. 'I have had news of Mr Cornhill,' she disclosed.

'So have I,' I said.

At this she burst into tears. 'Oh, Mrs Chalfont,' she said. 'Why do you smile?'

CHAPTER THIRTY-FIVE

What imp of destiny had plucked Emma from her resting-place when discovery was near? It was a mere sound – a gasp – yet one drawn from a great depth, from a well run dry and lined with stones. Jack Whaley heard it. The sound dismayed him. He had been in the army and heard men die. He followed that unnatural labour for breath to a small room at the top of the house.

The moment Emma entered the inn she knew something was amiss. There was a taut air. Instead of the customary brisk greeting, Jack Whaley, when he caught her eye, looked immediately away.

'Jack?' she queried.

'Sit, Emma.' He gave a sigh. 'I have news for you.'

'Tell me now,' she said. 'I have to put these flowers in water. It is almost time to start work.' She had brought Jenny a bunch of violets.

'The little girl . . .' he said.

'Jenny? Has something happened?'

He lowered his eyes, looked guilty almost. 'She has gone.'

'No!' With a cry, she ran up the stairs. She had known this would happen, and soon, and yet had not prepared herself. How could she? She had made this poor sick child her family and her purpose.

She stood in the doorway of the small attic room. The bed was empty. So, removed already. She moaned softly, too stricken for tears. Jack Whaley came behind her and placed his hands on her shoulders. 'She's not dead, Emma – not yet, poor mite, although her time remaining on this earth is numbered by hours more than days.'

Emma whirled around. 'Where?'

'The workhouse infirmary. You must understand she is too sick to be here. I could not keep her at the inn. She may be contagious.'

Emma sat, or rather sank, where she stood. It would be better for Jenny to be dead than in the Poor Law infirmary. 'Did she cry?' Emma asked. 'Did she call out for me?'

'Aye. She did. The little creature seemed all in a panic. She begged us to leave her. She said she'd not be a trouble for the gentleman was coming for her shortly. She made no sense. Ah, do not look at me that way. She is best off where she is.'

'She will die there.' Emma spoke gravely.

'She will die either way,' Jack Whaley said.

Emma stood up wearily. 'I have to go, Jack.'

'But you'll come back? You know this is your home.'

She acknowledged this with a shrug that seemed a surrender to hopelessness. 'I do not believe I shall ever have a home.'

The workhouse infirmary at Clerkenwell greeted her with a familiar odour of sickness and chloride, its sounds of suffering. The tiny figure under the white sheet seemed already in a coffin. Only the tell-tale patches of damp on the linen and a rough exertion of her chest testified that she breathed yet.

'Jenny, it's Emma.' Emma leant over the bed. 'I am sorry I was not there. I am sorry they took you.'

A look of contentment transformed her face. 'Emma!' she whispered.

'Were you very afraid?' Emma murmured.

With an effort, Jenny opened her eyes. 'I was,' she said. 'I 'spect I feared it because I always knowed it would come. It's where the likes of me ends.'

'This is not the end,' Emma said. 'When you leave this life you will go to heaven. Heaven is a very wonderful place.'

'What? Like a palace?' Jenny looked briefly hopeful.

'Yes, dear, the most beautiful palace that ever was.'

The child allowed her eyes to close and fell back on the pillow. 'They'd not allow the likes of me in there. We was told that in the Great House. Heaven was for them favoured by the Lord. We was all sinners and bound for hell. I'm feared of hell. It's dark and cruel.' She turned on her side and began to whimper.

'Jenny!' Emma took her hand and breathed into that hot ear. 'Do you think they would let you into heaven if I was there?'

Jenny did not turn round but her head nodded faintly.

'Then I shall take you there. I will not leave you. You and I will go there together.'

The little girl slept. Emma kissed her and quickly departed. Her first object was to remove the child from that gallery of death. Jenny could not walk and Emma could carry her but a short distance. From her limited resources, she must purchase a conveyance. In a very poor district where fish and bacon and old clothes were sold along with other variable items, and poor little children hopped around barefoot to the music of an organ-grinder, she soon found the very article she sought. One wheel was bent and most of the paint was gone but it still possessed a creaky mobility. By determined negotiation a price was struck and she hurried back to the gloomy institution.

Jenny was in a slumber that seemed beyond any normal reach. When Emma tried to rouse her the small body offered no more resistance than her doll, Baby Daniel. The older girl took her in her arms and held her close. She stayed hot and limp but a small smile touched her mouth. Emma gathered her up carefully. Her heart was racing as she carried her from the room. As she reached the door a cry rang out: 'Where are you going? Bring back that child.'

Employing a tone of the most withering condescension (with a debt to Miss Wilcox), she said: 'In case you had not noticed, this is no longer a child. The soul has left the pathetic little shell by several hours. I am taking her for a decent burial. If you try to stop me, I shall report you for neglect.'

Before they could respond she hurried from the building and out to where she had concealed her purchase. She there installed the little creature into a battered but commodious perambulator. With shaking legs, she pushed the pram at a run. She ran for half a mile or more until they were out of the neighbourhood and part of an anonymous throng.

She had rescued Jenny. What now? It was too late to achieve their destination. For a long time she walked the streets with her sleeping burden. The day was already fading. The lamp-lighters climbed up and set a bloom on tall iron stalks. Humanity, in its infinite variety, was burnished by the serene light that showed up the struggle and the soul. Like her, each person had his own strange story and none paused to wonder at his fellow's. For the first time since meeting Jenny, she felt the misery of her rootless state. After all her time in London she had discovered nothing. She knew not if she was good or bad, rich or poor, waif or orphan. The little invalid who had

387

unquestioningly committed her trust and her affection was soon to return to her true home. Denied that small and limitless blessing she doubted her capacity to carry on.

To keep from thinking she continued walking. She headed for the river to be among her kind. She meant to walk all night but her arms ached from the weight of the heavy vehicle and her legs trembled with weariness. When she reached Westminster Bridge she settled down to wait out the night under the stars.

This was a different scene from the one she had encountered here on her arrival in the city. The summer nights were soft and brief, the company less dismal. A number of visitors to the city for the Exhibition, having found no lodgings, had bedded on the bridge. There was almost an air of bonhomie. Some shared food and drink and even raised a song. To protect the slumber of her precious cargo Emma found a spot at a distance from the merrymakers. She took the child from the pram and rocked her in her arms. She watched the sleeping ships on the river, their sails bleached by the moon.

Something woke Emma. It was a small hand touching her cheek. She opened her eyes and found that Jenny was conscious and gazing at her intently. 'Look, Emma,' she breathed, and that same hand pointed skyward. Emma looked up. The fabric of the sky was faded. The stars and moon had the cheap yellow pallor of glass trinkets. A church bell stirred the morning fog with a silver spoon. With a blush, the heavens began to groom themselves for day.

The dawn puts on her colours for a small invited audience of insomniacs, early workers, late-returning revellers and those who have no sheltered place to lay their head. An elect band of sufferers and sinners gets a glimpse of the earth new-made. The two children gazed upon this wonder. We shall not condescend the show with a description. Such shades are not found in man's palette. Yet those who see it know that Paradise is nearer than we think. It is so close, we breathe its very air.

'Are we in heaven yet?' Jenny asked, in a hoarse whisper.

'Not yet, but we go there this day.'

'Tell me again. What is it like?'

'It is more beautiful, more splendid than anything you have ever seen or could imagine. All the people of all nations are there and every treasure of man and nature.'

The child considered this and then she whispered, 'They will not let me in – not in a workhouse gown.'

'Nor shall they, for you will be the belle of Eden.' Emma produced from the bottom of the pram the diminutive gown of broderie anglaise purchased at the market. She dressed the little invalid, who croaked with pleasure.

The sun came up. It touched the mighty monuments to man. The ships on the river were bathed in gold. Then labourers began to emerge into the street. The clap of hoofs, the creak and thunder of carriage wheels, the cries of street sellers, the anxious piping of little flower vendors chased the sun to its own place of business. The sky put on a dress of useful blue, more suited to the generality.

She had promised Jenny what was not in her keeping. She had pledged to take her to heaven. Yet she knew a place that was as close to glory as any earthly imagination might aspire. They travelled there via two stately parks. Jenny had never seen so much green. A palace came into view, a curved canal and tree-lined walks. ''Tis very silent,' she sounded undecided, 'but it smells most clean.' Yet her shining eyes gave broad approval and she smiled widely until she saw people throwing bread to the ducks. 'Look, Emma! ' she exclaimed in distress. 'Those big birds are getting bread. We must try to save some for poor folk who are hungry.'

St James's Park gave way to Green Park. Jenny pulled herself up in the pram to peer at exquisitely dressed children sitting in the grass around their nurse. 'Well, I do declare!' she said. 'They children have their legs and yet they do not play. Oh, how I should love a good run around.'

They entered Hyde Park. It was at its most beautiful, the boats and little frigates darting across the lake, the flags, the music and, soon, the fragile splendour of the Crystal Palace. To those with received views of Paradise, the children's Valhalla might have seemed a tawdry counterfeit, but they did not think so and nor did any others in their company, the majority being poor working folk who had delayed their visit until the entrance fee was reduced from a crown to a shilling.

Before joining the gathering queue Emma went in search of breakfast from the numerous stalls selling souvenirs and refreshments. She thought to buy an orange but an adjoining stand made a bid for her custom. 'Would you not like to try my coffee? It is the strongest and sweetest in the world.' The speaker was a Turkish gentleman, small and brown-skinned, magnificently attired in a bright fez, ornamental tunic and baggy silk trousers. Jenny seemed entranced by this exotic, so Emma obligingly ordered his beverage. It was served in an ornate little cup from a long-handled tin jug. The coffee was thick as soup but had an instantly reviving effect.

She offered money but the foreigner pressed it back into her hand. 'Put that away!' he said. 'Put it away carefully.'

'You must permit me to pay,' she protested. 'Your labour deserves its reward.'

'It will get it,' he smiled, 'for I shall charge twice the price to those with money to spare. Now hide your purse. Keep it safe from thieves and vagabonds.' As they left, he gave them two cubes of a Turkish sweetmeat. It was soft and translucent, dusted with icing sugar, and the colour of a dawn sky. When they sampled it, it had a taste of roses.

'Oh, Emma,' Jenny whispered. 'What marvels there are.'

In the queue everyone was in the best possible humour. Two serving girls, their ensemble a rude impersonation of current fashion, confessed that they did not have the entrance fee but relied on their charm to get them in.

'Well, I am glad I have money, for my charm would not take me far,' Emma declared.

'You've charm enough for us,' they said, and they linked her by the waist and waltzed her around until she was dizzy.

Three lads, their response affirmative of the serving girls' allure, said they had walked all the way from Manchester, a journey of nine days. The excitement mounted as they drew close to their goal. Jenny was alert to everything, her eyes like burning lamps. Despite the length of the queue, it moved quickly and soon it was time to go in. Emma reached into her pocket for her purse and made a dismaying discovery. 'My money is gone! It has been stolen!' She conducted a second search and fruitlessly explored the pram. Behind her, the crowd grew impatient. The man at the ticket office eyed her wearily. 'Get along now, miss. You're not the first to try that on. Folks behind have waited long enough.'

Emma's eyes filled with tears but she averted this vision for she knew there was no appeal. She kept her gaze away from Jenny too. She could not look on that little countenance, alight with expectancy. 'Come, Jenny,' she said. 'We must go home.'

Jenny nodded gravely. 'I expect that were St Peter. I've heard of him. I knew he'd not admit the likes of me. Yes, Emma, we'd best go home.'

But where was home? Where could she now take the dying child? She was gripped by a sense of remembered dread so strong that all the gay spring scene around her seemed to vanish. They had no money. She could not bring Jenny back to Jack Whaley's. Behind her, the two serving girls passed into Paradise, apparently on the strength of charm alone.

'Impudent dog!' a voice cried out behind her. She looked around in alarm, and saw that it was the Turkish gentleman and that he addressed the ticket-seller. 'I have seen all!' He spoke in his richly accented voice. 'This child has been robbed and you add insult to her injury. You are a disgrace to Empire and a discredit to this magnificent display.'

'My job is to take money and nothing else,' the ticket-seller responded. 'I can admit no one who cannot pay.'

'Those girls behind me had no money,' Emma said. 'You let them in because they were cheerful and pretty.'

'I did no such thing!' he protested. 'They had a purse of money and they paid me from it.'

'Oh, it was them,' Emma said dejectedly. 'They must have taken my purse when they danced around with me.'

'God Almighty, little lady,' said the Turkish noble, in a decidedly altered tone, 'have you no sense at all? Amn't I after telling you before to keep your money hid?' He took a florin from a small skin bag. 'To uphold the honour of this wretched nation, I shall pay for these children.' He spoke once more with the accent of a Turk. He bowed deeply before Emma. 'Arthur Curran at your service.'

'Arthur!' She threw her arms around him. 'What on earth are you doing here? Why have you painted yourself brown?'

'I did a bit of business with a true Turk,' said he. 'He sailed over to sell his wares but he had bad luck on a wager and ran out of money. I came by some cash so I helped him out of his dilemma. But, sure, who'd want to see an Irishman selling Turkish Delight and Turkish trinkets?'

'I would,' she responded, with feeling. 'I have never been so glad to see anyone. But you must not spend your hard-earned money on me. You are a poor person trying to make their way as I am.'

'Take it, and welcome,' said he, 'for the money was not entirely of my own earning. A gentleman gave me it – a sort of involuntary loan.'

'Arthur!' she rebuked. 'If you go on stealing you will hang.'

'Never!' He was shocked. 'You'd only swing for forty bob. I always calculate the sum to a nicety. Any road, there'll be no more thieving after this. Didn't I tell you I would make my fortune at the Great Exhibition, and so I am. Here! You will need a little to spend inside.' He handed her a crown. 'Go on, now. The man is holding your ticket out.'

She stood on tiptoe to kiss his cheek. 'Thank you, but please don't steal any more. And if you must, don't get caught, for if they did not hang you they would transport you.'

Arthur touched his cheek. He looked surprised and thoughtful. 'That's a very serviceable pair of lips you've got there. Your face does not betoken poetry but your lips might be worth a line or two. If you ever took a notion for a Connemara Turk I'd possibly have a go at marrying you in a few years.'

As she took her tickets Arthur called after her: 'Your name, little lady? I don't know what you call yourself.'

'Emma!' She smiled as she went inside. Her first beau! Not a very promising catch, but with more manners and kindness than she had encountered in better-advantaged gentlemen. It surprised her that someone would wish to marry her. She had imagined her looks would preclude a domestic resolution. Thoughts of home and hearth were banished as they entered the great hall and gazed upon the display of one hundred thousand exhibits from every nation in the world. Above all these and sweeping the curved glass of the transept rose the leafy splendour of the great elms.

'Is that God's throne?' Jenny was captivated by red-carpeted steps that rose to a plush and gilded chair placed for the monarch and her consort.

'It would be fit enough,' Emma said.

'Why are there two places? Who sits by His side?' the child whispered. She considered a possibility and then shook her head. 'They'd not allow the likes of me up there.'

They moved with the crowd, which first inspected the general wonders: the marble sculptures, a Russian room composed of semi-precious stones, a pearl as big as a fist. All the products of industry and treasures of the world vied with curiosities and strange inventions. A group of poor seamstresses gazed with awe upon a new machine that could, for the tapping of a pedal with the toe, undertake the labour that used up all their days and nights. Emma joined a cluster of women jostling at a breathtaking spectacle of silks, damasks and brocades mounted on a tall structure of plate glass. Hers was the only sigh that was not composed of wistful envy at the splendid display of Spitalfield Silks.

An hour seemed to pass in the space of a minute. For Emma, the chief delight lay in Jenny's cries of pleasure at each fresh wonder. The statuary, the porcelain, the silver, the fine linens and wools (there was even a presentation from my home town of H—) were the handsomest the world had to offer. Numerous curiosities were also on show, to demonstrate both the earth's antiquity and its infinite capacity for change. There were organs upon which tunes could be played just by turning a handle, a carriage drawn by kites, a lump of coal that weighed a ton. They saw a giant fountain made of glass crystal and a smaller one that sprayed a perfume called eau-de-Cologne. She drew Jenny's attention to the Koh-i-Noor diamond. 'It's the largest in the world,' she told her.

394

Jenny shook her head. 'It's never! It's no better than a vinegar stopper. We are inside the largest diamond in the world.'

As the morning advanced this gem seemed to concentrate all of the sun's considerable heat. Ladies fanned themselves and several had fainted. Although she made no complaint Jenny was suffering. Her cheeks had grown flushed and her eyes were glazed. Her concentration became focused upon her breathing, which was dry and shallow.

Emma took her to the great glass fountain at the very centre of the hall and refreshed her with the water there. 'I will get something else to cool you – the coolest and nicest thing in the world.'

In the refreshment room all the most elegant visitors were enjoying the shade of the great elm trees while slovenly looking waitresses passed out pots of tea and ham sandwiches. A man was grinding ice and ladling a creamy substance out of tin saucepans. 'Raspberry or pineapple?' he inquired, when Emma approached.

'A little of each, please.'

'That will be three shillings, then,' the surly man replied.

She handed across this outrageous sum and spooned some ice-cream into the child's parched mouth. 'Is that not the nicest thing you ever tasted?' she asked.

'It is,' Jenny agreed. 'But, Emma!'

'What, dearest?'

She sighed. 'This is not heaven after all.'

Emma felt the blow more sorely than she could have imagined. 'Why do you say so?'

'There are no babies here,' she said. 'I thought I would see all my dead babies here.'

'Poor little girl.' Emma hugged her. 'You are right. It is not heaven. Are you very disappointed?'

'Oh, no,' she exclaimed. 'It is better than heaven by far. Heaven is only ghosts and glory. Here is all the marvels that poor folks made. It's just . . .' The beseeching eyes that she raised were full of tears. 'I never knew there was anything nice in the world. Now I know it for a lovely place, I cannot bear to leave it.' She made a sigh. Her eyes closed. Emma lifted her from the pram. 'We'll rest now,' she said.

But where to find a place of rest in that great throng? All seats in the refreshment room had been claimed by the rich. In the great hall, working folk spread out on every remaining space the picnics they had brought with them. She pushed her way past swarms of gawkers at rubies and diamonds, at emeralds carved into little fruits, a tea party composed of stuffed animals, a mighty elephant with a magnificent silk carriage atop. These wonders no longer detained her. She sought only a quiet corner where she could cradle her little dying charge. Yet one exhibit did make her stand and stare. Of all the marvels it was decidedly the least spectacular. It was a black and white drawing of a girl. Emma recognized that girl. It was a likeness of herself. Above the head in heavy black was a single word: 'WANTED'.

So she was outlaw as well as outcast. It must be for the sum of money stolen from Fox Clough. She was overcome by yearning for the only place she had known as home. It seemed so far away, so undeserved. She felt that she could strive no more. Her wistful introspection was broken by a piping cry. It was Jenny whose eyes were open and her face radiant. 'Oh, it is heaven! Oh, look! Here is my gentleman!'

Emma looked. She saw nothing but the three-tiered splendour in its glass dome. Jenny gave a merry chuckle. She reached out a hand as if a familiar friend was by her side. Then she gave a low moan. She shut her eyes. Her head fell forward.

'Oh, help me! Someone help me!' Emma fell to her knees and laid the child upon the ground.

The jostling crowd became aware of illness in its midst. Squares of cambric and linen applied themselves to noses. As they backed away Emma found herself for the first time in a deserted space in that transparent mansion. The symphony of cheerful noise that had been its music now died away and no sound could be heard save the frantic wingbeat of a small bird trapped under the roof. Emma threw herself upon the slumped form of her only companion. 'Help me,' she wept. 'Oh, help me!'

A voice sounded close by her ear, a manly tone yet gentle. 'Have no fear.'

She felt so comforted by the utterance that at first she imagined God in His mercy was taking her to be with her little sister. Another more temporal providence then came to mind. 'Oh, Mr Ellin,' she cried.

CHAPTER THIRTY-SIX

The gentleman was not the one she named. When she looked up she saw that his aspect ill-matched his tone for he had a strangely unsparing gaze. As he drew nearer, his old-fashioned suit of clothing gave off an oddly musty odour. What, then? A detective come to bring her to justice?

'Who are you?' She wiped away tears.

'Not Mr Ellin, child, but his emissary.' His voice was so low she could barely distinguish any accent. Grey eyebrows thick as moustaches masked a shrewd expression, which made her think he must be some sort of legal man. 'Mr Ellin has been searching for you,' the man smiled. 'I am an old friend, engaged to help him. Come now. All your woes are at an end.' As if she was a feather he gathered her up. 'We are going home.'

What solace was there in that phrase: to be a child in adult arms, to shed her premature burden of responsibility, to hear kind words and a promise of safety. The exhaustion that follows upon months of struggle seemed to come over her at once. She wanted to let her lids shutter her eyes and to remain asleep until she was once more in familiar surroundings. 'Rest, now,' the man said. Yet she could not quite rest. The heat and noise of the hall affected her nerves. Apprehension plucked at her sleeve. A small, hoarse voice sounded in her head. *I wonder what a home is like? If I was ever in one I could think of it sometimes and it would be like being there.* She roused herself in a panic.

'Please, sir! I must attend to my sister.'

'Your sister?' The gentleman looked to the little figure slumped on the floor. 'Oh, I shall see to her. Only, dry your eyes.' He produced from his pocket a square of linen.

The incident that had repelled the exhibition-goers became a drama. A number of them began to pay attention. 'It is my daughter,' her rescuer reassured them. 'She ran away to see the Crystal Palace. I am taking her home.'

Why had he said such a thing instead of the plain truth? He began to move with purpose to the exit. 'My sister!' Emma spoke out in alarm. 'We cannot leave without her.'

'Yes, yes,' he reassured her. 'Mr Ellin said to bring her too.'

The unease that had earlier shown its face now developed a full set of features. Mr Ellin knew nothing of her companion. There was something strange about the man. The musty smell of his clothing was overlaid by an acrid odour that made her catch her breath.

'Please set me down or I shall cry for help!'

His hold upon her tightened as she struggled to be free. 'A high-strung young lady attempting to evade paternal protection?' He laughed. There was nothing of kindness in his tone now. 'An all-too-common sight, these days! No one paid much heed to your earlier hysterics. I doubt a fresh outburst would command an audience. Now, dry your eyes for Papa.' As the handkerchief was brought close she began to choke and cough.

With a limb of iron he forced over her face the chloroformed pad.

'Are you sure it is she? She looks a common enough child. Her clothing is plain.'

'Rest assured. She is the one.'

'Hard to believe anyone would offer a reward for her.'

Voices roused her from her drugged sleep. A reward? Who had offered a reward? Not the law! Only a dangerous felon would merit a price on her head. Whatever her crimes, she felt certain she was no murderess.

Cold water seeped into her clothing. A rank covering prickled her skin. She investigated an edge of it and found she had been thrown under sacking upon a thoroughly wet mattress. Cautiously she raised her makeshift blanket. The room was in darkness save a single shuddering drop of flame by which illumination she could distinguish her very odd surroundings. She was in a small chamber with mismatched and rickety items of furniture, all damp and half blackened. In the midst of this, at a sooty table, two men were in earnest conversation and refreshed themselves liberally from a bottle. By the light of the candle she could determine that one man was a short, miserable-looking fellow, with nervous, darting eyes. The other was strongly built with visage undistinguished but for the oddly luxuriant sweep of his eyebrows and, underneath them, his cold, assessing eyes. By these particulars she could identify her abductor. His jacket now hung grandly on the back of a chair and his clothing was as grimy as that of any ruffian.

'How much is offered for her?' the second man queried.

'No sum specified. Do not fret, Cooper. If he wants her he will pay whatever I ask.'

'Live or dead, she's not a beauty.'

'There's no accounting for tastes. Any road, it is she. Someone is willing to pay for her and that man has been notified.'

So it is to end as it began, Emma thought; in a dirty room where I am to be auctioned to a man, trailing my past like a prison chain.

Dejection and the effects of chloroform made her believe that, after all, her fate was inescapable. From the beginning, she had been destined for ignominious disposal. The few bright episodes that had intervened dimmed and grew insubstantial. Now they seemed but the bait that lures the doomed creature to the trap. Her dulled senses told her to sleep again. She was attempting to obey this directive when the conversation took a new turn.

'You mentioned another child, Lowry!' Her kidnapper was addressed. 'Might she not be worth something?'

'A piece of London refuse, cast up upon the banks of the Thames. I know the type. Any road, she were busy dying when I last saw her. She'll be cats'-meat by now.'

A surge of dread and panic made Emma fight her way back to consciousness. If only I had not left her, she thought. Oh, if I had not let her from my sight. She buried her face in the sacking to keep herself from sobbing. In her confused state it was not Jenny she saw but another small face, shining and clean, a perfect rose but surely with some outsize thorn to cause her such pain. The picture faded. It was replaced by the sad little object committed to her care. She forced her trembling legs to carry her from the bed to the table where the two men sat. 'Who are you?' she demanded. 'What do you mean to do with me? Why did you not bring my sister?'

The men were startled by the outburst. 'You should have tied her,' the one called Cooper said, and he trapped her roughly by the wrists. Even as she struggled her eye took in the items on the table. A flagon of rum, half consumed, was set beside a smaller vial. She recognized the latter for she had seen its like once before in the hands of her counterfeit mother, Eliza Brown. Her vision then encompassed another known object. It was the drawn likeness of herself last sighted at the exhibition, with its chilling dictate 'WANTED'. Close to, she could see that there was smaller wording underneath and that this imparted a different significance to the daunting imperative. In full, the notice read: 'WANTED – Information leading to the return of Emma. A reward is offered.' It was signed with a familiar name.

'Mr Ellin!' she breathed.

'You sound surprised.' Her kidnapper watched her shrewdly. 'Yet it seemed to me you were expecting him. It was his name you called when I found you.'

'Then I am not wanted by the law!'

'I hope not. We are felons enough here already. Were you expecting Ellin?'

'I expected no one,' she said. 'I imagined no one cared for me. Mr Ellin was kind to me when I most needed a friend.'

'What is he to you, this Mr Ellin? Not your father, I think?'

'He is nothing to me.' For some reason tears came to her eyes.

'Oh, come now, miss!' The one called Cooper leant close to her and she smelt rum on his breath. 'He must have some interest to offer money for your return. Is he, perhaps, the one who introduced you to adult life? You're not much to look at but there's some as likes young girls – the more child-like the better.'

'He is not!' Emma protested. 'His impulse is to virtue rather than its opposite. Mr Ellin is good.'

The men seemed amused by her distress. 'Do not fret! We do not dislike this good fellow. No – we like him! He must be rich to be so charitable.'

'He is not rich — except in intellect.' She was visited by a memory of her single conversation with a puzzling gentleman who addressed her as an adult and traded trust for trust. 'He lives very modestly. He keeps a small house and one servant.'

Both men now looked distinctly uneasy. 'How much do you suppose he will give for your return?'

A spark of defiance forced her to retaliate. 'As much as I am worth and not a penny more. How much do you suppose that to be?'

After a sullen pause Cooper took a sixpence from his purse and placed it on the table.

'Well, then,' she declared. 'I am scarcely worth your trouble. You might as well let me go.'

'We might!' The man called Lowry, who had brought her here, addressed her in a tone that was almost reasonable. 'Only we have already gone to trouble and expense on your account.'

'Mr Ellin will recompense you,' she promised.

'Why wait for Ellin?' Cooper grumbled. 'He sounds to me like trouble. If he is going to be stingy in payment why not just sell her to Mrs Keeley's house in Dock Street?'

'That would scarce repay our efforts. There's no shortage of girls on the streets. Yet you have given me a notion. Perhaps we could get a better trade from someone other than Ellin. This one being so young, we could send her to France. They pay a good deal for an unused child.'

'Don't send me away!' Emma's cry of consternation came upon a full understanding of her situation. Whatever slender chance she now possessed would surely be forfeit once she left English shores.

'Well, what a poignant picture you make, my dear,' her abductor sneered. 'I fancy there's many a man would like to make you beg for mercy. Yes, you shall have a Continental education.'

Her heart was beating so fast she felt certain she would faint, yet she forced herself to speak. 'I think I have already had that . . . education.'

'The d—l take you!' Lowry swore. 'The only pleasure left in you is to kill you. I shall do it myself.' He raised a fist.

'Wait!' The other stayed his arm. 'She may be bluffing to avoid her fate. I think we should send for Dilke.'

'What is to happen? Who is Dilke?' she entreated.

'He is a ladies' man,' Lowry said, and both villains laughed. 'For your own sake, my dear, I think it best if you try to rest.'

'I shall not rest,' she resolved.

'Oh, now! You ought to try.' Cooper held her by the waist and Lowry applied his handkerchief to the small bottle of colourless fluid. She tried hard to hold her breath but was overcome by the chloroform.

This time she awoke to a vague discomfort that seemed connected to yet disconnected from herself. Alarm roused her from her opiate state as she felt hands upon her body. She opened her eyes and saw a strange man intent upon some leisurely exploration of her most private self. Half paralysed by horror, she tried to cry out but only a feeble whimper emerged.

The newcomer spoke: 'You need not take fright, child. I am a doctor summoned to examine you.'

She wanted to ask why but the muscles of her tongue had been affected by the narcotic and she could only make a slurred and indeterminate sound.

'Well?' Lowry emerged from the shadows with an eager look. 'Do not keep us in suspense.'

'You may rest assured.' The doctor scrubbed with doubtful water and dubious cloth. 'She is a maiden yet.'

The words drifted on the air like the refrain of a ballad before coming to rest on her dulled brain. There was a sweet

404

sound to them. She felt tears on her cheeks. In spite of her dismal surroundings and the danger that surrounded her they were not wretched drops but a cleansing flood. The words were meant for her. The medical man had examined her and given his determination. She was a maiden. No matter that she was in a dark room in the company of those who meant to harm her, she felt that light had entered her. Her life was not a spent and sullied object. Unthinkable now that it should cease to be of value. It was a book unopened, a gift still wrapped.

'Capital news!' her kidnapper crowed. 'The Frenchies will pay forty guineas for a young lass whole. We'll not wait for Ellin. We'll put her on a boat for France tonight. I know a man aboard will keep her quiet for a sum. This calls for a drink. You'll take a drink with us?'

The doctor shook his head. He seemed to wish only to quit the place. By a very determined effort Emma managed to pull herself up in the bed and shape some likeness of a phrase: 'Doctor! Help me!'

This faint imprecation was all but drowned by the mirth of her captor. 'He'll not aid you. He's helped too many ladies in the past to rid themselves of little nuisances such as you. He is a doctor no more. Now, he's just a commonplace criminal who'll take his shilling and keep his mouth shut.'

She thought the doctor gave her a fleeting look of pity. Yet she pitied him even more, for his existence had been tarnished while hers, though in the gravest jeopardy, was yet undimmed. I shall have my life, she thought. I shall live it for Jenny. Be it no longer than an hour I shall live it with honour.

Afterwards she wondered if she had voiced this sentiment aloud. In her half-dream state she could not be certain but her kidnapper eyed her sharply and reached for the chloroform. 'I shall keep her drugged until she is safely in France.'

'Give her no more!' The doctor took the bottle from his hand and returned it to the table. 'At least not for the present! You may do her permanent damage.' His eye was then caught by the bill marked with Emma's likeness. 'She is not a waif!' he exclaimed in alarm. 'She is a missing child!' He lowered his voice. 'For heaven's sake, let her go. She may be of respectable family. This is more trouble than you need.'

'It is a long time since I have done anything for heaven's sake,' Lowry reflected. 'Her family ought to have kept an eye to her and not allowed her to wander unprotected. She is mine now and by the morrow she shall be where none will ever trace her.'

'You are wrong,' Emma vowed. 'I shall not go. I shall cry out and someone will help.'

'I wonder who?' Lowry mocked; 'myself and Cooper being the sole occupants of this handsome estate. There were some forty other wretches in residence until it recently caught fire. My own tenancy will be no longer than necessary for it is not quite comfortable owing to the furnishings having been sub-ject to the hoses and the floor being most unsound. Indeed, four persons might constitute a hazard.'

With an exclamation of disgust the doctor left.

'As to trouble,' Lowry resumed: 'the only bother I can anti-cipate is from our other piece of property, for she has an impudent streak. Tie her hands!' he charged his accomplice. 'Bind her feet and mouth! I'd like to have a drink in peace.'

'What of Dilke?' Cooper said. 'Aren't you afraid he'll squeal? He could go to the law or to this Mr Ellin for the reward.'

'What? Am I suddenly surrounded by ladies?' The villain seized the rope. 'I shall tie her.' He went at his task with a will. Emma tried not to cry out as the thick rope bit into her wrists and ankles for she felt it pleased Lowry to cause her pain. 'If Dilke were to go to the law it is he who would be the object of their interest and well he knows it.' The knots were made fast and then doubled. 'As for Ellin, he is a day's ride away. My letter is now a passenger on the mail train. It will reach him by tonight's post. He could not possibly arrive before the morrow.' He finished his task by stuffing a filthy rag into her mouth and tying it fast with a greasy neck-scarf. When all was done he surveyed his victim, then leant down with his mouth to her ear. 'Have no fear,' he spoke in the same coaxing tone with which he had first deceived her; 'you will never escape. You may grieve for your little sister but very shortly you will wish that you were in her place.'

Why does he hate me so? she wondered. Yet she knew the answer. It was because she possessed the one object we are given upon this earth that has no price, yet infinite value – her soul; and he had bartered his. To keep at bay her guiltless gaze he cast the sacking over her once more and stumbled back to the table to drink away his disillusion.

She heard the two men mumbling and the clink of bottle on tankard. Although she still felt drowsy the discomfort of her ties kept her from sleep. She passed the hours in praying. She prayed first for the soul of little Jenny Drew and then for those who had shown her the solace of home. Finally she asked mercy for others who, by their actions, had cut themselves off for ever from their true home. Those men were very drunk now. Their celebration turned to argument, her captor accusing his colleague of leaving him to do the work and face the danger. 'Now get out of here and organize her transport,' he snarled. The door slammed as the other left.

Presently all noises ceased. She lay very still and strained for sound. When silence declared its dominion she shook away the sacking. Her captor was slumped at the table. Watching to make sure he would not stir she carefully swung her feet to the floor. As noiselessly as was possible she slid her body down to follow. Lowry had made a useless parcel of her. She could not walk or crawl. Yet move she must, and before Cooper returned. By an agonizing effort she managed to inch her way across the ruined floor. Splinters tore at her face and the broken floor-boards proclaimed her passage with treacherous creak and groan. The short journey left her shaking and exhausted. Still, she must find a means of reaching the table. She worked her way to a sitting position and sat with back to chair. She would endeavour to pull herself up by her fingers. The pressure of her bindings had numbed her hands and for a time she could only fumble without grasping. In due course this activity brought blood back to her limbs and she seized hold of the chair leg and dragged herself upward. Progress was infinitely slow. Each time she pulled, the chair leg shifted with a squeal. All the time she kept an eye to Lowry, waiting for some flicker of wakefulness that would end her bid for freedom. She had raised herself as high as the seat. She had but to grasp the surface and ease herself on to it and she could rest awhile. Her quivering fingertips pressed upon its edge. With a lurching crash it fell to the ground. Her heart made a rival clamour as she saw the drunk man stir and mutter in his sleep. She rolled beneath the table and stayed there until she was sure he would not rouse, then cautiously emerged and edged around to the table leg. Pressing her back against it, putting her heels hard to the floor she succeeded, by a great effort, in raising herself to standing. Now she must lean back and find with her fingers the object necessary for her release. She realized that what she was about to do was as like to bring about death as rescue. She had no fear: *This day, God has given me a very great grace. Whether He chooses to call me to Him or spare me for a useful life I shall not succumb to that wicked man's design.*

Her fingers stroked a cold surface. She pushed. The bottle made a ghastly din as it toppled and the dregs gurgled over the table. Emma gasped. She had upset the wrong object. She trembled so much she was unable to move. Her face was not a foot away from that of her kidnapper. The man breathed some oaths. He did not open his eyes but his hand reached out for his tankard. It fumbled, then sank and was still. Quickly! I must act quickly! she thought. Her shaking hand reached out again, found its goal and nudged. The candle fell. She turned to see what she had done. In spite of her determination a choking cry arose behind the unsavoury rags that bound her mouth as the flame threw out eager yellow feelers, then bounded across the table to consume its half-eaten meal.

CHAPTER THIRTY-SEVEN

The evening post scattered its sociable seeds on Deerfield. It brought conversation to the dinner table or imposed its silencing burden of care. To Mr Ellin it meant the end of a long quest begun in pity and ended in atonement. A mission undertaken partly to relieve an increasing sense of boredom with his own life had become – as Mr Cornhill had proposed – his second chance. He would have gone to any lengths to find Emma. A return trip to London had yielded no word. His handbills, posted anywhere they might be seen, brought no information. He had come home to face defeat. Now he read the words that might spell his own redemption. *The girl is found.*

Why, then, did he not rejoice? Why shake his head and sigh? It was because of what followed upon that blessed phrase. An ill-scripted message couched in terms of thinly veiled threat spoke of 'sum to be negotiated' and warned against mediation by the law. It was signed by that most malign of foes, 'A Friend'.

'No benevolent hand at work here!' he ruefully concluded when he came to Fox Clough to show me: 'I believe she may be in very great danger.'

Again he went to London. Upon arrival, he did not instantly fulfil his assignation but paused briefly for another call: this time to the police. He showed the ransom note and copies of his bill. 'I shall follow the directive,' he said. 'I have offered a reward and I will pay it. Yet I suspect villainy.'

The constable studied the message and the pencilled sketch: 'Put away your money, sir. It will not be needed now.'

'What is it?' Mr Ellin was dreadfully alarmed. 'What do you know of her?'

'Do not distress yourself, sir,' the constable urged. 'She is where no more harm can reach her.'

She had overturned the candle. Bound and gagged she could not scream or shelter her face from smoke and fumes. Small startled sounds issued from the back of her throat as the flames took hold and the dying house began to shed great tongues of fire and shafts of timber from its beams. When the blaze was in full possession of its prey she flung herself upon her captor to wake him. Lowry was startled from his stupor. He looked in bewilderment at the inferno and then with muttered oaths pushed past his victim and out of the door. Emma watched his exit in dismay. She had assumed he would take her with him, that someone would see a girl bound and gagged and come to her aid. She was alone now with a more ruthless enemy. Out in the street she heard the commotion of fire bells, yet there was no time left. In spite of what she had earlier asserted she was very frightened. To defer her fate she sought to escape the worst of the heat. She flung herself to the ground and began her painful journey, choking and sobbing, back across the floor. She reached the bed with its dripping mattress. Like any frantic animal that burrows underground, she nudged her way beneath it. The fire bells sounded right outside the house now – too late, she judged.

Why is life so short and death so long? she thought in dread as hoses were turned upon the building and it began to come apart in a plague of rain and fire.

Mr Ellin found her in a hospital bed. He took fright to see a ghostly thing, a small and solitary wraith, a face all bandaged. To trace a sound in her sightless world, her head turned this way and that, like a blind fledgling, he thought. Then a voice came out of that muffled countenance. In strong tones it proclaimed that the bandages served only to rest her eyes, which had been hurt by smoke. 'Sit by my bed, sir,' said she. 'Hold my hand and let me hear your voice so that I will know it is you. Please forgive my appearance. I am lately come from setting a house on fire.'

'My brave girl!' he uttered, for he had heard the story from the constable.

'I am not brave,' she said. 'The fireman who found me was brave. Although more severely burned than I, he risked his life to save me.'

'Thank God your life has been spared.'

'It has been spared in more ways than one.' She spoke with quiet fervour. 'And thank God for it.'

Mr Ellin felt humbled by such composure in one so young. He could not boast as much dignity. Her small hand with roughened skin was so affecting that he almost welcomed her bandages, which afforded him privacy for an unmanning show of emotion.

A week after this there appeared upon my doorstep a surprise party. The party comprised Mr Ellin and Emma. The surprise was the appearance and demeanour of that young person. I had anticipated a sick and shabby stray. Months of rough living might have wrought any manner of adverse change on a weak and nervous child. I was prepared for it. I was determined to reclaim my consignment in any condition. Imagine my surprise at finding upon my threshold a clean, well-dressed and assured young girl. There was no doubting it was she. There were the same solemn grey eyes; the same features whose want of conventional feminine prettiness had offered such affront to the Misses Wilcox; the same lack of sham and sentiment that could discompose even one so eminently sensible as myself.

'My child!' I took her in my arms and the tears I had not shed before for danger of a flood now fell freely. 'At last you are home!'

She held me, too – that slender body taking its share (and no more) of maternal comfort before moving back to hold me in her level gaze. Those grey orbs were eloquent as ever to those with whom they would discourse. 'Not a child,' they said. 'These eyes have seen too much for that. We must be as equals now.'

My long-held scheme to pamper her, to substitute in her the child I had never held, must be revised. Her new-found self-possession merited its tribute of respect. What grand plans I might have for her future must await her approval. Before I might indulge myself by indulging her, I must afford her that greatest luxury known to human relations: I must listen to her.

I transferred my tears discreetly to a linen square and governed my feelings. At length I was rewarded by her return for a second embrace and then a kiss. 'Yes,' she said. 'I am home.'

Great preparations had been made for this homecoming, which had been signalled via letter. We proceeded to the dining-room where supper was waiting. I had prepared every dainty and tempting thing in the hope that Emma might pick at a morsel. To my surprise and relief, she made a good supper, after which she commenced to clear up.

'Leave that for Mary,' I said.

'I am sorry.' She sat again. 'When I see a used table I begin to tidy it without thinking. It is how I earned my living. There is so much to tell that I scarcely know where to begin.'

'The morrow would be a good place,' I said, although I longed to hear her news. 'Tonight you must rest. We have all of the future to catch up.'

'Yes,' she said. 'I can begin to think of a future now, even though I am still without a past.'

I glanced at Mr Ellin. He shook his head to answer my unspoken query. 'It is a long story,' he said to Emma.

'Not so long a story,' I ignored his look of appeal. 'And Emma has waited long.' I turned her once more to face me. 'Your mother was a good and beautiful lady who brought you into this world fourteen years ago. Your real name is Emma Osborne.'

'Who found this out?' Emma said. 'Was it Mr Ellin?'

'It was Mr Cornhill.'

'Who is Mr Cornhill?' She looked surprised to find a new persona introduced at this late stage.

'He is the gentleman you knew as Conway Fitzgibbon — the man who rescued you from that wicked woman, Eliza Brown.'

'Then — he was good?'

I bent my head. By an effort I managed a reply: 'As good a man as ever lived.'

Mr Ellin looked at me sharply but Emma noticed nothing. She was lost in her own history. 'What of my parents? Are they alive still?'

'We do not know. Every effort has been made to trace them.'

Her expression was forlorn but she managed a smile. 'I have you and Mr Ellin. You will be my family.' She came to me and embraced me and then, on an impulse, did the same to Mr Ellin. 'Mr Ellin has been so kind to me,' she said. 'I owe him everything. It makes the loneliness of my journey worthwhile to know that this kindly shadow was behind me all the while.'

Mr Ellin now had all the appearance of a cat fed on cream and herrings.

'My room!' Emma said then. 'I have thought of it often. Is it still there – exactly as it was?'

'Apart from a few improvements. I hope you will find them to your liking. There is still a nice bed in it reserved for you.'

'Oh, I should so like to sleep in a soft bed again.' She attempted to stifle a yawn.

'Go and rest now, my dear.' I kissed her.

Mr Ellin still watched me. When Emma was gone he said, 'Thank you, dear friend. Thank you from the bottom of my heart.'

'The past has worked all its mischief now,' I said. 'Let it slumber.'

'Gladly,' he assented; 'yet I wonder if there is not some fresh ill.'

'What do you mean?' I busied myself at the fire.

'Something happened in my absence. I feel sure of it. Several times this evening I saw a look on your face that, for all the happiness of this occasion, spoke of misery. My dear Mrs Chalfont, won't you tell me what has come to pass?'

At this my carefully contrived reserve deserted me. I allowed my hands to cover my face and wept most bitterly.

'What is it?' he appealed in dismay.

'I had not meant to speak of it yet. I did not wish to spoil the evening.'

'Are we not friends?' he inquired. 'Is not a privilege of that connection the sharing of bad tidings as well as good?'

'Mr Cornhill is dead.' I spoke abruptly, knowing there was no other way I could impart such news. 'He was at the French port of Marseille and contracted cholera.'

415

'Poor fellow! How terrible!' A sympathetic silence ensued. When I had recovered enough for conversation Mr Ellin said to me: 'Was he alone?'

'He was endeavouring to help a woman who had fallen into the hands of Felix Osborne. Mr Osborne has yet again disappeared – dead or alive we do not know and should not, I feel, seek to discover. It is time to put the past to rest.'

Yet it was not so easily subdued. Directly after Mr Ellin's departure I went to my chamber. I was worn out by the emotion of the evening and hoped to lull my body into sleep. As usual I lay awake, haunted by demons of desolation. 'Finch!' I whispered, and was answered by a mournful chorus of regrets. I tried to make a pact with wisdom and acceptance but my arms ached for the only contact that would ease them and my soul was tormented by mocking cries: 'You could have saved him if you had loved him.' I had loved him almost to distraction. My failing was that I could not accept him. What had he seen in me, that dear, driven soul? I was never more than a middling sort of person. I think he looked to me for that commodity he denied himself – for comfort. Yes, I could have comforted him. And I had not.

I woke with the dawn feeling drained, yet not quite bereft. A child beneath my roof would be my beacon of hope. I went to Emma's room to give myself the pleasure of her slumber. She was not asleep. She sat up in bed gazing fixedly at some object. It was the small portrait Finch had sent from Marseille.

'Who is it?' she asked. 'Who is the lady in the painting?'

'Do you not know?' I asked her softly.

'I do not think so. Yet the sight of her causes me such sadness I cannot bear it.'

What should I do? To make her face the object of her distress was a hazard. I had done it before and had caused much ill. And yet the past is a part of the very fabric of one's self. To be without it is to see in the glass a clouded image.

'Look again. Look at her eyes! Do they not look familiar?'

Again she gazed. I felt her tremble beneath my touch. After an interval, she emitted a most woeful cry. 'Oh, my poor mother!'

The missing pieces came slowly, wrenched painfully from a protective sensibility. I made no effort to hasten them. There was other business to attend to. We needed time to build the trust that had been interrupted at the start. We were much occupied in filling in the pages of annals that lay buried in the months of parting. She told me of her time in London, and of her little companion called Jenny Drew. I recalled my time in Fuchsia Lodge and the brief reunion with the man I had loved from my youth. Such easy fellowship awaited us now, ready for picking as fruit come into its season. After a full week in her company I could scarcely believe she had not been a daughter to me all her life. Yet she was not my child. I was reminded of this on a pleasant morning as we pegged linen to the wash-line.

'I remember my mother,' she said then. 'Why do I not recall my father?'

'You were very young when he went from your life,' I told her.

'Yes, I was four.' She looked surprised. This fragment had taken her unaware. 'No! That was not my real father. My real father was . . .' She frowned into some inner distance. 'I can't remember. The man who died – I did not love him. I only loved Mama. Everyone else seemed against her. They took her away. I was very frightened and I think she was too, yet she kept saying she had a kind friend who would help her. After that they would not let me see her.'

'Come inside, Emma,' I said. I left the rest of the linen seeping through the basket on to the stones and led her to the kitchen. 'Come and sit down.'

Submissively she let herself be guided. In troubled silence she sat. Her eyes had grown very large and dark as if she was four years old again and suddenly deprived of her mother. Wide and alarmed they grew as she began to speak afresh. 'I kept asking where Mama had gone. No one would tell me. Then I heard the servants talking. They said she was a murderess and would be hanged.'

These revelations came not in a smooth narrative but in a rushed staccato, with a sense of wild scramble, like someone recovering papers blown away in a high wind.

'I knew that what they said could not be true. I had to go to the place where she was kept and explain that Mama was good, but they forbade me to enter the courthouse. I made my nurse take me there and waited every day on the steps. I could find only one gentleman who would talk to me and I tried to tell him how good Mama was. In the end they must have known they were wrong, for they let her go free. I thought it would be all right then, that we could go home, but Mama said our home no longer belonged to us.' She laid her head upon the table and began to weep.

'Do you remember where you went after that?'

When she raised her face she seemed to have shed the last of her childhood with her tears. 'Yes. We went to live a long way away in a cottage with a lady we called Aunt Matty, although she wasn't really an aunt. My little sister was born there.'

She broke off her fitful narrative and looked at me in astonishment. 'I have a sister! Mrs Chalfont, I have a sister!'

'Do you know where she is?' I asked.

She looked back into that place that, until recently, had been a vacuum, but which now held an overcrowding of pictures. 'She is called Sally.' She smiled excitedly. 'She looks just like Mama. She is as fair as I am homely.'

'How did you come to be parted?'

'We were not parted,' she said in surprise. 'I never left her from my sight. She . . .' Emma broke off, then gave a cry of distress.

'What do you see now, my dear?' I asked her.

'I cannot look!' As if it would exclude the vision she put both hands over her eyes. 'I do not wish to look.'

'No, don't look,' I urged. 'Let us occupy ourselves with something entirely inconsequential. Let us bake a cake.'

There are few activities so soothing as the sieving and measuring and beating that preface a bout of sweet baking. We worked together silently. The anguish that had marked Emma's face receded and a thoughtful look replaced it. She seemed very calm the rest of the day but in the evening, as she was reading aloud to me, she laid down her book and murmured, 'Now I know why I felt such pain when I found that Jenny Drew carried about a dead little child.' She looked up. She spoke quite flatly. 'My sister is dead.'

'Are you sure?'

'Yes, she died in my arms.'

'Was it in Miss Fitzgibbon's house?'

'No, in London. We were made homeless again when that good lady passed away. Mama said we would fare better in London, but she was not strong and it was such a long journey. By the time we arrived she was too weak for work and we had no money for food or lodgings. She said we must go to the workhouse. She was very brave. She told us nothing else mattered so long as we could be together. But when at last we reached our destination, it brought the discovery that women and children were lodged in separate houses. We would have to be parted there. It was too much for her. She had already lost everything in her life. She would not go in. She sat on the step weeping with her arms around us. Then, after many hours, little Sal said that she was hungry. Mama brought us to a door and knocked on it and told us to go in for our supper. She gave me a ring from her finger and then kissed us and went away to the women's quarter. We went inside and were washed with disinfectant. Our clothes were taken and our hair shorn. We never again saw our mother, for she died soon after.'

'And what of your sister? What of little Sally?'

She began to cry very softly. Tears ran down her face unheeded as she continued: 'On the day of my twelfth birthday they told me I was to be sent out to work, and to board away from the institution. Sally and I were to be parted. The poor little child wept so much it was hard to bear but I promised to come and see her at the first opportunity. When I returned she was not there. She had run away to be with me. I resisted all who endeavoured to assist me. I trusted no one now. In blind panic I went to look for her, searching day and night the streets of London. When I found her in a dustyard she was blue with cold, half starved and hopeless. Other waifs lived there, picking over refuse for something to eat, and oddly attired women with clay pipes, who made a living seeking objects in the refuse to sell. The only other visitor was a sinister-looking woman who came from time to time to talk to the young girls. She was very dirty and we were all afraid of her, yet she promised food and lodgings, and if one of the girls was hungry enough she went with her. I would not leave Sally even to find food. In that foul place I, too, became ill. I welcomed death, for I knew she would not live. Yet the God who spared my life declined to spare me her suffering. My sister died a hard death.'

Emma paused. She folded her arms across her breast and bent double as if to brace herself against an unendurable soreness.

'I would not be parted from her, even after her life was gone. The day came when I no longer recalled who she was, for my

420

senses had been assaulted by grief and illness. I was like a dumb animal, clinging to its dead pup. I remembered nothing, not even my name. Yet hunger influences even dumb creatures. I was barely conscious by the time Eliza Brown came. She took my sister from me and brought me home with her.'

The crying ceased. She sat up and drew her hands across her cheeks. She was quite still. She seemed dazed, almost emotionless. A faint sound escaped her lips. As she swayed forward I took her in my arms.

'There! It is over!' I soothed. She lay inert but with fast-beating heart, like a wounded bird. I wished to protect her from everything in life yet lacking that facility cast about desperately for some ray to illuminate her darkness. 'From all of this there is one good outcome.' I kissed her cold, wet cheek. 'At least you now know yourself to be entirely innocent of the terrible insinuations made against you by that wicked woman, Eliza Brown. You are, in every sense, an honourable young woman. Now you may properly mourn and, in due course, heal. It will take a long time but the day will come when you will be able to resign your past to God's will.'

The look she gave me was bleak beyond bearing. 'That day will never come. I wish my memory had not come back. There is nothing in there but waste and loss, and it might all have been different had Mama not been forsaken by her so-called friend.'

In spite of what she said, she did begin to heal. We made our mourning together like two black-clad crones. We prayed for our dear dead and moaned together like the winds of winter. When this was done, I consigned her to her true season. I invited Diana from Fuchsia Lodge to stay for the summer. The two young girls became firm friends. They lay in the garden with flowers in their hair. They picnicked by the beck and wandered arm in arm in the cemetery to read sentimental verses from the stones. In the evenings those long-legged colts would run together over the moors, full of energy and secrets. What confidences they shared I do not know. Both had known unhappiness and injustice. They could comfort one another as no adult could. In due course, by this alliance, a small miracle occurred.

One day when Emma came into the kitchen, she asked if she might keep a pet.

'Do you have a specific one in mind?' I asked.

'Old Eli Hirst, the poacher, has died. His dog was left chained and is half starved.'

'You may have a pet,' I said carefully. 'But Eli Hirst's dog is known to be a fierce creature. His owner trained him to attack. Might you not prefer a more biddable animal?'

'No,' she said. 'I know the poacher's dog. I promise I can tame him. I tamed a hawk when we lived in the country.'

A charming tale ensued. At the age of eight Emma had found an injured bird and brought him back to 'Aunt Matty's' cottage. She and her sister fed it by hand until it mended and became a loved and trusting pet.

Happy memories had now come to keep company with bleak ones. She recalled her years of living in the country with Miss Fitzgibbon, her mother and sister as an unbroken stretch of perfect happiness. From the wise old woman she had received a liberal education; from her good mother, the gift of an untrammelled childhood. The children had befriended a wild dog, and as Sally wanted a brother the stray was appointed to this position. With their new defender, the little girls lived a free and unrestricted life, never knowing the constraints that other girls have placed upon them. A whole portion of her childhood had been kept safe from fate and this golden fragment was a rich, sheltered pasture for her to explore.

Gradually, more and more detailed memory returned, names of people and places and other pets. In spite of all she had suffered I felt confident that blessed youth would absolve her of bitterness. This hope increased daily until a visitor came to call. He had brought a gift of strawberries for the two young girls and wished to present it in person to Miss Emma.

'It is Mr Ellin,' I said. 'He would like to see you. He has a surprise for you.'

On this occasion the surprise was the flash of warning that entered her grey eyes and the almost haughty manner in which she responded. 'I do not wish to see him,' she said. 'I wish never to see that gentleman again.'

'How can you say such a thing?' I asked. 'He has shown so much concern for your welfare.'

'A pity he did not show it for my mother,' she angrily responded.

'What do you mean?' I asked, although I had a clear suspicion.

'I have remembered the name of my mother's friend. I know who it is. It is Mr Ellin.'

'Do not put too much strain upon your memory,' I advised. 'It was all a very long time ago.'

'I recall it most particularly,' she insisted. 'Mama always talked of him and I remember thinking that his name – Mr Ellin – sounded like a girl's name.'

'Are you sure it is the same Mr Ellin?'

'He was a lawyer, as Mr Ellin is. Besides, Mr Ellin unwittingly betrayed himself by his own mouth. In a time when I was too frightened to speak, he offered to barter a little of his history for some of mine. Although he spoke enigmatically, it is now very clear what he meant.'

There seemed no further point in argument. 'Mr Ellin loved your mother,' I said. 'Wicked men poisoned his mind against her.'

'So it is true?' She seemed immeasurably shaken. She had not been certain after all. She had looked to me for confirmation.

'If it is true,' I proceeded with caution, 'is it not also a fact that Mr Ellin, by his kindness to yourself, has made recompense for his hasty judgement?'

For an answer, that intractable young person said, 'Please ask him to leave the house. If he will not do so, then I must.'

I approved her tone no more than the errand, yet I did not deem it an idle threat and I understood the depth of feeling that underran it. I went to Mr Ellin. Even before I spoke, he guessed from my expression.

'She knows!' He laid down his gift and looked crestfallen.

'She is as unyielding as you once were. She will not see you and refuses to remain in the house if you are here.'

He said nothing. His whole appearance bespoke dejection as he departed.

I did not like this disagreement between two people who were close to me. Whatever the mistakes of his hasty youth Mr Ellin had paid for them and had striven hard to make amends. I felt now it was my nestling who might need a sharp lesson in accommodation.

'Considering that you and Mr Ellin are not related, it is surprising how alike you are,' I remarked.

'Me? Like him? How can you say it?'

'In wounding your poor mother he caused no less an injury to himself. He lived a half-life when he might have known great happiness. He stabbed his own heart upon an imagined point of principle. It seems to me that you are now inflicting the same pointless damage on yourself.'

'There is a considerable difference,' she said. 'My mother loved him. I do not even like him.'

'You claimed him for your family not a month ago!' I reminded her.

'My mother is dead – and because of him.'

'Yes, and what of that good lady? Do you think she would have acted as you do now? Suppose she had been able to convince him of her innocence and he had relented. Would she not have forgiven him?'

This conjecture gave Emma pause for thought, an interlude that brought such a look of melancholy that I almost wished to drop the argument. 'Yes,' she said sadly. 'She loved him to the last.'

'And would she not wish you to do the same?'

'What? Love him?'

'Forgive him.'

'I am not her,' Emma said.

'Well, do not say it with such pride,' I urged. 'By all accounts your mother was blessed with a perfectly sweet nature. The same might not be said of yourself. Your present objective ought not be to satisfy your feelings of resentment, but to make your poor mother proud of you.'

'It would seem I am a disappointment to both you and her,' Emma retaliated. 'I am not sweet. Perhaps in nature I take after my father rather than my mother.'

At once I had to go and put my arms around her. 'That is not true,' I said. 'You are headstrong, but you are thoroughly good. I am very proud of you. Your mother would be too.' At this she patted me and wept and apologized, and I had to realize that I was no longer the custodian of a child, nor yet the companion of an adult, but the natural opponent of a moody adolescent. The strength and clarity that charges young girls on the verge of adulthood would, for a time, be overtaken by the conflicts of transition. Yet this, too, was a source of pride. I would be the one to guide her to womanhood. I treasured this keeping. I even valued our conflicts. We were like any mother and her growing daughter, a loving dame and her too-strong cub in tender tribal tussle.

As she lay on my shoulder she whispered, 'When Mr Ellin found me in London he was so kind to me I almost did feel I loved him. Perhaps because of that the bitterness is now the greater.'

'Sometimes our feelings are too intense for us mere mortals to manage,' I murmured back. 'It is best to place them in God's keeping.'

Yet I felt sorry for Mr Ellin. He bravely kept a check upon the progress of hostilities. Each time he got the same result and departed in singularly hangdog fashion. He had begun to devote himself to good works and had taken an interest in the child workers of the parish. Although everyone said how kind he was, still Emma set her face against him. His persistence seemed at times pathetic yet I perceived both strength and courage in his campaign.

'Please tell her I have a message for her,' he urged, when a fresh endeavour was rewarded with the customary negative. 'This news I must impart to her myself.'

'I am afraid she will not see you,' I (again) apologized. 'May I not pass it on?'

'Yes. If she will not see me then it must be you to break the news,' he said gravely. 'It concerns the child she called Jenny Drew.'

At this the young object of his commission burst upon the scene with undignified haste and seized him by both lapels. 'Tell me, Mr Ellin,' she begged.

CHAPTER THIRTY-EIGHT

One day in spring Mr Ellin came to see me. That panther tread, which undisturbed the angels of the house, that pleasant face and undemanding mien brought with it its customary sense of well-being and earned its welcome.

This was not the same spring. The planet had passed through another quartet of seasons and returned to where it might bask once more under harmless skies. The year had brought an excessive measure of both grieving and healing. Mr Ellin was more his old self now, although a new self too, for he had become a great force of good in the community. He had been instrumental in setting up a little ragged school for the child workers of the neighbourhood (and I had transferred my teaching skills to this academy). Yet he still liked buttered muffins and his seat by the fire.

He claimed that favoured spot. 'Mrs Chalfont, I have a favour to ask.'

'What, not a story?'

He settled his languid frame at leisure. 'Over years a story may unfold.'

'I have an hour to spare,' I said. 'Let me have an instalment.'

'I shall not waste a moment of your time,' said he. 'The favour I ask is your hand in marriage.'

I have to own that the surprise of this request almost sent a circle of stitching spinning to the floor.

'You wish to marry me?' I played for time.

'Now that Emma has consented to be friends with me once more, I would like us three to be together. It is as she said on the night I brought her home – we are her family.'

'So!' I said; 'the idyll you envisage has you and I growing grey in harmony while a certain young person flowers to womanhood in our care.'

'Do you not think we would be very happy?'

'Look carefully at this picture,' I urged. 'There is the whiskered patriarch, and on either side a female in his keeping. Now, answer quickly – towards which one do his affections lean most decidedly?'

'Mrs Chalfont! They incline as yours do – towards the child. From what I have seen, that is how it is in many good marriages. Yet I feel, and always have felt, most cordial towards you. I number you as one of my closest friends. Have we not been the very best of companions? Do we not amuse one another? Have we ever known a moment's discord?'

'No,' I agreed. 'I own that our friendship has always been true, but it has been temperate. Surely relations between a man and a woman require no commitment unless succession is the object, or passion demands it for decency's sake.'

I was amused to see something like a blush upon that equable male countenance.

'Mrs Chalfont – I did not know you thought of such matters.'

I bent to attend to a complicated embroidery knot so that he would not mistake my smile for ridicule.

'My dear friend,' he blustered. 'We are no longer young. Surely passion – for decency's sake – takes a secondary role in the relations of the mature.'

'I can assure you, dear sir, that it does not.'

He looked quite confounded, as men always do when women act independently of the character that is assigned to them. Could he possibly be as guileless as he appeared? Had he forgotten the day he came upon myself and another in the summerhouse at Fuchsia Lodge?

'You and Mr Cornhill . . . ?' An uncustomary confusion now broke up his every utterance.

I nodded.

'But Mr Cornhill is . . .'

I sighed. 'Yes, sir. Mr Cornhill is dead.'

'Dear lady, forgive an unpardonable intrusion. I knew that you and he had old acquaintance. I saw that you and he . . . I should have known.' At this the blush became a positive crimson. 'Forgive me, madam. I thought the fellow rash. I believed he had taken advantage of your passive nature.'

'You think me passive?' I said. 'Yes, I wear a coating of that condition. It makes a useful cosmetic for the older woman. Yet passivity has no source in nature. It is an injury we inflict upon ourselves – a laming of the spirit to halt its reckless rush into danger. I think you must recognize that as well as I do, for in that, sir, we are two of a kind. Yet passion is not so easily tamed. It will sit as quietly as any well-trained hound. But it is not quite subdued. It merely awaits its summons.'

He was silent a long time. Then he reached out and slowly touched my hand with his. 'The object of my passion will not wake,' he said softly; 'nor yours, my friend.'

I applied a friendly pressure to that limb and returned it to him. 'I have been twice blessed. I do not anticipate a fresh upheaval to my poor heart. As for your heart – it appears to me quite a green field despite its camouflage.'

'I liked the look of you in that field,' he said.

To tell the truth, I quite liked the look of myself in it too. William Ellin was good-natured, amusing, appreciative of comfort and of feminine company. He was, in short, everything that Finch Cornhill was not. He would not deride me for a paucity of spirit. He would ask nothing of me and yet would reward me with kindness. Still, there was something secretive about him. As with most amiable men, affability was a defence of his private self. Only a great emotion could beckon forth that self and, like Finch, I believed my quiet friend to be capable of great things. It was for his sake more than mine that I returned his gentle offering.

'Now, do not sit there looking so enigmatic,' Mr Ellin pleaded. 'Take pity on this newly landed gentleman and his deserted park. Whom would you put there to pasture? Surely you don't mean to assign it to Miss Wilcox?'

'No. You might have stood a chance with her once, but I think she might elect to gambol in lusher prairie now that she has gone up in the world. I hear she has cast her bonnet in the direction of a widowed duke whose daughter presently attends her school.'

'What, then? Should I cast my hat at this duke's daughter?'

'Forget about her, sir. She is as dull as a cold potato. Emma refers to her as the *pomme duchesse*. Speaking of whom, how do you view Emma?'

'What do you mean? She is a remarkable girl.'

'I mean – do you consider her a child or a woman?'

There was a moment's hesitation, a look of puzzlement which passed across his brow and gave me my answer.

'She is not a woman,' I supplied. 'Yet not a child either. In a very short space of time she will have crossed the threshold from one to the other. You know, she is almost sixteen now.'

'Why, of course I consider her a child,' he protested. 'I was a suitor to her mother. I am more than twenty years her senior.'

'My husband was more than twenty years my senior,' I reminded him. 'I do not envisage Emma as a flighty young woman susceptible to romantic wooing by spoony young men.'

He looked quite dazed at this and lost to himself. He said nothing except softly to murmur her name.

'My dear friend,' I said. 'We have answered one another. I cannot and shall not be your wife but, rest assured, your good friend I shall always be.'

'I thank you for your frankness,' said he. 'I think at this moment I value that friendship more than anything. Yes, I do love Emma. I love her sharp brain and her bright spirit. She has more thorns than a wild rose, yet that wild rose is sweeter to me than any cultivated bloom. I swear I had not considered her affection in any but the purest light. The mere idea of her as a full-grown woman who would face me as an equal – that is pleasure enough. I could not begin to contemplate that she might ever belong to me.'

His confusion made me laugh. 'My dear sir, Emma will never belong to anyone but herself. As to where she will lodge her affections at some distant date – why, sir, I can scarcely get a clear picture of her past, never mind her future.'

That past had plucked her from a place of privilege and cast her into a valley of destitution. She had been dispossessed, abused, accused. It was an arduous passage for one so young, yet she had emerged strong and unafraid. Heaven grant her life would be calm from this day forth, that the smile which had begun to remould her resolute mouth would have long tenure. And yet she herself might choose the hazardous road. The God who kept her safe on her travels never fashioned her for satin and silk. This was made clear when she insisted upon knowing the full history of her father. 'Then I renounce the name of Osborne,' she declared. 'It was not my mother's name. I will keep the name of Emma Brown.'

'Are you sure?' I said. 'Your father came from good family.'

'I prefer the freedom of being a nobody,' she decided.

'Eliza Brown brought no honour to her name,' I reminded her.

'That is true,' she reflected; 'yet although she might have wished me dead, it was she who gave me back my life at a time when it was almost gone. It was she who sent me in pursuit of myself – a self I might not otherwise have found. I have made up my mind.'

I did not doubt her resolution. I asked if she would consider the name of Chalfont and to this she happily agreed. When the time came for her to take another's name I could only hope that life might place in her way a gentle and accommodating partner. She could do worse than the gentleman who currently languished at my hearth.

'I am not good enough for her.' He sighed (with something of a swain's self-pity).

'No,' I agreed; 'nor ever will be. And she would think so too – and make your life a merry hell in an effort to bring you up to scratch.'

'I have lived an idle existence,' he said. 'Even if she could not love me, I would like to earn her admiration.'

'You could take holy orders,' I teased him. 'As you know, Mr Cecil has recently become engaged to marry Miss Adelaide Wilcox. The bride-to-be is ambitious for a more significant living for her spouse and is using her new-found influence to effect. This town will need a dedicated and active curate – one with a spirited and needlesome wife who would bring bread to the poor instead of taking tea with the rich.'

To my great surprise he did not laugh at this jest but looked very thoughtful.

This village has some interesting times ahead, thought I.

Let me advance you now a little into the future. Six months have passed since my conversation with Mr Ellin. He now has a new occupation. He is poorly paid, yet always has some offering for the poor. Recipients of his alms all say the one thing: 'Mr Ellin is a gentleman!' So, without land or any mansion, he has achieved his rightful estate.

He is my regular visitor still. I like him better each time he calls. We have invested our histories whole in one another and our sympathies remain intact. He and Emma exercise their fine intellects upon each other, a sport that makes him seem ten years younger and her a decade advanced in maturity.

Emma is now my legally adopted daughter. No more the forlorn waif who sat in a corner of my drawing-room and could not open her mouth for terror, no more the embattled adolescent, she is my friend, my staff. When she is at home we discourse on many subjects. Sometimes I see her as a wise companion, more astute and far-sighted than I will ever be. At other times she reunites me with the idealistic young woman who set out for Happen Heath on the great adventure of her life. Then I feel that my destiny has, by its complicated path, fulfilled its journey and brought unity to a passionate heart and a moderate soul.

Emma writes daily but I do not see her except in the holidays. She and Diana have gone away to a new school – a good and progressive academy that appreciates the fine feminine minds it teaches and does not try to subvert them to fashion and snobbery. Emma is happy, she progresses well. From her letters I can tell she greatly cares for me, but she is a young woman with goals of her own to fulfil. Yet I do not pine, or pace my dear husband's polished floorboards or lament the empty spaces in the house. Lately (as I mentioned) fate has placed in my path a companion and an interest.

A little girl, ill in hospital a long time, was recently released and, having nowhere else to go, came into my care. I opened my door, found on the doorstep (in the charge of a nurse) a diminutive figure clutching a wooden doll. She peered over the threshold, looked around suspiciously and in gruff tones inquired, 'Is this a home?'

I answered in the affirmative.

'Would such as me be allowed inside?' she whispered.

'Most decidedly,' I assured her; 'because it is your home. Step inside and see how you like it.'

At this her angelic countenance lit up with a smile so full and radiant that I felt myself not to be in the presence of an earthly being but a heavenly one.

'Are you a mother?' she asked me.

'Yours, if you like,' I said.

She took my hand, we sauntered in, and when we had done a thorough inspection of every quarter she clapped her hands and danced around, lopsided on her lame leg.

Jenny Drew is mine. I claim her for myself (although she is Emma's beloved sister). It was Mr Ellin who saved that little life. At Emma's behest he set himself to discover what had become of the mite. Dying, she had been cast back into the workhouse. There he found her, unconscious but still claiming a meagre ration of breath. At his own expense he lodged her in a private hospital. A series of specialists, paid for from his purse, have reduced his assets to a point where he is dependent upon his income as a clergyman. Yet in every sense that matters he is better off than when first he came to this town. He is a happy and hopeful man. He has useful occupation. He is valued and loved.

434

Life in the streets has left Jenny with a residue of that racking cough. She still sometimes has visitations from a mysterious gentleman not visible to me. At times I fear that He may yet try to claim that angel for His own but I will give God good contest for her. He has already taken too many of those dear to me. Besides, I feel there has been a celestial exchange for this little existence. Jenny Drew, who should have died, survived. Finch Cornhill, who should have lived, is dead. Although he could not give his heart to the poor children for whom he campaigned, he would have offered his life for any one of them. By his tireless work he yielded his breath that they might breathe a better air.

Jenny questions me endlessly about the people in my life. She is a model student in the school of family, love, avowals, betrothals. This little woman earnestly absorbed the story of my life's great passion and gave her gruff summary.

'He sounds a worthy one. He'd not make us snug on his knee. Worthy folks is all bones, like pauper stew.'

My miniature philosopher put all in perspective. Finch was never worldly. The humdrum comforts that succour other married couples would not have anchored that soaring spirit. His ardent nature knew no moderate clime. He was sent to give me a taste of Paradise, whence he has now preceded me.

He is laid to rest in our village churchyard and we are finally come to accord. I understand at last the fierce, imperious fire of his ardour. Lovers are right to make impossible demands. Only they can see what is best in us. Only they have the power to call it forth. Even death does not end affection's transforming power. It merely modifies it. No longer beset by earthly jealousies, our lovers cease to ask, 'Are you true to me?' Their memory makes the humbler charge: 'Are you true to yourself?'

Perhaps at some future time, in some perfected state, we will meet again. I do not seek to hasten that day. For the present I feel blessed enough by the company of my dear living and the memory of my darling dead.

Today Jenny and I are on our way to visit one of these. Together we go to the garden, pick the last and best of the summer flowers and set out on our little pilgrimage. A black (but not dark) shadow follows. It is the dog rescued by Emma after his owner, the poacher, died. Demon by name and by nature, that savage beast became a lamb in Emma's care and, in her absence, the adoring protector of Jenny Drew. With his change of character, we renamed him Seraph.

A fresh breeze is blowing as we make our way to the cemetery. Yesterday it rained and today there is the feeling of a world washed clean. Trees mantle the valley with shadow and cattle bask in fields of gold. Jenny pauses on the path. ''Tis Paradise, it must be.' Her verdict is delivered. A sound then sails full and liquid down the descent. It is the bells from the village church. I sense that our century has woken from a long sleep and will see great changes for the good. Prince Albert's epic ark of empire became the emblem of a new age. In certain quarters (such as Fuchsia Lodge) the limbs of furniture are clothed for decency, and ladies preserved (like pickles) from the harsh realities of the world. Yet good must acquaint itself with bad. Dissipation thrives in the dark and can be vanquished only by the bright fire of its opposite.

At a graveside, Jenny and I kneel together (for she imitates all I do). Seraph lies with head on paws and watches her. When I shed a few tears Jenny sheds them, too, to see me cry and Seraph comes to lick her for comfort.

'Who lies here?' Jenny says then, in her rough, practical voice.

'The man for whom destiny shaped me,' I answer.

'What was his name?' she asks.

What epithet is etched into that timeless granite? Whose grave do I keep fresh with my tears? I pull back the brambles that in summer will be bright with roses. The clever little creature makes laborious sense of the graven symbols (for I have been teaching her to read) and deciphers the name of my designated mate. Which name? Reader, you must decide.

AFTERWORD

The first two chapters of this book are the work of Charlotte Brontë. Written after the completion of *Villette* and before her marriage, it was to be her last piece of fiction. Would she have completed it? Brontë biographers Lyndall Gordon and Juliet Barker, who introduced me to it, believe she would. Indeed there is evidence of her intention to do so. On a night in 1854, she remarked to her clergyman husband: 'If you had not been with me I must have been writing now.' And she ran upstairs to fetch the manuscript, brought it down and read it aloud. Arthur Bell Nicholls' mild observation that critics might accuse her of repetition for again using the setting of a school, may well have condemned a brilliant beginning to the bottom drawer.

The fragment, giving the working title of *Emma*, was published in the *Cornhill Magazine* after her death, with an introduction by Thackeray. Some changes had been made by her husband, who altered the name of the schoolmistresses from 'Fetherhed' to 'Wilcox'. It is the *Cornhill* version upon which my novel has been based.

I wanted to keep Charlotte's voice alive in the book and so have incorporated some lines from her wonderful letters. Brontë scholars will readily identify these additions. I have also included a sequence from an earlier novel that Charlotte had begun and abandoned. This dramatic fragment, *The Story of Willie Ellin*, introduced the character who became Mr Ellin in her subsequent (this) work and I felt he was due his designated past.

The development of the plot was in part inspired by Charlotte's growing interest in social conditions in London, which she visited on a number of occasions after her success, and where she soon wearied of the tourist attractions (including the Great Exhibition) and dismayed her hosts by visiting Bethlehem Hospital, the Foundling Hospital, Pentonville Prison and Newgate Prison, at which latter site she spoke to a young woman who was to hang for the murder of her child, and held her hand.